CHRISTINA STEAD

was born in Sydney in 1902. She trained as a teacher, but in 1928 she left Australia for Europe, where she lived in London and Paris, working from 1930–35 as a secretary in a Paris bank. She went to live in Spain, but left on the outbreak of war and with her husband, the novelist and political economist William Blake, she settled in the USA. From 1943–44 she was an instructor at the Workshop in the Novel at New York University and in 1943 she was Senior Writer for MGM in Hollywood.

Acknowledged as one of the greatest novelists writing in the English language today, Christina Stead's first work of fiction, a collection of stories, *The Salzburg Tales*, was published in 1934. Since then she has published eleven novels: *Seven Poor Men of Sydney* (1934), *The Beauties and Furies* (1936), *House of All Nations* (1938), *The Man Who Loved Children* (1940), *For Love Alone* (1944), *Letty Fox: Her Luck* (1946), *A Little Tea, A Little Chat* (1948), *The People with the Dogs* (1952), *Cotters' England* (1966), *The Little Hotel* (1974) and her most recent novel, *Miss Herbert* (1976). She has also published another collection of stories, *The Puzzleheaded Girl* (1967). In 1947 Christina Stead left America for Europe, settling in England in 1953. She now lives in Australia.

Virago publish *For Love Alone*, *Letty Fox: Her Luck*, *A Little Tea, A Little Chat*, *The People with the Dogs*, *Cotters' England*, *Miss Herbert* and a selection from all her great works, *A Christina Stead Reader*. *The Beauties and Furies* and *The Puzzleheaded Girl* will be published in 1982.

CHRISTINA STEAD
A Little Tea, A Little Chat

With a new Introduction by Hilary Bailey

Virago

First British publication
by VIRAGO PRESS Limited 1981
Ely House, 37 Dover Street,
London W1X 4HS

First publication USA, 1948
by Harcourt, Brace & Co. New York

Copyright © Christina Stead 1948

Introduction Copyright © 1981
Hilary Bailey

Printed in Hong Kong by Colorcraft

British Library Cataloguing in Publication Data

Stead, Christina
    A little tea, a little chat.
    – (Virago modern classic)
    I. Title
    823[F]   PR9619.3.S75
    ISBN 0-86068-176-9

INTRODUCTION

"I WAS BROUGHT UP by a naturalist, and I *am* a naturalist. I see what I see, and if you see what you see, you understand it. That's all", said Christina Stead in an interview for the Australian Broadcasting Commission in 1980. She added, "I'm not at all critical. When you're a little girl and you look in an aquarium and you see fish doing this and that, and snails and so on you don't criticise and say they should do something else." This is a valid statement about her own manner and method.

A Little Tea, A Little Chat opens with a long chapter about Peter Hoag, a figure almost irrelevant to the main part of the book, a mere valet or spear-carrier, a New York fixer, middleman and general gopher for the bigger New York money men. He can get anything for anyone – "he got passports and passages, silk stockings and medicines, narcotics and income-tax arrangements; he knew abortionists, skin-disease charlatans, psychoanalysts and face-lifters, lobbyists and lawyers, restaurants and bordels. He was in on arranged marriages and divorces, seductions and criminal discoveries." He knows also, says Christina Stead, that each of the men he serves "must find a fatal woman and a fatal day". Hoag is described from the colour of his tie to the pictures on his wall, right down to the last dollar and cent he draws from his dubious activities. In this way the reader finds out straight away what kind of a world this is but through the detail, not because the author delivers lectures or makes statements. Like a biologist, Christina Stead points out the features of the animal and its environment – we, the readers, come up with conclusions about the nature of the beast and whether we like it or not. It is Hoag, running around New York on his various errands, who first comes across Mrs Barbara Kent, down on her luck, and introduces her to Robert Grant. Thus, quite accidentally, in the unpromising surroundings of an old loft over a fur company, Hoag finds Grant's fatal woman and his fatal day. Grant is a cotton dealer, a big, strong, rich, practical, fast-moving, shallow, bored, grasping, lecherous, ruthless and hypocritical man. During the course of the book he betrays his friends, robs women and causes a suicide. He is never cleared of the charge of supplying materials to the enemy in time of war, he drives a man mad (and rushes round immediately to the man's house to reclaim a borrowed scarf) and spitefully denounces his son's girlfriend to the Mississippi police. No deed is too large or too small for Grant as long as there is some personal profit in it. But the author tracks him minutely and never comments. She describes a large, marine creature with a fusiform body, lateral branchial clefts, a tough, dull, grey skin roughened by tubercles. She mentions predatory habits – and the reader knows that it is a shark.

Christina Stead is, indeed, one of the most gifted, and at the same time most bizarre of the writers of her time. She appears to have no direct antecedents and, at the moment, no successors. She is a genuine original. Perhaps the reason why she has been compared with D. H. Lawrence is simply because both writers seem untainted by a literary view of things – their vision is unique. They see only through their own eyes.

Christina Stead was born in Australia in 1902. She came to England in 1928, married a businessman, William Blake, and moved with him to Paris and then to New York. Now widowed, she lives in Australia. Each of the countries she has lived in have provided her not just with settings, but with the real content of her books. *The Beauties and Furies*, for example, which was her first novel (her first two books were collections of stories) concerns an Englishwoman who leaves her dull English husband to go and live with a lover in Paris. The city itself seems to dominate the affair – the cafe life they live, the hotels, the people, the whole sensual atmosphere of the Paris of the '30s – far different from the respectable and plain-living London of the time – all condition the outlook of Elvira, the runaway wife, and affect what happens to her. The setting of the book, in short, is part of the action.

Similarly, the three novels Christina Stead published towards the end of the 1940s and in the early '50s, all set in New York, have a different kind of subject matter, the characters are different, and again it looks as if the city conditioned the action. It is as if Christina Stead instinctively recognised that if Paris is for lovers, New York is for action. Even Letty Fox, in *Letty Fox: Her Luck*, although looking for love, is always on the move, trying everything, grasping at everything to see what it is made of. Edward, in *The People With The Dogs*, shifts about, meets people all the time, has a finger in every pie. The skirmishings and manoeuvres of *A Little Tea, A Little Chat* are incessant. In this atmosphere, Christina Stead seems to say, no one quite knows what they want but they're ready to try anything in case there's something in it for them.

The later novels, set in England, have yet another tone – it seems impossible not to recall the Australian naturalist's daughter who enjoyed *The Origin of Species* and *The Voyage of the Beagle*. Did she then wonder if people, like animals, adapted to their own environments? At any rate, she sniffs at atmosphere quickly and finds the subject to suit it, a process, I suspect, which is mostly unconscious. Robert Grant is part of New York, fast, self-interested, capitalistic and far from nature. There is no difference between his attitude to money and his attitude to women. They are both there for the taking, if he is quick enough and cunning enough. But this exploiter of men and women is nevertheless captured and exploited by a woman himself and we wonder why. Most of the women around Grant want something out of him. He knows this and makes sure, like an old gunman, that he shoots them first. Grant will cheat a woman over anything – a pair of stockings, a car, a couple of buildings.

So how is it that, in these dog-eat-dog surroundings, Barbara Kent gains her ascendency over Grant?

Christina Stead is too realistic to make her ruin Grant, knowing that the Grants of this world are incapable, out of old habit, of allowing themselves to be ruined. Nevertheless, she obsesses him. The relationship represents what he has come to, in his boredom and egotism. In Barbara Kent he meets an indifference and selfishness as great as his own and, significantly, he tires of her when he thinks he has got her and wriggles out of the matter when she really needs, or seems to need, his help. The scenes between Barbara, now Barbara Downs, and Grant when they discuss whether he is to buy her out of a divorce case, in which he is involved (although he suspects she may have organised it to cheat him) are classics of threat and counter-threat, hidden and open, and of shiftiness and hypocrisy. She threatens him with publicity, pleads for money and falls on his mercy as the innocent woman he has betrayed. As she twists and turns to get what she wants Grant grows more obstinate, starting by promising a cheque, then, as she grows more pressing, becoming more evasive, "You have me, sweetie, if no one else stands by you, only don't come here. I'm packing . . . I'm going to Cuba." And then, "I had several big shocks financially . . . My funds are tied up abroad, can't get a cent out. Just pay my hotel bill and keep my family." The joke is really on both of them for they do, in some sense, love each other. The habit of mistrust, greed and deception prevent either of them from fully realising it.

Grant and Barbara make the Macbeths look open, candid and honest in contrast. And not surprisingly, for the Macbeths lived in a moral world and knew when they left it. Grant and Barbara have more or less abandoned all standards, although both use the language of morality when it suits them. And Christina Stead makes sure we know this goes further than domestic chicanery. It involves a suicide, madness and treachery. After Pearl Harbour, Grant actually suggests to his associate, Robert Flack, that they should send war materials to Japan. When Flack demurs, Grant just shouts, "My dear boy, when the golden harvest has begun, take a scythe in your hand."

The world of *A Little Tea, A Little Chat* is a stark one, and, in fact, although Christina Stead, by the manner of her writing, which is fluent, documentary and unmoralistic, gives the impression that she is neutral, just telling it like it is, the truth is that her work is permeated generally by a profound, if stoical, pessimism. She is not, after all, a scientist. Scientists can be neutral and objective for they have a limited area to study and established criteria for their observations. The novelist has the whole world to work with and he or she chooses what to select and how to present the information. We see, in a novel, what the writer sees.

The whole question of pessimism is complicated – the optimist calls the pessimist gloomy, the pessimist responds that he is just realistic. But on a simple and primitive level it can be seen that Christina Stead does not deal in hope or reconciliation. Happy endings in her novels are rare. *For Love Alone* and *Letty Fox: Her Luck* end happily, with the marriage of the heroines, but otherwise the characters seem to stay locked in the worlds in which they have previously existed, and these worlds not having been happy ones, the absence of change is a disaster. At the end of *Cotters' England* Nellie Cook, having destroyed everything, turns to spiritualism partly, we suspect, to try to heal her own radical despair, partly to achieve control over something, even if it is the afterlife. It will not work for her, we also suspect, because she has not changed. In *The Beauties and Furies* Elvira, the erring wife, is forced by her lover's deceptions to return to her husband. She has not made a decision, just accepted the better of two bad alternatives. Eleanor Brent, as *Miss Herbert* ends, has suffered many vicissitudes but stays locked in her own self-destructive dream. And at the end of that most harrowing and moving book, *The Man Who Loved Children*, readers must feel glad for Hennie, the desperate mother, when she commits suicide and ends her frantic, ever-losing, never-to-be-won battles with life. And similarly almost sorry for the others of the family who must go on living with the father, Sam, who will never change.

The final moral of Christina Stead's work is not only that no one ever wins, or very rarely, and usually by getting married, but that, events having come to no good due to the follies and self-deceptions of those concerned, there is no possibility of change. Nor do her characters reconcile themselves, nor do they fully understand what has taken place. It is a grimmer version of human affairs than that of real tragedy, where at least there is some resolution, some feeling of significance.

This steady state view of the world, where nothing really alters, naturally implies an absence of rewards and punishments. In *A Little Tea, A Little Chat* we are likely to sympathise with Edda Flack, the daughter of Grant's long-suffering associate. She dislikes Grant for his treatment of her father. On the whole she knows him for what he is. When she tries to get a job in Washington and remove herself and her father from Grant's sphere of influence we rather hope she will succeed. But she has already failed in a love affair and now she fails to get the job. Her intentions are good, but she is too weak. Again, Livy Wright, one of the less crooked of Grant's women, not only loses him, but two houses she was trying to buy. In fact Grant buys them cheaply when she is at a disadvantage. As in nature, the moral is that the weak fall prey to the strong. If the relatively clear-headed and independent characters of *A Little Tea, A Little Chat* fail, so the villains go unpunished.

All this is masked, in the novels, by the continual movement of events. In all Christina Stead's novels people meet continually, bizarre issues arise, like the dispute between Goodwin and Grant over the ill-fitting underpants bought for Goodwin by Grant, the search for keys to fit Grant's hatbox.

In such speedy worlds, Grant's world, the weight of different actions is not gauged; consequences are not examined. A ridiculous script reading, a few missing shoe covers are as important to Grant as a quick act of treachery in time of war or the destruction of a life.

Meanwhile, all is overlaid by Grant's voice – one of Christina Stead's brilliant, histrionic voices – fluent, lying or telling half-truths, accusing, exonerating himself, using language to baffle, persuade and mislead. Caught up and fascinated by the whirl of activity, ears full of Grant's dominating voice, we lose sight, in part, of what is really taking place. It is very lifelike. In essence it is a grim picture of the world, light and swift on the surface and frightening underneath. Christina Stead's books are indeed strange fruit – they entice at first but leave a bitter taste on the tongue.

Hilary Bailey, London 1981

Chief Characters

ROBERT OWEN GRANT—cotton speculator and dealer

GILBERT GRANT—his elder son

MRS. BARBARA KENT, then DOWNS—the blondine

MRS. JONES—her mother

MISS PAULA RUSSELL—her friend

MISS LIVY WRIGHT—friend of Grant

HUGO MARCH—Wall Street man

ALFRED GOODWIN—Grant's friend

DAVID FLACK
EDDA FLACK—his daughter } —friends of Grant

MISS ROBBINS—Grant's secretary

To my friends
AIDA and **MAX KOTLARSKY**

A Little Tea, A Little Chat

Peter HOAG, a Wall Street man, aged fifty-six in March, 1941, led a simple Manhattan life and had regular habits. He lived alone in a furnished apartment, at $110 monthly, on the eighteenth floor of a residential hotel in the lower East Sixties. His apartment was in the corner of the building, with two sets of windows, one set overlooking Madison Avenue, and the other, the cross street. The people below looked so small that they seemed to walk like two-legged fleas, and the cars so small that they were like potato bugs that could be scooped up by the hatful. The apartment consisted of a lobby about a yard square, a living room with a divan on which Hoag slept, a bathroom, and a small service kitchen, used also as a bar. The whole was carpeted and the ceiling not too low. The walls were painted green and decorated with six pictures showing small boys and dogs urinating, and, on two small veneered tables, Hoag had albums containing pictures with similar subjects. He had on a bookcase, three bronzes: the first, two dogs round an umbrella stand with a dripping umbrella; the second, a European import, *Mannekin Pis*, brought by his sister for him from Antwerp; and the third a head of Abraham Lincoln, given to him by one of his best friends, Hugo March, a stock-exchange broker. In the bathroom were several notices stolen from men's rooms, and in the kitchen a picture of bluebonnets in Texas, a state in which Elias Brown, Hoag's partner downtown, owned some oil property. Another of Peter Hoag's friends, now dead, had reorganized a bankrupt Southwestern railroad, and Hoag had helped in the affair. This friend, dying, had left Hoag $5,000. Hoag liked the Texas picture better than the others: the others were witty, but this gave him pleasure. He and March would look at it together, while he mixed drinks for March, after five o'clock, or cooked him some eggs and bacon; they would talk over the oil wells and Texas, and say the bluebonnets were a lovely flower. If anyone came from Texas, they would bring him up to the apartment to see the picture, which, however, had only been cut out of a *National Geographic* magazine. The oil properties had founded Brown's fortune.

Hoag had as many friends as he could count, all Wall Street men, stock-exchange and insurance brokers, bankers, men who ran bankrupt railroads, insured stockyards, were produce merchants and shipping brokers. About five of these were now his intimates —Elias Brown and Hugo March, stock exchange; Saul Udall, railroads; Arthur Pantalona and Francis O'Sullivan, plainclothes Government agents, Fraud and Narcotics Squads. About the first three almost everything was known by the six, about the last two, very little; Peter Hoag was the only one dear to them all. He was really loved, and not only by these men but by a number of others, all men of considerable active wealth, not mere merchants, but industrious, successful, crafty men with networks of control in the United States and Canada, not commercial princes of the first order, but men of principles identical with those of the first class, each one of whom, given some sort of break, might emerge (at least so each thought) as another Du Pont, or at least marry his child to a Du Pont. These men were well aware that the age of monstrous personal achievement had passed and that dynasties were now the order of that extraordinary one-time democracy, now territory of financial oligarchs. . . . These men loved the United States intensely, ferociously, with terror and greed.

Peter Hoag appreciated these men; his certainty that each of them loved money and lechery, above all, that each must find a fatal woman and a fatal day, made him irresistible to them as a friend. He was a rich deposit of sex lore and table talk. Peter Hoag got liquor in prohibition days, when O'Sullivan had been a revenue agent; he got passports and passages, silk stockings and medicines, narcotics and income-tax arrangements; he knew abortionists, skin-disease charlatans, psychoanalysts and face lifters, lobbyists and lawyers, restaurants and bordels. He was in on arranged marriages and divorces, seductions and criminal discoveries; he knew and did everything that was necessary to his friends, and was easy of approach, candid, honest, and tender. It was said no woman could, or at least would resist him, though he was a short, plump, carelessly dressed personage, with an ordinary pear-shaped face. It was not only as a fixer but as a friend that he was known to strangers, too.

He was given many secrets, because he would only make use of these confidences, if the time ever came, in an honest way,

4

that is, if he thought the time had come to put his friend into relations with another man who would buy this secret, or become a partner of this secret, or cure this secret, or find a lawyer for this secret. Thus he was the most private friend of men who live entirely in a world of private relations, unrevealed partnerships, profitable acquaintance. Peter Hoag looked frail and was supposed to have stomach ulcers, tuberculosis, heart disease, and social diseases, at various times and according to his own fancy, but he outlived many of these rich men, and it had become the ritual of this society to leave something to Peter Hoag in any will. From one he got $1,000, from another $10,000. One would say, "Hugo told me he put in The Rabbit for three grand—I wonder what the goddamn Rabbit has got now." The answer, "I'd like to see the lining of his goddamn safe-deposit." "Which one?—he showed me three separate keys." The Rabbit pretended to be poor. This amused them. Whenever they needed money, he was able to get it for them from someone: they said it was his own. They would calculate the interest themselves, and whatever favors he had done them, then make a discount, and halve it, and this would determine the amount they put in their wills for him.

This trade of running messages and being helpmeet cost Peter Hoag his whole life. If he lay awake in bed, he invented combinations, and soon fell asleep. In the morning he felt spry, got up as soon as his alarm rang, made his coffee, an easygoing expression on his face as he reflected on his work for the day. Saturdays and Sundays were also workdays for him. He saw the same bunch of boys in the week ends, and while they played golf or drank Scotch, they meddled with the same lives, tinkered with the plots of the preceding week, and laughed over new tricks to play on some newcomer or old crony. They not only were birds of prey, but loved to think of themselves as eagles in their flights and vultures in their hovering.

2

On a Monday morning in April, 1941, Peter Hoag washed himself carefully, put on a plain blue suit of English wool, and chose a small-patterned blue silk tie. He had three errands before he got down to Elias Brown & Co., in Beaver Street. First, he must make an unannounced call upon a widow, Mrs. Anne Warder, who had put in a fire claim on an insured apartment she had near Madison Square. Next, he must visit Sam Banks, a lawyer in a side street near Grand Central, to receive a legacy of $3,000 from the estate of one of his Wall Street friends lately deceased. Third, he must lay the foundations for a plan the boys had matured during the week end; as follows: to give a banquet in an uptown hotel, in honor of the forthcoming marriage of a Washington woman with a corporation president with whom she had lived for five years.

The plan was Saul Udall's. He and others of the boys had been friends of the woman and had thought of a wedding present for her. They would first obtain bond flotations for the corporation, which was in a bad way. Then the woman would marry, in honor bound, this man who was in love with her, but would obtain first of all an agreement for community of property. Then, she would divorce the fool when she had mulcted him and would marry Saul Udall, who was preparing to leave his wife. In the previous months Saul Udall and the woman had met every other afternoon in a room engaged by him. Saul Udall was one of the heroes of this crowd of friends and conspirators. His pranks made them rock with laughter. Udall wanted to divorce his wife and marry this Washington woman, after she had plucked the fool, and so told his wife that he must live alone because he had some spinal weakness and must have diathermy. At home, he stayed in bed; in town he was up all night with the girls. As to the corporation president, this plan was sure to run smoothly, for Udall had already practiced it on the person and life of another dull corporation president, who had been jerked into his place by influence and college friends. His picture had appeared in the Wall Street pages as new President of Corporation X, but everyone had known the truth and laughed loud. Udall had floated a bond issue on false figures; money was stolen by Udall, but in such a way that the President appeared to have stolen it. The President committed suicide in an unusual way, by falling off a stone balcony in his nightshirt in winter. Udall's entire circle wallowed in laughter and handshaking for weeks: they regarded it as one of Udall's great pranks. Now they had no doubt that through the Washington woman the control of the corporation would soon be in their hands.

Udall did things in a grand manner, too. For example, he had just sent to all his friends—Hugo March, Peter Hoag, Pantalona, about forty Senators, and members of the stock exchange—a book bound in morocco with gilt edges and vellum pages, handwritten

6

and illuminated, which reproduced a long, tearful poem from some acquaintance upon the death of his wife, an answer to Udall's condolences. "*An example of true love*," said the first page, and the circumstances, with Saul Udall's letter of condolence and the names of man and wife, were inscribed. Hugo March admired this so much that for Christmas he had ordered from the same illuminator a little book containing the remarks of a iudge in Oklahoma about the duties of citizens to the State, the remarks having been addressed to an out-of-work handyman who had cut loose and stolen an automobile. It was Peter Hoag who arranged all these things with the illuminator; they relied on him in all matters of taste.

Mrs. Anne Warder was thirty-one years old, a plump blonde, confident and confidential, a businesslike sort of woman. Hoag's mission was to look through her things before she could set the stage for the insurance investigator. He found her in her dressing gown, the place upside down, as it should be at that hour, but on looking through her closets and chest of drawers, he found that she had already burned holes in things, especially in some out-of-date inventory, such as a couple of suits in wool and silk, a torn fur coat, and even in some new underwear of too bright a pink. The taper was lying on the vanity table when he came into the small dark bedroom. He made an appointment with her for cocktails that afternoon, and he had liked the whole way she carried it off. He wetted his lips and thought he might get married; at any rate, he knew the woman was his type.

Sam Banks, the lawyer, was a boyhood friend of Hugo March, and was well known for his talent, the saying that he "never lost a case," and his ability for work. He shared a suite of offices on the fourteenth floor of a Fifth Avenue building—it was the thirteenth floor but called the fourteenth. Sam sat with his back to the windows, in shirt sleeves, reading a brief. He said, "Hello, Peter," and went on reading. His secretary brought Hoag a check, which he countersigned, and sent out for the cash. Hoag sat there, while Sam went on reading his brief. Presently, Sam said, "Excuse me, I'll be here all day, I don't eat today," and returned to the paper in his hand.

Hoag looked out the window at the roofs below him and thought about his lunch. Each day at lunch, which was always either in the fish restaurant or the tavern, downtown, the boys matched billfolds to see who was carrying the most cash on him. Hoag often won the bet, and probably would today: this was

7

why he took the legacy in cash. No pickpockets are allowed in the Wall Street area below Fulton Street; they can take the subway through these preserves but not get out and not operate even underground till the region is past.—Hoag was perfectly safe. Every day he helped out some man or other with a few hundred dollars; he got it back the following day. . . . Hoag thought he would get a fashionable photographer to take a picture of the banquet they were giving to the Washington woman and her new husband; they would send the photograph to all the known men she had slept with. All the men in their set admired her for her ability and the way men ran after her. Now she had two more men who would marry her. Sending this photograph would suit her very well and would be a tribute from them. . . . The money came, Hoag nodded and left Banks's office, got into his car and started downtown. The car was lent to him by Hugo March, a handsome dull-green roadster used at other times by March's son, Claud, who was now at a smart private school.

He stopped, however, to get a new tie, and it was after eleven when he reached Twenty-third Street. He decided to go to Luchow's for a sandwich. Passing through Irving Place, he was held up at Eighteenth Street by the lights. A woman waiting on the curb and going in the same direction attracted his notice. She was bareheaded, with fair hair roughly brought back into a knot on the nape of her neck; she held her head up and was crying, and she carried in her hand a very small broken paper valise, sewed up and tied up with string. She went on walking beside Hoag, who had slowed down to look at her. She was remarkably strong-looking, clear-skinned, apparently about twenty-five, dressed in a jersey dress with a shapeless beige wool jacket over it. At the next light, Hoag parked his car: they were in front of the old opera building on Irving Place, now a cinema for foreign pictures. When he opened the door, she looked into his eyes and stopped.

"Won't you come and eat some lunch with me over there?"

She put the paper valise on the back seat of his car and nodded, at once turning toward the restaurant.

They sat next to a large mirror. The light fell on her head. The restaurant was beginning to fill with well-fed, hungry, energetic, successful men. All looked at her. She was a woman used to men. Her cheeks were full, the chin noticeable, the facial bones large and high, smooth. Her eyes were narrow, oval, violet, with a darker outer rim. The eyes were set level with the face and a

8

little close together, and her front face appeared flattish. She had a full mouth with a protruding lower lip. Only a slight heaviness round the jawbones and a disappointed expression, a light fold from nose to mouth, showed that she was past her youth. Her eyes and hair were the extraordinary features of her head. The eyes were calculating but resplendent. Her smooth hair left the forehead bare but grew into lanugo round the temples and neck; and the empty temples were also animal.

Hoag was gallant with her, eating a piece of bread if she selected it but put it back, choosing something from the plate of hors d'œuvres if she had touched it first, listening softly without offense, smiling just below her eyes, watching with a clever intentness. She smiled. It was a little smile, with close teeth, but her eyes at once smiled too; she had a friendly expression when she spoke to the waiter. She was carelessly frank with him. All that he saw about her excited his business instinct.

She was Mrs. Barbara Kent, born in England of immigrant parents, one White Russian and one without a country. She could skate, dance, ride, speak several languages. She found herself alone, without a profession, at nineteen. She tried modeling in Paris and some American brought her to New York.

She had not the local figure, could not model, and lost men, could scarcely be bothered with them. She was thirty-two, but if well fed, rested, and well dressed, could pass for twenty-three or so. But her "mind was old: men had given her too much trouble; she wanted to settle down." She never listened to a word men said: "at three o'clock in the morning it was only one thing." And they were stupid, all were stupid, the newspapers were stupid. "You are stupid, too," she said, looking up from her plate, "there is one thing only with men." Kent had been a New York drunkard in his fifties. He had beaten her, and when she had run away had divorced her; result—no alimony. Since then, in New York, she had drifted about. She had been living last month in a furnished room in Twenty-first Street with a store clerk who worked late hours. She had invited a man up to her rooms and the store clerk had come home to find them together. He had only been able to say, "Get dressed, get dressed quickly, get dressed and get out—both of you get out."

That man had no money. Since then, she had gone back to haunting some little bars on the East Side, between Twelfth and Third Streets, where she washed in the back room. Her change of clothes she left in a laundry. They washed her clothes and gave them to her when she paid. They were tired of her in the bar, told her to take a walk. She did not like to drink, only wanted to find a man to rent a room for her. She knew there were call houses in this district for business men and she had been going to an address when Hoag met her.

"There are some things I can't do. I've never worked in an office. I can't take orders from a man. I'm not naïve. Now that only leaves a few things open to me. I'm too well educated to do a lot of things. I'm used to holding my own with men. I can manage. I just need some introductions."

In the evening of that day, he met Mrs. Anne Warder for a short time after the close of business, then went to Madison Square where he had arranged to meet the blonde Mrs. Kent. She was sitting on a seat near the statue of Farragut. When he came up, she said nervously, "I'm not used to sitting in parks; I don't like the attention; it's very disagreeable to me. You should not have made this kind of appointment. I hate parks."

They walked over to a place he had in mind, below Twenty-third Street, and went up the wooden stairs of a small loft building, just off Sixth Avenue and near a church. Two out-of-town women passed them on the stairs, talking about the price of furs and the wolf jackets they had seen. Hoag said, "The sexton from the church sends them here. They come to town with a bit of money to spend on New York clothes and he sells them a fur jacket—they are trying to put over wolf now; they like the sound."

He knocked at a door with an old, painted notice-board, saying "Goodwin Furs." Inside, in the bare entrance to a small, dusty loft, Hoag introduced Mrs. Kent to three men: Alfred Goodwin, tall, bent, with black hair; a noisy, athletic young man, also dark, called Delafield; and Robert Grant, or Robbie. This man, husky, tall, fair, with fine blue eyes, a square-set fleshy nose of extraordinary size, and a powerful chin, gave her one sharp glance and turned away. The other two looked her over.

She went and sat down on a cane chair near the dirty window. She was very tired; she had been sitting all the afternoon in parks. She wore what she had worn in the morning, her one-piece dress without ornament, the beige jacket, and her run-down shoes. Some hairs straggled from the loop on the back of her neck. She sat quite still. She had been introduced also to two women who hovered behind the men: Mrs. Coppelius, a small brunette dressed in black, and Miss Celia Grimm, a Gotham business type, with expensively dyed, dressed and lacquered hair, afternoon clothes, a blonde-brunette.

After a few moments, Mrs. Kent noticed that there was another woman present, a young blonde with regular features, who was at the far end of the loft putting on her hat to go home. She now came toward the group and waited in it, addressing the men and women familiarly; they called her Marty. Suddenly Robert Grant turned to Mrs. Kent and said brusquely, "This is Martha Ammamam." What name? Grant looked at her in surprise and repeated sharply, "Martha Anderson"; but he gave the woman several side glances after he had heard her voice. She noticed the thin, fine hair all over his large dome, still a salty blond. He was at least fifty, though his eyes and skin were very clear.

The men began to speak in low tones and the women to feign indifferences. Mrs. Kent knew the men were discussing her chances with them. The windows were shut. The revolting odor of furs and their preservatives filled the place. Grant turned twice and looked her over. "Like a pound of tripe," she thought to herself, "like a dirty rag." He turned back to Hoag with a headshake.

"Now this girl," said Grant, taking Myra Coppelius by the arm and shaking it, "you remind me of Laura, you're like her, like the woman who nearly ruined me—I nearly broke up my home for her." He stood back and screwed up one eye like a watchmaker. "Not very—but, good grief—better-looking—but, the wiry type, too: all springs, coiled—and—you're very bonnie, bonnie, wee. But perhaps I should beware of you! That woman nearly did for me! I nearly gave up one hundred thousand dollars for her! I nearly handed over an apartment house to her. Dangerous 'ooman. But you're sweet," he said, turning a sweet flashing smile on Mrs. Coppelius. He turned to the men, "That cow in the corner—she won't do! Don't see what you see in her! Looks like a scrubwoman."

Grant turned to Mrs. Coppelius, "Rain in the desert: thirsty man dying of thirst—can you believe it?" He went on with a laugh like a thunderclap, "I was walking down Fifth Avenue thinking, just thinking, believe me, my very thoughts at that moment were, My life is a blasted heath. I hadn't seen her for months—forgot she existed. I make appointments with women —a little tea, a little chat, mind you, nothing wrong—nothing doing. I don't like them: I'm a parched, thirsty man. I want an

11

oasis. They don't know the word! Now, in front of me, a rose—a passionflower! And Myra has been in New York for two months all alone in a hotel room. What a waste of life! Let's go," and he started for the door.

"There's Mrs. Kent," said one of the men.

Grant was on the landing, the door ajar against his broad back. He rumbled, "I don't want that cow. I don't see it."

Goodwin came back into the room smiling and beckoned Mrs. Kent to her feet; and when she reached the door, said, "Look, Robbie, please do me a favor and drop these girls wherever they want to go. I've got to catch the six twenty-seven, we've got guests; or you, Hoag." Hoag put out his arm to the unfortunate blonde woman, whereupon Grant mumbled, "No, I'll take them, come on," and hustled them down the stairs, himself at the back, talking audibly to someone, "But the blonde looks like a laundress, her dress is spotted; why should I spend taxi fare on a cow like that when I don't see she'll be any use to me at all!" and "Hang her shoes!" and "I got no time to dress up a dish for myself. I got no need for fancy looks. I'm no pervert. I got no time."

He hailed a taxi downstairs. Mrs. Coppelius said she would walk; and they spent a few minutes by the door while Grant took her address and telephone number and sketched some hasty gallantries. The men left. The blonde Mrs. Kent, holding her broken valise, stood by in the same cold, womanly way, said good night in rather a gentle voice, and turned toward the taxi with a beautiful droop of the head. Her columnar neck and fine shoulders were turned advantageously away from Grant. He gave her a startled glance. He now recalled her. In the presence of the men and the other women, she had had only three moods: a dejected indifference, a contemptuous indifference, and an abstracted nervous pose, as if thinking thoughts persistent and habitual.

Night had come. Grant knew nothing of this part of town and was casting round for some little bar, an Italian restaurant for about $1.50 where he could feed her, look her over, and make up his mind about her. He started to talk over restaurants of a cheap order with Miss Grimm, who presently said she had an appointment but would take the taxi uptown with them. Grant became angry with her. They got into the taxi, the blonde silent.

The lights fell on her face, plain fair hair, and neck rising nobly from the low-cut dress. After Miss Grimm had left them with a very dry farewell, Grant said quickly, "Where did you meet Peter Hoag?"

"He stopped his car and picked me up on the sidewalk."

"You had trouble, eh, little girl?"

She was silent for a while, then, negligently, "Hard luck hit me."

"There's always some man behind it, when a woman's in trouble." He moved against her.

"I have nothing against men; men have been good to me."

He cast up in his mind, judging by her appearance and type, what she must be used to and what small sums she must have accepted. She was quiet, did what he wanted, all without skirmishing. He felt he would spend an hour or two with her, put off a cocktail appointment, see Goodwin's wife, Betty, with whom he was having an affair, later in the evening. It would teach Betty a lesson which she needed. Betty Goodwin was a spoiled British libertine who drank too much. He redirected the taxi to his hotel, saying, with his hand on her knee, "Long-distance call I'm expecting from Jigago, business—"

He then lived just off Fifth Avenue, in the lower Fifties, in a big old hotel with a gay lobby, but pleasant, old-fashioned suites. The pair went upstairs, taking with them the small paper valise. Grant was completely indifferent to the looks cast at Mrs. Kent's dress and valise. She appeared to be also.

The bedroom was white, paneled, with tasseled lamps; there was a lounge with mustard velvet cushions, armchairs similarly upholstered, a yellow satin coverlet on the bed. His bed had been turned down for the night. As soon as she had put down the valise, he took her to the lounge, being always a brief and hasty man. Her hair came down, and when he came back into the room, she was twisting it up again, in a beautiful pose. Her hair, her dress, fitted the lounge; suddenly he felt shame at seeing her in such a poor dress. Although it bored him to do so, he offered her a Martini, getting out the bottle which was marked with inkmarks to see no servant stole. Then, feeling the glow of the drink, took her out to the cheap Italian restaurant he had first thought of.

They sat behind the restaurant, in an old flagged yard, full of dirt and overlooking an excavated lot, in which garbage was dumped. Some lights were strung across the yard at rare intervals, and a dim crowd of midtowners were drinking wine cocktails, the specialty of the place. Grant did not invite her to have any, since he had already given her a Martini, but presently softened and bought her a glass of wine. It was a pleasant night, the stars were shining, and they could see the clean check curtains and tablecloth in the home of the Italian superintendent of the apartment house next door. A young woman in black lingered by Grant's table to say hello to him, but he did not introduce the woman. Later, he told Mrs. Kent about her—Gussy, the wife of an American who had fought in the International Brigade and been killed in Spain. She always wore mourning, and was doing very badly; he, Grant, helped her out. She tried to make commissions by shopping in antiques for friends furnishing apartments. She was a brave little woman. He said he was against Franco, and Franco would fall; he heard from another woman he knew, who was also on the right side, that the British were dropping supplies and soldiers and ammunition by parachute into Navarra: "Mark my words, the British know which way the wind is blowing."

The blonde Mrs. Kent said she was a liberal, she would be a radical, only she had come to think of these things too late. She said it was a credit to a man like Grant to be so liberal. They had brandy and instead of sending her home as he had meant to do, Grant took her back to the hotel again, and leaving her in the sitting room, telephoned from his bedroom, putting off Mrs. Goodwin until next day.

This time she undressed and he saw her strong and well-proportioned body. When he asked for her address, she gave him one far uptown, where her friend, Miss Paula Russell, lived.

Grant dismissed the blonde about ten and did not think he would ever see her again. He felt he had made a mistake in bringing her back the second time. He went to bed as soon as she had left, as he always got up at six-thirty.

He was a cotton trader, had made his money in cotton. His mother, a tough, coarse old woman with an incomprehensible accent, had worked as a girl in Lancashire mills. He knew cotton from boyhood. He dabbled in numerous items on the produce exchange but not for his sole account. In these ventures he allowed numerous acquaintances, as Goodwin and Delafield, to sign the documents. He always had the impression that these adventurers would make a mistake and that whoever lost—the seller, the shipper, the purchaser—he would be able to wangle a profit out of it for himself.

3

One day the following week, the woman called Paula Russell telephoned Grant at his office and asked for an appointment with him, "I must tell you something you don't know about my friend Barbara Kent; but it depends upon the kind of man you are."

Grant feared a conspiracy or holdup and refused to see her. The woman interested him. On the telephone she had a made-up voice which suggested the easy woman, fruity and dragging, underneath hard, tingling. Grant thought one day he would see her to size her up. That day he saw Martha Anderson, the fur-loft blonde who hoped to get into modeling, or Hollywood, and who had some test photographs to show him. They went to his rooms for "a chat and a little tea"; and then with Miss Anderson, he met Alfred and Betty Goodwin, Betty's sister and brother-in-law, and Delafield for cocktails. Later, the other men having a business dinner, he took the two sisters home, and they entertained themselves, with drinks and various extravagances, before they went to dinner. He thought the sisters corrupt girls, a bit wild, but friendly to him, honest in a way. They would often tell him what their husbands said about him behind his back: they "thought it was a shame and we defended you." They agreed with his political ideas, though their husbands did not, said they hated fascists, sympathized with Jews, thought Negroes should have political equality, though they should not be allowed in uptown restaurants (the women were more liberal on this than Grant), and said it was a pity about Spain. They called themselves "fellow-travelers." Grant said he wouldn't go as far as that, but he had always been a radical, and for the people, that was because his mother was a millworker. He told them not to read the best-selling trash but to get hold of Bellamy's *Looking Backward*; it had been his bible when he had been a lad.

Grant returned the wives to their husbands after dinner; and then met Gussy, the widow, whose lingering at his table had rather touched him on the previous night. He took her out with Miss Grimm, the brunette-blonde, to The Casino, a fashionable cheap night club. They ate steaks, fried potatoes, French salad, drank black coffee and brandy, saw the usual Russian night club routine. Grant was a little nervous because the Russians sang a Red Army song. The girls were delighted and clapped heartily. They spent a dull time repeating a lot of radical bywords, and Miss Grimm asked Grant to contribute to some Communist fund.

Grant laughed and said, "I'll see you tomorrow for tea and a little chat about this, Celia; I don't like to rush into things, I want to know more about it from you." Presently he rushed Gussy to the sidewalk, thinking he would spend the evening with Miss Grimm, but Miss Grimm took him to The Golden Tassel and there introduced him to a Negro musician, who sat at their table. Grant felt ashamed and kept shifting about awkwardly and turned very red when Miss Grimm danced with the musician. He carried it off by dancing with her himself, but he could not help speaking to her about it: "I'm a socialist, but you don't want to lose your head; I don't doubt you, a sweet, nice girl, so serious about your ideas, feel friendly toward this colored fella, but think what it looks like."

Miss Grimm told him he was backward. They had an unpleasant talk about it, and he saw her into a taxi without getting a fresh appointment from her. When he got home he telephoned Miss Paula Russell and asked her to have a cocktail with him next day at the King Cole Room at the St. Regis. He identified himself by saying, "I am a man of about fifty, blond hair, not too much of it, large head, big build, five-foot-ten. I'll wear a light gray suit and carry *The Nation* and the *New York Post*."

It was a light, sunny afternoon. He was a little before the hour, as always. He liked to look the women over and perhaps make an appointment or get a telephone number before his companion arrived. A well-dressed, short, sinewy brunette went up the steps before him. He looked her over with ferocity. She was young but harsh. Her figure was made of two hard triangles, the padded shoulders square and the hips appearing not quite so broad, and squarish, the waist small-appearing. She looked about and sat down. Her eyes, black, were almond-shaped but set in a hard, straight line and in clefts. She had a square forehead with a peak of black hair, and her glance already exploited him. He smiled.

He took a table near. She asked for a light. It took them a few minutes to find out that he was Robert Grant and she, Paula Russell. Mrs. Kent had led him to a profit after all. He thought, I hope this isn't my fate; I hope this isn't another Laura.

She began to talk about herself at once. He liked this, for it gave him a quick, personal approach to her. She was French, born in Algeria, and brought up in Marseilles, where her family kept a *pension*.

16

Said he, "You look as if you had some Arab blood; my great-grandmother was half Spanish, so we're both half-breeds." She protested that by accident she looked partly Arab, she was as *white* as could be. "Perhaps I have an Arab temperament."

He invited her to his own hotel, to hear a news commentator, Quincy Howe, at 6 P.M.; he never missed, he said. On the way there, they both praised the news commentator, and both said they were leftists: Miss Russell was a friend of Soviet Russia, Mr. Grant also. The U.S.S.R. could extend her influence in the Far East to the neighbors on her borders; on the other hand, she should not go too far, to excite the envy and hate of Western Europe: she must know her limits— "There's a limit to all things, especially in politics," said Grant. Miss Russell said she thought Russia should get out Hitler and Franco and writes notes to the U.S.A. about the treatment of Negroes, who were not even immigrants, real Americans and how talented, but treated like dogs. Grant frowned very much at this; and said, "Yes, but she knows her limits: she's an international power, she can't meddle in our affairs; she has too much sense." They talked about war, depression. Miss Russell knew a great number of headline personalities in South America, Cuba, France, and elsewhere, though not the U.S.A. or England. She was engaged to a man in the hotel business in France, and had come here on a holiday before settling down.

Grant listened to his radio news, gave the girl a drink, and had what he always called a party with her. After the party, he still thought a great deal of her, was shocked at her corruption, but could not help seeing that she had not the slightest feeling or respect for him: she remained just as she had been. It intrigued him. She was more a man than a woman, he said to himself. He took her to dinner, putting off an appointment with Mrs. Betty Goodwin, who pestered him with telephone calls. "It will do her good," he said to Paula Russell. "But I got no time for her. She gave me a tie, very sweet; but there's too much of her psychologically."

At dinner he asked her about Barbara. Paula's relationship with the drab blonde was a pleasing riddle. Here she, Paula, was a figure in the world, knew publishers, undersecretaries, and business men richer than Grant and March, knew well-known German and French writers. "But what sort of a friend? You said you wanted to warn me against her. No need, I assure you. Now if you had told me you wanted to warn me against yourself

17

—that would have been in order. I got to watch out for you."

"I won't bother you."

He said hastily, "It's very sweet and kind of you to take this interest in a woman down on her luck. I wouldn't have given you the credit for it. But you're like me—you're like me—I'm supposed to be a typical Scot, a cashbox for a heart, and I'm helping out two friends of mine, the Flacks. I'm looking after them. Why not? Some day I'll ask myself, 'What did I do good in the world?' Eh?"

"Barb's a dangerous woman."

"I do not see the danger, but I'll ring her up and look her over. Give me a chance to see you again."

She gave him her number, and added, "Barb's gone away to Florida with a man who is very fond of her, an old man."

"How old?"

"Fifty-nine."

He frowned, "That's not so old."

"Old enough to appreciate Barb."

"How did she get to know him? I thought she was down on her luck."

"Hoag introduced them: Barb can do a lot with a fur cape on her back."

"Don't see it, don't see it!"

"Barb's quite lovely, but I don't think you know much about women."

"You're a strange sort of woman, selling another woman, a rival, like that. Now if it was yourself you were trying to sell, I'd understand. Is he rich, your fiancé?"

Paula said coolly, "I don't care for money, I'd rather marry a man who can do something, show me the world. Do I want to spend the rest of my life in a hotel?"

"That's me. You know what I'm looking for? I'm a lonely man. My wife is a narrow-minded Boston girl. I'm looking for a well-bred charming lady who can run servants, run a farm, I'd buy her a big house, fix it up for her. She's not a bad woman, my wife. Now I'm small-town, but I always had big ideas. In America, small-town is supposed to be a guaranty of romance, lifelong happiness. Two youngsters met on the stoop, married in the Presbyterian Church, got chained up to an icebox and a couple of lace mats and they lived happy ever after. My wife likes the country, but what she means by country is a country club. Sit around, drink whisky—not for me. I had a straitlaced

18

upbringing. I like a fine life, not that gossip and swilling. They don't hold me. She can't hold me. She knows I slipped away and she's hanging on, but it's too late. And look at me, I want to go to Trieste, I want to go to Soviet Russia. Wish I could do something good in the world. She thinks people are laughing at us here in New York. She hates them. I don't give a damn. They laugh. They don't know you exist. That's how I make my way. They're so busy laughing you get to their pockets without being seen. And honestly, mind you, all honest. I had a strait-laced upbringing: I'm an honest man. Don't like cheats. And then I'm a bit of a radical, and that's what I like here, they're all radicals. I'm not a Red, mind you, but a bit of a Marxist, good philosophy, helps you to see things in the right perspective. Made money for me, being a Marxist: I know what's coming. The Reds go too far, dreamers, but a Marxist is practical."

Paula spoke about idealism. She knew Red leaders in several fermenting countries, she said. They had different ideas, not so sordid, they wanted to organize the State.

Grant interrupted, "Organize, I could have done that, if I'd have been brought up in a different country where there was a law to stop me putting my hands in other people's pockets. Now the best I can do is to keep my hands out of my own." He laughed, and went on, "But never mind all that. I'm looking for someone to co-operate with me. My life's empty. I feel frustrated; not in business, but in life, my heart is frustrated. That's my problem; looking for consolation and not finding it—I waste my time in bars, going out with wrong 'ooman; I'm looking for a high-class girl."

She flattered him a little, repeated her story about wanting a man who could show her things, said, "Women still want to be captives to corsairs," and Grant said, "I'm looking for a high-class woman, with sex-appeal, too. Egyptian sakel!"

They made a date for the next day. Grant was intrigued, thought he had met his match.

As soon as she had gone, he telephoned Betty Goodwin, who came to meet him in a bar, even at this late hour, and he told her, "I just met a woman, she's my style, a bit too clever, though, and she thinks she'll work me for a trip round the world."

At this, he slapped his knee, and even his confidante, an anguished, loyal friend who was his mistress also, smiled. Grant went on, "She's like me, a bit too much like me. I know I'm no angel. She knows all the answers. I don't like that in a woman, eh? What do you advise, eh, lay off?"

She was unhappy and began to snarl and show her teeth.

He said, "You're dangerous, too possessive. I couldn't take up with you: you'd hurt me too much."

She began to cry. He patted her arm, smiled, "I'm afraid of women; a woman nearly did for me once—one went after me with a revolver—an accident, a misunderstanding. Flack went to see her and explained it was all a misunderstanding."

"You promised to marry her, of course."

He gripped her arm and burst out laughing, "You'll do, you'll do."

Betty said, "I know better than to hold you to what you say when you want to back out. You're a welcher."

He frowned and patted her arm. "I know you're my friend, you never let me down. But what do you think of her, first she meets me, wants a trip round the world. I must look like a gold mine, eh? Or do you think she really took to me, eh? Give your advice!"

4

One day in May he saw Barbara Kent walking along Fifty-seventh Street with an Army officer. She was well-dressed with a noticeable handbag and strange hat. She was lingering at the windows of an expensive dress store with the man. Grant walked rapidly past and then returned in time to see her face to face. The man was a typical B.P.O.E. dignitary, broad, about forty-five, with steel-blue eyes, Indian cheekbones, and gray hair.

"Public Nobody Number Five Million; I can cut him out. One of them chair warmers."

He followed them into the restaurant across the street, and when the blonde went downstairs to telephone, followed her. He made an appointment with her for the following afternoon, and rushed upstairs. He was impatient to see her, "I'll have it out with her: what about Florida, what about the elderly gent? Just a story between the girls? Or that gun moll wanted to get my eyes off Barb?"

He saw her every day for weeks. In the meantime, he had several disappointments. Miss Celia Grimm would not go up to his room with him and said he only "gave lip-service to socialism." He felt ruffled and cheated, for usually his radicalism made his girls trustful and either cheap or for nothing: a radical girl should not take money for love. He put his failure down to her interest in the Negro people and complained about her: "She is a kind of invert or pervert I think. I take her to The Golden Tassel, and she dances with a Negro fellow."

The other failure had been with the telephone girl at the office downtown, a handsome girl in black, whom he had seen dancing in night-clubs with several men. He had given her a box of chocolates once, at another time five dollars to get some gloves for herself. Now she was engaged, and leaving to marry. He was so indignant that he discussed with Miss Robbins, his secretary, the possibility of making her give back the five dollars. "She knew she was going to cheat me, if she's going to get married. I'd like the fellow to know what kind of woman she is. See if you can get his address. Say you want to give her a party."

Miss Robbins refused. He said, "Perhaps you're right. Perhaps I didn't attract the girl, eh? After all, I don't always win. And they don't know what's good for them, eh? Their privilege."

For the time being he was in a good mood, but when he went through the front office and saw the girl sitting there with the earphones on, he fell into a fury again. He waited for her at six o'clock, putting off an appointment with Mrs. Betty Goodwin, but when he came up with her, instead of asking about the price of the gloves, his old habits got the better of him and he began to murmur, "Lovely girl, congratulations, don't know why you wouldn't try to make something of me instead of some young fellow." In the end, he took her to a bar and had drinks with her, but got no further. Going home in the subway, he thought, She always gives me the impression she's taking me over. Don't like that.

Meanwhile, he had an interesting subject of conversation with Miss Russell. Why did Miss Russell lie to him about the elderly man and Florida? They had tea and a little chat several times about this. Paula did not like his new interest in Barbara, because as Grant put it to himself, "She has seen more of me than is good for her; and then, like me, she's possessive, she's greedy, she is from the Land of Grab," and he believed she wanted to break off her engagement for him. In the White Bar, in Fifty-second Street, where he took his conquests when he became used to them, and where a good many handsome models and salesgirls went after work, Miss Russell, dressed in summer black, told him, "Barb and I don't really like each other. Barb went

21

off the rails at sixteen and men treated her badly, threw her out like an old shoe. When I first met her in Paris—"

"—in Paris!" ejaculated Grant.

"—she had bracelets, diamond, gold, platinum, up the elbow, service stripes; then she was seventeen and had seventeen of them. She struck hard luck and in a couple of years she had eaten them off. She was in a divorce suit in London when she was twenty-two. At one time she was married to a man named Madison who was madly in love with her and thought her a pure young girl. He took her out to the Coast to get her into the movies. She was dazzled by Hollywood, and though she didn't care that much for Madison, she thought by going out with movie people she'd get a chance. She takes a good still, but she can't act. Her husband died, she married a man named Kent and lived in Los Angeles in a little suburban house for two years, but she got tired of it and started to get into trouble with men. She began getting friendly with married men they knew. Then Kent left her, divorced her, she had no money, and she started getting men into jams. At first, it was accidental. Some man insulted her in the street and she won a suit. I think she wanted to marry again, but no one pleased her because she was ambitious. She hitched her wagon to a star. She's quite honest really—serious-minded. She never had the strength of mind to go through with any marriage. She got sick of men so soon. I don't think she really cares for them. She's not a gold-digger at heart, but she finished up gold-digging. She has too good a head for figures. She can always calculate the chances. What's the use of marrying somebody with flat feet, some jerk, and so dying of old age at thirty? Look at me—I don't want to marry but I don't want to roll round, either."

Grant said, "Roll round with me and I'll show you things you haven't seen yet, you're only naïve, you don't know much, you're only young yet."

"I don't believe in any man any more. I'm tougher and smarter than Barb. Barb has moments when she goes romantic and thinks someone will do something for her. She always lets the right moment pass. She never calls the turn, and wastes their money. She skims off the cream and when the men get tired of her, she tries to make them do something for her. She has them eating out of her hand. When it's too late, she tries to make a profit."

"I thought you said she calculated everything."

"So she does, but she hasn't the patience. She's only a plunger: she has no technique. She's restless. No man ever made her happy."

Said Grant, getting restless, "She's like me, no woman ever made me happy. Sometimes I thought I met the right woman. Take you. You wouldn't take a chance with me. That 'ooman in Boston, my wife, is no good to me. Never loved me. Now when it's too late, she tries to make me come back. Just like Barb. It's a type—stupid. A woman like you could keep a man. I'm looking for an oasis in my desert, a rose on a blasted heath. Barb's not my type at all. First time I saw her, I thought, she's just a scrubwoman. She looks down and out, dissolute. You look well kept, good breeding."

"Barbara's had a lot of money spent on her, but she's just a tramp," said her friend; "sometimes she could have taken a bath in Goldwasser."

Grant mused, "She doesn't look like that, but you never can tell with women. Some of them are all on the surface, all on their backs, you might say; others are like old wine: dirty outside, cobwebs—the better, the more you taste, and it stays on your tongue. I don't see much of her. Dangerous, eh? Not the sort for me to play around with. I'm looking for romance. My heart needs a home, a cradle, eh? I've used myself up, played too hard. Now I need a woman, a mother, a sister, a sweetheart, a friend. That's what that cow in Boston doesn't realize. I need a mother now. She could have me back. But it's too late now. Now I've met you."

The interview had the usual successful ending and Grant was interested to see that a hardy quick girl like Paula Russell, with only occasional misgivings, was beginning to believe that she could replace *Laura, the dangerous love*, in his life. She was beginning to think about marrying him.

He was easily bored these days. Two years ago, he had arranged a partnership with a talented young cotton broker named McMahon who had put in $60,000 to Grant's $40,000, and who, though he required Grant's signature for checks, could deal in his own name. McMahon was active, but, as it seemed to Grant, when he felt flush of animal spirits, the young fellow took long chances, perhaps to impress Grant, who had promised him the management of a new firm in the Argentine. Two youngish cotton dealers, who had been with him for fifteen and seventeen years, meanwhile watched over Grant's interests in the firm. These men had been promised partnerships in Grant's old business which he proposed to put on a new footing in New Orleans very soon. The air of New Orleans did not suit him, he said, at his age. This business he had delayed from year to year. Now it looked like war, and it must wait till the war was nearly ended or quite over, for Grant suspected that all basic commodities would be differently controlled after the war. He was marking time. In the meantime, the two youngish men, James and Butters, remained devoted to his interests. He promised the general managership of the new house, and sometimes a partnership, to each one separately, conferred with each in secret, and taking each aside at times, deplored the other's lack of talent. It was simple: he would say, "a nervous, capricious sort of fellow that I saved from a very awkward situation, and who is grateful, but who perhaps overestimates my devotion to him. I want results. He made that mistake in '36," and this of each one. Meanwhile, he got Flack, in his spare hours, to help him with a *Memorandum on the Supply and Distribution of Cotton, Given the Redundant Inventories,* cotton being then the outstanding surplus of the world. This memorandum, a secret, and exhibited separately to James and Butters as his own rough work, was to bear the names of Robert Owen Grant and Mr. James or Mr. Butters, as the case required. Flack, meanwhile, had been promised a percentage of Grant's cotton exchange profits, in compensation for these consultations.

Grant's brain which had been functioning, to his own profit, with uncommon energy since the age of four or five, was now empty and ached. He had no more need for money, as his estate was settled in respect of his elder son; and the other boy, a weakling, he considered only as "a contingency." His will was drawn up; there were only two beneficiaries, one of them the "contingency," the other, Gilbert. The only problem for him was to make legitimately his current expenses, about $30,000 yearly, and since he could make any reasonable amount in any one year, he also spent very freely. He made his $30,000 in a few hours daily and through his organization, on the Cotton Exchange.

He had no hobbies. He could not read more than a few consecutive sentences in any book or newspaper unless they referred immediately to himself or his interests. Thus he might read a few words on Robert Owen, a few on Lancashire, a few words on cotton control; but in general he missed all the points. He well knew this and would throw down newspapers in the faces of his friends and managers, saying, "What's the point? What's he getting at?"

He spent many hours by himself. He jingled his money, walked up and down, pouted, frowned, sighed, thought of writing to friends long forgotten, recollected injuries done to him by the dead, called women, bought new clothes for himself, tried to think of some little thing, some out-of-the-way thing, like a buttonhook for gloves, that some freak friend wanted, the kind of thing that would take hours or days to unearth. He had little pleasure out of his own real hobby, libertinage; and he gave none. Women fell away from him, but he did not know why; and he retained only the venal. He had little to muse upon. Few women he knew wrote letters, and most of these contained requests for money, put in some roundabout or clumsy form. He kept what he got, and would conceal them, for further meditation, in various places: in the bottom of the dustcovers over his many suits; some were in his collarbox, some in his hatboxes, some under the paper lining of the drawers. Every time there was a question of moving, or of sending clothes to the cleaners, he had some interesting hours, during which he would lock the door of his apartment while he went over everything looking for *the private matters* he might have *caché*d.

After he had left the place, gone on a trip, or after the clothes had left for the cleaners, he would fret about some intimate letter or bill which he thought lost. Then he would run backwards and forwards between the cleaners and his apartment, and send his secretary over the same trail, or even some crony, like Goodwin.

In June, at the settling of accounts, he deferred payments to Flack till the end of the year. Edda, Flack's daughter, sent him in the mail a caricature of himself. Flack defended his daughter. They quarreled and Flack left off jackaling for him, for the time being, saying that he would get another job easily enough. A cotton speculator in New Orleans had offered Grant a participation for the sum of $25,000. He was a rising man, everyone whispered his name; but Grant had thought up a few schemes for going in with Bentham, this speculator, without putting up a cent. Flack now said, "Bentham will go in with me, for my brains, quicker than with you for your prestidigitation: from you he wants money, but he would go in with me for my wits."

Grant was not sure that this was not true. He watched angrily

and used friends as spies. What was Flack doing? All he heard
was that Edda Flack, the young daughter, had got a job as a
comic-strip continuity artist. No one knew what Flack was doing.
But the report was that Edda, the daughter, kept telling everyone, "Let Robbie Grant watch out, he will tread on a banana
peel." Grant was uneasy. Flack had been his best friend for long
years.

5

About July, 1941, he found himself in this becalmed area. He
had no pleasure from his friends. He was tired of being invited
out, town was going to empty soon. He had made many concrete
promises to many people and he was tired of their faces round
him. He went to Boston to see his wife and Andrew, aged seven,
the son remaining at home. He did not like the boy, an interesting, tender neurotic who clung to his father and cried every time
he left the house. He blamed his wife for the boy's sensibility.
Mrs. Grant was nervous, difficult, and tried to divert him with
her garden and the new gardener. The boy was more clinging
than ever. Grant thought all the time of the blonde. She seemed
to be with him. The third time he had given her a fair bit of
money, she had spent it on clothes. She had not murmured at
the small sum, not said anything about another meeting. One
day she said she needed more money, he had given it to her.
She knew an old woman who had been good to her in Washington. He found out that the address and name were correct, and
then gave her money for the old woman. She always pleased him.
He would sit on the lounge and mutter hastily, "I just made a
bit of money, what do you want a check for?"
She took it, after some little hesitation, the sum a little larger
each time. He liked it. He thought: My fault if I offer it. She
never apologized, demurred or said she would pay back, but
only, "I need it."
He had begun to buy what she needed. He paid for photographs of her and silver frames for them. She was simple, gentle,
easy to get on with when he gave her money. She never refused
him, made irreducible feminine reasonings about everything,
which he believed in, prattled personalities, friends she had picked
up, lovers, and told of them with the fragrance of a past innocence—it was in Germany, Switzerland, France, Belgium. She
had few moods of any kind, except when he, in a temporary fit
of avarice, refused her money. Then she paid him out. He

26

admired this. At present he had a winning streak. In July she received money from abroad from her father, James Alexis Jones, who went by the short name of James Alexis. Grant said he had brought her luck and she brought him luck. He had begun to see her every afternoon. He resented the other men she went out with, and while in Boston this time, he made up his mind to get her to move to a midtown hotel at his expense. He had become tired of Miss Russell: she was a campaigner. She had a bad influence on Barbara.

When he returned from Boston he had his plans made. The blonde woman went to live at the fashionable midtown Grand Hotel, a place with bars, restaurants, a night club, a roof garden, coiffeurs, dress shops. It was the resort of business and society people all day long. She began to dress to suit the place and to send him her bills, not only for clothes. She changed her airs to suit her position and quarreled with him. He often went to see her early in the morning but was not admitted. He would sometimes taxi uptown at midday and find her still in bed in some fine negligee; in the afternoon he would find her just up, very handsome, soft. He was delighted to take her out. They would go shopping almost every afternoon. On Sunday he found her in bed drinking chocolate and reading the comics. He reproved her for her laziness and the disorder of the room. She was untidy, would rather buy a garment than repair it. She complained that she needed a maid. She needed hundreds of things he had never bought for a woman before, all to keep her in order. She never seemed to be able to assemble a complete toilette. She was not the sort of woman to spend all the afternoon looking for just one kind and color of gloves. She bought rashly. He had fretted and marveled in Rome at Laura's energy for so small a thing as a pair of rose gloves. Now he saw it was a kind of economy and smartness, and he admired Laura for this long distance in time. The blonde had not her quality and was a waster.

"You will never have a cent," he told her regretfully.

Barbara frowned, "Mother did all that for me; I am too miserable thinking about myself to bother."

Her mother was in Ireland, she said, working for some wealthy Anglo-Irish in an outlandish castle with portraits, tapestries, horses, dogs, children and Catholic peasantry. Grant had seen numerous letters from the mother who wished to come to the U.S.A. He said, "A woman your age doesn't need a mother." Suddenly he laughed. But the blonde, "You will never understand that mother is the only one who never let me down. She's an old-fashioned woman; she keeps me straight."

"Get her over!"

"With what? I have no money. I'm always one day from the street."

"Don't talk that way, my dear girl."

"That's your story."

"Don't be a grasshopper, be an ant; imitate me: put something by for a rainy day."

"I'd rather die. I can't fight my nature."

"You make me worry about you, Barb."

After a pause, Barb continued, "Mother is just a poor grandmother living with those back country squires, taking care of their ignorant little girls. It's not pleasant for me to think of my best friend working as a nursemaid."

"It does you credit, Barb," he muttered.

He had her on his mind more than any other woman. How to reform her? She, meanwhile, spoiled by him, took no thought even for the afternoon. He would find her in her dressing jacket, discontented, because the dress she had set her mind on wearing was soiled. She did not bank any money nor get up a wardrobe to help her through hard times. He had to keep buying things for her: he bought her two or three fur coats, dresses, underwear, merely out of anxiety about the time when he should leave her. He thought, I must help her through the hard time she doesn't foresee herself. She is a child, she is naïve. She doesn't try to keep a man. Now look at me. What a sucker! When will she get a sucker like me again? But she doesn't think about herself at all. Not like that pig Paulie, always on the make. You've got to say that for the blonde.

One day he saw her sitting with her naked back turned toward him and her thick long hair coiling over one shoulder. She turned to him. He saw the light on her skin, how fair it was. He thought of this all day and night and called her to himself "The Blondine." Next day he found her lying on her side, all her fair skin exposed, her hair in its loop at the nape of the neck, her arm curved round the neck of a toy Angora cat she always had on her pillow and took to bed with her. She had once had a cat like that, deaf, she said, which slept all day and mewed all night. She preferred this one. The woman, the cat, the pillows, and the expanse of linen moved him. "The Blondine," he said to himself, "how she is wasting herself."

But as he had foreseen, he tired of her. All this took months. It was autumn. Miss Russell and the blonde sometimes quarreled, though usually friends, and both remained in the same relation to Grant. Mrs. Kent did not use her opportunities to meet richer men than Grant, though Miss Russell urged her to and gave her a very despicable account of Grant's character. Mrs. Kent became surly, fretful, self-indulgent, and told Grant that he stood in her way. She seemed to be trying to lose him. Grant meanwhile had seen too much of her. He had pursued his usual habits, meeting other women every day and carrying on intrigues of all calibers with girls in the office, girls introduced by cronies, of living promiscuously and entirely for himself.

The woman seemed pleased to be left alone and this was no cure for her. He had long ago promised to marry her. Now he told her he never would marry anyone: "He had suffered too much from women; and he could see she would make him suffer." She did not even try to rake up his promises. She told him she was tired of him. He raged and determined to stop paying her hotel expenses; but the next month when the bills came in from the most expensive stores in town, he paid, after his usual cautionary hesitation, and even sent her flowers when she telephoned him and explained in a sharp, cruel voice. He sometimes felt he could not get on without her and yet he hated her when he felt that she did not love him, was sucking him dry. "I'll send her back to the street," he said to himself. Meanwhile, he had arranged for the mother to come from Ireland to keep Barb company.

One Sunday after a quarrel, when he had found her in bed at three o'clock in the afternoon, he told her the affair was finished. She must pack up, find somewhere else to go. On this afternoon, he telephoned Mrs. Coppelius, the little dark woman, who had been the wife of a scapegrace physician somewhere out in the Middle West. Coppelius was not her real name. Her husband, a physician, a gay person, met too many women in his calling. She felt the disgrace, especially because she loved him deeply. Whenever any serious affair was going on, she came to New York, lived in a hall bedroom, and got a job as a salesgirl. When the affair was through, the physician would call her back. She had refused to see Grant for months, saying that he was only a man-about-town, that she would have been interested in him if he had been serious. She explained to Grant that she was "too passionate—she believed in love" and it was no use her getting into an affair with a man like him, "with a painted heart." Grant, though he protested that he was only looking for a woman to fill his life, did not like this and left her alone. Once when he insisted strongly, she had had a cocktail with him and gone up to his apartment and had undressed. But she would only kiss him. She said, "I do it to show I am not ugly, and that it is only because you don't love me, I don't—." He was indignant but puzzled by her act, and she remained in his mind as a very odd, attractive, almost girlish figure. Before she went, she explained, "I would fall in love with you, but to you I am only a woman you take upstairs." His future troubled him a little. He wondered if she were like Laura, the great romance of his life. Laura was a Roman woman of good family and wealthy, who had left a rich, successful Milanese business man for Grant. Laura was his greatest trophy, had captivated him for years, turbulent, shallow, fickle, passionless as he was.

That Sunday evening he made up his accounts and found that the expense of the blonde for six months had been $23,000 more or less. "Too much, little Coppelius works honestly for a living, she's Sea Island-staple, the other's rotten." He sat in his hotel some time, but did not ring Mrs. Coppelius.

He telephoned Martha Anderson, salesgirl in Goodwin's fur loft. He assured her her stills were very good. He thought she might get an agent to promote her in Hollywood. She had a mother to support. Grant held out hopes of a loan, and the girl put on her hat and came to see him at once, in the White Bar. He told her she was a real beauty, would certainly make her way, and that he was interested in her career. What he wanted was a woman of character: he was tired of drunken pigs and lazy sows and women he had spent $23,000 on for six months of boredom. He told her about Laura, about Barbara, and about Miss Russell, "an adventuress," and about his wife, "a sweet woman, an angel."

"If I had a woman with ambition and looks—who wanted to go on the stage—I'd be proud and glad to help her and not even ask anything from her." He repeated this, embellishing it. When he said he had to make a long-distance telephone call, she went upstairs with him, and he amused himself for a while. But though she was a handsome young woman, she was obedient and serious, and her smile was not seductive.

When she went he sat down quite desolate in front of his sun lamp and thought over his position. It was very difficult for him to think about himself. He could not think about his sexual life. This was repugnant to him. He thought, "I need a sensual woman. I can't help it." He tried to think about politics. He smelt a big change, big money, but he did not know from what quarter it was coming; he was afraid of the autumn, he did not like the looks of anything "in the political sphere," as he liked to say, and yet he smelt money too. He would follow his instinct but he must have someone to listen to. Out of a flood of opinion he would pick the one that meant money, yet he felt that without guidance he would lose a lot of money.

He always tried to read best-sellers, especially about international politics, reportages, spy rings, books about Trotsky, whom he secretly admired because "he had stood out on his own," but whom he felt obliged to criticize because of his few Stalinist friends; and books about Mussolini, though he was obliged to make bluff objections for the same reason. . . . He sought vaguely for some life-plan and some political views. As he sat grousing to himself, a temptation came to him. He longed to speak to David Flack as in the old days.

Flack had understood and admired Grant's youthful business energy. Grant then had only $30,000 and the meeting took place a few months before Grant seized the opportunity to make half a million dollars out of a certain agency that was given to him by an old English cotton firm which was too rich, too old, and too widely distributed—one of those mercantile empires which do not belong to the modern world. . . . It was not then too late in the day for Grant to establish his own small dominion. He presently had relations in many countries, even in India and elsewhere. He did it on his own. He had no political or financial friends.

During this time, David Flack, a financial journalist, was his friend, gave him intelligent information on financial markets, and steered him through the welter of daily-paper politics. David Flack was a Marxist. It became Grant's fashion to call himself a Marxist too, but only among people with empty pockets and few chances.

Flack's daughter, Edda, was a slender, sharp-tongued young brunette who naturally disliked Grant. She had drawn a caricature of him, showing his woman-hunting nose, and the thin yellow hair trained over his head. As he had often brought Edda a cake of scented soap or a bottle of toilet water, he called the whole thing "uncalled for, and unwomanly." She was too sharp, she had no charm. She was seventeen and always was ready for a tussle. Flack himself had always been a yielding, loving person, though tough in the wits. Grant locked the caricature away in a drawer but took it with him wherever he went—he could not throw it away.

He felt his passionate genial manhood, his old experience welling up in him; he wanted to go and throw himself between them, as he had so often done, give them an idea of his exploits; but the caricature kept sticking in his throat.

He called up Mrs. Betty Goodwin and arranged to meet her the next afternoon. Betty and he were a seasoned couple by this. They thought nothing of their afternoons together, but would chatter about barroom personalities, mutual friends, and business affairs before, during, and after their encounters. Betty, on the telephone, gave him enough opinions on the events of the day to keep him going during the evening, but at night, he was restless. His brain was going to sleep; he was afraid he would miss a big hand. He could not see into the future, and he worried, as he had often worried lately, was he aging? If so, to hell with the world, he would have the wildest time he could before he collapsed altogether. Did he have ten years? Twenty?

The next day as he rushed through the corridors of the Cotton Exchange to the street, he thought he saw a familiar figure; but he rushed on, perverse, romantic as a lover. When he returned to Hanover Square, he found a note for himself from David Flack; it was David Flack he had seen. As soon as he got back to his hotel, he telephoned his old friend and a meeting was arranged for the same afternoon. Grant put off Mrs. Betty Goodwin.

Grant was overjoyed, his feelings overflowing at the coming meeting. "Falling out of faithful friends, renewing is of love." He went to a Turkish bath, had a shampoo, manicure, and suntan and was perfumed all over. He put on a suit never worn before, and new shoes.

"She will see. Edda will see I am not the man she drew. She'll be sorry she lost me, she'll appreciate me more, see my good points, perhaps she gave him the good advice, Go back to Robbie, he muttered to himself.

He rushed out to get some mixed cocktails and brandy and cakes for the event.

"She called me avaricious, she'll see I'm generous."

They arrived slightly before the hour, David Flack's old way. David Flack and Robert Grant actually kissed each other and wept. Then they started walking about the room and declaiming about the market and the political situation, the likelihood of war, what Grant should do with his accounts, trust funds, and property abroad, and the new industries in Mexico and Brazil, all just as in the old days. Grant said, "You and I are going into this thoroughly, David. If war's coming, I want to make a profit, that's all. I'm too old to fight, all I can do is to make a profit, eh?"

Edda sat and grinned. He noticed her pretty legs and at once addressed himself to her.

He said boisterously, "I've changed. You know, it took me two-three months to get over that picture you did of me. But one day I said to myself, 'Let's be fair. Who is right, Edda or me?' I looked in the mirror. Mirror, mirror, hanging on the wall"—he burst out laughing and hung on to the mantelpiece, gesticulating— "have I got shoulders like a prizefighter? Yes. Have I got a big nose? Well, not so big as she made out—but she was a girl, then. I said to myself, 'Are you going to keep up a grudge your whole life against a girl, a schoolgirl?' "

The girl laughed out loud and said now she was used to men. She was a floater but wanted to be a journalist.

"A writer! A writer? I can give you material! You want to write reality! I can give you stuff—a best-seller. Just come here every day, any time you like, I'll just give you my life. Make a writer's fortune. In my office is a table, a typewriter, I'll dictate to you. You write a book. I'll give you all the details. Just take it down in shorthand."

"But I'm working, Robbie: it's paid work: I can't afford to speculate."

"My darling, I feel I'm floundering from day to day. I'm looking for an affair big enough for me, enough to engross me, take all my energy, all my heart—without absolutely committing me for the rest of my life, ha-ha! They're all short-lived in my family. All got thick necks, red faces. My two brothers are dead. Listen, darling, trust to me. I'll make your forchun. I'll take you to winter resorts, we'll go to Mont-Laurier, even Europe. Rich Americans are still everywhere in Europe: this is your passport! Ha-ha!" He slapped his pocket.

"There's a war on. The Germans are sweeping through the Ukraine."

Grant changed countenance, "If the Russians lose, it's the Dark Ages. We'll go and hide our heads somewhere, there'll be nothing to live for." There was a pause. Grant suddenly cried, "They've got to win. They use talent. They got new methods. They have the same idea as the Americans. Don't ask who their father was: don't ask if they wipe their nose on a handkerchief or throw it in the gutter; they got no handicaps, they take 'em from the farm, they take 'em from the factory, they take 'em from the schools, they take old men and teach 'em ABC, they'll win, they have what the U.S.A. had. Now it's Valley Forge. They'll come out the other end. Trust me, I have a hunch. Let's drink to them. Let's drink to us!"

He rushed to the closet, brought out the drinks and the cakes, got the glasses, did everything himself, saying, "Just wait a moment: let's drink to our reunion." He overfilled her glass in excitement and ran to get a cleaning fluid and a clean towel for her dress. He got down on his knees, briskly rubbing away and murmuring words of consolation; then up with a snort, and to his drink, which he drank at a gulp. "You don't know me, Edda. Now you know me better. In Canada they have women in Turkish baths and my woman told me my face looked forty-five, but my body thirty-five; a masseuse ought to know. My conscience is younger than that. I kept it young, virgin. Didn't use it!" He burst out laughing, "I've reformed, Edda. Also, you didn't know me. No good making fun of people. Got to see the good side. I've reformed. I had a girl this year, right here in this city, who appealed to me physically, but she was very selfish and I held off, for there was a deep attraction there; but I knew one day I would wake up and see her bad side. The blondine was honey, physically, but no character. I left her. I'm fifty, I thought this year, I've got to remake my life. My life's a desert, I said, I'm looking for an oasis. My life was a well gone dry, eh? You see, I was looking for another Laura."

His face shone, he shouted, "There she was at seven in the morning, sitting at the table per-r-fectly gr-r-roomed, and on the table everything sweet, nice to make it look appetizing. I said, 'Look, Laura darling, you need your sleep, you're not very big, and you don't rest enough; you entertain too much.' But she would get up in the morning for me, and she drove me to wor-rk in a powerful car, like the wind, like a racer, and she only weighed

34

a few pounds. She kept the house wonderful, in the house everything perfect, a perfect lady. Why don't you take a few notes?"

"If you think I can't remember that—"

He filled up their glasses urgently, "And in the morning, in the morning my head is clear, I'm practical, I have no illusions, every morning I said to myself, 'If there's anything wrong, I'll see it.' But I said to her, 'I'm going to pay you a compliment, it's a great compliment, and if any other time, it happens that any other man says it to you, you'll know it's sincere and a great compliment, for a man can see in the morning. You look so sweet in the morning, Laura, I want to kiss your hand.' And she took it as a great compliment."

He sat down. "Always looking for another. I am sorry, but I can't go back. She caused me too much sorrow, gave me too much hurt. I plunged into another affair, headfirst, when I got away from her, but I didn't like it, it was like this Paulie, woman you don't know, but it was only to set up competition in my heart. Maybe I was outclassed; I don't think so. Something else—the 'ooman's not loyal—not Sea Island-staple. A woman must be loyal. Wholesome. Constructive. Not a destroyer, not a grave-digger morally. She, Laura, the Roman woman, broke down my morale. Told me I was only a roughneck, a business man. I said I never pretended to be aught else. I told her, 'I relied upon you to build me up, you pulled me down and made me a laughing-stock.' Well, I didn't marry her—but she prevented me. Now, little girl, just to show you don't know me—you called me—mr-mur-mur too, Mary, my wife, an angel, just to show you, I'm looking to get married; I'll easily get papers because she has someone else too— only it's funny, I don't like that. I thought—at least she's loyal, something the other cows haven't. It broke me—morally."

The young girl laughed bitterly, "Love affairs always break you morally."

"Correct," said the father admiringly.

"Don't agree with you both at all, and as I happen to know something of your father, David, he is moral and he thinks I'm immoral."

Her father gave Edda a tender warning glance, which Grant caught.

He said roguishly, "Yes, listen to me, David knows me; my great affairs have been Continental women, I don't look for them, but they have been, and this time I'm looking for one too— I found one, beautiful, modest, she draws back—I'm a hothead, eh? She's a physician's wife. She loves him but he two-times her. A bad business. It disappointed her: she's suspicious about men. I said, 'Leave it to me to educate you.' I said, 'If you're the right woman, life's an empty well, if you fill it up—you can even fill it up with tears—you're my woman. I'll teach you about loyalty.' I said to her, 'I'll buy you a lavaliere, you'll find out about loyalty.' She said, 'Don't buy me anything, I don't want anything, that would spoil everything between us.' Eh?"

He grinned genially, "Listen to what I say. You don't know about life yet. You could write down my life and it would sell like hot cakes. Better than that what's-a-name fella's. Damn fool has five thousand dollars in every bank in the country, I heard, because that's all the guarantee the Government gives. A business brain like that can make a best-seller? I can—I mean you can. I give you the idea free, absolutely free, want nothing out of it."

David said, "We don't want an idea to sell, Robbie, we're interested in you as a friend." He kept on laughing like a foal whinnying.

The young girl assumed an enigmatic expression.

Grant frowned, "It'll sell. Why waste it? Here you have a golden opportunity. I give it to you on a clamboard. It's a question of real experience; not like that stuff they write—"

Said the young girl insolently, "I've seen you in action, five years ago, and if you ask me, you don't know anything about women. I have a theory about it: those who have too many know nothing, like a man who sat up all night eating candy."

He listened, smiled eagerly and vaguely like a five-month-old infant, stretched out his plump hand, said confidingly, "You don't know, my girl, I know women, I flatter myself I know women. Only the women don't know me. Only for themselves. Now any woman could take me over. All I want is a woman. All I need, I don't need nothing else. . . . This woman I met—a few days ago, the doctor's wife, my oasis, a little pond in my desert, I told her all I want is a woman. She could take me on. She wasted her opportunities." He meditated; he poured some more drinks for himself and David Flack and, already beginning to stagger a little, told his life history, and his mother's—the Lancashire mills, his father's last days, lying on a bed, Grant out making money at seven years old: "I'll tell you my story and give you a for-r-mula and it'll be a best-seller, better than that fella; and I swear to you, my word of honor, I have no interest in it, only to see something true written. It's got to be wholesome. I knew nothing wrong till I was nineteen or twenty, late development, eh? And I did nothing wrong till thirty-six, thirty-seven. Now you mustn't think of me as—mur-murmur—or the way you drew that caricature— that pulls down, that's a grave-digger; you must build up, then it sells. The people have the right instinct; they don't buy what's unwholesome. Young people make that mistake. No experience; and they like to pull down the generation before. For argument's sake, my young friend, a story I have in my head, just came to me. A young woman comes from Europe, from Poland. I met her there, say, she told me some story, I found out it was true; honest fine mother, honest family, young woman in love with her husband, a doctor, but he sees too many 'ooman, he plays with fire, she meets a man who suits her, that she admires, and he brings her to New York City. He's an American, wholesome, a constructive type. She has a father who has gone to Canada and made money in furs, a fortune in the New World. She stayed behind, married to a doctor. As soon as she meets this American, she realizes he is her fate; but she's modest, she draws back. He says, the American, 'I don't ask anything from you, just tell me what I can do for you, I'll teach you to forget, I'll teach you a constructive view of life. What is your ambition?' She says, 'I wanted to make a career on the stage.' Eh? She's pretty, she always wanted to go on the stage, but her mother wouldn't let her. Her mother said, 'It would take you away from me.' She remained a home girl, you see, then married a doctor, a narrow life. This American says, 'I like to construct,' says he's a moral engineer; 'I like to construct lives, too.' Now, Edda, make it simple, don't be clever, don't be sardonic—I beg pardon, I don't mean anything wrong, but no words like—mur-murmur—like you said about me, unnecessary, uncalled-for: people don't buy spoiled goods. Give them pure goods, nice colors, you see. You wouldn't try to sell ladies' scarves, ankle-sox to girls all black and gray, with holes in. Well, stories must be the same. Or make it a play. But, no, more money in books."

"Plays!" Flack cried, laughing madly, elfishly. "They're a gold mine, you dumb ox. *Tobacco Road* made millions, and it's not constructive, it's morally off-center, calls for the inspector of drains. I saw it, said it wouldn't go a week—went eight years. That's what my opinion is worth."

He laughed and repeated this several times.

Edda said, "I, too, thought it wasn't constructive enough. People don't care about what's constructive. They like to think the poor have a good time after all by sitting in the sun and spending the day in lechery."

The merchant frowned, "Don't like it, not my style. It won't go."

They shouted at him, "It went, it went all right."

He looked at the girl for some time and repeated more than once, "Our story will be constructive. Don't care if that fella made a forchun. How much did you say?"

He reflected for a minute after the figures and drank another glass of liquor. He suddenly came back to Edda and cried, "Maybe one lechery play—the fad will pass. Ours will sweep the country— my plot, take notes, for argument's sake, it must be wholesome. And the American mer-r-chant—builds up Poland for her. He sells furs—need them there."

In the end the two men, merrily drunk, the girl sober, put on their hats and went out, walked several blocks to clear their heads, and parted with great expressions of friendship on both sides. Grant cried, "I'll make your forchuns, both of ye, I'm in a winning mood, I'm beginning on luck and I've changed, I'm bringing a lot of people luck and no interest in it, take my word. I wouldn't even take a ticket in a lottery: waste of money. If you could buy the tickets from the winners—I can see the point—then advertise Grant's Bank paid out the following winners—but go into it? No, I don't pay out a hundred to one, which is what the people do. One man wins a hundred, loses more than a hundred. Not for me. With cotton, I work; with women I've a forr-r-mula. No losses. Well, sometimes one or two, but at the end of the year, if my accounts don't come out on the black side, I'm blue. Red, blue; black and I'm in the pink."

6

Early on Sunday morning, that is, about nine-thirty, he telephoned. "Excuse me ringing you so early on Sunday. There's a good reason for it, believe me, my girl, you'll make a forchun. I could not sleep all night thinking of our plot and I got some very good ideas. Now, have you got a pencil, jot them down and it will make your book a best-seller."

"I'm not writing a book," said the girl.

Grant was speaking urgently right into the mouthpiece, "I had just now a wonderful idea for my best-seller, I got to tell you now before I forget: I know a man Kincaid, found out the Jewish racket, you know what that is? Gentile finds out that Jews like Gentiles who like them, and he always makes a business of it.

38

This Kincaid, just to sell, pretends the British are the Tenth Tribe of Israel. He met a man, Solomon Greenstein, Jewish, whom I met in London, by the way. Kincaid, he was not allowed in business for some reason, and was doing illegal business, black market, in stopped currencies. He had his room behind Solomon Greenstein's picture business. Greenstein sold phony pictures, and made big money, false Raphaels, Rembrandts, etc. You can see them all over Bath, Liverpool, and other places. All wooden nutmegs. One time Greenstein made ten thousand pounds. Now, these pictures were Kincaid's and Solomon Greenstein was only his employee, junior partner, so to say. So Kincaid spent three thousand pounds on a bronze door with the ten commandments in Hebrew and Moses and all the prophets in the Old Testament, Obadiah, Isaiah, I don't know all the names of them fellas, I did once, just like some famous door in Florence, I think, only out of the Old Testament. There was the seal of Solomon on it and some green stones, so that customers would think that Solomon Greenstein, instead of hiding his Jewishness, made a terrific parade of it and was proud of it—except, you understand, that it was Kincaid who did it. Kincaid even thought of changing his name to Cohen, but he figured that 'Kincaid and Greenstein' were better, faced both ways. Now this Kincaid came to New York and brought Greenstein, who is a bit of a Johnny-Raw, and Kincaid hires several floors in a storage warehouse uptown, all for himself. When he sees the numerous Jews in New York he is even more tempted to change his name to Rubenstein, but he soon sees that a Gentile who goes in for Jews has a very easy time, so he still sticks to Kincaid. This time the pictures are his and he says he has a Jewish grandmother; since Hitler, this made him a Jew, so he felt satisfied. Also, he read up on everything Jewish like a real Scots scholar, and learned the Jewish alphabet, he learned to read Yiddish, and thus caught on to one of the great weaknesses of the Jews, who think Yiddish is a private speech, not just a form of low German, and if anyone can read or understand it, are sure you have Jewish blood, even if you can also read Russian or Arab. Believe me," said Grant, chuckling, "my dear girl, the Jews can say what they like, they are bair-rns compared with the Scots for a profit, and you know all the Jews in Dundee are meese-r-rably poor. In Glasgow, of course, everyone, of whatever origin, is miserably poor. However—"

"Let me speak." David Flack had come up to the phone and

was crowding his daughter toward the wall. "What does he want? Let me speak."

"Father wants to speak to you!"

"Listen, my girl, you're the artist in the family, tossed all night, thinking of our hit. You and I can make a hit of it. You and I. I only want the glory; you get the money, you see. Listen! Are you taking it down?"

She said impatiently, "Damn it, I can remember anything you can imagine."

He chuckled, "You've got plenty of the Scot in you, you must have had a Scots grandmother—"

"Lead on, Macduff," said Edda.

He said seriously, "A man, Englishman, Scotsman, what you like, that's for you, the writer, to decide, is in Warsaw during Hoover Food Administration, he knows some Polish, he goes to Warsaw, he sees this woman, Mrs. Lawrence; he brings her over to the U.S.A., he says to her, 'Eat something, you're beautiful now, you'll be a model over there, I'll stake you to your future,' that's what he says, and 'I don't ask nothing from you, I'm reshaping my life.' He brings her over, sends her to Hollywood, pays for her photographs. Now make it simple, straightforward and honest. No wisecracks. That's unnecessary. They got lost in the crowd—"

"What—I don't understand."

"Coming from the boat, they got lost in the crowd, she doesn't speak a word of American, and she goes about saying, 'Robert, Robert—'"

"Robert? Is that his name?"

"Any name you like, that's for you to put in, you're the writer, you got to imagine that, I'm giving you the plot. She doesn't find him, Robert or what you want, and she falls into the arms of this Kincaid!"

Edda listened dumbly, while her father hovered near the phone, saying, "I'll speak to him later."

Grant continued, "Now make a note of all this, it's br-rilliant, it's new. Let me tell you about this Kincaid."

"But is there a real Kincaid?"

"You change his name. This Kincaid, when he sells a picture to clients in this forty-two-room loft, he tells about his Jewish grandmother and Hitler, tears open his shirt and shows jewels, bronzes round his neck, inscriptions in Hebrew on jewels, you understand he bought somewhere. He tells them at night, he says the Lord's Prayer in Hebrew and he wears a yellow nightshirt with a swastika on it."

Edda laughed loudly and said, "You mean the Star of David?"

Grant became annoyed, "Now take this seriously, my good girl, it's a plot, you fix it up if you see anything that's wrong. He says they came from the Temple at Jerusalem, he is descended directly from Solomon the Great through his grandmother, and from Albertus Magnus through his grandfather, and there is strong reason to believe Albertus Magnus was a Jew. These heirlooms descended to him prove it. Well, naturally, he bought them all. He is a wonderful char-r-latan, also very romantic. Very romantic. He saw a girl in the street one time, a beautiful girl speaking some language he didn't understand. He made inquiries until he found the girl was speaking Polish. Now say this Polish girl is the girl, that's my idea. Then he married her. But she met this Polish doctor, who spoke Polish too, and she fell for him, a very seductive man, knows women, and she left Kincaid for him. Then she found out his true nature. And I said, 'Let me prove to you what a man can be like. I'm looking for a woman; my life is empty. It's up to you.' I said to her, 'A fair field and no favor, you prove to me you're the woman I'm looking for. That's all I ask. That's what I'm looking for.' There's your plot. . . . What do you think of it?"

"You're crazy. Here, Father wants to speak to you. I'm not a writer and I wouldn't try to break in with an opium dream like that."

"It's true, it's true," he kept crying out as she gave up the wire. She could tell from her father's conversation, as he tried to get Grant to talk business, that Grant was asking for her. At last her father relinquished the phone. Grant at once cried, "Now, my dear young lady, you must take this seriously. A great opportunity. I bring luck. Make a forchun for you. I want nothing. But I got ideas. Out of real life. Not stuff, like that young fella. If he can make one million dollars we can make three million dollars, because it's real life."

They parleyed a bit, and he kept on pleading, "My dear girl, just for me, do me a favor, take a note, my dear girl, this is real life."

He continued with his plot, "Friend of mine, Goodwin, was in fur business and ginseng business. He sold to priests and Chinese." He was offended when she burst out laughing again. He said, "You

41

ought to settle down, Edda; you got to look to the future. This will make you a forchun."

"Ginseng might. But go on."

He rushed forward enthusiastically, "He was in the London Hotel, I think Twenty—I don't know—some street. He saw a lovely girl in the subway. After following her home he got to speak to her. It was a vacant lot. She stopped, she was frightened, and she started to say something. He said, 'I'm serious, I'm in love with you, love at first sight.' He took her out. I was there that time and I had another appointment, but I saw her and I took Goodwin aside and said to him, 'Alf, does this girl mean anything to you? If not, I'll serenade her.' Alf said, 'Not a thing, she's too serious, go ahead with your serenade.' I went back to her, her name was Myra Coppelius—"

"You mean Kincaid went back to her?"

"Eh? Well, she was looking for someone. Me too. I said, 'Look, little girl, I like your face, I'm lonely. I'm awfully sorry. I got an appointment now. I didn't know I was going to meet you. You appeal to me. Will you meet me tomorrow for tea and a little chat?' She said she would. She said, 'I'm looking for someone and I've got to find the right one sometime.' Well, I didn't like that and at the same time, it gave me an in, don't you see? Too serious, Alf is right. But we met. She wouldn't tell me her name, only Coppelius. She has a room uptown, all by herself, but I don't know where. She is married to a Greek Orthodox doctor. She told me she was through with casual affairs. She wants to go on the stage. I said to her, for argument's sake, I mean Kincaid says to her, for argument's sake, he would like to spend money on her, just a pleasure to give her a chance, see if she would make him happy. 'For there's only one thing keeps me awake at nights, and that is to be happy,' I said to her. I want to be good. If the fascists win, I've got to be good. If the Russians win, I want to be good. I want to end good, not bad."

"You or Kincaid?"

"Eh? Both, both—it's the same, where a man is lonely. Now that is the plot. A million dollars, eh?"

"What's the end of the story?" asked Edda.

He shouted, "Edda darling, I'm not dressed yet. I'm walking up and down like that—what's that black tiger, that black thing?— I can't eat. Last night I couldn't sleep. I'm thinking of my book. It will be a wonder. Just put down what I say. I lived it. It's me. It's real, don't you see? Something those fellas that make one million dollars don't know. It will make three million dollars. I looked in the best-seller list just now, what kind of stuff are they writing? Trash. Something about green leaves, black idols, I don't know what gibberish. No wonder no one reads them. Wait till we get to work on it! All right, I won't bother you now, get your bath, get dressed, and come up to my place. I'm waiting for you. And bring David too; he's got good ideas though he doesn't know how to market them, no salesman. Leave that to me. You'll live in clover. I give you the ideas, I'm the salesman, you just write it down and get David to tell you how. . . ."

While Flack was in the bath the telephone rang. Wet and naked, he heard Grant's hurried, pleading voice, "You come to my hotel five o'clock, is that too early? And later I'll take you to a cabaret, anything to pass the evening, but it's to tell you my idea I want."

Flack, pleased, said, "Anything to please the poor bastard, his ideas burn a hole in his head and he has nothing to do on Sundays; he's a lonely old bastard and we ought to cheer him up."

At five, therefore, of this windy, gritty October afternoon, they went to his gaudy hotel. Grant opened the door instantly as he had been standing by it, kissed them roundly on both cheeks, took the girl by the arm and ran her to the lounge in front of the fireplace. He ran to his closet, got out his liquor and three glasses and brought them to them, resetting the scene of the previous afternoon.

"To our best-seller—and I like your title, Edda, it's a sure hit, it's a wonder, you'll see, we'll plaster all the windows with our best-sellers, them fellas will turn blue with envy. *All I Want Is a Woman*. That's it! We got the title, we got the plot. We got the girl, a pretty woman, sincere, attractive. Every man will want to —want her. Every woman will be jealous or else think, I'll go to the hairdresser, get a new hairdo, and I'll be like that woman, Myra—" He planted a fat Louis XV armchair in front of the girl and whispered loudly, "Say I shelve the blondine? Or say I'm tangled with the blondine? Doesn't matter. I send Coppelius to that Sarah Bernhardt School in California. I tell no one. It's a lottery. She is a great success, on the verge of a brilliant career, the most fame you can get, headlines, picture in the paper, name on Broadway, four-and-half stars at the least, but she says, 'I'll come home and cook your breakfast for you, Robert!' Whatever his name is."

He lunged forward, got up, plunged about, and repeated this

development some twenty times, walking round and about, standing in front of them, with them laughing at him, he laughing somewhat, but only with joy, communion. He kept on telling the story, salting it with, "What do you think of it? Give me your frank opinion, what do you think of it? You're laughing at me! Edda always laughs at me. Don't take me seriously! That's a weakness in you, you're not old enough to know it yet."

David Flack cried, rolling out of the lounge and laughing, "No, no—no, no, Robbie, we don't laugh at you, we respect you terrifically, we know you're a genius. We don't underrate you, make no mistake."

Edda was ashamed, "No, no, no, no. I know you've got plenty of originality, only you don't know this business. I know it's a business. I know a man like you thinks he can conquer any business—because he's original, because he can sell."

He listened carefully to all she said. His face became serious, then he smiled, he turned to Flack, "She knows me, she knows me! One of these days she'll see the sort of man I am, a constructive view. I haven't always done good, but I haven't done any evil either. I swear it!" He solemnly raised his hand and rolled his beautiful blue eyes.

They continued to make protestations of friendship and understanding for several minutes, and Grant busied himself with the drinks. Then, off again, he shouted, "Let me give you a perspective on my story," and he went through the whole thing again, explaining and crying, it must be positive, true romance, true love. "That's what the average man believes in and I'm an average man, I just want to find a woman. *All I Want Is a Woman.* It would make me. If I'd met the right woman to begin with— who can tell?"

"I don't believe a woman makes a man," said the girl.

"I knew many beautiful 'ooman. Knew as friends, not always stayed at the friendship stage. I don't say I always loved and I know they didn't always love me. Don't know why. You can't always hit the mark. Now I know that everyone is looking for his romance. Even the worst. It is their one good point: one good spot in the heart."

"Like the curate's egg," said David Flack, laughing and rolling, his spectacles shining at a dozen different angles in five minutes.

Grant frowned, "Not egg—this Solomon Greenstein, now, he married a lame woman, said he wanted to look after her. Is that

44

a good egg or a bad egg? You see! You see? Don't judge a book by its cover. Be a builder, not a grave-digger for civilization, eh? Love is mysterious: you can't explain it. It might be anybody, why not me? That's what I say to myself—why not me? Am I bandy-legged, am I deaf and dumb?"

He sat down and was silent for a few minutes. David Flack, dragging himself out of the pleasant listening daze into which he had fallen while the shouting was going on, had begun to speak when Edda unexpectedly said, "I have got an impression! I can see good settings for it—"

The merchant sprang to life again and started shouting, "What do you think of it? Give me your frank opinion—" David Flack remonstrated with him. He sat on a chair, simmered, muttered, but let Edda continue for a minute or two, when he suddenly shouted, "I shelve the blonde, you see, disgusted; attraction, but no character; and this woman—"

"What blonde?"

He mumbled for a while something about a woman in Canada, a woman in Rome, a woman in Warsaw, some of these women were blonde, some not, they could not make out which.

He said with less assurance, "You see, you got to give the man some constructive traits, he's a no-good, a jerk, Kincaid, you can buy him for five cents in some respects, but in other respects, he has a streak of gold. You can have the woman make him over if you like. You're the artist. And the girl's got to have character. I say to the blondine, 'You're beautiful, but I don't love you, you can't hold me: you gave me too much pain, and it's character that counts.' And the other is famous, but she is real Egyptian sakel and she prefers to come home and make breakfast for me. I have character too—a renunciation scene, very good—'No, no, no,' I say—'no for you, and no for me—I mightn't love you if you weren't famous.' 'No, no,' she says, 'fame means nothing to me, I want to come home, make breakfast for you, I prefer that as a career. Besides, I owe it to you. You paid for me at the start. Now I love you. That's your profit.' 'All right,' I say, 'then we'll both do something glorious, we'll go back and rebuild Europe, Poland, Italy, somewhere, I'll show them how to grow or distribute cotton. I'll show them cotton machinery. Even the Soviet Union would do—' I go and find out about the *saboteurs*—and you sing, or dance, or act—you are famous, you take your fame with you."

"Let me think, don't talk any more, Robbie, let me think."

"Another drink," he said, rushing toward her, but wobbling, for

45

he was already tipsy and so was her father, laughing and bobbing, squirming and repeating, "A movie magnate, a Hollywood success."

As she sipped the drink, he said, "Not thin hair, it's unnecessary. Sign of ill health, perhaps. You can be loved if you're eighty-two, but people want something simple; no need to have thin hair, it's uncalled-for. They don't understand—why put in big nose, wart on the cheek, harelip, cauliflower ear, no legs—?" he started to shout and laugh—"bald head, thin hair, wall-eye, why? Why? People think this writer has no character. What do you think of it?"

Edda burst out crying, "Like a drum, your one crazy idea. Like a bad headache. I'm getting out of here. I don't want success. I want to die young."

He was thunderstruck, and said softly, "I'm sorry, pardon me, I withdraw it, I'm sorry—no idea, excuse me, my girl—got carried away—"

She finished her drink in silence. The man went on apologizing and David Flack suddenly sprang to the fore, "Edda has a hundred ideas a day. We've got shelves there, covered with drawings. She sits in the subway and does drawings of dozens of characters. Each drawing is an idea. She has thousands of ideas, a capital of ideas, like Edda Incorporated, capital one million ideas. Do you understand, Robbie? And you only have one, one miserable idea. You're like a man with one cotton plant in his back yard, talking about cotton to Robert Grant who's been buying and selling cotton and thinking about boll weevil and living on the work of sweating black peasants all his life. He sprays his one bit of cotton with a watering can and you buy or sell thousands of futures in Beaver Street."

Grant's face lighted up. He sprang forward. "You're right, I see it. Excuse me! I see it. I leave it to you. You're the artist! But just give my plot a little thought. I say to her—'No for you and no for me—'"

Edda said, "I'll write a book about you, Robbie." Her face had begun to glow. She smiled at him.

Grant shouted, "Why not? I'm a man! But not central me; central Europe too. Look, we'll write about the new world, a new world, that is. The U.S.A. has new values, doesn't know how to use them. The old world needs new values U.S.A. has—that will be our theme, not me, see. Of course, you got to have human values too. Look, in Europe they all compounded a felony. They put up with Hitler. The whirligig of values, see. In old times a king threw his serving man out the window, no one would talk to him, they wrote him down in books, called him Pedro the Cruel or something; now, not. Everyone talks to Hitler after Munich, you get pretty women saying he's handsome, and statesmen saying he's brilliant,· and young boys saying he represents their ideal. You see? We'll have that in too, no one can say I want to write only about myself. We'll have everything that keeps people going. *Inside Poland*. But no, your title, *All I Want Is a Woman*, that's better. All I want is a 'ooman," and as he left them at their door, he called to them from ten yards, "All I Want Is a Woman!"

7

He threshed home, much excited by the project. It was early. He put in a call for Mrs. Kent's hotel, was told that she had gone the day before, without leaving a forwarding address. Grant telephoned Paula Russell, who was sharp with him. Barb had taken their quarrel to heart, thought he was getting ready to throw her out, so she took the first step, she went. She had other choices; Barb was not the one to leave herself unhedged.

"I had no intention, no intention at all of doing the 'ooman harm, not my way," he grumbled. They had a few minutes' talk in the course of which Paula arranged to see him the following week, if she were still in town, "But I may join Barb."

She would not say where Barb was.

He was dismayed. He spent hours worrying his suspicions, not to feel the emptiness. He loved the woman.

"I often asked myself if I loved her; now I know I do. This is love to feel my heart bruised this way. To worry this way about a tramp is love."

He tormented all his friends with it, called up Hugo March and Peter Hoag, "What should I do? Get after her with a detective? I'm used to her, I want her; she's no good, but neither am I."

The next week Barbara telephoned him at the office at ten in the morning, apologized for the trouble she had given him, and asked him if he was attending to the bills sent on to him from the Grand Hotel. "Don't take it to heart so, Robbie, don't go telling your troubles to the whole town, like a whipped dog. It was only a little tiff, the course of true love never did run smooth."

She was speaking fast, and as always, her voice which began low had risen to a pinging note, a note which irritated and piqued his nerves. When she used this tone, she had something at heart. He scolded, "You shouldn't have done this to me, very inconsiderate. I don't know if I can forgive it so easily; put me in a funny position, you can understand."

She said it would blow over, he would forgive her. She would forgive him too, would see him soon, but not just yet, for she was now Mrs. Adams, had married that Burton Burstall Adams he had met several times. Adams was a dissipated Army man of their acquaintance. Grant had long shut his eyes to an affair between them, thinking that as Adams was always drunk their rendezvous must be unsatisfactory. He felt this victory of Adams like a blow.

"You don't love him, Barb, I know; you must leave that sponge. Come back to me. You don't drink at all."

"He married me."

Grant blew up. He had spoken of marrying her too; but she had played with his affections. He had told her she only had to win him and he was hers. He must see her at once, "All a mistake."

"I can't see you yet, Robbie. I have to get my alimony and I want to get enough to live on, so I'll be careful till I do."

"What harm is there in my seeing you with Paulie?"

"Mother will be here on Tuesday and I must spend some time with her after our separation."

Grant had forgotten the mother, although he had some time before arranged for her passage through some business friends. He said, "You want to get your mother a nice little apartment."

"Yes, I think you should find some place, make some arrangements for her."

"I'm very busy, my sweet. I don't know what you do all day."

"Surely this wouldn't take too much time or trouble."

"I want to see you, sweets. I can see you at your mother's?"

She had a biting voice. He shivered. He said suddenly, "A hideout for you and me? All right I'll get mother a room, but promise to ring me tomorrow, sweets. I'll let you know where I got the room."

"Mother will be very disappointed. I told her you would take better care of us."

"But she knows you're married to Adams, good heavens."

"I can't very well saddle Adams with my mother at this critical time. He can always say I overload the expense sheet."

The next day she telephoned him, found out where the room

was, but would not meet him there. They must never meet at her mother's room, until she had sure grounds for divorce.

In order to meet her regularly, therefore, he promised at once to open accounts for Paula and Barbara at two uptown restaurants, where he had relations with the maîtres d'hôtel. The girls would eat at these restaurants every day; and eventually would both go to take tea at his apartment. In this way and through the corruption of the girls he felt that he played tricks on Adams. This idea made them very gay at times.

By the middle of November, the blonde was tired of waiting for a New York divorce and had so managed Grant that he had agreed to pay the expenses of her mother and herself to Reno. When she returned he was to go to Reno himself, divorce his wife, and come back to marry Mrs. Adams. He said all this several times to the mother of the blonde, whose apartment he visited regularly in the hope of seeing Barbara alone. The old woman, refined, white-haired, with a disagreeable voice, but good taste in dress, was full of poses—she hated the Jews, the radicals, and business men. Grant could not understand a sensitive woman like Barbara. She supposed Grant had to marry Barbara, but she had always wished Barbara to have a position in society and she was disappointed. Barbara was taken in by everyone, had no sense of character. Grant groveled before this false refinement and the old woman pursued her advantage, "You have done nothing for us!" She would add, "The proof of the pudding is in the eating, as you Scots say, Mr. Grant."

In the end Grant bought Barbara some clothes, some jewels, set the mother up with a fur cape, and arranged for Miss Paula Russell to travel with them as a companion. Before November came to an end, the three women had gone off, at his expense, and although he telegraphed flowers and daily inquiries to their hotel in Reno, he heard nothing for a while. At last Miss Paula Russell wrote to him that they had all been very blue and nervous and the expenses of the town were very high. They had been quite miserable to find themselves in a town like that with funds so low. Grant again telegraphed and sent an express letter, "I feel like flying out there now."

The mother immediately replied,

I fear there would be little room for you. But as soon as the divorce is through I am taking Barb to the Coast, where

49

she can have the proper medical attention. All this has been most trying to a nervous system like hers. I say nothing of myself. With me it is merely old age; old age cannot be remedied. It is a good thing. One resigns oneself and suffers less than the young. People of our age, Mr. Grant, are better off than Barb. In Los Angeles Barb hopes to meet old friends, always the best rest-cure. Of course, the poor girl is quite run down and quite psychotic. (I would say, afraid of men; but that will not last long, I trust.) Many thanks for the telegrams. I passed the envelope on to Barb, as you requested.

Grant showed this letter to the Goodwins at his next cocktail hour. He swore the old woman was a perfect lady, she wrote in such a cold tone. Betty Goodwin cried, "Oh, Robbie, they're a pair of bloodsuckers!" Grant laughed weakly, "The old lady I don't know. Paulie I don't know. But the blonde is different: she was brought up a one-way girl. She doesn't see things our way. My wife's a parasite too. But she didn't rape me! I swallow my medicine. I can't marry a Grade-A woman and expect her to walk in a procession on May Day. Can't have your cake and eat it. Her mother likes the Germans, thinks they're gentlemanly. Just shows how innocent she is. Once she was in a *pension* in Germany as a girl! She's still a girl. I send her gloves and I tell her Hitler is no good. My propaganda. The Reds are all fools. You can't convert people with words. Got to be gloves! Ha-ha— The French convert people with gloves and perfume; when they're Reds the whole world will be converted. Ha-ha. With the workers they say, 'You'll get better living conditions.' With Barb what do they offer? She'd be worse off under Communism: have to work as a shopgirl. She knows it by instinct. A weakness of Red propaganda. Now I would write a pamphlet, saying, 'Look here, girlie, all the women have fur coats, lipstick, and get a dowry from the State.' Eh?"

Betty told him Mussolini promised this. He shouted fretfully, "And Mussolini isn't entirely wrong: he knows human nature, otherwise how could he hold them down all these years? Of course, Italy's a backward country."

For over a month he received nothing from the wandering women but hotel bills, which he paid promptly, asking only with each one for a note of thanks from Barb. At the last, Barb wrote him a short note,

The weather here has been wretched and we have had no company. We went to the movies two or three times but no good shows. I am not well and shall be glad to leave here. It is a dull town and not the kind of company one is used to. There are few people one can meet; but I am not in a state to meet anyone. My nerves have been very bad and I have had to think mostly of myself, which is what I wanted to avoid. I go out occasionally for fresh air but I am not one for solitude and soon return. Yours very sincerely, Barbara Adams.

With this she enclosed a photograph showing herself in sweater and ski-pants, hair blowing loose, on a mountain side with a strong, squat, handsome young man, and a dog. She wrote on the back: Barb and friends. She looked young, simple, and beautiful, which Grant immediately wrote to her. He enclosed an envelope with the word *Barb* on it; inside, a check.

This was their last interchange for months. He waited and waited, and as the time lengthened, ran to all her friends saying, "Explain to me why I am faithful to her. She has taken my money, the alimony and disappeared into the blue beyond."

Paula, a dangerous woman, had put her up to it. Perhaps she had got a nervous disease and was shut up, or dead. Who would tell him? Paula was the kind of girl to grab everything and disappear. Perhaps Barb had got into the papers under one of her married names and he had never seen it. He did not show the photograph nor tell what his worst fear was.

8

It was early in the morning of December 8, a Monday, that Grant called Flack, with an immense, jovial, mysterious excitement, asking if they had heard of the Pearl Harbor surprise attack the day before. He shouted, "What's the idea, eh, Edda? What's the idea? Force us in against Germany, make us crazy with two enemies at the gates, make us send troops to Europe, make us fight for the Soviet Union, eh? Crazy, eh? Miscalculated. Glad it was the Japs and not the Russians. Ho-ho. You and David would have been in trouble! Ho-ho. Didn't mean that, just a joke, my dear girl. Tell David to get down to the office as soon as he can."

The city was released. The war-tension of months, the uncertainty, were at an end. It was like news from Mars: they had never thought anyone would dare to attack them, mighty nation that they were, but it had only the effect that the first hard punch has on a strong youth. Everyone was downtown. In that morning, Flack and Grant sold all Grant's Government bonds at superb prices, many others being ashamed to sell at that moment, and they bought steel shares which had fallen since people were nervous, not knowing which way things would turn. Grant felt the absolute freshness of his youth that morning. He calculated all day, walked briskly round the downtown area, listened to rumors and the thousand projects which had already sprung up. In the next few days they all considered what primary produce would be needed in war, as well as cotton, he went with Flack in a car to look at old disused piers and sheds in the Hudson, he wrote letters to all his correspondents in Europe and elsewhere, and considered forming a shipping company in Valparaiso to send contraband of war to Japan. Flack was found sufficiently pusillanimous to shake his head at this idea, while laughing. Grant shouted, "My dear boy, when the golden harvest has begun, take a scythe in your hand."

"I'll ask Edda."

"She'll say no; but I'll ring her up and try to perr-suade her."

They spent days in the office now, Flack being once more apparently Grant's factotum.

They wrote to England, Switzerland, Chile, the Argentine, especially those interested in dyes, shipping, and the export of such general merchandise as can be used to disguise arms, ammunition, rare chemicals, drugs. Downtown, everyone was in a rare state of pleasurable excitement, of hope. The marasmus had passed. Brains churned. Everyone went out handshaking and deploring with the ear cocked for the moneyminting half-word. One of their acquaintances stopped in the middle of Broad Street to shake his head over the war news, clasp hands and declare heartily, "When I was four a fire swept the whole block in which my family lived. My father, mother and sisters took shelter with some neighbors. I collected all I could, vases, chamberpots, pictures, dusters, and took them to a vacant lot. A woman came along and said, 'How much do you want for the vase, sonny?' I sold it. I sold the lot. They thought I had gone in the fire. Everyone got their insurance, I had pocket money: no one lost by that catastrophe, as they say in the papers."

Flack and Grant would meet several people, then rush back to the office to talk things over, write more letters.

"I want to do something my size, we sue a Government, for

52

argument's sake, Beaver, Broad and Co. have five hundred suits a year against the Government in peacetime: look at the chance wartime gives you! A Government can't help treading on your toe, infringement of contractual rights, property damage, property falsely sequestrated. I have that stuff of Laura's, they think it's Italian, it's mine, at least I can prove it, there's that. We must look up something else. There are the other Governments too. We can easily think up something. They'll get in a pack of white-collar majors, paper shifters will go to war without knowing anything about business and we can't miss this chance. We can make a forchun, my boy, without undertaking any contracts, nothing where you might get in the wrong. Let them get in the wrong. I'll have the law on my side. That's the principal thing in a suit with the Government: then the same letter-file majors don't know what to say. And basically, my dear boy, Government is honest: don't know how to wriggle out of it."

They spent some time bathing in this flood of opportunities and plans, and the German declaration of war on December 1 gave them fresh prospects. David Flack drew no salary but was content with the promise of percentages in this new world, excited, upset.

"We got a blood transfusion, they gave us a blood transfusion," declared Grant every day.

His love for the blonde had disappeared like an empty transparent thing, some cast shell of a sea-animal. The thought of the money nagged but for the moment. "To hell with her: I'll make it back overnight; we'll put it in profit and loss," said Grant.

He had been moldering for years with the world closing in on him. This new international outlook gave him an interest in new women. At the moment, he found himself virtuous also. He picked up a Spanish woman of great beauty, in one of the big hotels, took her up to his room for the usual long-distance call, and when he came back from his bedroom with his coat off, found her sitting just as she had entered, chaste, still, touching, without a smile, on his sitting room lounge. He did not even kiss her. He took her downstairs again, gave her a drink, and after waiting a moment for the flame to stir him, took her back to her hotel in a taxi. He thought his virtue might melt in the taxi, but it did not. Instead, he said to her, "What were you doing in the hotel?"

"Waiting for men."

"Why do you do this, you're not suited to it?"

"I'm a widow, and have no money."

"Have you been successful?"

"This is my first day at it."

This gave Grant intense pleasure. He made an appointment with her for the next day. She did not keep it. He told Betty Goodwin all, adding, "I let her off and that set her on the right path; she's gone home again—a beautiful woman! I could have had her and I gave her up of my own free will."

When out with Sue, a wealthy libertine trying to better herself by radical frequentations, he met again Celia Grimm, who was collecting funds for refugees from fascism. He promised her that he would contribute "When you convince me—that's your business, isn't it? You see, I am a socialist myself—I gave a five-pound note once in London, to one of the ugliest women you ever saw; but she made a brave speech— I'm not tight in the purse-strings like you think, but you've got to appeal to my sentiment. That's something your radical friends don't appreciate. They don't enlist human nature on their side. Say to a man with money, 'Give.' He won't. But enlist his sympathy, tell him children are starving, they need fresh air, milk—take time off, take him around in a car, show him sharecroppers—he can't stand it. He's only human."

He expressed a desire to meet "these Negroes of yours and see what you see in them—you see, I'm trying to understand, there's no prejudice in me."

He was taken by Celia Grimm and the warmhearted libertine, Sue, to a party given by a Hollywood writer in an apartment in a run-down house on Park Avenue. Here he met some permanent celebrities of the circles in which Celia and Sue lived. He delivered several of his speeches about human nature and was not greeted by the applause he had in cabarets from his "Communist" girl friends. He was naturally humiliated and thought they were at fault. If Miss Russell, who said she knew the Marxist circles of several European and South American countries, and the blonde, and Gussy the International Brigade woman and other cabaret radicals agreed with him, this society, obviously, was simply trying to push out an intruder, a business man.

At the party, Sue became infatuated with a stranger and left without a good-bye. As he took Celia Grimm to her parents' home in a taxi, he held her hand and told her that she was right, he had got over his race prejudice. He realized the Negroes had charm, personality, they were different from us and probably knew more about love. Miss Grimm's reply to this was not what he expected, but he took no notice of it. He was not even disappointed that she did not kiss him good night. He was anxious and elated. He had made an appointment for the next afternoon with Mrs. Wood, the wife of one of the Negro celebrities. He had plunged into it. After listening carefully to what a group of people were saying, and learning a few phrases, he had gone over to Mrs. Wood, sitting by herself on a red velvet settee.

He told her he was a newcomer to the radical movement, though a socialist all his life; that he believed in the rights of minorities, and a few other things he had learned; and said that now, looking at her, he knew his intelligence, which had acted first, was really just instinct, for she appealed to him as a very unusual woman. He saw that the gulf between the races did not exist, and that if it had been created by first a feudalism and then capitalism, it could be bridged by understanding and, especially, love. He asked her if she believed in love at first sight; said that he now, tonight, had proof it existed. He liked her looks, she looked like the kind of woman he had always been searching for—only due to his old-fashioned upbringing and to being at heart an Englishman, and to having spent so much time abroad where he had no opportunities of meeting women like her, he had never thought of looking at them. Now it had come to him in a flash that love was no respecter of persons nor of race. He did not want anything wrong. He wanted to assure her of the purity of his intentions. Would she meet him the following afternoon, in some quiet place for tea and a little chat?—he wanted her advice. But she must tell him where, for he was practically a child in the world, went out little, rarely met women.

The Negro woman, whose husband was a great ranter, and who was tired of sitting, evening after evening, on a settee, red velvet or bare cane, was overwhelmed by this attack. She told him where to meet her: it was in a bar in the Village where the mingling of races was possible, a Spanish bar known only to the radical élite.

Grant was extremely flattered at being taken to this bar. He put money in the jukebox, danced with her. She was a remarkably elegant and light dancer.

She was very simply dressed. He wanted to get her a pair of gloves. Then came the problem of where to buy the gloves; they could not enter his usual stores together, and where to meet more intimately. These new obstacles interested him at first, but very soon began to bore him. He did not care for the pursuit nor for adventure. Ever since his early manhood, since his

55

marriage, he had bought women; most had been bargains and most had made delivery at once. He never paid in advance: "I got no time for futures in women."

In the end the woman arranged it with a friend. After two or three meetings in one week, he failed to call her up. Once or twice she left a message with the hotel clerk, but she never dared to call. He went back to his uptown bars.

9

He spent Christmas with his family as usual but returned to spend New Year's Eve with the Flacks, as was his custom. He thought of them, since they were not money-seekers, as good luck. Once the New Year had come in, he dismissed them and either went to bed or to a cabaret, but he feared to bring in the New Year with bad people. With the Flacks this year he found Edwin Burgess, a poet admired by Flack who "did not sell ten copies." Grant was enchanted, and took Burgess and his chubby, young, dark wife along with him to dinner, and then back to his hotel to see the New Year in. They listened to the radio and sleepily drank brandy. He looked at them with oyster-eyes and smiled. A cream-skimmer, he thought, a profit-taker, a man sitting on the backs of the poor who entertained such singularly poor and honest persons on New Year's Eve, had every chance of avoiding the evil eye for the year to come. The superstition went further, with him, as always, trapped him. If this man sold only ten copies and was yet a fine writer, he would be willing to write, on a percentage basis, Grant's best selling idea of *All I Want Is a Woman*. He took the man aside, into the other room, and made an appointment with him for the following week. The wife was quite pretty and so discontented with her life that she was surly. Grant spoke to her a moment as they waited for the signal on the radio, took her hand when they sang *Auld Lang Syne*, and made an appointment with her in town for the next week. He felt he had his reward when a few days later, a Sunday, a friend telephoned him in the morning to say that he had seen Barbara in Jacksonville, Florida, with a young naval officer. He had traced the girl to a hotel for Grant's sake and found her living there with her mother, still as Mrs. Kent. Grant telephoned the Flacks and rushed down to them in a taxi. Edda opened the door.

"Where's Jacksonville?" said Grant.

He kissed Edda on both cheeks, rushed in, whirling hat and

cane, "Where's Jacksonville? Is it chic? What's she doing with a young naval officer?"

Flack came out, putting on his dressing gown, and grinned, "First town in Florida you hit going to Miami! It's not chic, it's fatback and grits. How the hell do I know? Who?"

"Give me some of that like a good girl! I mean the blonde," said Grant, taking a cup of coffee off the table, draining it and holding out the cup for more.

"What blonde?"

"The blondine, Mrs. Kent, Mrs. Adams—the one who got divorced. Never wrote. Don't understand it. Got to get my silver tea tray back. Silver picture frames. Took me for a ride—taught me a lesson."

"If it isn't too much to ask, would you mind putting a little order into your gibberish," said Flack.

"That woman's kept me in the dark since Reno. I'll find her. I'll take the train. I'll surprise her."

"That would surprise me," said Edda.

"Listen, my boy, Davie, can't go there myself, got to stay in town, Sam Uzzazuzz is in town, Jigago, want you to go, Davie, pay you the out-of-pockets, do me a favor, hunt her up and her party. Taught me a lesson. But she'll pay me back."

But Flack refused to go to Florida and so did Edda, in her turn. From their apartment Grant telephoned several hotels in Jacksonville, without success. He made Flack go out and get a list of hotels in Jacksonville. They telephoned all these.

Flack wearied, said, "Perhaps she only went to the hotel for a cocktail on the way home."

"That's it, that's it! Where would be her next stop?"

The next day, Grant got to their flat before eight in the morning. He had traced Mrs. Kent to Washington. From their flat he now telephoned Washington—for the fourth time that morning, as he confessed. He told them his hopes, fears, sorrows.

This went on for nearly an hour. At length he believed that he had found the hotel, something in the porter's voice giving him a cue. He therefore asked Edda to telephone the same hotel and ask for Mrs. Adams in the name of Mrs. Goodwin. This was done. The porter at once replied that Mrs. Adams was staying at the hotel with Mrs. Jones, but was out. Grant rejoiced, and began talking fast, telling the whole story over again, mixing up his ideas that she was innocent, and had been ill and had bad luck and had lost faith in him, with notions that she had betrayed him, was a cheat, and brought bad luck to all men. Presently, he took them out to dinner at the Brevoort. Grant, still full of joy, did not know what he was saying and certainly not what he was hearing. He went on talking madly, "If she's in Washington, it's only natural, as one day she told me she had been connected with a legation. She's a very bright young woman, understands all the details of business. She had some schemes for smuggling currency and furs to Mexico, also perfumes; naturally I didn't listen to her, but they were all right—that is to say, some holes in them, but if you picked out the good from the bad—but there's nothing wrong about her. What if she went out with a young naval officer? There's nothing wrong in that. I let the poor girl down, I said I was through with her. She lives with her mother, poor girl, that shows a good heart and her mother's an innocent old woman, born and brought up a lady who doesn't know where her daughter gets her money, when she gets it from men. That is—she does something not quite correct, not quite clean—now she fleeced me of forty thousand dollars and gave me nothing in return. And I told her, 'Be good to me and I'll give you anything. You call the numbers and I'll get them for you, if you're good to me. Just you name it, I'll get it,' I told her. Can't blame her if she took money after that.

"There's always a man behind it. She told me that Schlaugenberger, that ace she knew, seduced her as a young girl, wouldn't marry her, set her on the wrong track. . . . She's innocent, that girl, I swear it. I can't get along without her. Tried to, can't. That's flat. . . . And a thing I don't often talk about, never in public, never to you, Edda, never to your father, but it's the secret, she's honey to me, I'm a honeybear, and she's got honey. She's sweet when she's alone with me, she's—" He went on pitiably talking about her as she was in love, with a big, drawn, hungry, old face.

"What if she has no use for me now? I got used to her. You don't think she'd go with any young fella she picked up? A woman might—wartime, it's a kind of patriotic feeling—but no woman falls for that braid and that clam kind of face."

After weeks and months of pretending, even to himself, that he was looking for a soulmate, someone to finish his days with, of running round furiously in lecheries that lasted and lies that glittered only for an hour, this all burst out of him, his need for the blonde woman. When he saw they were sitting silent, he shouted, "But I'll get over it, I'm only anxious to make her pay for all she did to me, the money—that's lost; but the silverware, the furs—I'll make her give it back. There are skeletons in her closet. I'll make them rattle. It isn't the money, I'm not mean—not avaricious—if it's a big love affair I give big pay—but if she'll come back to me and say, 'I made a mistake, it's you I want, forgive and forget,' then I will do the handsome, too. 'Let's start a clean sheet,' I'll say. Forgive and forget. But no naval officers. What's your advice, Edda? You're a woman! I'll take your advice. You know by instinct. Tell me what to do. Does she love me? What's your opinion?"

The girl had been casting her eyes over her shoulder toward the big-faced man who was chiefly listening to them. Several people could hear Grant and were smiling faintly. Edda said abruptly, "It's my opinion you're sunk, you'll never get any lower. That's my idea."

This pleased him. He went on to show that he was glad he was "in her clutches," that he admired her venality, her conspiracies, and admired her and himself for the large sum of money he had spent and the way she made a fool of him. He said complacently, "Yes, she buys me at one corner and sells me at the next! I don't claim she's innocent. But I'm no good, either. Birds of a feather. You're right. I'm sunk. I'm sunk. I met her when she was just a scrubwoman. I thought, What the hell do I want with this bloody cow? Then I got into her 'clutches.' "

He told them the story about Peter Hoag. "I thought he'd pulled a boner. I rang him up and said, 'This time you put money on the wrong filly, Hoag.' He said, 'Wait and see, she carries my money and she'll come in at the post.' He was right. I'm sunk. She torpedoed me."

They sat long over brandy-and-Benedictine, as he retold his tale. It had begun to snow. A blonde woman gaily dressed, who had come in out of the snow, brushed past their table and was hailed by Flack. She greeted the Flacks and made to move on, but Grant had become tense, his eyes shone, and his face was merry. She was Sophy Manfred, but just back from Reno and—"Now call me Buchanan, I want to have no more of Manfred, call me Buchanan."

Grant looked at the others to guess what she might be, then took out his little red address book and murmured, "Are you just back from Reno? That's trying on the nerves. I had hard luck just recently; maybe we could console each other."

The woman was smart, small, lusty. She wore her blonde hair

59

piled high, a black and white silk blouse, a red suit and a fur coat. Heavy bracelets jingled on both arms. Grant called for drinks and stroked her arm. She gave him a quick stare, looked at the others to guess what he might be, leaned across the table and cried huskily, "O, Edda and—may I call you David?—please, wait till you hear what happened to me this week. Bundy, my stepdaughter, said, 'You must go to a psychoanalyst; if you don't go, after what happened to you, there never was a woman like you before nor will be again.' 'But why go to my psychoanalyst?' I said to Bundy. 'You know as well as I do that he cannot cure himself, why should he cure me? Isn't his own wife a case of nervous breakdown and didn't I see it from the moment I rang at the doorbell?' She opened it and I saw at once; I said to myself, 'A more miserable, more unhappy woman does not exist; whatever your troubles are, Sophy, they are probably a mere fleabite to her troubles.' And this doctor cannot see a mental crisis like that in his own living room—living room; it was worse and nearer home than that, for later she told me everything. I visited him several times, and one day I waited for him in the sitting room and she was there, and I saw she was jealous—of me, perhaps, and I said, 'Darling, why do you look so ghastly?' And she burst out crying. After we had a long talk I went away and never went to see the doctor again. 'Quite right,' said Bundy, 'but there are other men. . . .' My dear Edda, I feel black and blue, I have been lacerated morally, mentally, and spiritually! What that man did to me—even at this distance of time and space—let me pour out my feelings to you, and you will find it interesting, too, for I have made up my mind that this story ought to be preserved for the good of humanity. How a man can take a perfectly innocent, trusting woman and subject her to attacks in the dark, bludgeonings, a blunt instrument is not in it, spiritually, I mean, of course, and all the while she is feeling her sore head and thinking, I am at fault; she carries about a guilt feeling which makes her the monster—the whole thing is a novel! I have a name for it—*The Perfection of Murder*. Don't you like it?"

Grant burst in desperately with, "Like it, like it: but I got a better title. Listen to me, I got a name and I got a subject for a novel, a best-seller will sweep them into the Atlantic; I'll guarantee it will be sold to Hollywood before it's so much as in print; it's about a man, Kincaid, who is restless and takes a woman from Rome, the wife of a doctor—"

Sophy broke in—"What did I tell you? Great minds think

alike. A doctor's wife who gets into trouble and her husband either cannot or will not see what is the matter, himself the disease, or the criminal, or whatever you like to call it, the thief in the night stealing her—her mind, if you like—*The Thief in the Night*—what do you think of that for a title? But I like the other. Or, better—*The Night Side of Dr. Jones.* Eh?"

Grant burst out laughing, and stroked her arm, "Good grief! You're the girl I've been looking for. You appeal to me. You're blonde—you're not as blonde as the other one, but you've got character and she has none, and what I want is character. I'm looking for the right woman and I want one who'll be a sweetheart, a sister, and a mother to me. Three women in one. How do you like that for a title?"

Sophy stopped, stared, burst out, "What did you say your name is? Do I know you?"

He told her, and asked for hers and her telephone number. She stared at him for a moment, her thoughts astray, and said suddenly, "Listen, darling, this is real, you couldn't invent it: I went through agonies, torture, mental and physical torment, over that man. He's a monster, but one with invisible torturing hands, a giant insect of steel with antennae of silk. That's how he got me. He got me into his toils and then took pleasure in seeing me writhe; he wrapped me up and carried me off to his lair, that is the only possible description of our marriage—if you like to call that marriage, when a man with a twisted brain and a demon in his soul takes the body and soul of a young woman and tears it to pieces and eats them alive, body *and* soul. That's a scientific description of my marriage. Wait till I tell you the details, darling! You're a decent man. You have no conception of what a man of the other sort, the nether-world of men, the apemen who look like men you might call them, do to women when they carry them off to their lairs—legally, mind you, legally! He called me the River Nymph before he married me, then he said I had no soul at all. He called me a machine. He treated me as you don't treat machines, you handle them with care. All the while, sitting there quietly, in a quiet apartment with all the conveniences you can imagine—oh, I supped off gold, if you like to put it that way—he was a silent, invisible torturer. How can you explain that to anyone? Only a book, a play could do it. And I am going to do it, because I lived through it. Whatever your imagination, darling, you couldn't invent it. Truth is stranger than fiction. No psychoanalyst could explain it to me as I can see it myself. I'm going to call it, perhaps, *Death with Arms,* eh? Or, *The River Nymph?* A hollow mockery."

Grant said, "You're the kind of woman I need. What I want is a blondine with your character and your head. I want your advice, little girl. Edda here and David here are going to write a story about me. If you've been in torment, I have, too. Perhaps I haven't been torn to pieces, but my heart was sore. That blondine did that to me. I can sympathize. When can I telephone you?"

"Now look—what is your name?—I don't know who you are, but I like you. I can see you're sympathetic, I'm never wrong and I know it would surprise you, a man like you, to know how some men can behave. I want to tell you the whole thing, not to give you an earful, it won't bore you, but just to restore my faith in men, for I've been dragged in the mud at the tails of four horses, the four horses of the apocalypse it was for me, and if you're thinking of writing a book, Mr. Grant, it has to have a woman in it. I'll give you the subject, you can't go wrong, it'll be the truth, and call it *The Life of the River Nymph.* Write down what I tell you, it's written in my heart's blood and you'll get the Book of the Month. You should learn something about women, for that will give it reality. What do you want to write about Roman women and Rome for? It is about a real flesh-and-blood woman —like me—I've given you all the details. Do that, and it'll be a raging success. I read all those books and I tear my hair, I'm eating my heart out, and I think, O, why don't you write the truth about women? The truth is here—the truth will make you free, the truth is black but constructive—" she pointed to her breast.

Gladly Grant burst in with, "Good grief, you're right. Three women in one. I'm glad you like my idea. When can we get together? The truth is constructive."

"Why don't you come up to my apartment now? But I must warn you, I'm serious, I'm not just looking for a good time. I'm not that sort of woman, don't make a mistake about me. I just want someone to confide in, I want to lean my head on your shoulder spiritually to restore my faith in humanity. A heart-to-heart talk with a woman is the best thing, but an honest, fine man, like I can see you are, will be the next best thing. I'm not flattering you. I always tell men exactly what I think and they know where they stand. I haven't had much luck lately, and I'm looking for some luck."

He said dully, "What I want is a blondine with your head. A woman with two heads."

"I like your other title best, *The Life of the River Nymph*."

"You're right! It's true." He shouted this, stretched, and got up. They parted in the snow, the Flacks going home and Grant going toward Washington Square, where Sophy Buchanan had a new apartment. Grant turned back to Edda to say weightily, "Now like this little girl said—constructive, no clouds, no long noses, no thin hair, constructive!"

10

It snowed for twenty-four hours, and for three days was full winter. David Flack had caught a cold on that first snowy evening and could not go out. His daughter stayed at home from work to attend to him. Grant was concerned and visited them twice a day at their apartment, to unravel with them, piece by piece, the mystery of the blonde, what she might be doing in the federal capital, and why she refused either to come to New York or to let him visit her there. On the third day there was no snow, though it was very cold, then quite warm with sun in the morning and the afternoon, a snow-gray sky, ice on the roofs, the snow overhangs melting, a tinkling, falling, with the trees turning from white to wet black, and much snow in the gardens. Opposite the Flacks' home, in an old garden, a huge iron bell stood, the snow upon it. Grant stayed nearly all day in the apartment, eating all that was set before him, and saying kindly, "You're not well, my boy, need a little bouillon." He would rush to Flack, fix a pillow, stand in front of him, considering, go back to his chair, cross his legs and plunge into his confidences.

"How did you like Sophy?"

Grant hesitated, then laughed in a troubled way, "Couldn't make her out: got the better of me, don't know if she meant to or not. Damn woman chewed my ear off about that River Nymph, and the dog, that boarder too—" He laughed and made David and Edda another confidence.

On the first snowy evening, the evening he had met Sophy, he had gone home with Sophy meaning nothing wrong, just for a little chat, and had no idea the damn woman thought he was a writer who wanted to write her memoirs. He got up from his chair, did a two-step, shook his head gaily and cried, "Me write her memoirs! That's rich! But it was an obsession, a fixed idea."

63

He found her amusing and then a fine type of woman. She appealed to him and she had had a rough time. He thought he might console her. "I'm looking for someone to fill in that lacuna: that lacuna with a tea tray and a silver frame." She offered him a drink, but he didn't drink, so she had one herself, and there was a little dog there, he didn't know what kind, which barked at him when he kissed her. She was standing up and talking on and on about the damned River Nymph and she simply brushed him off without thinking. He threw his arms round her and planted a big kiss on her—h'm-h'm—and the little dog rushed at him, clasped him round the leg and bit him. Every time he tried to get closer to her and make her forget that River Nymph, the little dog got jealous and barked or tried to bite him. He begged her to shut the little dog up, which she did at once. It had all been thoughtlessness on her part, she was a one-idea woman—the River Nymph, Dr. Jones or Bones. He thought, "Now the coast is clear," and he had just made her a little interested in himself when the door flew open and a man with his hair on end and his coat half on rushed out of the apartment shouting, "I can't stand it, I can't stand it, I'm going for a drink." Grant was ruffled, very ruffled at her hiding a man in her apartment; but she said it was only the boarder, a very nice man who wrote articles for the little magazines and had sworn solemnly to her that he had no interest in women as women. Just the same, the whole thing had put him off. He did not know what to make of it. What should he do? He stood in front of Flack and asked solemnly, "What do you make of it? Eh? Give me your advice."

Flack groaned. Grant rushed to him and pulled the rug around his knees, "Eh? Eh? Take a little rest. Do you think she's sincere? It wasn't a *mise en scène?* I'm a bit dubious."

Flack said nothing. Grant looked at him with melancholy interest and shook his head, "I'd do better to try to get something out of that blondine. Give me something to live for—" and suddenly he threw back his head and let out a full-throated, bellowing laugh, "Eh, but what a woman, my boy; I was a fool to let her get away." He then talked about what they would do when spring came. Perhaps he would get the blondine out of his system if they all three went away.

Grant was contemplating buying a big old house on an island in the St. Lawrence, a Victorian mansion which no one would have but which appealed to his old-fashioned manorial tastes. There they would go, all three of them. They would go into the

Canadian fur trade, with Goodwin, open a branch. Europe would need furs, any kind of furs, rat furs, cat furs, after the war; better to look ahead then! "Give the trappers a few needles, or radios. We can buy any grade and store. The war will ruin the European fur trade. The Russians will be ruined. Any skins, worth a forchun."

He had proposed a trip to this island and house in spring. They would all three go. He asked Flack, on this snowy day, to write a letter with him to Spatchwood, formerly his manager in the cotton trade, in England. Spatchwood had lost his money through the confiscation of a Jewish firm in Germany by the Nazis. He was now doing odd jobs, trying to make commissions. Grant had given him many introductions, but no money: "I can't give handouts to everyone, the world's poor."

Flack sent a letter this day, apparently as Grant's agent, requesting Spatchwood to hire engineers, plumbers, architects, anyone necessary, in order to give the picturesque old place a thorough inspection, and to draw up estimates of costs for remodeling and making up-to-date. Grant repeated, "But put in, we must keep the façade, the façade has charm: it's romance incorporated. And put in there must be one suite of rooms with a boudoir for Edda. She's going to live with us all her life, if she doesn't get married. And if she does get married, I'll just close it up. I won't use it. We won't stay there the whole year round, mind you. We'll go to Florida; when the war's over, we'll go to the Mediterranean. I've got a chalet on Lake Como we can go to, just the three of us—when I'm in holiday mood. The rest of the time, I'm either making money or looking for the right woman."

He stood with his back to the snowy gardens and built up his dream for the house: "When spring comes, we'll go up there and look over our house. Retire. Keep out of mischief."

"Mischief is what I'm looking for," said Edda.

Grant said, "I'll bring you, I'll woo you, I'll buy you, little girl."

Flack sighed. Grant said, "Get him some bouillon, Edda; listen, Davie, Flack, listen just this once. We'll work out a scheme for me to send to the newspapers, a scheme for a British-American Cotton Board which will please Wall Street, Lombard Street, and the public, too. Monopoly, international control, will be the big moves after the war. Let's get our names in now. A position for you, Davie, Edda can get in with someone as a typist and I'll put my fingers in the pudding but I'll do public

65

service, too. I'll only take ten per cent. Them fellas want to hog the lot."

"That's why you'll never be a Rockefeller," said Edda.

"No, no, my dear girl, there's something real underneath all those fortunes. Real ability, real goods, industry, management."

David Flack became lively, "Furthermore, you never make money if you're looking only for that. Money is an abstraction. In the end you fail. Money doesn't exist. It only exists when it's married to something else, a love-match."

"That's very basic," cried Grant.

"Money has no children; all those posters and those slogans are wrong: 'Make your money bear fruit.' Money has no fruit. Money is the water you water the tree with, that's all," said Flack.

"Yes, even the blondine is real, her body, her hair is real," said Edda thoughtfully.

Grant frowned, embarrassed by the word body. He cried out gaily, spreading his hands toward them, "It's only a plot of ground bearing some wild wheat, don't know how it got there, an accident, between a little hill with an olive tree and a stony patch, and you can hardly get to it because the boys there are always driving bulls up and down, black bulls. Them boys like the bulls to run at you. They know how to manage them with a little pointed stick; they think you're a half-wit if you don't. The bulls could gore you, toss you, the boys just laugh. They like to see you run. That's about half an acre, that patch. I saw ripe wheat there, ripe wheat of wheat height; the sun was setting and it changed its shade in the broad sun and the setting sun, like very blond hair—it was yellow, not shining sometimes, and shining and weaving and braided, all in order and brushed, moving in all directions like when she bends her head and neck, softness—in all directions. A compound of silver and bronze, a sun-lavender, and blue and all these shades going over it like clouds. The sky was that violet blue. The road bent there and you could see the city on top of the rock, a dry rock, and the valley is dry, but fit for olives, good for olives. The nights there are dark brown, you see nothing, you can hardly breathe. That splitted rock is dry but sweet down where the water runs—it reminded me of myself; and that bit of acre with the wheat reminded me of the blondine. The two of us and you see they are real. The blondine is real. And you know, I have my shady side, but like they got in the grain trade a bowl of seed in the office—you must

66

take a bit as you go in as a compliment to the office—it's good luck, she is like grain, like bread, too, and if I take her, kiss her, it's not what you think, something bad, not all bad. Perhaps some of this shipment of wheat has a bit of rust on it, but wheat is not bad. A woman can't be bad. The speculators can be bad. Hoag sold the woman."

He paused, as if astonished at this truth. He murmured it over several times, as if to apprehend it.

"You see, Hoag, he's a no-good guy, maybe a petty, rotten man, but his seeing her in the street like that was like me, suddenly seeing that patch of wheat from along the road; and in spite of those two black bulls, one on each road, I had to go along and look at it. It was just what I wanted. The dry hill, the stony patch, and the plump wheat some peasant planted there. Now I see a lot of women in the street, I don't think of their—body—never, never, never until I get them upstairs—not even then until I—until—they are like all the wheat you might see all over Manitoba, or all over the Ukraine. There's some good in it. If they can be bought and sold like cattle—cattle too are good for something. Now this blondine has been corrupted, you see, like good food is adulterated in capital cities and countries where they have fraud everywhere. She's innocent. The blood of people is stored up in banks, and it can go bad, but was good, and it can be sold by gangsters, but it grew up free, it flowed free—like milk, like water. Now that blood can be accessible only to monopolists and gangsters, and so can the blondine and so can wheat. They can all be allowed to the people only at high prices, and so there's a sort of poison, rust, a rotten dew on that blood and that wheat, and even on my blondine, and so the wheat and cotton is whored. Why the style we have here of cheated-wheat and cheated-meat and whored-bread and tainted-cotton, I mean, only for gangsters—look at me. If I'd been born in a land where they wouldn't let me put my hand in your pocket—not yours, Edda—I'd be a good commissar. But I'm corrupted. I'm a profiteer. Will I sit by and let the others take the pickings? It's asking too much."

"Look, I didn't say body in a wrong way. The word body is a good word, too," said Edda, ashamed. "I know the blondine is a beautiful woman, though I never liked that high, narrow forehead of hers, and the hollows in her temples. It is the face of a peasant—I don't mean peasant is a wrong word," she cried again.

"And supposing she goes back to the gutter! Some naval officer takes her, he's a high-flier, a highjacker, and he leaves her and she goes back to the gutter again, and supposing he ends as a drunk, that's a double tragedy."

"Who? Who?"

"In your book, this man wanted to build up and he ends as a drunk," he explained with droll melancholy.

"Your schemes on the side are like speculation in blondes," said Flack.

He frowned. "No, no—I'm honest. I'm looking for that little patch of wheat, I want an oasis."

It was four o'clock, time for his usual uptown "session." He left.

Edda said angrily, "And to think I've seen him myself picking up one-dollar sidewalk speculation women! Why do we know this man?"

But Flack burst out into a tender, hopeful praise of Grant—as he had been in his youth; and of their future, "Bear with him; it's for our future. He's a big bull himself, snorting and tearing up the turf. He always speaks of our house, your boudoir—"

"I hate him," cried the young girl, bursting into tears.

Flack looked at her for a minute, and then said, "I know you do. If you say so, I'll give up the whole idea." He spoke earnestly and looked resolute though disappointed.

"I know he's kind and good. But I am jealous because he can love wholesale—he has money to secure it, and I have none and none! He throws his wholesale in my face without meaning it."

The next day Grant was back again. He walked about looking uneasily at the clock and said he was waiting for a telephone call. "Better here, better not at my place, might get blackmailed." He had employed a private agent in Flack's name, asking for information about the blonde in Washington. He had already heard by phone at the office that she was dancing at the Diplomat Hotel with naval officers; that she was out every night. Grant had bombarded her hotel with telegrams and telephone calls.

"Perhaps she thought I was cooling off? Perhaps she treated me to my own medicine? What should I do? What do you recommend?" And all the time laughing anxiously, appealing to them with downcast face and fresh, simple glance, confessing his activities, his suspicions. He had sent one of his office men down to Washington to trail her. Parkinson said she was dancing at the Diplomat Hotel. She might be a spy.

"Oh, she's a spy, of course," said Edda.

He became restless. "I can't believe it. She's always talking about her mother and how cruel her father was. A girl wouldn't do that with her mother around. Her mother's always on deck, reads her mail, I think. She's an innocent old busybody, that's all. No, no, I refuse to believe it till all the evidence is in."

"Well, I've been invited to March's place for some week end and I'll make it this week end, if he wants me. I'll see what the boys can do to find out," said Flack.

Edda laughed, "Oh, she's a spy: that is your big affair."

Grant became very gloomy, "She can get men, why should she work at spying?"

Edda laughed, "Men aren't enough for a woman."

Grant frowned.

11

On a Saturday in April, 1942, Flack went to 44 Wall and met his friend Hugo March about twelve. They got into the green roadster to drive out to March's home in Pennsylvania. He had few week-end guests; people avoided the Pennsylvania cottage, though March was generous with drink and food, and close-lipped, and as crony as any gangster.

It was a fine, cool day. The country showed faint signs of the change of season.

"It's as fine as anything in Europe," said Flack as they drove down a compacted dirt ramp into a broad, saucer-shaped valley that would be green, lush, soon.

"That's something I'll never know, but I'll take your word for it and want to hear no more about it," said March, in his slow, sinister way. He drove fast and steadily, a short, fat creature, sunk into the seat, flesh hanging in folds everywhere, bold, round, clear blue eyes staring at you from the mirror, thin sandy hair, a square chin not yet engulfed. After a moment he continued, emphasizing each word, "Any American that takes a boatride out of this country is crazy. Of course, if the Japs slam you, you have to go after them and even accounts; but they are crazy to dress American boys in soldier-suits and send them over the other way. Nothing good ever happened over that way. We have goods to export; we don't want to export Americans that make the goods. I never could understand what you and your friend Grant—and the others—wanted to gallivant in Europe for—for my part—I don't see why they issue passports to Americans.

You'll find in the *Congressional Record* that Senator Whittington —my friend—said the other day, he personally would refuse them. So would I. You'll find those people who go abroad have never seen their own country. They have never seen Pennsylvania. They are afraid to go through New Jersey. They tell you people gyp you in Connecticut. They are a pack of noodles. They're afraid to go west where Abe Lincoln came from. Anyone—that's my opinion—who turns his back on the Statue of Liberty—deserves to stay wherever the hell he thinks he's going. I wouldn't let them in again. I'd say, 'Take your damn bit of paper and do the needful with it, when you get over there with the dagoes and heinies. Leave this country to those who like it. . . .' But I'm damned if I'd let one of those goddamn s.o.b.'s take his American money with him. I'd make him try to do business on the other side, in the peanuts those monkeys use for money. Why not put the cheapskates in a concentration camp and say, 'When you get out of this goddamn Coney Island you'll be glad to see any part of the U.S.A., even the bit just outside the barbed-wire fence'?"

Flack laughed and made a sympathetic speech, first placating March, then growing eloquent upon the pleasures of travel, "And it wouldn't do the American boys any harm to see the other side had bath-tubs too, sometimes."

March waited in dead silence till he had finished and then, "All that don't mean a good goddamn to me. I wouldn't let Americans travel and they shouldn't let one of our boys pass the seas. They got nothing to teach us. If there's any fighting to be done, we'll do it at home. And I don't mean on our cans, I mean against those who don't want to work. That doesn't please you, but your opinions don't please me."

All this was delivered as a quiet monologue and the remark at the end in a much softer tone. March laughed, "Well, come on, give me a stump speech."

"I don't fall for sucker bait," said Flack.

"You fall for Red bait. The whole world's going to hell without our aid. Let it, is my remedy. We got a big enough country. All we've got to do is to sit on it. No good ever came out of meddling in other people's affairs. It don't matter who's right, it don't matter who's wrong, you get that rainbow in your eye and you pay the damages. Why did the British get us in? If we'd let the Japs mind their own business in China and clean up the Reds, we wouldn't have had a Pearl Harbor. We don't give a good goddamn about Hitler. I don't know one good American who cares if he dies or walks all over Europe. Do them a lot of good. But who cares what a pack of starved mongrels do? I got a Great Dane out at my place. There's a little bit of fluff, a white snarling little mutt, comes past and snarls round his feet. My Great Dane looks the other way, he makes believe he doesn't know he's there! My Great Dane is the U.S.A.! And that's what we'll do—make believe the rest of the curs aren't there. We've only got to tend to business, and make our own money. If there's something we don't like in our country, we'll fix it up our own way. A guy who lets wind about Russia and Hitler and whatnot ought to be locked up. He's either crazy or a traitor. You'll find his mother or father wasn't born in this goddamn country, or he don't want to work, born lazy."

They drove on and on. The hills were rising and growing black; their vegetation darkened. They began to go through ugly road-side villages. Presently, they passed a village, a railroad spur-line, and through a notch between two hills which were hardly more than outcropping coal seams, so dark were they; and then out into a great sullen valley, both limbs opened wide, unresisting but repelling.

"This is my country." March pointed to a low, plump knoll covered with plucked-out native growth. He smiled, "My place is there, but you'd never get a glimpse of it from the road."

"A hideaway?"

There was a long pause. Then March, with a chuckle, "It could serve—for a hideaway. I put in all the woodwork myself. It's right on top of the goddamn rise; and from my study window you can see a hundred miles, it looks like. I can see a deer moving ten miles away. I could shoot him ten miles away, on a clear day."

They switchbacked up a long, raw, hidden drive.

It was stony country, worthless for farming or orchard; and March had got a hundred acres very cheap. The house was not on top of the rise, but on the crest of a lower slope. The spur rose about it some fifty feet; and all the scrub had been cleared from this part of the hill.

The house had been a farmhouse, consisting of a large kitchen, narrow bedroom, and leanto. To these parts were added a series of small rooms and porches downstairs, and a second story, small, awkward, sitting on the ground floor like a housing on a horse. The entire house had been fitted with heavy oak panels, and the second story with marble-plated bathrooms, glass-and-chromium showers, and mirrors. The furniture was bird's-eye maple, with brown and yellow cushions, curtains, hunting prints, and a few cheap ornaments. The study had a bookcase with detective novels, a collapsible bar, several closets with sliding panels, an Army cot, a brick fireplace with heavy firedogs. The small leaded windows were fitted with double locks and bronze screens. Doors were few, but the farm bedroom, now used for a dining hall, opened toward the valley. The study had a door which opened toward the valley and on to a drop of about ten feet, there being no step or porch beneath it.

They had lunch early. There were, with Flack, only March and his wife, Angela, his son, Claud, and two unexpected guests, March's fourteen-year-old daughter, Muriel, nicknamed Fairy, a buxom, languid, sly-eyed child with fine skin and hair, and Davis, a nineteen-year-old friend of Claud, who had brought Fairy from her convent school apparently on a sort of escapade.

The cocktail sandwiches and the meal were prepared and served by a good-looking forty-year-old woman called by March "Violet" and by the others, Mrs. Downey.

When Flack complimented Mrs. March on the soup, she sang out, with pretty plaintiveness, "I don't know what's in it, I didn't even taste it, you noticed. Perhaps there are hairs in it, perhaps face powder, she uses some rice powder his mother used to use," she looked with a wicked smile at March. She continued, "It's not my doing; it's Mrs. Downey's. Everything here is run by Mrs. Downey. She is the real wife, not I."

Claud and Davis and the daughter covered this up by youthful byplay; March frowned and Flack, who had never met Mrs. March before, rushed into the breach with one of his long, hilarious improvisations. March said, "You needn't put on a song and dance, Flack; Mrs. Downey's manager here because I want her and I pay her and anyone who opens her goddamn puss on the matter is out looking for trouble."

"Everything here belongs to Mrs. Downey. This is not my home, I am no one here," continued Angela March naughtily, and she smiled a little, like a beautiful young cat, which smiles deeper and deeper and looks into your eyes just before it reaches for them.

Mrs. March was a youthful, deliciously formed woman, blonde, in confectionery colors, very pretty, very gay. March looked at her across the table and spoke to her for the first time since he had entered the house: "If you don't like it this way get into the goddamn kitchen and hustle your behind."

The wife seemed pleased at this opening, "How can I go in there? She runs everything. I don't know where my own pots and pans are. I would not be welcome there, you know. I could not have a cocktail, but I am sure Mrs. Downey had a cocktail in the kitchen."

"Did you forget to take Mrs. Downey a cocktail?" March asked his son.

Claud laughed without embarrassment, "Oh, no, she got one—two, in fact."

"That's better," said the man.

Afterward he explained the whole business of Elias Brown, his friend. The marriage with the Washington woman had fallen through. The banquet had been magnificent. They had sent the photographs to all the Senators. But Udall's scheme was foiled by two lawyers down from Chicago who were counsels for the receivers, and who had a vested interest in the bankruptcy and dreaded the day when the railroad would become solvent. These boys obtained a temporary bankruptcy financing, enough to keep the railroad alive but not to put it on its feet. In the meantime they foiled Udall's other scheme which was in effect to obtain control of all the railroad president's assets while crashing his reputation and indirectly leading to his suicide through the destruction of his earning power. The railroad president was at present bankrupt and the hero of this widely whispered story; but—strange to relate, women are funny cattle—the woman he married had suddenly taken to him and stood by him, and she told the boys to go and play in another back yard. She told Udall to stick to his original wife, she knew too much about him, she did not believe he would do anything but swallow the whole of the money and leave her out in the cold, too. Said she, "I'd rather be married than president."

The boys thought ill of her for this, though they admitted you never could tell what a woman would do when she got married.

March went on to discuss the future of the U.S.A. Hitler had the right idea in some things, so did Mussolini, only they were two-cent administrators. What they needed were a few billion dollars, the organizing ability of men who could handle dollars and government. Just to show Flack how wrong he was, he let him into a great secret, which was that March's "friends were organizing all the time behind the scenes to take over"; they had their men, they had the money, they had the key positions, and they had an army which they would use at home, not abroad. The U.S.A. would be turned into a magnificent producing machine, producing for March and his friends. March said in his wise, ponderous way, with his dewlaps moving slowly as he champed out the phrases, "I'm not speaking of fraud, grand larceny, some grand swindle as your friends over the other side try to make out. I mean legal procedure, strictly honest business, all-embracing scheme for government that cuts overhead by ninety-five per cent. The government has to be a different sort. Look at the money thrown away on the workers. Have unions with millions of dollars only used to upset industry and waste our money. You want to cut out all those high-paid union officials, with cars. A state within the state. We'll have one state only. Modern government is a halfway house to monopoly, not the kind we have now, with the boys filling their own pockets, but a stern, sane monopoly. You have to have monopoly: it's economical, efficient, progressive. This Government stands in the way of proper monopoly. Monopolies are now run with the Government in mind: there's a scratch my back and I'll scratch yours policy. Government doesn't intend to do its duty. Government is Tammany on a big scale. It wants to be popular. A true monopoly wouldn't worry about being popular, it would be efficient. Because of this Government, with Tammany façade, you have plenty of waste. Birds who don't know their elbow from their foot do buying and selling. In the monopoly state, the biggest monopolist in the steel business runs the steel business, and that's government. We revoke the Wagner Act and all those brakes on industry and let the wheels turn. Your friends over there have never been in business and they don't understand efficiency. What they say about capitalism is a horselaugh. They have an idea of monopoly; only ours is better. If they could take a gander at Radio City they'd wish they had one too. You can build Radio Cities out of our production, plus our efficiency. But you haven't seen the half of it yet. Only let us stay at home and work, and not play with toy soldiers.

"Now take insurance, that's one of the fattest markets in the country, and it makes millions for anyone who touches it. The poorest son-of-a-bitch in the country works his hide off to pay insurance and see what happens when your automobile runs into another car, you try and get the claim. If you can sit it out, you get it, but you got to sweat for it. Me and my friends, we're living entirely on inefficiency; but I'm an American patriot and I like to see efficiency. I could live on efficiency and make more out of it than I make on inefficiency. . . . Well, I'm no reformer and if the goddamn suckers want to keep me fat this way, O.K. I'm not going to live on aspirin trying to make the country run better. But I got friends in Washington who are reformers, and they want to organize this country so they squeeze every last ounce of energy out of it and every last penny of profit; and those little weasels over there can have their wars and their Hitlers, they'll show just like a Mexican jumping bean in the hopper of hell. Let them wear themselves out, we're just getting into our stride, why, we didn't even find a formula yet, but those wizards are working it out. Now this s.o.b.—Mussolini—he thought he had a good idea with his formula, the corporate state; but what's that? Ice-cream soda for school kids. No American would want that kind of salad dressing. We only want one thing and that's more efficiency and all the wheels grinding twenty-five hours a day, and this'll be a country like there never was before on the face of the earth since we parted from the goddamn monkeys."

"But, Hugo, you never talked like this before. He just sits there drinking whisky," said Angela, opening her eyes.

March said, "She's putting on some act and I don't like it. If I never talked like this it's because I can't talk to a feeble-minded moron."

"You see what I am to him," she wept, her whole attitude pretty artifice and protest.

"Keep your puss closed or I'll put something in it you can't spit out. There's only one real woman round here, she does the work and you're an ornament."

He said to Flack, "Let's get out of here and get a breath of air."

Mrs. March sulked. March shifted his glance to Fairy, who had been giving young Davis secret touches and lascivious glances, shielded as she thought by her father's serious speech. March flipped a titbit at her across the tablecloth, called attention to her well-developed figure, her pretty face, sparkling, oval blue eyes, which resembled her mother's.

"Gently, Fairy," said he, noticing her right hand on Davis's thigh. A cloud passed over her face, she shifted in her chair, let her hands and wrists play scales on the tablecloth, and burst out laughing, a foolish, open-mouthed laugh, with a weak rictus.

The young admirer, Davis, an intelligent, dry-minded youth, smiled at March. He was the prospective son-in-law. Fairy went back to her public flirting, touching Davis on the collar, neck, ear, hair. March looked at this for a moment, and said in a strange tone, warning, firm, "Fairy, now behave, my little queen."

She straightened up and dropped her soft underlip. In a few minutes, when her father had started to talk about the s.o.b. in the White House (meaning President Roosevelt), she went back, with side-glances of daring, to her play, Davis smiling but not openly encouraging her.

The father said, "Wait till you hear something. What are you going to have on your fifteenth birthday, Fairy?"

She laughed at him.

"Come, come, little sweetheart: what is Father going to give you?"

The mother frowned and tapped on the tablecloth. The girl laughed, "An evening dress."

"Yes, the week before her fifteenth birthday, if she is a good girl and goes back to school and does not run away again, remember: my Fairy and I are going into town to get the very best evening gown we can buy, I don't care if we go to Bergdorf's, or wherever you like, and we'll spend two hundred dollars, if you like. And I'm going to throw a big party for you, sweetheart, aren't I? In the Iridium Room, on the Astor Roof, anywhere you say."

"Cut low," said the girl.

"I don't approve of it, but what I say doesn't count," said the mother.

"I promised it and what I promise I perform. But until then, Fairy, you must wear the dresses they give you at school. Father will be angry. Father will not give you the evening gown."

"Décolleté, décolleté. I won't go back to school unless I can have a new dress now."

The father spoke in warning tones again, and she drooped; but he added tenderly, "When you are fifteen you will get a diamond bracelet, too."

"A wristwatch," she said.

"Go out now, Fairy."

He glanced with intense, covetous fondness at the strange girl who was not even looking at him but at Davis, and flirting again as foolishly as a young dog. "I want it, I want it. I have pretty shoulders, Maxim told me."

Her father watched her go out with an expression of fondness and doubt, "She's so innocent for her age. I'm glad she has picked out a good boy like Davis. I told Davis she'll have a hundred thousand dollars when she marries and I'm going to let her marry at seventeen, if she wants it. She doesn't know what it's all about now; she's just like one of my white chicks out there. I keep her caged up, too, it's better."

"He married me at seventeen too; I regret it. I'm sorry I didn't get a chance to see life," said the wife impudently. March took no notice of her. Angela said shrilly, "She's too young to have a boy or get married, but of course what I say doesn't count."

March half rose and looked cruelly right into his wife's mouth, "I'll come round the table and smack your puss in a minute; stop your goddamn clacking, I'm sick of it."

"I'm going upstairs," said the wife.

"Scuttle up, if you don't I'll tread on you," said the man.

The wife ran off. However, at the door, she stopped, was smiling again, seductive in the pale blue velvet slacks she had been wearing since before lunch. She said naughtily, "I'm going riding."

Presently they saw her, smacking her crop against her legs, pulling on white gloves. She had a blue ribbon in her hair. The men looked at her as she walked through the house, through the kitchen. March said roughly, "I've got Claud keeping an eye on his mother now; she's been up to her tricks again."

Flack knew nothing of her tricks and said nothing. After lunch they sat in one of the porches while March drank four or five heavy whisky-and-sodas, then they took a walk, to see the land. Presently March became sullen. "Where did the goddamn bitch ride to? I'll shut her up." He told Flack now his wife was certifiably feeble-minded and he intended to have her put in a private asylum. She had no more decorum than an animal.

Davis had taken the Fairy for a drive in the car. Presently they came back, excited and mischievous. The Fairy had had two cocktails, although they were forbidden to her. "It's all right if it's with you, Boy," said March to Davis, "but otherwise it's not allowed."

The young girl laughed foolishly and said the boys always gave her cocktails; her father could not stop her. "They'll do anything I ask them. They'll kiss me, too, if I let them; they let me do anything if I let them kiss me. If I could wear a midriff evening dress, they'd do anything for me," said she, stretching in the seat. The father looked at her with touching belief, "You mustn't say those

77

things, Fairy; you don't know yet what it's all about, queenie," he murmured. "You'll go back to school and when you're a woman you'll wear your evening gown."

The young couple got out of the car and went indoors, declaring they would find some drinks in the kitchen, even if "old Downey" tried to stop them. "I hate that old bitch, she hates my mother."

March seemed happy now that his daughter was at home, but as nightfall approached he became more vindictive in his remarks about his wife. Presently she rode in, tired, querulous, and called to an as yet unseen man to take her horse. She strolled in, pulling off her gloves, and asked her husband for a drink.

"You know goddamn well you can't drink."

The wife, turning to Flack, said, "Because I'm supposed to be weak-minded, you know. Well, I will drink and I do drink, if not with you, then with others, who are kind to me. I have friends; he doesn't know I have people who are sorry for me. I have a friend Marie, haven't I, Hugo?"

"Yes, she has a friend Marie, and Marie is a goddamn fine woman, and if it weren't for Marie I'd shut you up tonight. Go away and get yourself fixed up for dinner; you can't eat your dinner in pants, the way you did your lunch."

She laughed and strolled off upstairs. The husband said, "She knows she can't get away with anything. And I mean what I say."

After dinner, the young couple set off in Davis's car to take Fairy back to her convent school.

"Mummy'll come and see you next week," cried the wife.

"No, Mummy won't come and see you next week. Mummy'll stay away," said the husband. And he took his friend away to the smokeroom, explaining that one of the reasons for sending the daughter to the convent school was the silly, weak behavior of the mother. "If I could, I'd take her away from her altogether. I've told the school I'll take her away if they allow her mother to see her."

At eight-thirty the host, having drunk several more heavy whiskies, fell to snoring on the porch couch, and the son and guest, after reading books in different rooms, themselves went upstairs. The next morning, the two men, become very friendly, were talking about business matters and March was once more showing his furniture and paneling to be admired, when on an impulse he began opening the desk, library shelves, bar, and cupboards. He slid aside a double panel under the bookcase and showed a collection of modern guns, revolvers, hunting rifles, guns for street and field warfare.

"I can sight and pretty damn near kill a deer at ten miles—or a man. I could get anyone coming up that drive." Then he bent down and looked round at his friend, his heavy face suffused with blood, his large blue eyes clouding. "I've even got a sub-machine gun amongst others."

"You're not the only one who collects guns, I know; but the others collect Civil War stuff," said Flack, somewhat uneasily.

March straightened up, "And I spent money on what can come in useful, no antiques that'll go off backwards."

"Expect a private war up here?"

March pushed to the panel, which concealed the heavier guns, and locked the door, saying, as he put the keys in another drawer which he locked, in his habitual ominous tones, "It-could-be. I think—we—are—damnwell—living our whole goddamn lives in a state of siege. There are too many smart monkeys about for my liking."

Flack changed the subject, dragging in Grant's affair for the first time—"a woman he played around with and got involved with and who has been dancing with officers in Washington. I wanted to save him from himself and suggested that she might be on the police records, she must be."

March poured himself a drink, sat down, "It's not that dishface blonde that he's been chewing my ear off about? What was her name before she married this Adams? Just that, and where she was born. Has she got a friend, heavy sugar—? Easier to trail a woman by a man."

The next day, Flack made the only other reference to the matter as they drove in, early in a sparkling morning, almost spring. He said, "Robbie telephoned Washington from our place and from his own and God knows where else. They'd have him down, the idiot, perhaps as her friend, he's always making a mighty noise, a chorus boy imitating the heavy—it was pretty indiscreet, any way you look at it, if she is a spy."

"What the hell gives you the idea that she's a spy?"

"There's a war on and they use women like the blondine."

"Don't she get enough out of Grant? Is he busted?"

"He paid forty thousand dollars for her in one year, then gave her the gate. She always has a hedge. She married the hedge. It was no soap. He spanked her in public or something—who cares? That's all in the day's work to a girlie like that. She has a delightful friend, Paulie Russell, who spies on her, hoping for a few hot dinners from Grant, a couple of bottles of perfume—she's the soubrette. It's better than the Salvation Army, though she has to sing psalms for it and listen to Robbie's line, 'I'm a radical, I'm a romantic,' Jesus C. Christ, you don't know him—and then she wears better clothing than the Army lassies. Probably Grant promised to marry Paula, he always does; it's the short road to what he calls the honey. The girls soon find it conspiracy in law for him or them to agree to break by fraud a signed contract, viz., marriage, and they get mad, especially the kind Robbie picks. Then they leave him, or they truly do him damage—the old honeybear always talks too much—or they decide it's easier to be taken on again at cheaper pay. The Hollywood method; throw him out, he'll come crawling back: Grant's own invention though —no marriage, a cocktail about once a week, or at first six pairs of stockings at Christmas, but the following Christmas, two pairs, and the next Christmas a jar of marmalade—ha-ha-ha—he works them down to bargain prices. Then he drops them altogether, unless he uses them as a floorwasher; but he never lets up on his sweet song and he keeps plenty of houris hanging round, all at different stages of his System, as he calls it, and not even a ground plan before him, all in his head—what a brain, it could have been used for something better, as he said! He gets them at last—and if they're leftists, at first—to sell honey free. It's the System."

"It sounds cheap. How do you know he has any money?"

"I've gone over his list of securities. I know the address of his trust funds and I've witnessed his will. I'm his do-all and net-nothing."

"What do you want to lick his behind for? It still sounds cheap, keeping you for a yes-man. It don't appeal to me. I offered you a participation. You could have done better with me."

"He keeps me to be his no-man, don't you understand? You know damn well I'm a leftist and I have to speak my mind. Now with your crowd of bums, I have to drink whisky every evening at five and say nothing. I can't do it, Hugo. I prefer that guy with all his faults and his strange, sweet song. I tell him he's going nuts when he begins to think he's Mussolini. He goes to all newsreels in the hope of seeing Mussolini behaving like a chimp on a stone balcony."

"I thought he was a radical?"

"He's a radical like I'm a Dupont."

"I still don't see what's in it for you—you got to pay your rent."

"He's asking Edda and me along with him to Rome and to Lake Como after the war."

"Where the hell's Lake Como? Do you want to go fishing?"

"He's got a chalet, that's a kind of cottage, and a house in Rome."

"And he's taking you free? Tell that to the King of Denmark. Why should he waste dough on you? I guess he's taking you to see the etchings, as he says."

"You don't understand Robbie, Hugo. He's a tenderhearted man and he never forgets he was once a poor boy."

"If he never forgets he was a poor boy that's a good reason for him to hate poor boys." March made a loud Bronx cheer, and continued, "Well, be that as it may, and I think you're, frankly, nuts, I don't think he's got any money; anyhow, in Wall Street, I go on a rule: every man is worth one third of what he is said to own."

"Grant is worth much more than one million dollars," said Flack sharply.

"That's not peanuts; but they said he was worth more. What is his object with the blondine—is it a payoff or is it honey? That's sweet, I love that!"

"He says he wants to make her disgorge: she got valuables out of him. It's a question of vanity."

"A sucker for women."

"He paid out one hundred thousand dollars once—all told. I knew him then, too."

"What makes him think this one is a spy?"

"She knows someone in a legation."

"That's all he knows?"

Flack said that was all. March turned up the radio. The swing tune came out clear and sweet on the brisk morning air.

"I love that," said March. Presently he began to talk about stocks and bonds with Flack. "I presume Grant is doing pretty well in the market if he pays you for your advice."

Flack made no reply. In the afternoon Flack brought Grant to Beaver Street to meet Hoag and March. Said March, weightily, "I understand you want to find out about a certain party, a woman. I have an informant I have contacted this morning. My informant is Edison Furnivall Carter, you can check up on him, but you can't talk to him; he doesn't talk to strangers. I did Carter a favor, and he does me favors. He just informed me he believes he recognizes the name of the party you are interested in.

81

He's not sure and he won t commit himself until I confirm the bona fide of my party. To do me a favor he'll take a gander at the documents for me, or get a man he can trust. He don't usually do it, he has clerks for that, but this is the kind of thing you wouldn't want a clerk to be in possession of—am I right? Question One: What do you want to know? Question Two: Will you pay a sum of money, say five hundred dollars, to a patriotic charity, sending the check to Carter, whose reputation is of the highest? Question Three: Do you want to try some other method first, as hiring a private dick?"

This composure upset Grant. He walked up and down the office. He looked through the glass partitions into the general office. March asked for money and all he offered was a three-barreled name. Flack, at once sensing Grant's mood, recommended that instead of spending so large a sum as $500 which March had mentioned to him, Grant first of all employ a Washington detective. This would cost perhaps much less since they might find out something the first week. On the other hand, it was like taking a lottery ticket while the other was a sure thing: he would know at once, perhaps tomorrow.

Grant walked up and down. March continued in his full-stomach voice, "I personally wouldn't spend five hundred dollars to find out about any cow in the U.S.A., and I think you're a sucker if you do, but it's your poison, and you're the doctor. No blonde is worth five hundred dollars to me," and he added a commonplace obscenity which made Grant writhe.

He said hastily, "I got to find out who she is, because she tried to take me over. If the detectives are in with the real S.S., can you trust them, or do they split?"

Lazily March said, stretching his short, fat legs, "They split both ways, one for you, one for partner, two for me; but what do you care?—you get your share. I mean they're whores, but if you want to try it that way first, I can get you the most honest of the whores, he's a pal of my good friend, Francis O'Sullivan. But O'Sullivan's a sick man; he's waiting to retire and I think he'll go in with this Grey, Samuel Doncaster Grey, that's the private detective. That's how I know about it."

Grant anxiously walked up and down, "I never buy without a sample! Would I buy raw furs without a sample? They'd send me tips and tails perhaps. I want to see the goods first. Let them give me a couple of lines—only a couple of lines—and then I'll see what they've got and pay if it's worth while. But they can't plunder me because of a woman."

March said contemptuously, "Suit yourself, it's your show. If you'll pay, there'll be maybe a song and dance, maybe a strip-tease, maybe a good spy story; if you don't pay, the curtain won't go up, my good friend."

"I can't believe it, butter wouldn't melt in her mouth."

Flack cried, "You don't think they choose cross-eyed hunch-backs for spies?"

March said, "Better than a winsome blonde who dances with attachés in the Diplomat Hotel."

Grant walked up and down, "She's always in bed. And you have to be up bright and early to be a spy."

"Not a lady spy; she works at the other end of the clock," said Flack.

Grant stopped in front of them and declared, "Look, I know some fella got her fascinated out in California and some gigolo at Saratoga—"

"First I heard of that," said Flack, laughing.

"Never mind, and at Washington she's in with some naval fella. She's pretty, she wants a good time. She wants to get married. What does that prove? No, no. I know the answer. It doesn't suit me to pay out five hundred dollars to get the same answer out of the machine. I don't know these friends of yours. Maybe you don't know them. Five hundred dollars—I want a sample before I go into it. Five hundred dollars—and then I hear— We don't know the lady: you've got war-fever."

"O.K. by me, let's forget it. I wouldn't pay out five hundred dollars for any blondine—I love that!—and as for a White Russian or whatever she says she is—"

Grant walked up and down. "She's fascinated by the gigolos in uniform. I'll tell you the kind of girl she is: she's lazy but she's honest; selfish, but wouldn't take a penny but what she feels she's entitled to. That I'll swear to. She takes money from men— good; who doesn't? Your own wife does. She's selfish, she never did for me what that other one did, she stays in bed till twelve, she wouldn't make a good wife. My own wife, do you know what I had to do? Send out the laundry, count the laundry, ask the servant to sew on buttons. I was a young fellow, didn't want to bother her. But my blondine—well, I'll tell you, she has a weak-ness for animals. She used to keep a little bird flying about the apartment in Paris when she was with that skating champion.

He objected but she clung to it. When she moved to the U.S.A. she brought it with her. She said the bird didn't like New York air. She let it out every day; one morning she found it dead. She cried when she told me, she said—it just died, quietly, without a sound; and she burst into tears. By Jove, she wouldn't cry for me like that perhaps. Never mind. She said it in French—she learned French in Lausanne. She said, '*Il est mort comme ça, tout tranquillement.*' She had those—what is it?—Siamese cats. At first I thought it was an ornament on the mantelpiece. She had a little white cat, with blue eyes, deaf; she said they're always deaf. And that lazy 'ooman would run after those animals—I couldn't stand them myself—giving them water, cleaning them—worrying when one of the cats went whimpering round the place because she wanted—wanted—honey, I suppose, just like me."

He blushed. He paused; then continued, "And she wouldn't even clean a pair of gloves for herself. You may say she's tough with tender spots. But she was nice to me, too, at times. You may say she made me pay through the nose. But I'm not ashamed, I'm not ashamed. Why does some little fella write anonymous letters to the income-tax about me? Because he is jealous I can pay forty thousand dollars for a woman who is no better than the next one. But—I offered it to her! She didn't beg it out of me. She didn't dun me. Of course, she knows how to get it without asking."

He was sitting down, pulling up his cuffs and coat sleeves, showing his large, blond, hairy wrists and hands. He passed his large hands over his hair. He got up and looked at himself in the mirror, rearranging his hair and tie, "I won't say she had a great passion for me—maybe; it isn't possible. A long nose, thin hair. I didn't quite understand her. She thinks I let her down. I did let her down. I want to be fair."

"What do you want me to do—burst out crying?" asked March.

The three sat silent for a while. Grant's unraveling, self-interrogation went on for another half hour and Flack, ashamed of wasting March's time, said, "Why not try this detective, Grey, for a week?"

They discussed the cost. Grant held out "for proofs first—this detective could keep me dangling."

"It's a cash-first business. You'll need my recommendation to get a detective to do it even on a weekly basis," said March.

Grant could not make up his mind.

March burst out laughing, "Well, now I've seen a great lover in action."

Grant frowned, "I got to know first if there are files on her."

"You expect fancy women to let you sample first?"

Grant would not answer.

"Well, the first time I've seen a great lover in action," said March.

"I got to know there's a file first."

"What files? Is this to be Treasury, Immigration, or State Department?" inquired March.

Grant was confused. He looked to Flack, "How do I know? For all I know, it's a myth, it's an idea of Flack's, not worth a baked bean."

"Don't say me, Grant; you know—"

"All right, all right."

"It's no business of mine. You just have to make up your mind whether you're going to spend your money on aspirins or on finding out! I'll give you my opinion, which you can have without spending a nickel—you're a fleecy lamb if you spend one more cent on the damn blonde; I'm one hundred per cent with you there. You'll do better to keep the five hundred dollars in your pants, or give it to your boy friend here."

"I don't know anything about all this. I'm out of this picture. For me women aren't something you can buy," said Flack.

"A real woman can't be bought," said March, looking sidewise at Grant.

Grant squirmed and fought with himself, "I spent twenty-four hundred dollars in sterling silver I brought from England, and I ordered a silver dinner service; and she's got a silver frame there. Two hundred and fifty for photographs—she went to the best photographer in town, they made her look like a Du Barry. She's all right as she is, but they made her look better. I'm out a fur coat I got from Goodwin, wholesale, eighteen hundred dollars—"

"That cost you eighteen hundred dollars wholesale? It's murder," said Flack.

Grant frowned, "I'm not talking about the forty thousand dollars."

"I'd like to take that blonde into my business," said March.

"She met a Christmas tree," said Grant.

"Well—what is it to be—a Sitz or a Blitz?" said March.

Flack said, "Come, Robbie, you've kept us here two bloody hours and we still don't know where we're going to start, or if at all."

85

"I'm damned if I'll spend another five hundred dollars on her—and no honey," cried the miserable man.

The other two burst out laughing. March said, "Look, my friend, I think you're crazy and it's none of my business, but I'll ask my friend Morales—"

"Who's that?"

"Someone I know in Washington, to do a little exploring. Would you say the State Department secret files would be the best, if—only—mind I say only if—if there's funny business?"

"All right, all right. Ask your friend Morales."

"He won't do it for nothing."

"What does he want?"

"I'll see, but not five hundred dollars, less than five hundred dollars. He's under an obligation to me."

"Telephone me tomorrow," said Grant, as if to a clerk.

"I'll telephone you—at your office—since I'm doing you a favor —when I goddamn please."

Grant and Flack went out, talking emotionally.

"This Morales—he gives us names, not the goods," Grant kept crying fretfully.

"You've got to trust March in a case like this."

"I drew a report on him; it was better than I thought," Grant agreed, with respect.

Two days later March let Flack know that there was "something for him from Washington." Grant sent Flack to March and met him afterwards in a bar just off Broadway. Flack said, "You can't ask more from March than this. He got Morales to make a preliminary inquiry and he went to bat for you, said you had to know whether it was a wild goose chase. Morales says she is being watched, there is a file on her, and she has several aliases, Kent, Adams, Brown, and another they won't state. You are in honor bound to give March the amount Morales asked—one hundred and fifty dollars. It's nominal—it's very cheap. And I want to say one thing, Robbie: if you try any three months', six months', and nine months' notes techniques with this baby, you'll never hear another word from him. I know March. He's tough, and he never forgives."

"The information's dear at any price," cried Grant. But when March called him about the $150 owing next morning, in his slow, hard voice, Grant said he'd send a boy over. March called him two hours later and said something had happened to the boy with the $150 check. "There are no vouchers, only cash talks,

86

Grant," he said sweetly. Grant then sent a boy over. No sooner did he send the check than he felt a curious exaltation. He rubbed his hands, telephoned Flack, and said, "I think at last we're getting somewhere."

Nevertheless, he would not authorize "Morales" to do any more work. Morales would not say in which department he had found her. It was not enough for the money. He would use a detective and not the detective mentioned by March but one he would find himself. He asked Alf Goodwin to do him a favor, go to Washington, do an errand in the Department of Commerce, and at the same time set a cheap detective on the trail of the blondine. "Anyone could trail her, a three-year-old child could trail her. I know her habits. She's always in public, except when she's with her mother."

At the end of the week he had the following report from the detective, James, picked by Goodwin: that Mrs. X went out for long drives with young naval officers and a pro-Franco attaché, who was evidently very fond of her. The attaché had given her papers in a restaurant. She had been followed to a pharmacy, and had handed the sheet of paper to a pharmacist. It turned out to be only an old European skin balm. Cost of this inquiry—$70. Grant read it through and through and thrust it at Flack.

"Nothing," said Flack.

"Nothing!" Grant sat silent again. He said, "Weakness for uniforms: fell for that gigolo attaché!" He thought again, turning the pages, remarked, "Very reasonable, seventy dollars, very reasonable. Should I have him go on?"

"What can you find out in a week? What are you doing it for?"

"She's got under my skin. Cheaper than that Morales—and told me more. But what does it prove? If I employ him on a week-to-week basis, he'll dole it out to me, just feed me enough—a serial story. Nothing doing. It'll be his market. I'll never get seventy dollars' worth."

"It's your lunacy," said Flack.

Grant could not make up his mind and took the report to several friends, Goodwin, friends of the blonde, business associates. At last he came back to Goodwin, "Have patience with me, my boy. I'll tell him to go on another week, but he hasn't got carte blanche. No carte blanche. I want results. If he don't turn up something serious next week, it's all off. It's up to him. Tell him that. If this doesn't work, I'll go back to March and see what he thinks."

The next day Hoag came to Grant's office downtown, casually, but mentioned that March had seen his friend, Edison Furnivall Carter, who had asked him in the course of conversation what was all this about Mrs. Kent? Carter had hinted that there was something in it, and "his friends," whoever they might be, would like to know more about her. He could not give away Government information, but he guaranteed Morales, knew him.

"Think Carter gets a cut?" inquired Grant.

"Of a hundred and fifty dollars?" said Hoag elfishly.

Flack said, "Carter is an intimate friend of"—he named two well-known statesmen—"and is known to be incorruptible."

"A week-to-week basis can last from here to Kingdom Come and I'll be none the wiser," said the unhappy man.

"Why don't you put down a lump sum, let one of Carter's men do the work, remove the file, and have a peek at it? It'll cost you less in the end. But you have to pay first. You're not dealing with blue-sky peddlers, phonies; you're dealing with incorruptible men who are doing March a personal favor," Hoag said.

"Favors and incorruptibles always cost more, you know that," said Flack, laughing excitedly.

"You're not on the Curb, you're on the big board, this way," said Hoag. Hoag took back with him a check made out to Hugo March for $500.

The next week this surveillance had a welcome end. Goodwin's detective reported that Mrs. Kent and her mother had left Washington without a forwarding address, but had taken the train to New York. He named the train. A friend of his had seen the pair at the other end and followed them to the Hotel Charles Wagoner. The report cost $70 plus $50 for the friend. Grant gladly paid the bill, and said the $500 was as good as thrown down a sewer, he had always known it. He was on bad terms with Flack, March, and Hoag for several days. With them he sulked. Meanwhile, the chins of all his other friends and acquaintances wagged madly, set in motion by him, as over innumerable dinners, teas, and cocktails he discussed with them the possible meaning of the blondine's life in the capital and of her departure and of her life now. For she refused to see him, would not even speak to him on the telephone. He asked hundreds of times, perhaps thousands, "What does it mean? What's your interpretation? Give me your advice—what is she up to? Has she some game or is she an innocent woman?"

However, one day, about midday, Flack, who was miserable under this cold treatment, telephoned Grant who was delighted to take him back into his following. He begged Flack to go at once, with Edda, if she was available, to the Hotel Charles Wagoner, to watch for the blondine and her mother: "See if Edda can get an afternoon off—I want her to see this cow too; I can't leave the floor till two-forty-five—then I'll join you."

On the protestations of Flack he only stormed, "Look, Davie, do me a favor. If Edda is working, all right, though I'm disappointed, I thought she had more liberty—go and sit in the lobby of the Charles Wagoner—at least you've seen plenty of photos of the blondine. You can have lunch first. Don't spend too much time talking. Get a sandwich. We'll have dinner tonight. I want to go over with Edda and you—ask your advice. Tell Edda to put off any appointment, if she has one. You needn't get to the *Cha-Wagner* till two. She never gets out till then. I want you to tell me what she's doing, what she looks like, who she's with. If you miss, if she goes out before two, I'm half inclined to believe them tales of that Morris—"

"Morales—"

"The trouble with that Morris is, if he's lying it's wasted, and if it's true, I don't want to know it. Ho-ho."

Flack protested that he had an article to write—"on excess profits"; that Edda would refuse to go and sit two hours in a lounge, even if she were free; and that neither of them had the faintest interest "in your lunacy." Grant was angry; he also cajoled. At length, Flack went to the "Cha-Wagner," at two o'clock, saying dolefully, "But after this you hire a professional dick, Robbie."

"Wait till three-fifteen; I'll take a taxi as soon as the market closes."

When he joined his friend in the lobby of the Charles Wagoner, Flack had seen several fur-loaded blondes of the type described by Grant. He had found that Mesdames Kent and Jones were still in their room. Grant asked to speak to Mrs. Kent. He came back from the house phone with a disturbed expression. "Of course, it's the blondine, though her voice was lower, muffled, or the wire was bad, or she spoke through a handkerchief, but she said she didn't know me."

The two stood about. The desk clerk observed them. Every

time the elevator came down, Grant turned and stared.

This went on for several days. The men waited, either together or separately, from noon to dusk, when Grant usually had an appointment. When Flack said he had work to do, Grant exclaimed, "You're working with me; we're together from now on. I'm fixing up our house."

When Flack, nervous, expressed his loathing of the foolish intrigue, Grant would say, exercising his sweetest smile, his most affectionate manner, "You're my brother! I never had a real brother! You're my brother! Bear with me—I know it's dull for one who doesn't get the honey; and I don't want the honey—I just want revenge, just a whim, bear with me—it's only a matter of a day or two. Is it money you're anxious about? Take money."

And he would drag out a handful of change, or even half pull his pocketbook from his breast pocket.

One of these days March came to Flack and asked him if Grant could really be as rich as Flack thought. "The monkey always shies away from talking about the market. He don't join in; and there's this obsession about the blonde; he doesn't act like money to me."

"You forget, his father and mother were Europeans. Robbie has a lot of that in him. He doesn't talk about money because, first, he doesn't want you to know he has any; second, he sincerely thinks it's vulgar."

March said, "If it's an act, it's too deep for me."

Flack explained with excitement, "He loves luxury—to the luxurious, money is vulgar."

"I can understand that kind of luxury. If a man finds what he's been looking for all his life, forty thousand dollars is peanuts to pay for it. But tell me, who saw the receipts?"

Flack laughed. "I didn't."

"But I could give that blonde a job in my business. She can roll 'em. You mean to say you waited four days in the Charles Wagoner? What's he giving you? I wouldn't hunt other men's moose. If you want my two cents, let him muddle through, if he's so British, his own way. It doesn't put any soup bone in your stew."

"He's taking Edda and me to Canada to look over his Hoot-Owl Hostel he's bought in the St. Lawrence; he says he's making it over with a boudoir for Edda."

"This fellow gives me the heebie-jeebies. I can't make head or tail of him," said March.

12

They reached the middle of May, 1942. March telephoned Grant to tell him he was sending Hoag over with an important message. Hoag told Grant that a secret round-up of spies was rumored and that March's friend, Carter, and his "top secret-service contact," had been advised of the movement of the blondine from Washington to New York and of the simultaneous payment into a New York bank of a large sum of money in an account which the blonde regularly drew upon. Although there was nothing implicating the blonde directly, it was released to March that the blonde had known, as a girl in Prague, a German skating champion who had got her into the spy game. At present they could not put their hand on her—"that is the way they put it," said Hoag—but she met numerous people of all nationalities mostly in some kind of official position, at strange places, and if not a spy, she might be a smuggler. She, who a few years ago had nothing, now had accounts in several banks under different names, one of them amounting to $20,000. Out of this she took large checks at regular intervals. Immediately after going to the bank, she would go uptown to the room of a man who had been her coiffeur for many years, a relatively humble coiffeur, to tell the truth, a man of Sudeten-German parentage. Before or after her arrival other strange birds would fly there, as manicurists, clerks, and so forth.

"It's overwhelming," said Flack, when he heard this.

"She's not smart enough."

"Didn't you tell me she was a great calculator? Also, she knows four or five languages."

"I always thought there was something phony between her and that coiffeur—Marcel is his name, Marcel. Never liked the man. He never did anything for her. Besides, she just winds it in a knot—that's what got me first. I myself gave her forty thousand dollars! She got it honestly. In trade," and he laughed robustly.

"Every blackjacker in Sing Sing has some sweetheart who believes in him," said Flack.

"Yes, yes. She loved this chauffeur. She bought a garage for this gigolo. Now this coiffeur. I know she had an affair with him. Knew before. It shows, at any rate, she's disinterested. Doesn't go for money. She goes for romance. She don't look like it—but I don't either. You should see that blondine in a café or restaurant! She's sweet, charming—to everyone there—not only men, women too. She's nice to the woman in the toilet, she's nice to the waitress. She can talk by the hour to the waiter and the manager, to the elevator boy, to the bellboy! She's a real democrat. I believe her when she says she's a radical. She must be. She talks to everyone in the hotel. And such sweet expressions—believe me, my boy, that apart from our intimate conversation—when she's with me—that woman is as charming with a waiter as she is with me. That's not a woman who'd sell out for money. And you should see her with that little white furpiece, that bloody white stuffed cat. She loves it. She sleeps all curled up round it, holding it to her chest—like a baby. It's touching. I swear I had tears in my eyes. I thought, there's a woman took the wrong turning, this bloody German ice skater at the bottom of it. The fellows suspect everyone. A woman goes out with a lot of men—you've got to suspect her. Everyone would, I would. But I've got to be shown. Show me. That's all I ask."

He turned pathetically to Hoag and Flack, and spread out his right hand, "Do me a favor, show me something! Give me a small scrap of paper, a bit of writing—a photograph—anything—just show me. You have no evidence."

"You can't believe you could be taken in," said Flack, laughing.

"By a woman I—by that woman? No. Im-possible. And then she loves a chauffeur, a coiffeur, a gigolo? Impossible. She's disinterested. It's love."

"Have it my way! She's a tramp and she'll take money from anywhere for her turtledoves," said Flack.

"No, sir, no, sir, no, sir."

"You don't get anywhere by roaring, 'No, sir.' Save your money. I don't care."

"No, sir, take it from me, sir. Impossible."

In the end he agreed to March's proposition sent by word of mouth of Hoag, to pay any incidental expenses in Washington for March, who was going there on the next day to see his friend Carter about some other matter. Hoag said, "It's serious; it's not the kind of thing you can interfere with. There are personal reasons why Carter can't appear in such a thing, especially with this spy scare on. You'll have to be ready to put up one thousand dollars to have a partial transcript made of certain files. They won't be all the files, but they'll be enough to convince you of part of the story."

"I'll pay one thousand dollars to be convinced, but they ought to give back the money if they're wrong."

"Carter doesn't act on a whim. He's doing this for March who is sorry to see you being taken for a ride by a dangerous woman. He doesn't care what you do with women, but he does care about you getting mixed up in a business like this."

Grant became very anxious before they were through, and Hoag went off carrying with him a check for a thousand dollars made out to March, who would cash it and plant the money where it was needed. Grant paced up and down the office. Without telling Flack, who might relay the news to March, he presently rushed uptown to Goodwin's loft and told him everything, adding, "I've made up my mind to check on their story, to see if I'm being shown the etchings. If it's etchings, I'll make them pay back every cent with interest."

Goodwin left him to consult the detective James. James recommended his friend Bentwink, a "retired Washington man." This man, Bentwink, a likable gray-headed six-footer, about fifty years old, had a small gray Ford which, from now on, was stationed in the cross street in the fifties in which stands the Charles Wagoner. He arrived there before eight in the morning and did not go away till ten at night, being relieved at times by an assistant, and sometimes by Grant, Flack, and even Edda. Of these only Grant had seen the blonde woman. Mrs. Kent left her hotel at twelve or after, usually with her mother. She went to the same restaurant, the same shops, and then home. She never stayed out late and, in fact, was so abnormally circumspect in her movements that she never received anyone at the hotel, spoke to no one in the lobby but the clerk, the bellboy, and the doorman, and would not speak to strangers on the telephone. Bentwink had a plan of the hotel. She could leave by one or two service doors; perhaps she did, for almost certainly she escaped their watch. If she went out the front door of the hotel, she would not take a taxi in front of the hotel but would walk to the corner. Once she walked past the watching car and looked furiously at Bentwink.

"What's the use!" cried Grant.

"An honest woman doesn't take two taxis to go to *Longchamps*, she walks," said Flack.

"That blondine never walks," said Grant.

He passed sleepless nights. He arrived at the waiting detective car at eight in the morning. Impatient of the long sitting, he would get out of the car, rush past the hotel door, pounce about on the corner of the block, walk up and down the other side of the street, so that the most nondescript man would have been noted, far more a man of his height and manner.

To make matters worse, March, who had been in Washington, sent for Grant to come to his office and there showed him a sheet of paper, unsigned and undated, which read as follows:

This party is known to be an experienced agent, having connections through a German coiffeur with an enemy country; and is believed to be the local paymaster. Is considered as being in a key position. Send in any information you pick up about this party.

Grant, nearly frantic that he could not in six days get the addresses and times of her appointments, said furiously, "Why doesn't the Government arrest her then? It's unpatriotic. I don't believe it! What's 'this party'—what's 'key position'? I want the facts, I want the names. What about the German coiffeur?"

March laughed at him coldly and assured him that Carter had told him enough to convince him, "And I'm a hard bird to fool. I think you're not only playing with fire, you've got your big fist right in the red-hot coals and you don't even feel it, you're so woman-struck. Look at you paying out a private flatfoot to do what the Government is doing for you! Do you think she doesn't know that sleuth is waiting there in the car every day? You can tell from the way she behaves, she does. No wonder she went through your pocketbook. You're not born yet. If she weren't too hot, I'd give her a job in my business—but I wouldn't touch her— for honey or money." He looked at Grant with a sinister grin.

Then he smiled in a better way and relented, "Grant, you don't want to land in the pen for a woman. You're not that much of a romantic. I want to save you from yourself. I'm no Galahad, but I've seen friends of mine get tangled with a dame before this. It don't happen to me, but it happens. I'll do this out of personal regard. I kept looking around when I was in Washington, and I spotted a certain party I know who is in a jamb—a big gambler, no luck and no sense, I took him out, got him drunk, and though he didn't spill as much as I had hoped, I smelled embezzlement from his song and dance. I did some more fishing, on my own, it's a private sport of mine, and I figured the amount he'd taken. Now I am sure this boy, who's been up on charges before, can be bought for two thousand dollars, but cash. He's an official in the F.B.I. and has only to ring a bell and say, 'Bring me the file on a certain party,' and they bring it, no questions asked. I'll ask

94

either for a complete transcript or for the file itself. At any rate for enough to convince you—and flashlights of your sleepytime gal, if you want 'em. Though I'd as soon rent my bedroom to a real, live rattlesnake. Now, I give you my personal guarantee. But just tell me what you suspect—for if I can throw them something, too, it'll help; and I'll see what I can get on those points. I understand the files on her are voluminous. And remember, it's cash. You can't buy even a wrong guy in the U. S. Government with maybes."

Grant held off for several days, but as March was going to Washington again and began treating him with contempt, and as Bentwink, the detective, had no results, Grant gave a written promise and he did pay $2,000 in a check to March, when March came back and presented him with a bill of charges written in mysterious terms. Upon receiving the check, March delivered the following document:

KENT, Barbara, alias Adams, Jones, Paul, Texier, born in England, 1908, father Richard Texier, Luxembourg, mother, Maria (Popovna) born in Moscow, the mother without a passport, "White Russian." Went to school in Lausanne, ran away, met German skater Braun, lived with him, when cast off by him went to Paris, lived with artist, "Paul" (other name not known). Paul's means of livelihood not known. Braun then and probably now in German secret police. After Paul, lived with correspondent, Paula Russell, in Switzerland. . . . (Her Washington relations are left out.) Closest friend, Paula Russell, American-born, who introduced her to James "Alexis," Boer-Dutch, called British, magnate, with whom Russell and Kent have close relations. Kent went with "Alexis" to Saratoga, and to Palm Beach. . . . (Here followed an account of her relations with the gigolo, the chauffeur, known to Grant.) Paymaster for the East Coast spy-constellation known as the "Ursus" ring. . . . Meets regularly for conferences—Alfred Goodwin, Betty Goodwin, Paula Russell, "Alexis," chauffeur Wilson, coiffeur (File No. ——) and File Nos. (five numbers omitted). . . . At present apparently estranged from Robert Grant (File No. ——). See Hilbertson, New Orleans.

Grant read this in silence, rot jingling his money, wrestling with the air as he usually did. When he looked up his face had changed color and lengthened, "Good God!"

"It's a knockout blow, isn't it? You know how to pick 'em. I couldn't have picked that bird out of the basket if I'd tried for a year. I love that. She's so innocent. You're naïve, Robbie."

Grant, after a pause, said, "But they've got my name there, a file number."

"You give a nest egg that size to a rag and a bone and a hank of hair of that profession, and you don't expect the police to take down your telephone number?" asked March with awful joviality, the quotation ringing in the room.

"Give it to me," said Grant, suddenly grabbing the paper. He rose, hooked his stick on his arm, and made for the door. "I'll let Flack look through it and see what he makes of it."

"David will make out that two and two are five, which they sometimes are," said March. Grant heard his peals of laughter as he got to the staircase. He ignored them.

13

He began going out regularly with March, because of the file on himself. How could he get at it? What, at least, was the number of it? He'd try his own relations in Washington. Surely, for the money he had paid, and cash on the nail, he could worm some more out of his friends in Washington? Grant took Hoag out twice by himself and asked him to see how the land lay, when next he was in Washington.

Meanwhile, Hoag was once more the center of gossip and fun. He had married Mrs. Anne Warder, the attractive widow whose clothes he had once inspected for fire damage. Anne had turned the trick by pretending to be pregnant, said the "boys," laughing noisily over every luncheon; but Hoag held out that she was pregnant and that he would be very pleased and proud to be a father at his age. The jokes took on a different color.

One day March said to Grant, "You never did as well as Pete, anyhow: she bought satin sheets for when they were married; and she's bought him a little car."

"Wish I could do it, don't know how he does it," said Grant.

"You better ask him, watch his style."

"She must like him, if she bought him a car," said Grant, smiling rosily.

Hoag's affair stretched over several weeks and Grant's miserable involvement was never discussed by the circle of friends, even though Grant now went everywhere with them—to their fish

96

places downtown, to their taverns, to their particular Italian place in the Village, and uptown—he went everywhere with them, pitiably trying to bring the talk round to the blondine, edging in a kind word for her or a vulgar anecdote, endeavoring to talk bawdy which he had never done, and falling back on his venereal adventures because he could never remember a joke, and even now blushed at the filthy behavior of others. He liked to think himself both a moral and an immoral man. He did this by assuming that the world was a hard-working, well-behaved, respectable place in which a few devil-may-care men and women, pricked on by their own temperament, found vice irresistible, discovered, but kept to themselves, the great secret that there is gaiety in vice, like the son of a teetotal father astonished at the worth of wine. This could not be reconciled with the pedestrian view of March and his friends that corruption, vice, and crime were the essence of human nature, that the fools, the lambs, did not know it, but the wise soon found it out.

Grant was reduced to talking his heart out to Peter Hoag, who suited his tongue to his company. Grant told him all he knew or imagined. Hoag said he was a fine fellow, not "a loose mouth like these boys," and that Anne would be pleased to see him one night for dinner. Grant was happy. Since he could talk only of himself or, at best, entertained but one of any company, that is to say, some pretty, accessible woman, he was rarely invited out. Hoag said, "Mrs. Kent owes me something, though I never keep that kind of accounts; and I think she'll come to dinner with us if I ask her."

Grant slept all through the night of this day, and dreamed of "something colored." It seemed to him there were fields of colored cotton, blue, red, yellow, with a windbreak of trees, shining, tossing in the sun.

In the morning before he went to work and in the afternoon after the exchange closed, he visited the detective Bentwink in his car. Grant had lied to March about this, pretending to have dismissed the detective, who had found out so little. But Grant believed in what he called "my system of checks and tallies."

Mrs. Kent met the chauffeur twice, the coiffeur three times, and once had dinner in a restaurant with James "Alexis." Once she had been seen walking up Fifth Avenue with a young blond man; she was often with Paula Russell. Grant thus kept living with the blondine at a distance and became part of her life in a way that had never occurred to him before. He was now in her confidence, knew her friends and lovers, and interested himself in the spy business for her sake. He read books called *Inside This, That, and the Other*, and revelations of espionage, infiltration, influence, and the venality of the press and café society. He at last went back to David Flack, who liked international politics, and laughed at "the Wall Street gorillas whose only dream was to run barbed wire around the U.S.A."

One night he and Flack were sitting in the gray Ford, some six hundred yards from the blonde's hotel, talking about the no-strike pledge of the unions, both declaring vivaciously that "labor should never give up its rights."

"I was a poor boy myself and I know labor had to fight for every right, however small."

"It would be different if there was a Second Front, if there was any possibility of their really helping the Soviet Union," said Flack.

Grant trod on his foot. He believed this, but it embarrassed him when Flack said it in the uptown district.

"You're only a messenger of fate, a forerunner. After the war, Mr. Bentwink here won't spit on you, he'll have lots of work if he doesn't want to retire," caroled Flack.

Bentwink laughed. Grant moved forward suddenly, nudged Flack, trod on his foot. He frowned, "Bentwink, do you want a cup of coffee?"

It was getting dark. The two men were away only three or four minutes, but when they returned, Flack was waving excitedly from the car, and saying, "Jump in!"

The blonde and her mother had just left the hotel. First he had observed the doorman looking down the street. Next he saw the blonde and her mother, heads ducked into shoulders, shoulders up and veils down, trotting to the opposite corner. They had hailed a cruising taxi and all one could see of it now was the taillight where it waited at the intersection for the lights to change.

The detective put out his cigarette, and they went in pursuit of the taxi, which was held up in Fifth Avenue by a light. They followed through a number of quiet streets and saw the women in the car turn and observe them. The taxi put on speed, so did the following car. The taxi drew up suddenly at the marquee of a restaurant-bar called by its street number. The two ladies got out and entered the bar. The Ford drew up immediately after and

Grant went in after them, telling the men to wait. After some time, Grant came round the corner of the street, grinning a bit, disappointed.

"I paid the dragon in the ladies' room—no soap. They went out another entrance."

"Is there one?"

"Yes. I've used it myself. I taught it to her!"

He burst out laughing. The detective stayed near the bar; Flack and Grant went to dinner where they milled over the old subjects: markets, war, the U.S.S.R's chances of survival, the blondine.

"I'm not getting anywhere."

"Why isn't this famous spy on trial?" asked Flack.

Grant muttered, "That boy March—think he's taking pleasure in my pain, you know, bit of a sadist—started to ring me up every day about how they're catching spies, said had I seen this and that. I didn't read the blame things. I asked him if there was any danger—after all, I saw my own name on that paper—and he said, not yet awhile. They're letting her think she got away with it. She's too big. She's the key to hundreds of little cockroach spies."

"For better or for worse, then, the Government's leaving her her freedom?"

Grant smiled broadly, "Yes, she may get away with it. Hope she does, hope she does. Can't believe she's really guilty. I saw her poor. I picked her out of the gutter. But what about my file? I'd like to see it. March says Carter's annoyed and feels I've overstepped the mark—couldn't believe it of a guy like that, in that position you'd think he'd do it for the safety of the State, eh?— and now he wants three thousand dollars for a sample of my file —to show good faith. Ha-ha! Three thousand dollars is without good faith. You don't need good faith. Show's he's a do-gooder, eh? Money and faith. Starry-eyed. Never asked for money and good faith in my life. Why? You put in one or the other. You don't invest both. Shows March is a pushover for professors. Wouldn't think it of him? Them Pantalona and O'Sullivan! Anyhow, wants three thousand dollars for a sample of my file."

Flack laughed, "A sibyl! The more you pay, the less you hear."

"I'd like to see it!"

"Why? What do you think they have on you? You telephoned the blonde?"

"Don't put me off, this is serious."

"Unless you've been in some monkey business."

"Don't let me hear any more of it." He frowned and stalked along.

He continued to pay "the expenses of the investigation" to March and from day to day received messages which summed up much as follows:

That Mrs. Barbara Kent was the mistress of one James "Alexis," Boer-Dutch, not her father, who was suspected of being a fascist agent, working for Spain, Germany, Italy, and Japan, one or all of them;

That Paula Russell had quarreled with her because of "Alexis";

That Barbara often went to visit an old woman who ran a boarding house, on upper Lexington Avenue, the old woman, Sudeten German;

That "Alexis," just like Grant, pretended to be a "pink" and went round radical society seducing leftist women; and at the same time had a string of other women.

By July or August it turned out that Grant had spent over $5,000, sent in bills or in checks to March, and that he was now authorizing March to make inquiries in the Argentine, Cuba, and Mexico, where, March declared, she and Alexis were known to have gone during her uninformative absences.

March had business to attend to in Canada, a gold and asbestos mine which he intended to look into and in which, if the reports were favorable, it was already agreed Grant would be his partner. March had friends in all official circles in Canada, he said, and would inquire about James Alexis and the blonde while there. He had been tipped off by his Washington friends that the blonde *might* be wanted for smuggling: smuggling what? Say furs and currency across the Canadian border: wasn't that enough for the Honeybear? And who, said March, was Hilbertson? Another of the Honeybears?

Grant had become singularly gloomy and declared to March, Hoag, Flack and the boys assembled, "I'll go no farther; she's too hot to touch."

"Then we'll call it a day?" said March in his slow way. Grant became troubled at this question, and after a while said, "I'm in too deep. Go and see what they know. Alexis, I've met him; but Hilbertson, who is he? But as for the blonde, I'll swear she's innocent. But what kind of a gang has she got in with? I know her,

I'll swear she's too lazy. But what worries me are these names, names I don't know, they've got mixed in. It's worrying, very worrying. I like this 'ooman, you see. I'll swear she's innocent."

March, who was going to Canada for a month, offered to see Grant's friends to solve this mystery; and Grant gave him several private addresses.

14

In all this time, Grant had been haunted by living memories of the blondine. Morning and evening, when he shut his eyes, he virtually saw her and regretted his life with her. He was as busy as usual with his lot of little parasites. He saw as many petty harlots and "side-dishes" and "pay-girls," but the idea that he was getting old and would not have another great passion worried him. He expressed this to no one yet. He could never sit long in one place for fear of this and other disagreeable notions flocking round him. He rang up people all day long, made useless appointments which disgusted him further, and often got tipsy, a thing he had never done. One of his pleasures, when he had an empty hour in the afternoon, had now become to sit in the gray Ford with Bentwink, the detective, with the vague hope that the blondine might dart out of her hotel, thus giving him the amusement of a short, fruitless chase. As he sat, he ruminated over his affairs: they were not encouraging. One afternoon he had in his pocket a letter from Celia Grimm, about Mrs. Jenny Woods, the Negro wife. It asked him,

What have you done to Jenny? I don't know what will happen to her. She wants to leave her husband. She believes something you told her about people being equal in love. She thinks you mean it, I know. Do write to her at least telling her you are not serious. You don't want to be responsible for a tragedy, Robbie. If you don't do anything for Jenny, I shall think you about the worst man I ever met. I know you came into a world you didn't understand and it seems easy for you to cut a big figure; but why don't you think of the consequences of what you do? She thinks you are going to take her to some house in Canada, she says it is all ready for her and you. I know this is pure fantasy. But you must not play with people this way. Something will happen to you some day, Robbie. It can't go on this way, you taking people's lives for a joke. I don't understand how you got away with it this long.

However that may be, I want you to do something about Jenny—but what, I don't know. She thinks you love her and want to go away with her.

He was considerably depressed in the afternoon of this day, by the memory of Celia's letter. He was born for love, he could not help playing the game. He would have nothing to live for, all told, if he had not that. It was by no means his first insult.

He threshed about in his heart, trying to avoid, by feinting, these blows from friends and blood-relatives. Though he received many bitter, insulting letters from disappointed friends and hangers-on and mistresses, stupid attempts at blackmail, requests for money with contemptible promises to repay when the work was coming in, complaints, and even beastly language, which he never admitted, showed, nor acknowledged (though he always kept them as if they were some sort of magic), he writhed when the stinging phrases came back. He despised the writers, for only impotence spoke thus. The angry should act; the wronged should try to ruin him.

He went on preying now, as all his life, upon most of his connections. And he could not help it, it was his nature, they uncovered their weaknesses to him, it was too tempting; and it was his nature to put his hand into the pockets of others, to take up a spoiled business and try to make a profit out of it. He even misled many people, on the off chance, out of instinct. He did it even to keep his hand in when he expected no profit. He loved his game of life. He could "never resist temptation."

He thought thus to himself, gaily, but this was not his consistent nature. He defended his vice, but was unhappy for it to come to light, either to others or in his own sight. In the morning Flack had hurt him by saying, "In 1934 I made six thousand dollars for you on my signature; I paid you every cent although Hugo March told me I was a fool to do so: I got nothing out of that for myself. You know it too. Ever since, you have been calculating, and when your out-of-pockets to me and Edda nearly reach the three thousand dollars, no matter what I do for you as a general factotum, you will find some reason for getting rid of me. That is, if I don't make you another six thousand dollars. But I hate money. You can't help yourself, Robbie, I know you. This is not an indictment, this is a statement of fact." It was true about the $6,000 and the $3,000. Grant naturally made such calculations every day of his life. This was his proper life as a merchant. It was unmannerly to say it or make it a moral charge. He felt a slight dislike of Flack. He saw now where Edda got that hard part of her nature which had made her describe him, she a young girl, he a man to dazzle such a tough splinter of virgin, as "avaricious, long-nosed, thin-haired, with a sniffing belly." The pair became quite repugnant to him, for the moment.

He rang up Alfred Goodwin and Betty, went over to their flat for cocktails. There he told them all Bentwink had told him yesterday, but became restless under their advice. Alfred was in one of his flamboyant moods, promising to do everything and detailing amazing, improbable acquaintances of his, this "top name" and that "Winchellite"; best-sellers, Senators, millionaires, gossip-columnists. He kept saying, "Anything you want done, I'm your man, I'm Alfred Fix-it. I can pull strings everywhere. Bring it to me. I'll trail your blondine into the mouth of hell and back, if you want—" He became worse as he got more money in the black market. When Grant objected to obscenity, the dreadful Goodwin shouted that Grant must be "an invert, retarded sexually, lacking something" and did not stop there.

There was such a noise and it was so shameful that Grant could not make a date with Betty, and faced an empty evening. He went alone to one of the restaurants where Miss Russell and Mrs. Kent still had credit, on his account. He sat down in a corner eying the door, canvasing the women, hoping for a pick-up. He continued gloomy. In two days it would be Saturday, when he expected his son Gilbert from camp. He was obliged to keep on good terms with Flack and daughter, because Grant found the young man insupportable, although he did his best for him while he was in town. Gilbert was what Flack called "a coldblooded Hotspur" who was rationally intolerant, genially censorious, originally tedious. He "saw no reason why he should not speak his mind," a genuine puritan. Flack and Gilbert were of an equal purity of life, Edda and Gilbert equally difficult to get along with. After dinner, Grant took two brandies.

The restaurant was small, long, and narrow, with numerous small rooms, once bedrooms or even closets, turned into dining space. Grant had been badly placed by the owner, Pierre, although they were old acquaintances, because Grant and he had had some small financial misunderstandings. Grant had lent Pierre some money to start the place and had begun to take it out in trade. This was one of the reasons that the blondine and her friend had an account there. Grant and his friends had long ago taken it out in trade, but Grant still fought for a discount. Likewise, the bills for the blondine and other of Grant's free-living female friends were overdue. One of Grant's principles was to dispute every bill. He explained it thus, "If they're wrong, they'll correct it. In the first place. They won't overcharge me because they won't want a battle. In the third place, if someone makes a mistake it won't be Robbie."

"They put it on so you can have the satisfaction of taking it off," said Flack, making indelicate comparisons.

Grant only looked the keener at his bills and fought the harder, employing Flack many odd hours, Sundays, evenings ostensibly set aside for conversation, and lunchtimes, to prepare the figures.

Grant had noticed, over his shoulder, for some time, two women no longer quite young, on the dais, next to the restaurant window. The window was draped with lace and red velvet, according to Grant's own suggestion. One of the women wore an extraordinary red hat, with six sides, five small sides in front and a long base at the back. The crown was peaked, carried a variety of flowers and a veil. Grant noticed it because somehow he was reminded of the blondine. More, he was irritated by the woman's lack of taste. He had an odd impulse to improve the woman, buy her a more becoming hat. He turned his chair so that he could see "the woman with the hat." For a second, a strange, flat face with cat-eyes and pointed cat-lips floated before his eyes; then he saw it was Mrs. Kent. She was sitting on an upholstered bench and had sunk low into it. Her hat covered all her hair, except for the front of the parting. She looked haggard, and was rouged too much. The women were not speaking to each other but simply ate, as if they were at home, "in the kitchen, too," thought Grant. He began to take his fill of Mrs. Kent. Never before, since the first time, had he narrowly observed her.

She seemed composed, but he knew she was not quite at ease. She smiled a little to herself and fidgeted, although in a different way from other women. She fidgeted by being in constant, easy, rounded motion. She looked at her plate and all round her plate, at her knife and fork with interest, picked up the salt and pepper with the right hand as she took hold of her bread with the left hand. She ate with one hand while she fetched her handkerchief out of her bag with the other, raised her eyes to note any passers-by, to greet the manager and the waiter at every passing; she observed the tablecloth card, kept putting pieces in her mouth, chewing strongly with a semicircular motion, at the same time pointing her chin and jawbones toward the public, chewing, viewing with tranquillity, observing and at the same time reaching for a bit of bread. She felt in her bag again, not with the fretfulness of most women, but peacefully as if she had a century before her, brought out a mirror, actually observed herself as she was chewing. The other woman made some remark. Suddenly the blondine smiled with unspeakable sweetness. But it was not at the woman but at the waiter who had come over and bent over her, rather too low for good manners. Grant caught glimpses of the blondine as she lengthened the conversation with the waiter, as practiced a coquette with him as with a monied man she might expect something from. It hurt; and Grant thought, What does he do for her, what commissions? What is he saying now? Grant had used waiters, maîtres d'hôtel, and others such often enough for dirty purposes to know what the waiter might be saying. It was intolerable. He snapped his fingers for the manager and indicated that he was going to the other table.

It was only at a distance that she seemed to be aging. At the table, he saw that she was still good-looking. Now she had a cold expression and he remarked her violet eyes were angry. She did not introduce the other woman and Grant, sitting down, turned his back to her. The other woman, after stopping a moment, went on to finish her meal. One glance at her had been enough—a fat woman over forty, who looked like a bawd.

"Hello, Sweet!"

"Why are you having me followed?"

"I was advised to, I never wanted to, I didn't believe a word of it. Flack and his daughter put me on to it. They were indignant because you treated me badly."

"What about me? Why worry about these people who only want money out of you? They're just trying to take you over. You trust them but not me. Why should I talk to you again, Robbie?"

Grant looked over his shoulder questioningly. The older woman was looking hard at them, lips apart, showing false teeth. She smiled. The blonde said, "Mrs. Hutchison, my friend Mr. Grant."

"How is your mother, Barbara?"

"Mother is quite well, thank you—a little rheumatism. But she does not complain. She hates to give me anxiety."

"Sorry, sorry! Give her my compliments. Must come and bring her some of my special coffee and some candy."

"She won't return the compliment. She never got over the way you treated me. She does not understand that kind of thing. She was so indignant, she said to me, 'I am glad we have seen the last of such a disagreeable man, common business man, no gentleman.' She could not understand anyone not keeping his word.''

Grant looked nervously over his shoulder. The rouged Mrs. Hutchison continued to smile at them with porcelain teeth.

"Mrs. Hutchison is Mother's friend, but she's seen more of the world, she's more liberal. She knows all about you, Robert! She has seen my mental agony. I could not sleep for months. I would wake up in a sweat, wanting to scream. I felt I had no resource. You let me down. I thought, I'll never trust a man again. There was such a trouble in my heart—I felt I never could love again."

Grant turned and looked at the older woman. He murmured, "No idea at all; no idea of all that. You left me, Barb; I didn't leave you. One morning I ring up, one fine morning, I think I'll go over and kiss Barb good morning as usual and—gone, flown, no trace. What about the chauffeur? You got married!"

"After you left me, I had nothing. I had to look after myself in my own way."

He could not bring himself to say, under the eye of the grinning vulture, that he had given her money for the divorce. He only said, "Let bygones be bygones, then. Or we'll talk this all out later. If you've anything against me, I only want it brought out into the light of day and I'll put it right. I'll make good now, if I can. If it's not just imagination. I'm sorry you suffered, Barb. You know me, sweet. I want you to be happy. And I want to be happy. Let's go somewhere. I've got something to say," and he looked significantly at the older woman.

Mrs. Kent too nodded at Mrs. Hutchison, who said in a voice startling in its brutality, "I won't sit in on your conference. Why move? It's all right here. Good-bye," and in leaving she violently aped the manners of society.

They spoke only of idle things. Grant, after taking two more brandies, forgot all he had meant to say and taking her hand, implored her, "I want you to take me back. I can't live without you. I haven't been faithful, but your record isn't clean either. We've got nothing to settle up—too much accounting. Between us, no accounts. We've both been in the mud together. All right. You had mental agony; I had mental agony. I hurt you—you hurt me. You went crazy and ran away from a man like me. I went crazy and two-timed a woman—a woman—I two-timed, I admit it. But there's a vacancy in my heart. I want to marry you. Come back to me. I want to get rid of that cow in Boston and settle down. What I want now is a sister, a mother, a friend, a sweet-heart, and a wife. Three women in one. The last year has been a desert. When I saw you just now, I was dry and thirsty. 'There's my oasis,' I said. Let's go to the hotel, I want to telephone. You come along with me."

But the blonde woman refused. She had to go home to her mother; and she explained that it would be difficult for her to see Grant. Her mother must never know. "She has received a severe shock; she doesn't trust you any more. She was brought up so differently. She doesn't know that world has gone forever."

"Please come to dinner with me tomorrow night and I'll explain everything to you. I want your advice, too. You're always right. What you said about Alfred—Goodwin—worked out. He's crazy, that man. Talks like a Napoleon, a Mussolini. You were right. Let me come into your life again and I'll come with clean hands and clean heart—I'll take myself to the cleaner's—"

She laughed. "Telephone me about five; I think Mother is going out then with Mrs. Hutchison."

"Who is she? Don't like the looks of her!"

"She's just a divorcée who makes money by reading palms."

"I'd like her to read mine and tell me if you're going to forgive me."

The blondine was not at home on the three succeeding days. Grant, who had been going to dismiss Bentwink the next day, kept him on. Bentwink had nothing to report, and Grant felt that she had been at home all the time. He telegraphed her, sent her flowers, and wrote a note to beg her to meet his son Gilbert, now in town. "I want Gilbert to meet you. He's a great judge of character and if he likes you and you like him, I'll be settled in my mind about both of you!"

She answered him the next time he telephoned and agreed to meet Gilbert. The couple would meet before, over cocktails for a little chat. They met in the White Bar, which had been the scene of so many of their rendezvous. Grant showed the woman all his letters, from his family, his wife, his business acquaintances, asked her opinion on a deal just going through, complained about Flack and his son, received her advice remorsefully and humbly, kissing her repeatedly, and pouring out his loneliness. "Talk your mother over, sweetsie; we're going to make it up. You don't look very well and I feel blue. Let's think what to say to her." He promised her a good housekeeping allowance and comforts, and told her a good deal of what he had done against her since last year.

"You treat me like a criminal."

"You weren't quite honest with me."

"Wherever I try to lay my head, you hunt me."

"The main thing is, we're together. I want you to give me your opinion on what to say to my wife. I'm through with that 'ooman. She won't get any money out of me. We're together! Laura's relatives are dead and I'm going to tell her, 'I've been kind, a friend. Now you ought to take country air.' I've done enough for her. She hurt me. When the war's over, I'll get the house back on the Pinchem Hill and we'll go there, take a trip, that'll be our home if you like it. I'll buy you a big house in Canada, got a man working on it. You'll have two or three servants. Place upstairs for your mother. Or maybe another house is better. Ha-ha! We'll entertain and if you like we'll go into politics. Laura always wanted to have a salon, go into politics. What do you say? You seemed to take a great fancy to Washington. Or should we go to my farm in Picardy, make big cheeses and little cheeses? You've got the complexion of a milkmaid. Liverpool's a fine, busy city, too, chance to do something, but no entertainment—well, out with it. That bit of cheese can stay in Boston but we'll enjoy life. The new life. Build up, not sleep our life away. I've got enough Presbyterian in me for that. You and I rolled in the mud together, not our fault, a bit of the gypsy in us, a bit of hobo, street-singer, eh? Serenading for a living, eh? You and me, singing serenades, slumber songs. I don't mean to offend. Dust gets in your eyes. I whistle and the dollars roll into your pocket. Don't mean to offend. It's our being together again, makes me a bit of a poet. Know a man who writes poetry and he got two beautiful women; I never knew women went for poetry until then. Never mind, never mind. Now we can start to reconstruct. I've been looking for the right woman and now I'm putting my money on you, sweets. I missed you. Never expected to. Must be a love story."

She would not go home with him "for a long-distance call" before he met his son.

"My experience has made me cynical. You have to prove it to me, Robbie."

"I swear, on my word of honor."

"Once bit, twice shy. You won't get me again with that honey."

At that, he laughed, and she smiled so innocently that he did not know where to look; but she continued, "You know, Robbie, I think I am learning to hate men."

"No woman can hate me."

"I wouldn't put money on that."

"If I hurt them, they hurt me. No matter what I do, they turn on me. Like Flack, I helped him for twenty years, kept him when I didn't need him, he's nervous, got no stamina, and he put the idea in my head you're no good, he made me get a detective. They're no good. I ought to take your advice."

She said, "What do you want all those mental and moral cripples round you for? It's to flatter your ego. They only want a handout."

He murmured, "I got to do a good action sometimes, it's my nature. I need you to run me. I need love. If you're with me, I swear I'll make a clean sweep of the whole crowd."

"You hand out good money to those lunch-detectives, but you don't think of me."

"The fact is, Barb, they make me a profit, they pay a dividend: if I buy them a cup of coffee, you can bet they've earned it." He spoke earnestly and grabbed her elbow, continuing softly, "Trust me, Barb, I don't waste a cent on them. They pay me 1,000 per cent one way or another. Some paid a lot more than that," and his clear, sweet laugh rang out.

"And that's what you think of me too. Well, don't count my dividend in yet. You'll have to pave the way with five-dollar bills before I forgive you after what I know."

"I love you, my sweet; I'll do anything you say. You've got me and now is your chance to take me over."

15

They arrived early at the Little Bar where Grant had invited company to meet his son. Mrs. Kent at once went to the lounge to telephone and was away a very long time.

It was a small bar below ground level, out of a large lobby with a staircase, glass doors, palms.

Grant's first new guest was Mrs. Lawrence, a small, showily built business woman in her forties. A delicate nose veil had a design which cut her cheeks and nose into strips, like scars, a startling illusion. Her melancholy eyes now beamed at Grant, as she held out her hand: "It's wonderful to see you again. Your

Chicago friends miss you. We are always saying, 'When is Robbie coming back to make life gay?' "

Although she was a successful dress buyer, ran a fashionable dress shop in Chicago, had been married twice and had two children, she impressed one as a kind, awkward, single woman. She might also have changed clothes with some ancestor, a black-eyed peasant woman of the hard-working, unhappy type who never leaves her stone kitchen. She was never at ease and never perfectly dressed. Part of her dress was dowager, part flirt, part saleswoman. The general effect, at first, was that she loved to be genteel. She was a busy woman yet she felt bound, out of business, to act the home woman who does not understand. This gave her the air of a woman who knows nothing about men. After work, she lisped and simpered spiritually. She drew back, revolted at coarse discussion, never laughed loudly, dropped her eye as sadly as a dog when she was unnoticed: everything rebuffed her. Everyone felt obliged to chant: "Sally Lawrence is a charming, good woman, an excellent mother"; and this was exactly what Grant kept saying to himself, as he looked at her. But she had more flavor than that for him, because she owned two apartment houses and there was some romantic story about her private life, she was not entirely the white lamb.

Grant saw her attention was wandering. He grasped her hand and drew it across the table, "I like you, Sally! Where have you been all this time? Why didn't you come to see me, as you said you would? I've been all alone here and no one to cheer me up. Let's have a drink and be merry, eh? When are we going to have tea and a little chat by ourselves? Eh? You let me down, sweetsie; I expected you, I waited, and you did not come."

She hesitated, looking into his face, then smiled and was warmer, more abandoned, "I've been very busy; and I wasn't sure you meant it, Robbie."

He cried indignantly, "Mean it! I told everyone, you ask my friend David Flack, I told everyone, I found in Chicago my ideal woman, suited to me exactly: good business woman, owns houses, runs everything with a profit, handsome, a good dresser and nearly my age, a bit younger, of course, and that's what I want now—three women in one, the sweetheart, the wife, and the mother. Women are always older than men in one thing—they have more heart."

He shifted his chair and fondled her hand, keeping his eye on the lounge exit. He went on, "You like me a bit, too, don't you, Sally? You're the woman for me. As soon as I saw you, last year, I said to myself, 'There's my woman; I like her. She's honest, she has character, and she's handsome too.' You know me, Sally. I'm crazy, I'm unsettled, but it's not my fault. It's that shiftless— er—woman in Boston. She did nothing for me. Disgusted me with home life. I thought I wasn't made to be a married man. Then I saw you and I said to myself, 'If I'd met her twenty years ago, it would have been a different story. I'd have whistled a different tune all my life.' Supposing I had had that luck! I made my way: I've got what I want—in some things, but not in love. All I want is a woman. Then I've got nothing to wish for! If you would have me we could give up work and go and live somewhere. I've got a beautiful house on the Pinchem in Rome, a summer cottage on Lake Como. What do you say, little girl, do you want to get married again?"

Mrs. Lawrence became beautiful and almost voluptuous; but she looked puzzled and at length said, in her made-up voice, "We should have to get to know each other better."

He leaned back, looked round for the waiter, saying calmly, "I'll take you at your word."

He snapped for the waiter. Before their drinks came, she said nervously, "Robbie, I asked one of my friends to come along, I hope you don't mind."

"Delighted, delighted!"

"It's a woman, Livy Wright, Miss Olivia Wright. She's fascinating to talk to; she knows all the real estate in New Jersey. She's an agent."

Grant broke in with, "What do you say, what do you say, little girl? Think it over, think over my proposition. See if you can make me happy: that's all I want. Then we'll stop work, let the world go hang, and just enjoy ourselves! Give me your opinion. When can I meet you? Tomorrow, next day—tomorrow I can't— next day, yes, five o'clock. The White—no, noisy place—Manetti's. Five."

His eye, rising, spotted a vigorous, dark young woman standing in the door and looking the place over. Grant stared pointedly. She stared back at him, observed Mrs. Lawrence, and rushed forward.

Grant beamed. His manner changed entirely. He rustled and shone with his softest expression in eyes and lips.

"Sally told me about you but she didn't tell half the story.

She didn't say her friend was bonnie, very bonnie. You're a beauty—what's your name?"

After a startled moment, Olivia smiled, then laughed outright. "You're the fastest worker I ever met."

"It's my lucky day. Sally was the first. She brought me luck. Then she brought me you. My boy's coming. I want you both to size him up. Sally's a mother, got children herself, knows children. I'll take her word, and I want to know what you think; a woman's view."

"How old is he?" said Livy.

"Twenty-four, twenty-five," he muttered.

"Hard for a father to admit he has a grown-up son? Just like a woman! You must be a terrible wolf. I can see it in your eye."

He was astonished by her method, cocked his head, screwed up his eye, but kept smiling at her, and his eye was very light. He flushed slightly, "Nothing like that, not at all. I mean it. Mother takes no interest; I've had to mother him myself. Don't know if I've done a good job. Do everything for the boy—get him socks, shirts, see he gets his hair cut, send him chocolate. Want to know if you like his manners. A bit worried about him. Too stiff-necked. No give and take."

"Did you bring along your Mother Hubbard? I'd love to see you in a cooking apron though. I'll bet you beat up little hot biscuits in the morning," jeered the young virago.

Grant jerked his eyes upon her, looked sullen, stared, but she stared back. He melted into a grin. But he turned at once to Mrs. Lawrence and sinking his fingers into her plump arm, he cried, "She brought me luck! I had a big shock, Sally; and you brought me consolation. Chicago's a dull town, not my idea of a town, and I didn't see a woman there, for weeks, that appealed to me. Then I met Sally. My life was a desert, and then I find this oasis. What do you think of her, Livy? Is she an oasis or isn't she? I asked her, 'What can you do for me? Can you cheer me up?' But she let me down: she promised to come to New York to see me and she didn't. I don't know what to make of it. Didn't make enough impression, I suppose. You can't always succeed. She's gone back on me; let me down."

"I phoned you at the office yesterday and the secretary said you were out of town," she said in a wise voice.

"Yes, yes, little business, great shock—" he muttered.

"I called at your hotel and they said you had just gone out." She was earnest, the false glamor gone.

He raised himself, looked over her shoulder, stared round the bar at the other women, said coolly, "Well, my dear girl, you know me, I work hard. I don't work like I used to but hard, and Ben—" and he plunged into a bewildering business story, in which the phrases—foreign exchange commission, blocked currency, trust funds, French estate, sequestered properties, German occupation—alone emerged from a surge of mutter.

She listened to this with a calm face. Livy thrust her bust forward and cried, "What the hell is he saying? Your Romeo sounds like a solid fourflusher. It's as clear as mud. What the hell is it all about? Don't tell me."

Grant ceased. He had kept throwing glances at Mrs. Lawrence, and seeing that the story had not sunk in, he now leaned forward, patted her hand and said, "Well, begone, dull care. I'm here, and I can see you. That's enough. All's well that ends well."

At this moment his other guests arrived, Alfred and Betty Goodwin. He got up and bustled over to them, whispering to Goodwin, "Glad you came. The bloody woman has been checking up on me, eh?" He laughed outright and kissed Betty on both cheeks.

Betty looked the sharp, wire-haired New Yorker of about thirty, gaily dressed, with an air of uncertain, uneven money. Goodwin, now forty-two, fleshy, paunched, nearly six feet, expensively dressed but in the more vulgar Wall Street way. He had heavy black eyes, a well-shaped dark head, but a surly manner. He tossed his head, surveyed the public, smiled loftily. Mrs. Goodwin started some flip conversation, Grant repeated his standby about being rushed to death, business in and out of town. Betty said quickly, at this point, "How was Philadelphia?"

She was brushed aside by the ungrateful Grant, who had an impulse to shout: "Where's the boy, where's the boy? Goodwin, you're late, always three-quarters of an hour late. I'm rushed to death and want to have fun. I need luck. Mrs. Lawrence brought me luck. Then this one, Livy, Livy brought me luck. I had a great shock and now I want consolation."

Now Gilbert arrived, was introduced, the party was complete, except for Mrs. Kent.

"You're late, you're late!"

The young man ordered Scotch-and-soda, and said, smiling, "Now don't let Dad ration me: I learned to drink in the officers' club. Dad's only idea of how to spend the week is to go home and take a little stretch and drink tomato juice."

The women flattered the young soldier. Robbie, meanwhile, began craning his neck till Livy said, "Expecting someone?"

"A lady, she went to telephone, can't understand it."

"It would be a lady."

Grant frowned, and glancing at Gilbert said, "My wife's an angel, an angel, fine mother, I respect her. But she could be more active. Too languid, too inert. Could have made my life a paradise. I don't ask much. I like the home."

"Oh, I'm sure Mrs. Grant is a sweet woman," said Betty.

The boy smiled at her. Grant got up and declared that he had to telephone, had forgotten something—his partner. Livy turned her face away from the boy and winked.

Goodwin was now displaying a diamond and emerald chip bracelet which he wanted to sell cheap—$10,000. Gilbert looked on with surprise as the man seriously considered the bracelet and even looked round the little bar which was now packed, appraising the curious but casual glances coming in his direction. Gilbert could not believe that so much money was circulating, or that they threw money away like breadcrumbs. He, for example, even kept breadcrumbs to give to the sparrows on his window sill. It was a pleasure for him to think that they were stuffing their bellies with the crumb, living on it, that it was not wasted. The women examined the bracelet, tried it on. Goodwin let them feel it, kept looking for Grant, who was away a long time.

Gilbert asked, "Do you think you can sell that thing just by hawking it round?"

"You can sell a box of chocolates these days for seven dollars and the customer won't even wait for the three dollars change, he'll tell the girl, 'Keep it, buy yourself a sandwich.' Why can't I sell a little bit of junk like that? Last week I sold a bracelet for eighty thousand dollars, as easy as nothing. I can get any amount of this stuff and get rid of it the same day. This kind of money is just nothing to what's going around. This is just dung: you don't think that's any good, do you? Do you know what I'd think of any lady friend of mine who wore a thing like that? I'd say she was a —— and her boy friend was a ——. This is a real boom; but not a boom-boom boom, it's the genuine article, prosperity. We're always going to be like this, only better and I've only just got on my legs. I was crawling before like a louse; wait till you see the money I'll make the next six months. I'll be carrying it home in valises. I know what the score is and I know where to get the goods. And I can sell. Three qualities you can't do without in a day and country like this.

"Don't make any mistake, Lieutenant Grant, you're coming back to a different world, a better one too. You're doing a good job; and we're not asleep here. We're rolling it up so that when you come back you'll have nothing to do but walk into a job at ten thousand dollars a year, have a good time, and live on the fat of the land. What's eighty thousand dollars? A friend of mine sold a diamond and ebony lavaliere-and-cross last week—a quarter of a million dollars. Just a fluke, I didn't get hold of it myself. Last week, I made twenty-two thousand dollars on a deal. Do you know what this country is like? I'm asking you. You can't tell me. You don't know. No one knows but a couple of men in this country. This country is just bursting with inventory, all kinds, junk and good stuff; but it's the junk that's eventually going to make us rich. They don't know what to do with it. They're afraid to handle it. They're paying storage on it, they're burning it for insurance. Let me just dip my hands in it and they'll come out dripping gold. I won't burn it. I'll sell it. You'll sell it abroad. I'm just waiting for the war to be over and I'm the Victory Kid. You boys are doing the right thing and it's going to be good for you here when you get back. Democracy is right because it's American, and it's going to give us all security forever; and the kind of security you'd dream about for your mother or your sister. You want your sister or your daughter to marry a millionaire, don't you? Well, she's going to marry one, if he's only a goddamn bus conductor. When you've finished cleaning up over there, come back here and get in with us—we won't even waste time cocking a snoot at the pack of cockaroaches they call people over there. . . . Goddamn it, this country is a real country—I like it and if I like it, it's good, because I only like the best and—"

He looked at Betty who was kicking him under the table. "Skip it, Alf. Put on a new record. I agree with you. We all agree with you. He's a great one for skinning a skinned rabbit."

Goodwin weighed the bracelet in his hand.

Gilbert was silent.

Livy said, "Does your dad fall asleep in telephone booths, or is he dialing all the blondes in the city of New York; or does he have fainting spells?"

Goodwin said, "Your dad's losing his profit-sense. He could

have gone in with me last week, wouldn't. He drew back. Wouldn't put up the money. That's a weakness of his lately. Money sweats sweet sweat, sweet sweat like dew, like honey—" here he stopped and laughed, without noticing his wife's gestures—"and your father's the original Old Honeybear; but he's losing his grip. But you just leave it to me, Grant, I like you and I've got connections in Washington, in London, in Buenos Aires, everywhere you can mention that can't turn wrong. I like you, I'll take you along with me. Now your father lost a lot of opportunities this year. He made a big mistake with the field-canteen factory, and that warehouse full of electrical goods. But I've got a few tricks up my sleeve. All he's got to do is leave it to me. I'm helping everyone, it's my nature. I don't want to see you fighting for your country, for home and democracy and not make it a better world for you to live in here at home. Your dad will be all right with me and I'm doing it just because I feel that way. I'm doing it for everyone. Because I've got the power, you feel some years are lucky for you, and this is for me. How would you like to go in with me, Grant, when you come back? Why don't we buy you out of the Army now? I know your dad would do it any day, but he doesn't know the way to do it. Now I know a couple of people in Washington—Arthur, Ben, and Charlie, you know, Betty—and a couple of grand to them, let a bit stick to the fingers of about eleven people in between, you know—that's the way you do it—and you'll be out and home here quicker than you can send a telegram, 'Love and kisses, I'm discharged.' I'll cut you in on unloading the crap, you'll go out and scout around for me and smell out all that inventory. When Europe's ruined after the war and the kids are starving and the old people dropping dead like flies, everybody sick, and without any hats or shoes, you'll see: we'll make a fortune. They'll pay anything for a pair of old shoes, for a rubber tubing, for a shipload of left-foot boots, they'll go hobbling around in left-foot boots and pay ten times what you could get selling it down South or burning the warehouse—"

The women were drinking and smoking, paying little attention to Goodwin. Only Betty tried to interrupt this eloquence.

But Gilbert got up, seized his cap, put enough money for his two drinks on the table, and said, "We ought to have martial law and court-martial you. I shall never again walk into a place where I see you. If you think I believe your lies about whom you know in Washington or any Arthur, Bob or Charlie, you can empty it out of your filthy brain. I never met such a scoundrel! I'm going. Dad can get me at the hotel."

Betty Goodwin, however, after listening to part of the speech with a dashed, humiliated expression, picked up her things and said, "Come on, Alf, we're going, he's not going. You put your foot in it. I kept kicking you, you dumb egg. Gilbert's a patriot. He's drunk, Gilbert."

Gilbert started to denounce him again, "Drunk or sober—"

The other women intervened. Livy cried, "They'll go. You've got to stay with us, to cheer us up after this disgraceful scene. We need consolation."

16

After the Goodwins had gone, Robert Grant returned, walking in a thundercloud.

Livy and he said, simultaneously, "Where are the others?"—"I always believed in the resurrection of the flesh."

Grant sat down, the same in manner, looked round with an expression of misery, murmured, "Ben made a big mistake, without my advice; he's young, doesn't take advice, saw the accounts yesterday and asked him, 'How come?' He lost fifteen thousand dollars last week. One plunge. September cotton. I warned him. Nothing to laugh at. Nothing I can do about it. But of an argument. No good. I said to him, 'Ben, I told you I had advices to sell. You bought. Why?' He's boyish. Not serious. Honest man but not serious. Have to get rid of him. He can buy me out. I'm retiring from that business. I've got enough. Received a terrible shock. Excuse me. Where's the waiter? Some more of the same."

Gilbert had moved beside his father and listened attentively to everything he said, offered himself as a Galahad. Grant, with a grimace of brutal melancholy, drank deeply and looked about with heavy eyes. Suddenly, he sparked up, "All's well that ends well!" and he grasped Livy Wright by the elbow and thrusting a look at her, exclaimed, "You're a beauty! You appeal to me. I like you. I can see you have character—beauty, brains, and character. That's what I'm looking for."

The young man looked, smiling, at Livy and the other women. His face had an honest radiance.

Grant muttered, "My wife's an angel. Sweet woman. Good mother. But not to me. What I'm looking for is a combination of—mother, sister, and angel. I had a shock. Bear with me. His mother's a sweet woman. An angel. He knows I respect her. But perhaps I should have let her go a long time ago. She—find another man. Both made a mistake. All I want is the right woman. Big shock. Let's have another drink. I need consolation."

He looked at his son, "Your mother's a fine woman. But she never sewed buttons on my shirts. Never got up till eleven in the morning. A fault of character."

Livy said to Gilbert, "I envy you your gorgeous figure; wish I had a waist like that."

Gilbert said, "It's not so good. Too much Scotch."

Grant looked up, "Want you to meet David Flack and his daughter, Flack especially."

"They're some of your few decent friends, Dad. I like them."

"Smart man, daughter's very clever, but has a lot to learn."

Livy leaned across to Gilbert, "Here's a bit of paper. Jot down your exercises on this. I envy you that figure. I love tailormades. I'd better do some exercises, though."

She had a black dress cut in a low diamond neck, showing her white skin and the doughy spring of the breasts.

Grant leaned over to Mrs. Lawrence and began, hotly, "You're a real lady, you give me a complex. That's my trouble with you."

"Oh, I don't want to do that. How do I do that?"

"I'm not polished enough for you. I've got corrupted somehow, bumping into trouble. If I'd had a high-class woman with character, a beauty too, who was devoted to me, who would sacrifice for me, I'd be different. Love is sacrifice. That's the test. Sacrifice! Will a woman sacrifice for you? Then she loves you. I apply the acid test. No one comes through. Then you find your oasis was a mirage. A mirage! I know you know what sacrifice means! Look how good you were to poor James. What a wonderful wife! What a good mother!"

He took her by the arm. The other two had stopped their conversation.

Livy said, "What a line!" and the young man said, "Watch him put it over! I don't know that one."

Mrs. Lawrence turned to Grant with bright eyes. Grant went on, kneading her arm, "She's all right, your friend, all right—but too much a hoyden! Not my type. I like a quiet woman. I don't want to get a complex. Been hurt too much. You frightened me, you gave me a complex. You didn't telephone me. I don't say I always knew the right woman. Made too many mistakes! But

118

you show me you're the right woman. I'm afraid. I'm neurotic, now. And the trouble is, I'm afraid of you."

Mrs. Lawrence listened carefully, timidly, saying she did not want to frighten him, how could she, such an ordinary woman, frighten a man like him.

He became jovial, "You're dangerous! I might go too far with you, do harm. I don't want to harm a lovely woman. I'm a bad boy. Now Livy's a hoyden. I couldn't hurt her. She knows the score. You don't. You're gentle—you're a real mother. What do you think of my boy, eh? Like him? Fine boy! Good character!"

He turned to the others, but still wildly, still valiantly, proposed another round of drinks "and then we'll have fun, go to a cabaret and have dinner."

Gilbert said, "Yes, but wait till I've been out dining, wining, and supping with Dad for a week. I'm used to these whirlwind visits. He stuffs me in the morning, makes me toast and orange juice, which I detest, then it's brunch, lunch, tea, dinner and cabaret, where I have to take something and I drink all the time. I'll be a yard round before long. And then Dad's habit of resting. Who ever heard of resting in the afternoon and after dinner? I'll be fat. I'll will you my clothes when I get out of the Army. You reduce a bit and you can get into them."

"My legs are too short."

Gilbert continued, "Dad's tour of New York City—have you seen it? Take a compass and stick it right through the Barbizon Plaza. Draw a circle with a radius of half a mile and there you are, that's it. Dad's world. I was at the Barbi-Plaza last night, night before at Pommes Frites, tomorrow at Monte Carlo, tonight I don't know where, and what about the "21"? Do you know the Raleigh, beastly showy place full of war-rich like this brute who was here, and bits of chicken under bell glasses, and special ices? Never a good quiet spot among them where you can enjoy yourself. Showy places, showy women—you know, Dad, I've come to one conclusion and that is, that that is one of the reasons you go there though you don't know it yourself. Oh, Dad's a mystery to no one but himself. An oasis, he calls it: I'm looking for an oasis. The last week I've eaten in some damn rotten oases and paid through the nose. Dear old Dad means well, but I know, Item, he hasn't the shadow of an idea where we ate anyhow, and Item, he doesn't give a damn, though he has a good palate. But Dad's view of good food is—the less the better. If you get a twentieth of a chicken on toast and three sprigs of cress and one carrot with cream, that's a good restaurant. I'm no eater, but in between Dad's expensive meals I have to sneak off to the Automat. I just came from one."

Grant, at this, laughed.

Gilbert continued, "The truth is—I'm always finding out the truth; it seems to lie round in chunks so you can stub your toe on it—is—that taste can't be bought. You have the same things at a fifty-cent place, a dollar twenty-five place, a two-fifty place, and a five seventy-five place, only less of it each time. See how much you can pay for being magnificently hungry. Now I don't think Dad knows that. He's generous and he likes to give people a good time, so he just throws money out the window by the barrel."

Grant cried humbly, "Well, my boy, got no time for all that. Besides, you don't know New York. All highjacking. One restaurant makes a reputation, next restaurant opens just to steal the trade, and give the same dish for less. Soon as they get the trade, they start cutting down. Every six weeks you have to go to a new restaurant. When it gets known, you see a line all round the block. Have to take someone else's advice, go to a new restaurant. Then it's too late; either they have a line round the block or they raise their prices or they cut down on the portion. Why?—started with an angel and a cook. No money, big overhead, cutthroat competition. Feeding the poor is the only business. Even then, it's swill against swill. What can you do? Change management? Competition has bought the manager, or the cook, or the head waiter, next day, the restaurant's no good. . . . I want to eat when I go out. Have you got a table? What is good today? Eat, get out. Make a career of eating—haven't the time. I don't say it's wrong, but I like to get out. Go somewhere else."

Gilbert laughed, "Come on, let's have more drinks, before we move over to one of those places with an eighteenth of a chicken under a bell glass and a sprig of cress. Bread and butter extra, so Dad says, no bread and butter."

He called the waiter, in an insolent manner, and ordered the drinks, adding to the women, "Dad never thinks of those things. One of his weaknesses. I guess Dad needs me around to get on socially. He's more like a bear. Good-natured old bear." He put his arm on his father's broad shoulders.

Grant became angry, "Don't flatter yourself, my boy. I got on all right without you."

Sally Lawrence said, "Your father is a simply marvelous host, Lieutenant."

Gilbert continued, "Oh, Dad's a good fellow, his meaning is clearly to be generous and let everyone have a good time. But between meaning and reality, Dad will never learn, there is a gulf which well-meaning can't jump. Especially the ready-made, leap-before-you-look type like Dad. Oh, I've studied Dad. As a matter of fact, between you and me, I don't think Dad ever thought about himself, as himself—the way you and I do, as most people do. Dad, I say, never looked at himself from the outside once in his life. An extrovert, pure and simple. The first act of the thinking man, I hold: 'What am I?' Dad doesn't know what he is!"

At this Grant began to laugh and said, "Perhaps I know who you are. I don't say I do, mind."

Gilbert leaned back, crossed his legs, and was smiling at them, his handsome, smooth, bluish face lighted up with confidence and naïveté. He seized the opening, "There I differ with you. A man must know himself before he knows others or can manage others. I fancy you must spend, perhaps, the first seventeen years of your life investigating your own impulses, reactions, processes—even finding out you have them—before you realize the other man's just another such animal as you are. The day you know that, you not only grow up, you can manage other men.

"I don't believe I could swear, but Dad has never done that once in his life. Perhaps once. Some shock. Take shock! Dad talks about getting a shock. He gets shocks. But shock is supposed to give you a new vision. Now, I've always argued that shock is not enough. You must have maturity, insight. You can shock and shock a dumb animal and what does it know more than it knew before? It doesn't even know you're hurting it. It's shocked. Just like Dad. He gets a shock and tomorrow he'll trust the same pack of criminals and scoundrels he's trusting today. This Ben—this Alf Goodwin—this Betty, a vicious little animal—it's in their faces—Dad's gifted, if you like, I grant that. He cerebrates, but he doesn't think all round a subject. He has flashes of intuition, he's damn near what you might call genius, but he doesn't apprehend! Apprehension is a sort of crystallization, all over the surface and down to the bottom of the flask: it begins in one spot and spreads, like hoarfrost on a window. Now Dad's apprehension always stops at that moment of polarization. . . . I don't say I have anything like Dad's gifts, but one thing I can do he can't do, and that is see the causes of things, the roots of personality. His mind is like a flashlight, it's here—there—it's very bright, you see the time by it, but you get a spotty idea of the landscape—pale here, red there, a couple of inches of ditch there, a dog's print somewhere else—you can miss a haystack and a corpse—you have to wait for that gray morning light to see the whole layout. The gray morning light—that's my type of thinking. Now if you spotlight personalities the way Dad does, and you have a big generous impulse the way he has, you don't see them at all. They're like actors in a movie. I've given this whole subject a lot of thought.

"I said to myself, 'Why is Dad always surrounded by rascals— the sort of men no decent man would shake hands with?'"

Grant, nursing his knee on his leg, looked at them, with the expression of a young girl whose bosomy mother is discussing her before visitors. The others waited, drinking, talked into quiescence.

Young Grant continued, after looking happily into their faces, imitating his father's gesture, nursing his knee, "Why doesn't Dad do better in business? He has a poor understanding of his competitors. It's dog eat dog. Now you would think an animal would instinctively understand its enemies at least and their way of fighting, and fight back; and once it had won, leave them. A dog, though, fights a skunk and somehow gets the worst of it. Dad is surrounded by swindlers, crooks, cheats, and he doesn't even know it. Then a man has to have a broader view of life than Dad has. Dad is always telling me—I'm sick of hearing it, though I don't doubt he means it—Dad says to me, 'I've made enough to live on, you are grown up, and now all I want is some woman who'll understand me and make me happy.'"

The women repressed their surprise. The boy looked around with a manly air, observing his father's annoyance and deep flush, said with a smile, "I'm adult now and see things differently. When I was a boy I believed Dad when he said Mother was an angel and sweet—and she is too—and Dad's a fine fellow, you couldn't find a better; but in a way Mother is sharper than he is, and not so angelic as he is and—in a way Dad's more wrongheaded. In short, they're both fine people and not suited to each other."

He said with a twinkle at his father, "—that Dad, who is a nice old lad, even if growing weatherbeaten, is attractive still to women, especially women who don't just go for a young face and understand character, for I've noticed a thing or two, though

I shut my eyes, as I should—the same thing does not of course apply to my mother—well, my feeling is, to make a long story short, Dad, that if you and Mother were thinking of an arrangement like that, I should have nothing to say against it."

Grant looked in embarrassment at the women. He murmured incomprehensibly. Livy said, "You're all right, Lieutenant."

He paused and glanced around dramatically but without fire. "Certain types are poison. Now certain people Dad dragged me to dinner with, against my will if I may say so, last week, the Yabes: I made it a point of honor to quarrel with the Yabes. The opinions I heard there were the same inflation-profiteering opinions we hear from your rotten acquaintance, Mr. Goodwin, with whom I have just quarreled. We should speak up. *They* are not silent. If vice shouts from the rooftops, we can engage a brass band and have our slogans painted on streamers. I have made up my mind that while here I am going to protect Dad as well as I can. Parasites, bloodsuckers, will find themselves pinched off. Now I ask myself why it is that I, a novice, a newcomer to experience, compared with Dad, can see what is wrong and Dad cannot.

"In the first place, I see them with new eyes. He is used to them. But how did he become used to them in the first place? Because he has an amiable, lavish sort of nature. He sees and yet he prefers not to see. He wants company. He lives alone. That is one of the reasons, I say, he should perhaps make some arrangement with Mother. He is lonely. He tells me that till I'm sick of hearing it, but one has to give a man his due, especially at his time of life. I have the greatest respect for you, Dad. I think I understand the whole situation.

"In the second place, to continue my list, I have had army experience. I believe you can see more in an army in a month than you can in a year outside. I don't mind admitting, it made a man out of the schoolboy I was a couple of years ago.

"In the third place, this is purely personal because I am, so to speak, a kind of indifferent man, not involved with life. I have no ax to grind in life, if you like. If you need something, you smell out the people who can give it to you, but by a law of compensation which I can't explain, for it has no survival-value, you become blind to their dangers. The life of wanting, of passion, is a precarious sort of life. I don't say it hasn't its compensations, too."

Grant at this laughed a little and murmured, "Who knows?

123

Who knows? Perhaps the boy's right. Better to be indifferent. Only I can't, I'm corrupted, my boy, you see."

Livy said quietly to Grant, "How the hell did you get a boy like that?"

"Just like my mother, good north-country temperament, very solid, very honest," murmured Grant with some pride.

The young man, at the first hesitation in this colloquy, went on superbly, "When I say my vision is near perfect because of a quiet temperament, I mean it in both senses. Physically, first. The one time I went to an oculist, he told me he had never seen anyone so near the ultimate possible ideal in vision. This was an excellent thing for me, for if I have the slightest headache, I know it comes from some other cause and shall never ruin my eyes as I am sure some do. . . . Secondly, I mean, I have for some reason we shall probably never know, straight moral vision. In dealing with the men, I endeavor to act with perfect justice on every occasion. I weigh, and it seems to me I never could hurt a fellow or carry on revenge or prejudice. But I spend so much of my time weighing these things, and analyzing myself too, that my decisions always come to me in a flash, not only regarding the men, but also when I have some discussion with superior officers. I believe this is because I understand human nature. . . . This all occurred to me when I was about fifteen; for it was then I first began to understand Dad. It worried me. It gave me something to do, to—to protect him. Before that I felt I should protect Mother, for she has not been very happy. And I've noticed among Dad's few real friends, a similar protective feeling—they feel he's a grand old fellow (that's the way I put it to myself), he hasn't had all the advantages, though his natural genius makes up for all that, he's worked hard and hasn't made as much money as he wanted to, because these crooks are around him, trying to sweat him, and they think, the friends, we have no ax to grind, we'll keep him company and elbow out the gangsters. I think I've hit the nail right on the head."

"You're all right, Gilbert," said Livy seriously.

Grant burst in, vaguely, "His mother's an angel, very sweet, good mother, excellent wife, but now I want to go home, lay my head on her lap, say, Mary, I want a mother more than a wife, I'm tired, but she's lost interest."

The younger Grant continued, "You see, this is no new problem for me. I know my attainments are small, I've a mediocre mind, yet I got on remarkably well in the army, though no comet or anything like that at school; and after puzzling it out for some time—for I said to myself, I want to square things as they are with what I know about myself, for I do not believe in Santa Claus: why is it that a man not extraordinarily bright, certainly with no academic or paper talent, let us say (had to have a tutor for Latin, for example), and a man who frittered away a couple of years as I did—when I first went to college, you know, it was just as if the light of day had changed. You've no idea of how different the world seemed. I got quite punch-drunk. Strange thing, I really saw—girls, for the first time, if you like—I didn't work too hard the first two years. Thus, I had a lot to make up. This was another drawback of my nature. When I felt this new world, I wanted to examine it, really plunge in and experience it to the limit. What is this new angle on the world, so to speak? This wasted a couple of years for me, that is to say, the problem of women, which, by the way, I like much better than other problems. Yet in the Army I got on rapidly, and soon got the way of things. It at last occurred to me that it was knowledge of human nature that stood by me. Yet I swear that it wasn't till I was seventeen or eighteen that it occurred to me to really think about myself as an individual. I seemed to emerge from a cloud about that time. You could call that cloud the cloud of flesh, or the cloud of infantile personality, I suppose. My deduction is that Dad has never quite emerged from that cloud of infantile personality. He is obsessed by his own impulses. He sees the world as driven by the same, and he attributes these impulses to others. Hence, monstrous errors in choosing his friends, and even, one might say, of taste."

Grant had listened to the end with a grave face. He had been stretching his neck out of his collar, flexing his shoulders, though not jingling his money. He raised a hand, called for the bill, said they all needed dinner. The young man said, "I haven't half finished what I wanted to say but I can tell you at dinner too."

"After dinner."

"At dinner, if the mood is in me. I get a real pleasure out of analysis, don't you?"

17

He helped the ladies, and went upstairs beside Livy Wright. Outside he took her arm gallantly, and held it warmly after they had crossed the street. He called back, "Let's walk a couple of blocks, won't do you any harm, Dad, to get some fresh air."

He led the way, bending over the small woman, with an attractive intimacy. Presently Grant whistled a taxi and they went to dinner at Manetti's, Grant hoping that he might thus lay eyes on the absconding Mrs. Kent. She was not there. Grant went to the telephone several times, and when he returned, burst forth into some incomprehensible story, about "I'm helping everyone, having a good time, but not myself. G. for example came in, from Montreal, with a British passport covered with limitations in rubber stamps; he must return to the bloody island in six months because he was born in Poland, and the bloody island's nourishing Poles, won't let them out of sight, why I don't know, need food themselves and do nothing but feed Poles, say Edinburgh's full of Poles. 'What shall I do?' says G. He doesn't want to go back. He's British now, doesn't want to go back and mix with the damn Poles. He says Britain's too much like Lodz, real Polish Poles now. I say, 'Don't go back to Montreal, go to Ottawa, they're dumb in Ottawa, I've been there to see. Lose your passport, they'll give you another, no limitations. If they don't find the old one. Often been done.' 'Thank you,' he says: he fell on my neck.

"I thought up a scheme for rebuilding France when this is all over, and look at the possibilities in Russia. I have a scheme for the organization of supplies after the war, in Europe, if they'd only go socialist, that would save the people from famine. But they don't want that yet. Only one social organization they know, that's war. Money doesn't count. They've all lost the taste for sound money. Commodities made to burn—arms and after the war, cotton and coffee, just the same as before. Then they grab the state and make the people work for nothing. Don't know how to count in money any more. They don't even want sound money. What do they get out of it? They have to pay the people back the money they saved that was clipped off the payrolls. . . . They don't want commodities, can't sell them. . . . All they can do is draft the people, squeeze all the work out of them, make them work, reproduce and drop dead, when their work isn't equal to their food, Hugo March's paradise. Simple. Only way out unless we have socialism. . . . I want to help people; I'm through with egoism. I've been an egoist all my life. Not my fault. . . . But I have a weakness! I'm lonely. Give me some job, I'll help my fellow man. But otherwise, I'm looking for a woman, three girls in one.

"For argument's sake, I see a picture in a window, I think, There's a beautiful woman—I got to find out who she is at any cost. If she's as pretty as she's painted, and she's not married, I'll take her out and see if she's got character. If she has, I'll say, 'I don't know if you're the right woman. Prove it to me.' I can't afford to make a mistake; not a Mussolini, not a commissar. For argument's sake, say this woman is French. I'll say, 'Your people shall be my people, I'll go over and work out a food commission, they'll need it—no milk, no coal, no meat, no herds, no iron, no green vegetables, all eaten, stolen, strayed, killed.' . . . Thieving doesn't pay. If you start to live off highway robbery, you don't grow no vegetables at home; you forget how to work, your wife has no clothes, you steal clothes, but you can't keep on, one day they put you in jail, rope round your neck, your wife's gone out to beg her bread. Then I go to France, take my French woman, and I say, 'I want nothing from you. I saw your picture in the window, I said I'll marry you, even if you're deaf and dumb. I'll marry you, I'll take you to France and I'll do it anyway, keep my word.' What do you think of me, Livy?"

"I'll go along as your secretary as far as Paris, anyway!"

Mrs. Lawrence said, "Robbie wouldn't leave the U.S.A. Europe is going to be a shambles after the war. There's plenty to do here."

"I say so too! Now I realize that there'll have to be a change after the war and Europe will be the new world while we'll be the old—"

But hearing the gears beginning to grind, Grant interrupted with: "Would you take me on, eh? Going to be fifty years of capitalism here, want to go and see a new world coming out of the shambles. A chance to construct a new world and remake your life—how do you like that?" bouncing about, spreading out his hands, grasping both women by the arms, till the young man laughed away his own ill-humor and Grant was able to cry, "Let's go to a cabaret—the Golden Tassel—I've had a shock—"

Tipsy, gay, he bore them off to the small cabaret. Here Grant commonly met Betty Goodwin, because her husband despised the place. And the place was so radical still that Celia Grimm had once brought here Mrs. Wood, the Negro wife. At the Golden Tassel Grant made another trip to the telephone, came back with a furrowed face, and declared he was going to get good and drunk. He danced with the women and then with Celia Grimm, who was going from table to table of a large group of friends. He brought Celia to his table, told her about some novel he was writing with Flack's advice.

"The story of my life. I'm not going to paint myself all white nor all black: it's going to be human, constructive. *All I Want Is a Woman*, that's the name. A man, Kincaid, made a few mistakes but he never hurt anyone unless they hurt him first. And at the end he wants to be good. He finds a woman like you, and after the war they go to war-wrecked Europe and say, 'Take us, we don't want to live for ourselves: we bring the promise of America to blasted Europe, we want to recreate Europe.' "

Celia Grimm said, "You have such a good heart and do so much damage: I don't understand it. Do you know Jenny Woods has left her husband and she is waiting for some sign from you?"

"It's nothing to do with me, she's neurotic. I want no part in that. They're unstable, these colored people," muttered Grant.

"Won't you write a note to her, advise her, help her out? She believed you. I told her she was making a mistake."

"I want no part of it. Modern capitalism came down on a simple peasantry and they're unstable," said Grant.

"At least see her and tell her to go back to Woods."

"No, no, least said, soonest mended. If she sees me, she'll expect something."

"I'm afraid for her, Robbie."

'I want to keep out of anything unhealthy," said Grant.

"You'll slip on a banana peel some day, Robbie."

"Don't worry about me, don't worry about me: you see her and send her back to her husband. Do that and we'll forget all this and go to Rome after the war, eh, sweetie?"

He did not dance with Celia any more that evening, since at the end of the dance she refused absolutely to accompany him to his hotel. Just the same, towards the end of the evening, Celia introduced him to a very beautiful elderly woman who was looking for a companion, and Grant went with her to her apartment. She was richly dressed and her apartment was in an expensive block of flats. Grant told her that she was the woman he had been looking for; they understood each other right away. She must have been of unparalleled beauty at one time, but now all this had begun to crumble, it crumbled at a touch. She wrote Grant's address and telephone number down in her morocco-covered address book; but he never saw her again.

18

In some such manner passed the four weeks of March's absence in Canada. Flack, meanwhile, had written humorously to March, telling him that he wondered if it was worth his valuable time to pursue the inquiries for Grant, "since the poor old jackass is doing his best to get in with the harpy again, and I suppose it is a love affair, as much as he can understand one, so why not let him enjoy it? When it comes to clinches, I know who will win—"

He said as much to Grant in the office one day when they had received a demand for money from March, but Grant persisted in his idea of a showdown.

Flack said, "What is it worth, all he's told you?"

Grant muttered in his way, "Uzzazuzz—Hilbertson—New Orleans—h'm!"

"Who is Hilbertson?"

"Man I once knew in business; old man, retired now. Don't understand how he got that name."

"What about Hilbertson? Is he a spy?"

"No, no, no: knew him once, in on a deal: retired now."

"If you'd ever tell me anything straight, Grant, I'd help you maybe."

"Never mind, never mind, never mind! Let's go out and celebrate: forget all our troubles. Let's go to the movies."

March returned from Canada shortly after receiving Flack's letter. He had made a little money on his speculations up there, visited many addresses given to him by Grant, some till that moment unknown to Flack, had a tale to tell. He liked Canada the more he saw of it; he said, "It's a hideaway, in case I ever find the air of the U.S.A. getting less fragrant. They're a disciplined people, obey the law, never talk bawdy, pay their taxes, believe in God, King and country, hate the Reds and wouldn't stand for any goddamn bastard like Wallace; trouble with us is our democratic tradition. It'll get us out on a limb some day; we ought to take a line from our northern neighbors."

He was out of pocket some $2,785 on Grant's behalf, but he had found out, he said, from the generous, law-abiding, respectable R.C.M.P. much more than from his friends in Washington: "Son, she's left marks all over the map from Los Angeles to Ottawa. He picked a daisy. I'm beginning to think my friends weren't as frank with me as they might have been, but perhaps they have more on her. But when I compare them with British loyalty—what you pay for, you get in British territory. My countrymen, God bless them, want to take the cream off the top, and then get a profit out of the residue as well: the first is due to their wits, the second is theirs by law, and if there's any left, they'll make plastics out of it and sell you the junk for a dollar seventy-nine, as a bargain."

Flack laughed, "Yankee thrift. What's the news from the honest Dominion?"

"It's a sizzling anecdote. I want your opinion. Should we give it unvarnished to your Romeo? I'm beginning to love this. He picked her out of the gutter. It turns out she's a Mata Hari. Then he gives me an earache telling me she's innocent; then he wants me to get her criminal record. What is he, sick?"

"Just give me an outline."

It boiled down to a long and still continuing association with the old man called James Alexis, wealthy international figure, with confiscated estates in territory now occupied by the Germans and large properties also in South Africa and South America, particularly the Argentine. Grant and Flack had looked up Alexis and knew all about his holdings and his international relations, suspicious in wartime. The reputed wealth of Alexis was about five times that of Grant. To make it worse, he came from a well-known family, although he had discarded their name. His brother was a famous painter and he himself had written several political essays and novels.

"Prepare your Romeo for the bad news; and tell him it was damn good of them to mention Alexis' name for a couple of bedbugs like him and me. They only did it because I know Captain X, and I did him a favor once."

Flack said, "A tip. Find out who she met at Grand Central yesterday evening. Grant is half mad because she stood him up and at the same time met some European friend. He suspects the German skater, almost anyone, the painter—I gave you the list. He also suspects a fellow named Ruiz, who's a Franco agent. I may as well tell you, his position has changed. He's furious with her; and he's beginning to get some sense and see how repulsive she is, with her fascist tendencies. I said to him, 'Every harpy favors conservatism in the end, if not fascism.' They don't like work. What have they to hope for from the working class? Why are they playing with radicalism now? Why do half the tramps Grant meets say they're pink? First, because they think it'll please him—and then he, misled, thinks it will please them. Then, as one girl bitterly pointed out, he gets them cheaper, they think it right; and last, they are floating on the fringe of society, feel ill at ease, and they think that's true discontent. Grant and all wholesale swallowers of women, and all petty profit-takers, are restless, half in distress, they believe justice is not being done. A shark, hanging outside a school of dolphins which has driven fish into a beach to devour, probably would say he too is a liberal: there should be fish for all."

March frowned and growled slowly, "They want something for nothing—that's the root-drive behind EPIC, and old-age pension and workmen's compensation and all boondoggling, isn't it? And these damn fish, too. I wouldn't hand out a cent to anyone in the country. Then you'd have no pipedreams about getting the government to put in toilets for you and pay you for putting in too much cotton. People would learn to think ahead. That crowd around Grant live from hand to mouth. Aren't you all getting your pickings from him?"

Flack turned pale, "Am I?"

"I don't give a damn what your arrangements are—but if you don't, you're worse than I thought you."

"At a time like this, when every monopolist in the country is getting a handout, you object to the workers getting a handout?"

"The workers want to get paid for not working. The monopolists, as you put it, work day and night, they never let the country out of their minds for a minute. All the workers, as you call the steel gorillas, never think of a damn thing but going to the movies and kissing their girls and turning on the jukebox. Who deserves it—us or them? Don't forget to tell Grant, by the bye, that that little jaunt cost him two thousand, seven hundred and eighty-five dollars. And tell him with my compliments that I wouldn't pay that much for the Queen of the Congo."

Flack went back to the office and begged Grant not to go near the woman. "Pay March what you owe and let that be an end of it; you're a patriot with all your faults and your big blowing and I'm-out-for-myself, you don't want to be mixed up in such things, and since you give yourself out as a socialist—" he continued bitterly, eying Grant hard—"kindly have some respect for socialism. What would happen if your name came out in the press connected with such a harpy and a spy?"

Grant grumbled and shifted, apologized for his behavior of the night before, but had no excuse and would not promise.

"The damn woman cost me a forchun, a forchun, got to get

some return: throw good money after bad, but I'll make her sweat it out."

He felt uneasy, sank into himself, looked at Flack with a grudge, but at Flack's first kind word, he said, "My life's so empty, I need her. I'll go down with her if she's a spy. I've got to have the virtues of my vice. Why would James Alexis go round with a spy? She gets her money from him." He went on about James Alexis, of whom he was extremely jealous. Alexis, richer, famous for his personal achievements, not only had the blonde woman but, like Grant, went round declaring himself a socialist, better, "a Marxist." He actually had read Lenin and could argue about it. Grant's lip fell and he went on rumbling, "I'll do better than that fella. I need her. I'm as bad as she is. I'm no more a socialist than she is. She didn't read Lenin. I didn't either. I'll go down with her. I'll get my name in the papers. It'll be a sort of glory, the only sort I deserve. You're right. I'll drag socialism in the mud. Alexis couldn't afford that; he'd draw off from her. What am I? I'm not better than that 'ooman and I've never pretended to be. What do I expect out of life? I've wasted my life. I'd rather have a big splash of scandal, something to fill up with. My life's a desert. Then she'd have to come back to me and stick by me; no one would have her. Alexis wouldn't. He's got a wife and his family would get after him. Then he writes papers on economics and agriculture. He has a reputation. He couldn't do it with a scandal like that, a tramp, a spy. I'd come and rescue her and I'd say, 'Look, darling, I came when everyone else turned their backs. I stuck by you, now you stick by me. You hurt me, all right, I forgive you. Maybe I hurt you. We'll start from scratch. We'll go away to Monte Carlo or Rome or the Thousand Islands, and we'll spend a quiet time there. I'm tired of messing round, you've had enough.' With these connections I have, March, Washington fellas—not that I think much of them—the R.C.M.P., I could buy her out of it; and I will. Then I'll take her away. Get my name in the papers. What do I care for that—in Boston! It'll force my hand. I'm afraid you were right the other day. This thing'll force my hand. Force her hand too. There she'll be with all her cards on the table, stripped naked, in public. They want to give her a whipping. I go and say, 'Look, darling, this is where I stand by you. You didn't expect it of me, but now you see the kind of man I am. I need you, you need me—' I'll take her away where she can't spy!"

He driveled on. Flack nearly wept out of pity and boredom.

As soon as Flack had got down to studying Grant's investment position, Grant went into the outside room and telephoned Bentwink's office to call Bentwink off the job and send in a final report and account, and to Miss Celia Grimm's home, to ask her to get him a free copy of Robison's study of the Negro—he had seen a mention of it somewhere and wanted to get it: "Don't mention my name, just do it for me, sweets, will you? And I'll do something for you, I promise I'll see Jenny one of these days and see how she's feeling, eh? Don't want to do any harm."

Last he telephoned March and said in a mysterious voice, "See if the name—yesterday—was M. Yves Troland; I see he's in town and that's the French liberal minister she knew in Paris."

He waited till two-fifteen, doing business and nervous because of the expected calls; and then rushed uptown leaving Flack to "close the shop." His friends were not in at the Charles Wagoner; he left the parcel of toothpaste, aspirins, and so forth that his secretary had tied up for him into one packet, and went out again, once more to walk the streets. When he came out of a newsreel theater at Grand Central, he telephoned to Miss Livy Wright and had dinner with her. The woman seemed half in love with him and had put on a new dress with a low-cut bodice, which offered him her firm breasts. She was boisterous, rude, just as yesterday, but there was imprudence and abandon in her today. He took advantage of it and this seemed to flatter her; in a moment of passion she told him any woman could love him, no woman could help herself. It was a long time since he had felt so flattered.

When the woman left, he telephoned Peter Hoag about the promised dinner with Mrs. Kent, but heard that Mrs. Hoag was out of town. Then he telephoned the Charles Wagoner, from which he got no satisfaction. In distress, he telephoned Mrs. Goodwin, who at once came out to have cocktails with him at the White Bar; but when she had gone home, he felt exhausted, and knew he would toss all night. What should he do with his life? That no one could tell him! Only the blonde had known how to organize things to his taste: she was a consummate time-waster, not brilliant, but then she had found out Grant's physical nature at once.

"I don't regret anything. She filled my life, if only with headaches!" He tried to fight down the amount of $2,785 with March. March had rebuked him, "We're dealing with an honest country. You don't suppose you can buy them for peanuts? You're damn lucky you got it for that. They wouldn't have given it to you for five thousand dollars—not for ten thousand. And if you let it out where you got it, they'll shut up like a steel trap. It's not like this country, where eleven government monkeys stand in line, in Times Square, with their hands out asking for their cut."

Naturally, he had sent the check but he felt the blow. March had now cost him $9,500 with his research, and the detectives $680.

"Well, I'll take it and dump it into her lap and say, 'Explain this, my sweetie!' I'll get her back and it'll be worth it. That blonde is worth ten thousand, one hundred and eighty dollars—"

He took several tablets but had only a few hours of dull sleep. He got up as usual and began his ablutions, following a system which filled in more than two hours of his morning. He took a bath, a douche, a scented bath, a hot and cold shower, a footbath, a pedicure and manicure, a suntan from his special lamp. His teeth gleamed, his nails were buffed, and he wiped out, as far as possible, every sign of age. He emerged in fresh linen and a different suit, with a hot towel held to his chin with one hand, and he looked over his stores. After ten minutes' steaming, he applied eau de cologne, powder, hair cream, eyebrow dye, and while he put on his cocoa, he inspected his coat for the day. It was eight o'clock. He turned on the radio, rushed through the morning papers, polished his shoes, cleaned his teeth again, and was ready for work.

It was still far too early. In the old days he had been at work at seven-thirty. He still rose early, but as he had nothing to attend to but his personal affairs, his partner doing most of the business, he was at a loss. All his friends were still in bed, if they were not at business. At nine he telephoned Flack: Flack was in bed or bathing, for he did not answer. Grant went downstairs, started to walk down Fifth Avenue, retraced his steps, went into a florist's —to whom should he send flowers? He dispatched them to the Hotel Charles Wagoner, to Mrs. Kent; others of a cheaper sort to Mrs. Jones, whom he had begun to detest.

"Where a pup goes wrong, look at the dam," he thought to himself. He thought he would break her down, make her reply. She did not reply and no word came from the mother.

He did his business in a frenzy and spent half the day pouring out his miseries to Flack, "I feel like a scorpion biting its own tail and biting itself to death, when it thinks it's stinging the other fellow."

"If you would only study something, Robbie; you have nothing to fill that big empty head of yours."

"Behind everything in a man's life, there's a woman, you don't know that, Davie. If I had the right woman I might study—but it's too late now."

March telephoned to say that he had made inquiries and the man Mrs. Kent had met at the station had been the ex-minister, Yves Troland, now in exile. His informants also said that her ex-husband Adams was in town and that that was a danger for Grant, as the gigolo had been a love affair for her.

"She handed him all your money. Now he's probably come to collect dough from Alexis. Why don't you lay off her? She's too hot for my money. You're outclassed, Grant. I hear she's been bragging that she took your money and gave you nothing but a Bronx cheer. I wouldn't let any —— treat me that way. She buys and sells you. She told Peter Hoag you're just a tired business man who will end up by being kicked around by every woman in town who'll look at you."

Grant's eyes grew large and seemed about to fall from his head; he looked at the telephone girl to see if she was listening. He said, very low, "Where did you hear that?"

"Paula Russell, that sidekick of hers, Hoag told her. Miss Russell said she thought it was a damn shame the way you were being led by the nose. She said all your friends were talking about it. They'd like to find a cure for you."

Grant put down the phone and sank into his chair, overwhelmed with defeat. As soon as he could, he left the office and took a taxi uptown to see Mrs. Goodwin. At five he was having tea with the Goodwins and a couple of their friends, who included a middle-aged lawyer, named Walker. They all gave advice about the woman, Goodwin asking insolently how much he could take of such punishment from Barb, that if he took any more, he hoped he choked on it; and went on to say the whole thing had been Grant's fault. The women listened gloomily to this, but broke in at the end with their cackling: each had something against her. Only Betty Goodwin, to please him, said Barb was very lovely and had nice manners. Then the newcomer, the dark-faced lawyer, Walker, said, "Is it the pen or expulsion you want? I can get one or the other for you and you'll be rid of this bloodsucker. We can get her on twenty counts."

"Robbie, too," cried Goodwin, laughing knowingly. He went on to say what misdemeanors and felonies Grant must have committed—some he, to his knowledge, surely had committed—with the woman. He went on to the end shamelessly, showing Grant's passion in tatters. Grant, appalled, disgraced, listened to the end, saying, "No—no—that I never did—let them try that—I took a chance, but not a crime—"

But the lawyer listened to all, while Goodwin swelled with his role and Betty Goodwin's eyes became profound. At the end, there was a silence, one of the women sighed, and Grant said, "I've done everything for the woman. She's dragged me into a wallow. I'm sunk in up to the neck."

And in an abject manner he went on again, telling them a thousand details of his love for the woman and how she had mistreated him: "She is my vice, I may as well marry her."

As soon as he got home, Mrs. Kent telephoned, reproached him for not calling upon her that afternoon, and made an appointment to meet her mother and herself at once in the lobby of the Charles Wagoner. Grant rushed to meet them.

She was there, with her mother and Miss Russell. He had to sit through three hours of cocktails and dinner with the three women at Manetti's, and then conduct them back to the Charles Wagoner. At the door of the hotel, he simply took Barbara by the elbow, led her aside, saying, "Something I've got to ask Barb," and as soon as they were out of earshot he poured out a flood of words, with, "Let me get you an apartment. I want to come and see you. I'll do what you say. Here you're either not in, or you've got your eternal bodyguard. I have to talk to you. It's important, important for you. Something I found out about you. Someone I know went of his own accord to the police and made inquiries about you. It's to your own interest to hear it. A certain party. I must see you. Will you think over the apartment?"

"What are you talking about? I can't make decisions like this! Why do you rush at me like this, after abandoning me and treating me like a criminal for months? You have been brutal, cruel, to me. How can I trust you? You must make me believe in you."

She made as if to break away from him, she looked at a man who was coming up the steps.

"When will you see me?"

"Tomorrow," she said, after a moment.

"And all alone for once."

"Telephone me about two. I'll try to arrange for Mother to have tea with Mrs. Hutchison. If not, I can't leave her alone here in the afternoon. We're so much together; and I can't tell her I'm seeing you alone."

"No, no," he murmured.

"Please don't let us stand talking in the lobby. I detest that. Telephone me at two. And let me tell you, you talk too much to too many people."

He swore he would not talk to anyone about her any more, "I've done you wrong, I'll make it up to you."

"The whole town says I'm a spy—that's you!"

"I swear it isn't. I swear it!"

19

At lunch he met Hugo March and pressed him for every detail of the Canadian story. He felt sure, he said, there were things he had not told David Flack—and so it proved. Was it smuggling, currency, furs? Yes. It was furs, diamonds, currency, drugs; she could have been jailed long ago, if not that she always gave them a valuable lead as a collector of men. They only had to follow her to get many names.

"That's not quite fair—she has innocent friends, myself for example."

"Tell that to the judge."

Through some misunderstanding, or because they wished to warn March, his Canadian correspondents had sent in another report to him, the cost of this one, $1,000. March advised Grant, when he grumbled, not to get himself in wrong with the R.C.M.P.: "You're a friend of this beauty, and so you're on their watch-list. You'd better keep on the safe side. If you don't want any more information, I'll tell them to hold it."

"I know enough now to sink a ship. I'm getting rid of this blamed woman, you can tell them that."

"Speaking of sinking ships—aren't you doing ship-chartering and ship-reconditioning these days?"

Grant stared at him.

"It might be said that she is getting information from you!"

"Im-possible."

"What more likely? Your only way to clear yourself would be to show that you've tried to clear up the mystery of the woman."

"I can show that!"

"If you get any more information on her, you ought to turn it in!"

"That's going too far. Let them give it to me, not me to them. Besides, I don't see how she can do it all. I never knew her to work."

"She wouldn't have to work hard to get information from you. Suppose they think she got it from you. They don't have to be dainty about putting two and two together to make five."

Grant turned red.

Flack said she might have been part of the Schellenberg ring: "The Countess Exe—"

"Might be a good tip."

He took nothing to the Charles Wagoner, thinking that they had got enough out of him. When he went upstairs, he met the old lady, Mrs. Jones, alone. Seeing his stare of displeasure, she said that Barb would soon be there, but she had found out "their little plot" and she wanted to talk to him first, about his plans. Barb had mentioned an apartment. Did he seriously mean to separate mother and daughter? And for what? For what sort of an arrangement? She wanted Barb to marry again and settle down for good, it was high time. She did not believe that Grant would leave his wife, nor would she be willing to consider it for a moment, "I believe in the sanctity of the marriage tie; but as Barb was so pressing, I agreed to let her have an interview with you here, because I respect an honest feeling. We are only human, all-too-human, we cannot help our feelings."

It's sure, then, thought Grant, that the old witch does not know about my relations with her daughter. He muttered about "—sincere feelings of respect, Barb used to like me a little bit, I thought at one time, even loved me a little bit, and then she avoided me— I was brokenhearted, I didn't know where to turn. I must see her. She isn't fair to me. I'm only a man. I'm suffering."

The old woman smiled and said that this was what had influenced her.

"I'll marry her, I'll get a divorce and marry her. I'll take her to Rome and we'll all live in a house I have there."

"Not so loud, please, walls have ears."

"I beg your pardon?"

"My daughter never saw any signs of your making good, to use a vulgarism."

"She let me down too."

"Unfortunately, my daughter was not brought up to work and so she must be provided for. I say nothing about myself. Barb would never let me starve."

"My dear good woman, I offered Barb an apartment yesterday."

"She can't live alone."

"I want her to. Otherwise, she can live here and forget it! I won't pay for any circus. No expense accounts, no duennas. No girl friends. No shutting me out."

"I'll put it to Barb the way you put it, Mr. Grant," said the old woman sourly.

"Those are my terms. All or nothing."

Grant waited a long time, but Mrs. Kent did not return. At last, her mother said he ought to go, that she was tired and must rest. Grant spent some time in the hotel lobby, and then waited across the street, but saw nothing of the woman. He regretted that he had dismissed Bentwink—he could have sat in the car.

The next day, Mrs. Kent telephoned him at twelve. She had been unable to get a taxi and so had had dinner uptown. Grant shouted, "Why didn't you take the subway?"

Mrs. Kent merely asked him if he wanted to see her that afternoon. She promised to be there and to send her mother out, "I'm afraid Mother took things into her own hands yesterday. I have scolded her for it. But she doesn't know how things are between us, Robbie, and you will simply have to forgive her."

"If you see me—"

"Bring me a bottle of that Origan perfume, if you can find one that the storekeepers haven't made all water, and two bottles of Coca-Cola."

He put down the phone and burst out laughing, "I'll get that and I'll get more. She's checked up and found I brought nothing with me yesterday." He walked up and down the office, slapping his pocket and laughing.

She seemed to be alone. He craned his neck, whispered, "Where's Mamma, eh?"

"She went out shopping with Mrs. Hutchison."

She had gone back to the couch and was now stretched there in a négligé, with a Shetland wool blanket under her feet. There was a lamb's wool mat by the couch. She had her white fur kitten on her pillow. She looked charming, her hair in a loose knot on her neck, her neck still round as a pillar in this posture. He put down his hat, stick, parcels, and sighed, "Barb, you are as fair as fair can be."

"Wheel the tea tray over here, Robbie. I am lazy today, I don't want to do a thing. Forgive me."

His face fell. He flushed. He did as he was told, bending down, unfolding his parcels, showing them to her, and bringing a chair to her couch. The telephone rang. He said, "Let it ring."

"It might be Mother."

It was her mother. While they spoke, the blondine looked at Grant with her bright, interested eyes. When she put down the phone, she said, "Mother is anxious and says I must be very careful, she is not sure she trusts you. However—I am going to obey my own impulses, not Mother's whims."

Grant at first could hardly speak, for satisfaction. In an instant it flashed through his head that it was the mother who had engineered everything and that the daughter had no grudge against him. Nevertheless, she disappointed him.

20

The next day March had it conveyed to Grant that the blonde woman was in fact a part of "the Schellenberg ring"—this was part of the secret information his Washington informants had not wanted to let out at first. Flack became excited at this, and shouted, "A fine mess you're in! See if his informant associates her with the Baron von Dangen-Steinkeller—write down, wait, I'll write them down—here, see if she had anything to do with Von Papen, Ernest Haack, Lydia Oswald—I'll get a list here and you just shove it at him and tell him his Washington informants, for the money you've paid, have to tell you whether she has been in cahoots with these, any one—and if so, my dear boy, I'm going to ship you east of Suez, where the best is like the worst, or to Cuba, or to Mexico City, or anywhere else for a vacation, you dumb ox. A woman has a loop of blond hair and he has to follow her into the middle of a spy ring! Why didn't you take a warning long ago? You lost the wretched harpy; now you've moved heaven and earth to get her back—and at the last moment, when it's too late, I find you in touch with Von Papen, with all the rascals in the universe."

Grant felt very nervous. He had already confessed everything to Flack.

Presently, March sent a note over by an office boy, "My informants say that this party is connected with the parties mentioned. Names, dates check. Einam and Brinon through Von

D.-S. They are pleased with confirmation through you. Do you know more? M."

Flack tore the note from him in excitement. Grant's head whirled. His headache was so severe that he could not see the walls of his office. Flack shut the office, helped him into a taxi, made him some soup, put him to bed, drew the blinds.

Grant murmured, "I can't talk it out now, come to me at five this afternoon. I have an appointment with the blonde, put it off, tell her I'm sick. What a fool I have been! There never was such an imbecile. You're right about me. I'm a sucker. There are plenty of women. I have to pick out what's dangerous. It's my mixed blood—my Spanish ancestor; the Spaniards loved danger."

"Never mind those family portraits, she must be a good fooler if they gave her the job; you're not the only one she fooled. Don't blame yourself. You're the hundredth man she sold her line to. Hundredth—a thousand, nay, fifty thousand! Never mind. Sex has no eyes. Only feelers. Forget it. Go to sleep, old boy."

When he came back, he found Grant up again and shaved. He was meanwhile looking at a bit of paper, which he now showed Flack, "This is the list we sent to March. It's your copy to check. All the names check. I don't dare ask him any more. This is the end! To whatever I ask he finds the answer. The answer's yes. She must be one of the worst and the cleverest women in the world. You wouldn't credit it if you saw her there with her white cat. And yet—" he looked sorrowfully at Flack—"you don't know how she is at night, curled up like a little girl, her knees up, on her side, her hair in braids or just tied plain with a big blue ribbon, and white nightgowns, not always those pink, lacy things, but lawn, tucks. She says she wore them at school, French things, little lace, just like a young girl. She looks so young sometimes, with her hair spread out. She has a white Angora toy cat that she can't sleep without. It's like one she had that was deaf. She cries about it, because it made such a noise one night. She hit it, and she never knew it was deaf till afterwards. It cried because it couldn't hear her and couldn't see her. She kicked it; she says she had on a satin mule, but just the same—that worries her, years after! I can't believe it, my boy. If there are women like that, why, those women are monsters! I saw one of them in a shop once; she wanted me to buy it, I wouldn't have the little thing near me, it scratches—and blue eyes like she has—" He shook his head.

"So innocent, naïve-looking, and such depravity, degeneracy—it's possible, I'm not an imbecile, but still—why does she want me?

Eh? I'm no spy. It doesn't make sense. She must like me, anyhow! That's my conclusion. She must want someone decent, serious man, eh? I've tried to work it out all the afternoon."

Flack said, "This list we gave March and his information check."

"I know."

"They check a bit too well, it seems to me," said Flack after a while, in a sprightly tone.

"What do you mean?"

"Keep your shirt on! I've been thinking this thing over these last few hours. I saw the state you were in. You love her."

"Go on, go on."

"Keep your shirt on and let's go over this in cool collectedness. Doesn't it strike you that since the beginning we got the information we asked for? And wanted? Whenever we said, 'Does she know Freylinghausen?' she knew Freylinghausen. When we say, 'Does she know Von Dangen-etc.?' she knows V.D. Does she know Baroness von Einam?—yes; Von Papen?—check; Yves Troland? Yes! But we never get this information before we hand it out. We never hear a name till we mention it? Odd! Furthermore, if the R.M.P. have sold you information, they can hardly blackmail you into giving them information. The whole story doesn't hold any water but our own."

"You mean, he's holding out on us?"

"We are the F.B.I., we are the State Department, and we are the R.C.M.P.!" said Flack solemnly.

"Good God! We are! You're right! What fools! She's innocent."

Grant flushed, his eyes flashed, he lost his headache. He sat down heavily and said, "Let's just check to make sure, not get carried away by a coincidence."

They went over it all from the beginning, with, "What did you say? What did I say? What did we say to March? Are you sure? Who else was in on this?" They worked through their notebooks and set up the dates of the checks paid to March.

"Now I have another theory, a daring one, but we can try it; we can only lose."

"What is it?"

"Calm yourself. It's only a theory. It is this—how will we know if she knew even one of these people if we don't make a test? We'll plant a name on March!"

"Do you suspect March? But the fella's rich!"

"I don't say he did it. Perhaps he's met someone who thinks he's the sucker."

Grant frowned but after a moment became excited, "We should have thought of that in the first place: very good."

They went over and over it. Then they both started laughing and between them began to concoct a name. At last they hit on the name of a Belgian town, Schaerbeek, the Countess van Schaerbeek.

"We'll ask March to ask His Informants if she was connected with the notorious spy, the Countess Adele van Schaerbeek, who operated from—Lausanne?"

"There's no such person. He'd know that. Or his informants. After all, they have some files."

"What informants?"

"By George," said Grant, staring at Flack. There was a pause.

"It's impossible, im-possible, my boy," said Grant.

"Let's try it, anyhow."

"I don't like it."

"We'll say we were misinformed, printer's error. Easiest thing in the world. Who are we? Are we police?"

Grant got up and pranced around, "It's a wonderful idea, my boy. And if—if—it turned out to be partly, totally—or in any way, a hoax, boy, oh, boy!—and you found it out—I'd kiss you, we can be in Fifth Avenue, Fifty-seventh Street—never mind, if it's a sell—"

He came up, kissed Flack vehemently on the forehead, he jumped back, "I won't howl, I won't squeal, I'll be joy-crazy; I'll take you all out, I'll take everyone but that damn crook—"

He threw out his arms, laughed, threw back his head, opened his mouth, and laughed loudly, "That would be the end of my problem."

:"Take it easy! You don't know yet."

"It's im-possible. Give me the note, quick. Adele van Schaerbeek. Lausanne. He'll have it by special delivery tonight. Just found out from informant. We'll have an informant, too. Wake him up. Two o'clock. I'll say, 'Don't deliver it till two o'clock.' Let him think I'm crazy, woman-struck, he called me. If it's true—oh, boy, will he pay it all back, he'll spend the next six months in a sweatbox."

"He's dead to the world by this time; the last trump won't wake him up. Save your money."

"We'll send it over first thing. Where's Edda! Call her, tell her to come up and rejoice with us. I want her. Call Edda."

Flack did this and this was a blessed night for Grant. He kissed them both over and over again. In the night, Grant scarcely slept at first, for he was piecing together dates, names, checks, hoping —and again seeing the woman at her worst. Her mother's intrigues at times seemed the solution. "What if she is just a lazy, silly, harmless girl who wants to reform and thinks I let her down? She is sick of the life she leads. Poor Barb."

At another time he walked up and down with a scowl and finally came out with, "But what's the meaning of this name, Hilbertson?"

"Who the devil is Hilbertson?"

"I was in on a deal with him, a long time ago."

"Is it a secret? They could get that name from anyone."

"You're right, you're right, h'm."

21

The two conspirators could hardly wait for March's regulation two days to hear the result of the test. They did not telephone him, for fear he would suspect something. In two days they had a note, brought by his office boy. It said, "My informant is told that X made several trips to Lausanne prior to your meeting; and was guest of Countess A. v. S. in her hotel in Paris."

"Make him write it out in full," Flack said. "I'll go across and get his other details, as he calls them. Then we'll show him the record—"

"Will he write it all out? He'd smell a rat! I don't want a show-down. He took us for the Simple Simons of Green Goods County. We were, too."

Grant looked nasty. Flack hastened to say, "How do we know he's guilty? Why would he do it?"

"For eleven thousand, two hundred and thirty-four dollars."

"Is that really what you paid him?"

Grant looked guilty and confessed that this was the real total. He looked black, "Whether it's him or his informants, we'll squeeze it out of him. But why would he do it?"

"One: to take you for a ride. . . . Two: to get the money. Three: he and his crowd are genuine gangsters, I believe. Four: we don't know he did it himself. Perhaps he's only a catspaw. Five: they're so tough they take you for a lamb. You are—to them.

Sixth: you keep yapping you're British; to them that's equivalent to a Back Number."

"No one suspects you. You got me into this—you only meant to do me a favor, I recognize this—and you can get me out. I'll make him spit out every cent if I have to shake out his pants and his B.V.D.'s like Uncle Jack."

Uncle Jack was Alfred Goodwin's uncle, a small, worn old man, a gardener, who sold flowers in pots every spring. In winter, he sold candy and soft drinks, in a wayside shanty he had made himself. His earnings were all in cents, nickels, and dimes. Every night, when he entered his home on the East Side, he took off his trousers inside the front door, and left them lying there for Aunt Bella, his wife, to shake out. They had a large cider jar full of lead nickels. He was a good-hearted man.

"He took me for Uncle Jack! He filled me full of wooden nickels!"

Grant shouted with laughter. When he calmed down, he said in a businesslike tone, "When I've melted down his grease, the butcher won't take him in for war-fats. Let's think up a scheme."

He scooped out of his desk all March's reports and spread them before him in a disorderly heap. He said in his husky voice, "It can all be phony. Do you think he could dream up all that?"

"I already told you he didn't have to think—we gave him the names. You can't keep your mouth shut, for example. The whole town knows about this affair."

Grant frowned: "We'll get a scheme, patience is the watchword. We'll give him the British manner—naïvety, niceness. Boy, will we be naive and nice, Simple Simons: just the picture he drew of us."

"Here is my idea."

Flack explained that on the following Sunday March and Hoag were going to visit their friends Francis O'Sullivan and Arthur Pantalona at O'Sullivan's new house at Five Rocks, a spot on the flats, quite near March's country hideout, about ten miles from those hills. March had built a house for O'Sullivan at Five Rocks. The house was not yet finished. Pantalona, March, and others of their close circle spent every Sunday, when there was no work in town, fixing up the house with O'Sullivan. Flack was positive that next Sunday would find them all there, because he had been invited, with Edda.

"Peter and March called up Edda yesterday to invite her, the first time. He wants to make us sure. Maybe he feels he's been getting away with too much."

Near the house was a large, unfashionable golf course which took Jews to be members. March's crowd played there because some of their friends were Jews who came out for a game in the week end. Flack would get an invitation for Sunday dinner for Grant. Mrs. O'Sullivan was a motherly sort. Flack felt certain that O'Sullivan and Pantalona were two of March's famous "informants" or at any rate, go-betweens for him and his "Washington crowd."

Perhaps it would be smarter to drop in on the March outfit, at Five Rocks, without notice. Flack would say casually that he and Grant would go out to the golf course for a game of golf, and then would stop by to see O'Sullivan: what more casual, what more natural? They would have a chance to meet everyone and see what expressions they had when he and Grant dropped certain remarks. Flack said, "But I'm going to coach you, you're a bull in a china shop."

"Trust me! Trust me!"

"I don't trust you."

"It was you got me into this bloody mess," Grant said with a little ill-humor.

"That's right: everyone's guilty but Papa," said Flack.

Grant laughed but he ruminated with a disagreeable expression. Flack continued, "Oblige me by not putting in any of your cannonballs: you have the diplomacy of an elephant imitating a fan dancer."

"Leave it to me."

"You leave it to me. You're just there to lend weight to my words and to look as casual as possible."

"Leave it to me, leave it to me. Take my word, it's a conspiracy."

"Has March been rogued, or is he the rogue?"

"We'll get it all back. I couldn't understand him always standing there with his hand out, when you say the fella's got millions. I don't want to see 'em. You go, Davie!"

He walked up and down, his hands behind his back. He whirled round, his eyes gay, "You were all wrong, and I was right: she's no spy. She's just a lazy, shiftless, good-for-nothing tramp, she's innocent. Couldn't make head or tail of it myself. He just copied it out of the newspapers. For eleven thousand, two hundred thirty-four dollars could have done it cheaper myself. Some headache.

What a racketeer! He asked for it. He bought us and sold us. What suckers! We deserved it. But I'll get back every cent. Trust me. He hasn't seen me in action. I'll be British. I'll be Simple Simon."

"Don't worry. We'll get it back, if it's what we think. Don't forget—we don't know yet."

"I know. I know. I've an instinct, always had," said he, furiously.

Flack finally persuaded him to go out with him on the Sunday. Grant hung back, wanted to try to see Barbara, who had been coy lately. "And I don't blame her: for conscience-money I'm giving her the dinner service she's been hankering and hinting for—she'll get it. Oh, boy, she's got to make good, too. But she will. I've treated her shabby. She must have sensed it. The womenly woman can sense anything. You can't fool people in the love affair. It's too old; it's an old racket. It's hard to fool people, only not me and you," he murmured and chuckled.

He went to one of Barb's specialty shops and bought a very handsome service, one which had been pointed out by Barbara herself. It was to arrive on Saturday; he would come in on Monday. He kept frowning, "Damn this Sunday trip, you make it. You're a better judge of men than I am; I'm a better judge of women. Look what you thought she was—a spy."

22

On Sunday about eleven David Flack found him dressed but glowering. "What will Barb think if I'm not here just after sending her that? It'll look like a farewell gift. She knows I've been shadowing her."

"Don't hug the telephone, come on. She'll be there tomorrow."

"I'm not so sure."

"Will she leave a Christmas tree like you?"

Grant smiled. "I know; I am her Christmas tree. I don't think she found another like me. Not that James Alexis, not like me. I can prove it by the checks!" He roared with laughter.

They drove swiftly out to Pennsylvania. It was a cool, gray midday, not unpleasant. Grant jingled the money in his pocket, turned his collar, twisted his necktie: "We won't find out nothing from this junket."

"We'll see."

About one o'clock the hired automobile began running up and

down the muddy roads of a new development near the golf course. Some people near by had heard it was called Five Rocks.

"I'll find it, I've an instinct for such things," cried Flack.

Grant anxiously looked both sides of the road. The chauffeur seemed expert. They presently struck a muddy road called Riverside Drive, parallel to a stream, and in a moment Flack had spotted the house. "There's a picture of it in March's office: he's proud of it." There was a green car at the gate. The back was open. Inside, down a crazy-paved driveway half-made, the big stones standing in mud, was a group of people in Saturday morning clothes—March, Hoag, the O'Sullivans, Pantalona. Grant swaggered in with an earnest look, Flack very good-natured behind him. March's fat, short form was bent double over a heavy paving stone which he was lowering into place. His hands were muddy and scratched. He was not able to straighten up till the other greetings were over. His face was very red: the whisky-fed chops swaddling his great jaws flapped and settled back into his city collar. "What are you monkeys doing here?" he said nastily.

Engaging Flack swam forward, hands outstretched, teeth laughing, spectacles shining. He explained everything. March softened, wiped his hands, and said to O'Sullivan, "Butch, let's go into the house for a drink, I'm dry. Have you got a drink, Mary?"

There was some hesitation; then O'Sullivan said with great false heartiness, "We must have something in the pantry. You rustle up something, Mary. But while Mary's finding it—I don't know— We've just moved in here and we don't drink much— Why don't you bring in the rest of the stones, Butch?"

"Well—if you want to be a slavedriver, Butch," said March and went toward the car. He was in his city clothes, with a hat on. He leaned into the back of his car and struggled with another big, flat, gray triangular stone.

"He's a strong man," said Grant, a bit worried.

O'Sullivan laughed. O'Sullivan had the fresh face of a country boy. Pantalona, in a very dark gray suit, with his hands in his pockets and his shoulders bowed, went pacing up and down the grass, swinging his legs round small tufts. He had a slightly pitted dark olive skin and an emotional, cruel, coarse face with sulky eyes, the whole theatrically wicked.

"They say he used to be a gangster," murmured Flack, "and O'Sullivan got him in as revenue inspector. He's a wonderful bookkeeper and his mere appearance makes them come across. He

148

has a weakness, though: they can't send him into lofts. He's afraid of mice."

Grant shuddered and took a pace back, "Keep him away from me, if that's one of the Informants."

Flack said, "Mr. Pantalona is still going to his psychoanalyst, isn't he?"

"Yes," said Pantalona himself, gutturally, glancing up for a second and then looking down again and kicking a clod. "Yes, it'll take him eighteen months more to cure me. You'd be interested to know what he says." He had an unmusical slum voice.

March had staggered up to them and past again with his stone. He bent double once more and carefully placed it into the path. He was redder than before. "How's that, Butch," he gasped.

"That hits the spot," said O'Sullivan. Pantalona looked on morosely and went kicking his heels down the grass patch.

March said sadly, "Maybe I better get the others, three or four more of the damn things."

"Watch that blood pressure," said Flack.

"Oh, he's in training," said O'Sullivan. Pantalona came up to the path and looked curiously at March. His expression softened; it was not quite a smile that hung on his cruel mouth. O'Sullivan smiled gently and continued: "He built this house, Butch did, he put up the fence, he put up the embankment, and he made the barbecue with his own hands."

Seeing Grant's astonished look, O'Sullivan added, "I had gallstones taken out last month. Butch March did all that for me. Paid for the operation, too."

"Why not? Do anything for a friend," said March, gloomily. He went back to the car. His thick shoulders hung on the side of the car as he struggled with the stone. Pantalona stood there looking at this; he smiled at last, outright.

O'Sullivan said in his sweet, low voice, "Butch March insisted on doing this for me. He comes round the place as soon as he gets home. He insisted on doing all this for me. Can't stay away from the place. Like an uncle."

Mary O'Sullivan, who had come out to talk about the liquor, Scotch provided by March, it appeared, stood there laughing and stroking her folded arms, "Hugo March is a good friend, you couldn't ask a better."

"Butch is a good friend," said O'Sullivan.

Pantalona laughed outright. "He built this whole house for O'Sullivan," he said harshly, as if it were news.

149

March dropped another stone into place. Flack was chattering away, as if everyone was in a good humor. Pantalona, distracted, not following the talk easily, walked up and down beside the path March was making, talking to him as he waddled down again. He spoke in a low voice, March panted: it was some business secret. When the third or fourth new stone was in place, they went into the house. In the house, March revived, and showed the plans with an owner's and builder's pride. He opened the window seats to prove they were blanket chests, showed the fastenings, took them upstairs to see the plumbing, the bedsteads. O'Sullivan sat down and let him show his eagerness out. "Very nice, very nice," said Grant, quickly, jingling the money in his pocket; "very clean, very new." He cast little glances at Flack.

When they got downstairs, Flack went up to the little group—O'Sullivan, Mary, Pantalona—and after a few words, when they were all together and before the liquor came, he laughed, "I see your friend Carter does not hit it off with Roosevelt these days."

O'Sullivan laughed blandly, Pantalona not at all. Grant followed up with some remark thrown off the grindstone. March looked serious.

Flack said, "I've always heard Carter was a rigorously honest man, almost a professor in the White House; but I've heard some things about him lately—it may be rumor, or perhaps no man can keep clean in Washington."

"Ought to be some honest men," rumbled Grant.

March said, "Carter's an honest man. I wouldn't let my best friend say a word against him."

Mary brought the drinks. "Thanks, Mary," said March, and took a gulp. O'Sullivan and Pantalona drank fast too. Flack and Grant did not drink.

Grant said, "I don't doubt Carter's an honest man, but probably surrounded by—pickpockets. Man gets a bad name—his secretary takes bribes, he doesn't. Doesn't know about it. Some men have been martyred for their secretary. It's historical, isn't it, Dave?"

"There's always someone who'll pocket it," said March.

O'Sullivan laughed blandly, Pantalona said nothing: they drank.

Flack chattered away, "I know a personal friend of Carter, a professor, a friend of mine, from Rutgers. Didn't know till the other day when I mentioned his name. My friend thinks highly of him, is very indignant at the hue-and-cry after him because he was a friend of the President. Now he's reformed, anyhow. Heard a funny story about him. Probably newspaper terror. Someone after him."

"Think I'll go to Washington myself," said Grant, "think I'll take a trip, see the Secretary of Commerce about—bills of lading —got to see a man—"

O'Sullivan said tranquilly, "If you go next week, look me up; I've got a little place—like to see you."

"Thanks," Grant answered, "thanks, much obliged."

March got up, "Let's get out, get me fresh air, don't want to spend the week ends this way."

"He's a hog for the outdoors," said O'Sullivan.

March said, "I want you to see the barbecue, my friends, just the same, made it myself." He led them to the bank of the stream where a small outdoor fireplace stood, "Not finished yet, but will be by next summer."

"Ought to have it for this summer, don't you think, Butch?" asked O'Sullivan in his soft voice that the breeze blew away.

March looked grave. "Don't see how I can." They looked at the shallow stream and the water-ravaged banks; and then the two friends got into their car and went away in the direction of the golf course.

"Didn't get anything out of that," said Grant.

"March was embarrassed, and O'Sullivan was very curious."

"You think so."

Flack went over the scene with him in detail. Grant cried, "I believe you're right, Dave."

They went right back to town, Grant talking fast and shallow about his financial situation, because his mind was full of the woman. There was no message at the hotel. He kept Flack with him while he went upstairs and routed round, miserably.

"What's the matter with the bloody woman?" When disturbed and grumbling he said " 'ooman." "Is she holding out on me now? Is she angry?"

He telephoned her. The Charles Wagoner said she had gone out.

"When? Where?"

He turned on Flack, "It's your fault. You dragged me out there. I saw nothing worth the trip."

"I thought to get the goods on March was to be your life-object."

"You do it. I'm not going to let the bird fly this time with my birdseed."

"Do you think I have nothing else to do but be your Leporello?"

Grant cajoled and flattered, and Flack gave in, "But for God's sake, don't behave like a dancing bear."

He called Miss Russell next, with "Where's Barbara? I've got to make a confession to her. I've been bad to her"—and made an appointment with Paula for the evening.

In the evening he met Paula alone in the White Bar and babbled for a long time about his relations with March. He did not say, however, how much money he had spent, but "a forchun." Paula said, after a while, "I have a confession to make too, Robbie. I was angry with you because you were seeing Barb when you were seeing me. You treated me like a doormat. You saw me to talk about Barb; and then—you made love to me too."

He said nothing, but watched her coming out with it, "You showed me all Barb's letters and told me how she'd treated you, you said you were through with her too. I let you treat me like a dirty dishrag. That's the introvert side of my nature. I'm an introvert. I'm a masochist. I'm a pervert, I like a man to wipe his shoes on me. I let you do anything you like with me after I found out you were still crazy about Barb. But I knew all the time what you were doing to me. And the more you did it, the more I wanted you. I don't know what it was. I'm a kind of escapist. I'd rather be an old-fashioned woman, let a man walk all over me. And you're such a rough, strong sort of man, you bring that out in a woman. So when March came to me, I told him all I knew. He came to me right away. It was all my fault."

Grant had not expected this. He puzzled, turning it over in his mind. He and Flack had swept out every corner of their memories.

"But March didn't know anything at first—just little bits of lists—well, go on, anyhow—I'm thunderstruck— It never occurred to me— Does she know?"

"Then I thought I'd protect Barb by giving false information to March."

"Protect Barb from what?"

"Why should you ferret and worry into her private life? Isn't her life her own, because you once or twice gave her a check to pay the hotel? You think you buy a woman like you buy a pair of shoes!"

He said roughly, "The information—what is it, true or false?"

152

"I only gave one bit of true information—Barb told it to me—about James Alexis—the man she knew in Canada. I gave Barb the money I got for that."

"March split with you? With Barb?"

She was embarrassed, "Just this once, because it was your fault and we both hated you then; so did Mrs. Jones. You told everyone about Barb. I'm surprised no one else ran to pluck you—you were so downy!"

"Downy! H'mm—downy—and Barb knew?"

"She thought it was only fair she should get some of the money you were paying for information about herself. She gave it, so she should get the money."

He burst out laughing, went on for a few minutes, then, "I can't credit it—from you either. It wasn't clean. Why didn't you come to me?"

"We both hated you then. All fair promise, no cash."

He looked down. The dark, pit-eyed woman went on in a hard contralto, constantly breaking into bitter resonance and sounds like minted coin.

"If you had ever been threatened with a dispossess by a landlord, through unemployment or inability to work, or had dependents who knew nothing of the world you live in, or the way you live, or are trying to stand forward, yourself, without money, from a disagreeable background, you know it's very difficult to keep your poise and hold on to your sense of fair play. Any expedient that will keep you off the street is good management. You knew Barb when she was on the street. At a time like that a crook, a cheat, someone who would cheat your best friend to get you twenty dollars, is himself your best friend. That's the way March looked. Barb appreciated his friendship and help. Help comes from any hand. Beggars don't ask the pedigree of the people who give them nickels."

He waved his hand, "Look, my girl, I am very much surprised. Don't make heartbreaking speeches to me. I've been in the street. I was a poor boy, an orphan. That's why I'm a socialist."

"That's why Barb and I are on the people's side, only Barb hasn't my brains and she doesn't know what it's all about. If you suffer you want something better."

"Never mind that! Barb had only to ask me and she would have had the money if she had behaved properly to me."

He paused and reflected, "But where did he get all the other information? Flack says I told him myself. I know I didn't."

"You went on with it?"

"I spent eleven thousand dollars and more on a wild goose chase."

"What did they tell you?"

He flicked his eyes, "A lot of trash, no doubt. But I don't know—I don't know, my girl!"

They parted in ill humor. Miss Russell had gossiped scurrilously about Mrs. Kent. If Grant wanted her back he must share her with James Alexis. She advised him not to rent an apartment for her: it would only be for the benefit of James Alexis.

23

Grant was now resolute to get the money back from March.

"I'll get it back before Christmas. I'll bleed him—make it a white Christmas for the Marches."

He laughed considerably at this, repeated it many times to Flack.

"A white Christmas—all except the five hundred dollars Barb got. Let her keep it, but it's the last she'll get. She won't take me over again with her white cat and her white rug."

He was very angry with her and filled in the larger part of several days and nights raving to Flack. At home he sat by himself thinking of the kind of life he led, spending money, time, energy on sordid fantasies and scurrilous people: "They live in the sink of the earth and I'm sinking down with them." He had letters from his wife, who was indignant at his long neglect, but who put it so plaintively and modestly that he became tyrannical, and showed her letter to everyone, to his mistresses, and their hangers-on, "Just when I need a comforter, she thinks only of her own headaches. Always was like that."

Christmas was not far off and he was obliged to go to Boston then because of a long-established custom, but the idea of seeing the woman and the nervous, devoted little boy revolted him. He could not face people who lived so far out of his world. With them he must sit silent and chew his lip, gnaw his heart out.

When next he saw Barbara at Manetti's, he knew that her crony had told her everything. She looked pale and, a curious trick of hers, when she most needed make-up, she kept it off. She was ill-dressed. This characteristic puzzled and irritated him, "Just when she ought to try to win me over, she dresses like a village dressmaker!"

But Barbara was for the moment defeated and in his power. He became serene, spent his afternoons and evenings with Mrs. Kent, and devoted himself to recovering the money from March. He bought Barbara a teapot, some clothes, a bracelet she said she needed; he was sorry for her in her defeat. She was not like the many girls he had had, sulky, insolent gougers who were always calling for taxis. Barbara liked to walk round her own district, that is in the district between Fifty-eighth Street and Forty-fourth. She would go as far as Sixth Avenue sometimes on one side but never beyond Madison Avenue on the other side, and then only on certain blocks. That was the walk Grant liked best himself. She had one weakness, she liked to linger at shop windows, "window-shopping," she called it. Grant liked to walk briskly, with his eyes ahead, or talk urgently into her ear. But Barbara stopped at every window in this favored district of hers, and would glance upwards to first and second stories, at famous names. He had long ago become acquainted with the businesses and relative standings of numerous silversmiths, art dealers, and dressmakers. She would observe new names even on the fourth story. Her competent, thoughtful mind was a directory and a catalogue. She would never ask for anything as she trailed along from window to window, or made her observations about Spode, Wedgwood and Sèvres, Chippendale, Hepplewhite, but would become absorbed in some delicate thing, a lace collar, a pair of earrings, and would stand there pondering it, marking its workmanship, estimating its value (the things she liked rarely had price tags on them), saying, "That would look well on me, I suppose, but perhaps that would be better." After five or six stops, Grant, fretting and fermenting at her side, unable to tolerate the lingering any longer, would enter some store gallantly, buy her something she had pointed out. She would seem quite satisfied then, and would only glance sideways at the other shops they passed. If she began again, unable to resist the temptation, he would bundle her into a taxi and take her to some bar.

He told himself that now the chase was ended, his thirst for her had gone. He was just bringing her along, trading on her inert nature. He was well out of it. The trinkets he was giving were "come-ons." He would begin talking some of his goods out of her as soon as she thought him hers. He called upon the mother too, hinted at the "skeletons in Barbara's cupboard." He had received an anonymous letter, perhaps written by some jealous woman friend. This all put him in good humor. Each day, since his reunion with Barbara, he had been calling March, saying in a quiet, troubled manner that he was convinced there was something wrong about one of March's link-men. He was sure Carter himself was an honest man. The money for the wrong information must have slipped out in between.

"If I were you, I'd prod them one after the other and get a bit of it back. After all, you can expose them to their chiefs," he said.

He kept this sort of melancholy grumbling up for a week or so, saying that he was going to Washington to call upon O'Sullivan, he thought, and to have it out with him, for he understood March was in an embarrassing position, but O'Sullivan was a man of the world and could make up his own mind about which of the link-men had taken the money without doing any work. "The detectives are honest, do you think?" And he harped upon O'Sullivan, "He could probably put his hand on the man right away." March made one of his periodical trips to Washington, and at the end of two or three days was back with a check for $500. He said, "I shook him down. Once my suspicions were up, I had my eye on this man from the beginning. They only called on him once. There's a bad egg in every crate."

"Five hundred dollars in only two weeks. I'll get the tea service, too, you'll see, and everything else—what do you bet?" said Grant to Flack.

He had a consultation with Flack every day about the best way to frighten, tantalize, and unsettle March. The money came back very slowly. They began to think that March himself had money difficulties; but how? Grant thought of putting a detective on March's trail, but was dissuaded by Flack. In the end he sent him to snoop around Wall Street himself, and Flack brought back news.

March's wife had run up large debts and March had had to insert advertisements warning suppliers. Claud had stolen $600 from his father's pocketbook. The Fairy was in the country, address unknown—put away, said some; others hinted at a runaway match with Davis. Hoag would not deny; "in itself a bad sign."

"That girl's no good. Take my word," said Grant, rubbing his hands.

"Poor March," said Flack.

"His chickens have come home to roost, eh? Looks as though he plucked me for himself!"

"He has an enormous salary still, he can't be as broke as that."

"Let's get what we can on him and gouge him anyway."

"Obviously there aren't any documents—"

"No, but mental torture, moral suasion, eh? Will he pay up everything, what's your bet? Will I get it back, eh?"

Grant, profoundly interested and exhilarated, walked back and forth, going over their chances. He sent Flack out into the town again to pick up what he could about March. He kept muttering, "The fellow's a gangster, you can start with that. He plucked me, he plucked others, you can start with that. What did he tell us he met that gangster in a place in Brooklyn—what was that fella doing in a place in Brooklyn like that? Them fellas don't let outsiders in."

Flack protested, "One day I dropped into a Yorkville café and saw there a couple of gangsters. I had been to school with them. I started to talk to them and Butch Mahone came up and put his hand on my shoulder and said, 'No one touches the perfesser, here, see?' "

Grant had heard this before; he frowned.

"Butch died years ago. Hardly any gangsters live beyond twenty-four."

"Shoot each other? Don't eat well?"

"Jail fever; short-circuit."

"We'll short-circuit March. Find how to do it; we'll leave him in the dark and empty his pockets. Mental torture. Can we send in something on him—income tax? Do me a favor and spare me this morning, just finding out," he said at the end, seeing Flack getting touchy again.

For a few days, it looked as if, as Grant said, Fate had got March before they could get him. Some family scandal had blown the boy out of house and home, the boy was living high, gambling and drinking. March had had to pay up large debts for his son.

"It's good, it's good, but it's not enough. I'll get my money; and this'll be my bonus; looks as if God's giving me a bonus, eh?" Grant rejoiced.

"Don't talk that way."

"I should worry, my boy; he didn't have a heart for me. I'd feel the same if he did it to you. I'd feel the same. I'll rub it in. What can you expect? Give a boy a father like that, give a girl a father like that—what can you expect? It's asking for it. If my boy is honest and a gentleman, it's because I didn't spoil him, I made him an honest man. I respected his mother, I didn't waste money on him, I said, 'Choose what you want, make your own way, remember, always be honest and make your mother proud of you.'"

But Grant, while talking and walking, kept "Our March Operation" in the front of his mind. His face lighted up whenever Flack told him a new bit of scandal; at deductions he frowned, "I want facts."

He rapaciously enjoyed every detail of March's depravity. As soon as they had got in a full report on the boy's doings, he seized the telephone and asked Hugo March to lunch at the Bankers' Club, "good décor," he muttered aside to Flack. He said, on the phone, with a funereal sigh, "Very worried about this blonde; she's got me in her pocket. I think she's double-crossing me. I've got to have your advice. There's a name I want you to ask about," and he mumbled something, then put down the phone with a clap of laughter.

"He swallowed the bait. Now watch me land him. I'll torture him and he'll think he's being tickled."

They went to the Bankers' Club. There, Grant, without making any reference to March's family troubles, began: "Your brother Peter's boy Johnny is doing very well, I hear, in school. Saw him the other day—he seems like a fine, honest boy: has a future. Eh? What do you think? Has he a future? My boy, Andrew, I don't see much in him, but his mother says he's gifted. I don't know. He don't see much of me. It's better. Let her send him to private school and he'll learn to get along with others. I say coddling a child spoils him. Especially bad for boys. Girls—I don't know: you got to look out for them, never know how they'll turn out. Question is with girls, what son-in-law you pick. That's the only thing a father has to do. Otherwise, some crook gets them— especially men like you and me, marked down for their money. No sharpshooters, eh? Now, I'm not downy—they shan't pluck me, them sharpshooters. . . ."

Said March slowly, "I don't know much about education: I sent Claud to St. Paul's and I've done the best I can. The rest is on the lap of the gods."

"Well, I'm sorry I didn't have more education, but had to get along without it. In another country, different civilization, set of values, more education, I'd have been a better man perhaps. Now in Russia I could have been a commissar, wouldn't have taken any bribes, they don't allow it; first, it corrupts their buyers, their contact men: it gives them a bad reputation. If there was a law keeping me from putting my hand in my pocket, and in other people's too—ho-ho—why, I couldn't do it, I'd be a better man. As it is, others take, why should I abstain? . . . But if I could look back on my life, say as a People's Commissar for Fruit and Vegetables, and think I never touched a ruble not my own —I never even had a ruble my own—I just thought about fruit and vegetables, food for the people—or the American people, if we had American soviets—see, there ought to be some law to save us from ourselves. You and me, men like us, we see others putting their hands in downy pockets, we think we will too. Other guy's a sucker, I won't be. He's offering himself on the chopping block, make mincemeat out of him. That's what we think of. Eh? And there's not a damn thing means anything. You and me—the world's running the other way, should we swim upstream, against the tide? Wasting our bloody breath if we do. And yet what do we look back on, men like us? No family life, everything despicable, contemptible, no sense of honor. We picked our friend's pockets, our son picked our pockets—maybe, though God forbid—that's why I say education is important for a child, and the parents ought to keep their fingers off him; and then, once he's had the best, horsewhip him if he's turned out bad. I'll disinherit that boy if he does anything I'm ashamed of. I did bad things; my money's to see he won't."

March wore a Chinese expression: "Human nature's one thing you can't bet on. You don't know how anyone will turn out; so don't open your big puss too wide till you know what's going to happen to you."

Grant frowned. Then he went on quietly, "Yes, you're right. Take that chap O'Sullivan, looks like a nice person. He has a boy, hasn't he?"

"He has."

"Yes. Now, if that fella, that boy, young O'Sullivan, was to find out anything about his father, that his father wasn't straight, for argument's sake, it might smash him, break him. A big disappointment can ruin a young man's life. . . . Just an example. I took to O'Sullivan myself. Thought he seemed honest, straight-looking fella. You know about that money, those checks I gave you— It's just possible that O'Sullivan was sung a song and dance by the informants he got in touch with and that none of that money reached its target. For argument's sake, why couldn't some man along the line take the money and make up some tale and send it on to me—I don't know! How do I know the whole damn story is true? It don't check up with a lot of things I myself know. It's been bothering me. Here's a girl, I got her out of the gutter, I've taken her about, I built her up, in a way she's my creation; and now I drop her flat and because of some dirty story some fella made up. I feel I ought to recheck, through another source. I feel like facing down those informants, going to O'Sullivan and saying, 'Give me the name of just one of them, just to satisfy me. Do me a favor, just to save my face to myself, satisfy my pride, prove to myself I haven't been taken up to see the etchings—just satisfy me once, I'll say that I haven't been given the runaround—a woman's in this, her happiness is at stake—for suppose she's innocent, a young woman like that, and it came out that I was circulating this story about her, or that someone else was—why it might ruin her, she might sue for damages: it wouldn't look nice.' . . . Now I've got a funny feeling, mere instinct, mere intuition, that I've been sold down the river by some one man. Just to satisfy my pride, save my face to myself, I'm going to O'Sullivan and say, 'Tell me the name of one fella, I trust you all right, and I'll go to him and see what he has to say for himself.' How do you think that would be? You know him, how do you think I should put it?"

After a moment's silence, March said, "Well, I don't think you're right; you don't know O'Sullivan. He wouldn't stand for hankypanky from his informants."

"No, but I've got this hunch. I'm an old stock-market gambler, I like hunches. Grant me my hunches. Humor me—" he said, grinning graciously—"I'm too old to spoil, I've got this bee in my bonnet and I won't be satisfied till I've paid my pride this little bonus— I just want to see O'Sullivan—you can be there—and ask him, 'Do me this favor, name one of your informants and let me satisfy myself.' There," he said, flinging wide a great palm, "that's a naïve request, but I stick to it. I don't like to think I've been sold down the river. Keeps me awake nights."

March said, "If you've got this bee in your bonnet, I'll see O'Sullivan. I know him better than you. I'll sound him out, whether he knows this informant of his very well, and what his character is. And I'll tell him that you're suspicious, too; and perhaps O'Sullivan will get after this character."

"Yes, do that," cried Grant enthusiastically, smacking him on the back as they rose, "just to humor me."

He rushed up to Flack's home as soon as the market closed, and discussing the campaign, thrusting his chin in and out, his face smoking darkly, told him what he had said to March.

"How do you like that? Do you think I did it right? Do you think he smelled anything? Maybe he did. Let him. I think we'll get something out of him."

When he got his next check, which was for $750, Flack exulted. But Grant said, "Always paying back half. Does that mean a split that he can't get back, or does he think he'll get out of this with at least fifty per cent profit?—And did you hear any more about his boy?"

"Yes, they say he's left the city."

Grant rubbed his hands and walked up and down, his eyes sparkling. "Looks like the hand of God, eh? You can't get away with everything all the time. Give a boy a father like that, and he'll turn out bad. Serve him right."

"Grant, have some pity."

"Not for him! Telling me that rigmarole. Every penny! I want to know Edda's opinion. I'm coming home with you."

"Edda thinks it's a swindle, but he won't pay in full."

His face became overcast, "She does, hey? Well, I can only try. I'll give him waking nightmares, anyhow."

Grant waited till the daughter Edda had come home from work, and the two men sat down to eat, asking her advice, as they put the finishing touches on the "next day's play."

Flack said, "Ask him for the details, drive it home hard."

They telephoned March at his Connecticut home at six-thirty, and arranged a conference at his office the next morning. Grant went alone to March's office. He wore a depressed expression this morning and began his spiel in a low, earnest voice.

"Hugo, I've been having Flack make up my accounts for the year and I'm depressed, very depressed, to see what I spent for that damn blondine. I want to put it down in red and black, and learn it by heart and chew it over, so it will be a kind of lesson to me. I have to look out for women, always been my weakness. Now, I've got a kind of chart and what I notice, I have no details. To save my self-respect, I'd like to have a few details on the various bits of information your informants—I mean the regular ones, not that one fellow who was the weak link in the chain—gave me from time to time. Now this fellow Carter, is he your personal friend? I don't want you to tell any tales out of school. I mean, does he know your wife, your daughter, your son? Or is he a business acquaintance, one of your clients? It's unimportant, that's why I'd like to know. I'm like a man who shuts the door after the horse bolted. Ha-ha. It isn't funny: it depressed me very much.

I felt myself all over and thought, 'Am I getting sick or silly? Am I getting old? How old is this Carter? Why would he give me this information? Is he a man my age?' Perhaps if I went to him and told him the inside story, he might laugh at me—but he might take pity on me and say, 'Look, I'm sorry you've wasted so much time and money and I'll clear it up for you once and for all.'

"What I want is a line of demarcation: what she is and what she isn't. Now I'm establishing a plan of my own, and where I lack details, I thought of going to the people concerned and throwing myself on their mercy, saying, 'I'm an old fool, a woman bought me and sold me, now I'm through with her, but do one favor and I'll do you one any time: what is the truth? Tell me, so I can sleep at night.' Now, can you give me an introduction to Carter? And I don't care if you say, 'This is the sucker who fell for that blonde spy.' I'll see him and I'll tell him, Hugo March and his friends, Arthur Pantalona and Francis O'Sullivan, took my money and arranged for me to get a lot of information and saved my neck, and I'm grateful. Now, when was the first date you saw Carter for me? Then there was a later date, when Carter arranged for his Number Two man to abstract a file for him, wasn't there? So if you could give me a vague idea, January 17, May 5, I could include them in my letter to Carter, when I say I'm your friend, I'm the man in question.

"Oh-ho, don't think I'm angry. I'm not. It taught me a lesson. It's a blessing in disguise. Now what is the name of his Number Two man and this fellow, the embezzler who needed one thousand bucks—perhaps he's the one who bamboozled us, eh? No: you said you only saw him once—but give me his name at any rate and I'll speak to Carter when I see him. What name, when, where, you know, what time of day. I'll pin this fellow down. That's the weak link in the chain. Eh? I'm ashamed and I'm shameless. I'll go to Carter and confess everything. You just give me the names and dates and I'll go and say, 'I'm the one, I'm the sucker, I'm the one who paid out eleven thousand, two hundred and seventy-eight dollars for a blonde spy.' Eh? So just give me Carter's Number Two man and the embezzler, to begin with."

March looked sternly and thoughtfully at him. He said emphatically, "Perhaps I can sympathize with you: no one wants to be made a monkey of. But I suggest you let me handle this.

Carter's a big man, wouldn't listen to you, your blonde is only Number Seventeen thousand, eight hundred and forty-three to him. I'll give you names and dates if you still want them, but I think I can guarantee some satisfaction about that embezzler, for example. Now, why don't you leave this thing to me? I know the parties and I have private information it would not be fair to give you. With your names and dates you'd get no farther, while I, without names and dates, can push the fellow to the wall. And I'm beginning to think you're right about that embezzler, perhaps he did ditch me. You can't touch that type without getting into trouble. They're thieves. Why do business with thieves? A man like me comes along with a foolish request about a blonde, he thinks I've gone crazy, and he waits for the plums to fall into his mouth. So unless you're hankering for a list of names and dates, let me do the arithmetic for you and I'll guarantee to do better than you."

This negotiation went on for some minutes; a few days later, March sent Grant a check for $750, "in connection with the subject of our conversation the other day."

This banked, Grant and Flack found hilarity and profit in concocting "the new play," and on the following day, Grant, who had been showing friendly concern, tenderness, and hospitality to March, took him out to lunch and discoursed as follows: "Getting this money back from the bottomless pit has done something to me, made me avaricious. I'm beginning to feel that there was more than one crook in this affair—and I don't blame you, I blame myself. It was my blonde, not yours, and if I could be fooled I have to grant that you could be fooled, about the money. Now, anyone who pays out eleven thousand, two hundred and seventy-eight dollars for chasing a woman he's already got must strike a man temporarily short as a fat goose ready for the plucking. Now, how about this detective, friend of Goodwin's in Washington, this Morales? Now, that's your friend, this James is friend of Goodwin, but James is friend of Morales—I found out—"

"Well—" said March.

"One of those fellas might be dishonest. Now I'm going to take the trouble to send Flack to Washington to find out where James and Morales stationed themselves, a regular itinerary, and it's only my right, those fellas are obliged to send in typed reports every day, and I saw no typed reports, but those typed reports must be in their offices, so I'll send and take a look and say, 'Do me a favor, tell me where you sat or stood or walked while you were taking my money. If you can't tell me, I'll get my lawyer to look into it, unless you can furnish a detailed report that I can check on.' Because I can check on this and I will. It's become a sort of hobby with me, but I feel so humiliated at being taken in this way by that blonde, and now by those fellas, that to save my pride, I must get a complete picture. When I get that complete picture down in black and red, I'll hang it on my bedroom wall and it'll be a blessing in disguise. Now I don't doubt your friend Morales is all right, for he's a friend of Carter, but this other one—probably some man down on his luck would be glad to do anything and say anything for a few ten-dollar bills, eh?"

"Now, it's a good thing you mentioned this to me," said March. He lighted a cigar and leaned back in his chair, looking at Grant through the blue smoke, "I'm going to Washington this afternoon and I'll see my friend Morales if you like this evening, fit it in somehow, to oblige you; I don't see how you keep all this up. It would give me the heebie-jeebies. But I don't care what you do with your life or your money, and I'll do this for you. I'll check up with Morales about this fellow James. If you think James took your money—how much was it?—I'll check up and make him disgorge if I can. But if he's a crook and he's spent the money too, what will we do?"

"I don't like people to take me for a Simple Simon from Green Goods County because I'm fond of a woman."

"That would put us all in Green Goods County."

"Just to prove to the fellow he called the wrong number this time, I'd do my best to get it out of him even if he's starving, and has two paralytic children and an ailing wife," Grant laughed. He smacked his pocket.

"I can't say I disagree with you. I wouldn't coddle a thief."

Three days later Grant received back the amount of the checks he had paid to Goodwin for "James." He received this amount from March. Flack went over to see March, after a conference with Grant, and said what had been agreed upon, but in his own charming, friendly manner, "I don't suppose, Hugo, you got that money back from the poor devil. You must have paid it out of your own pocket. I feel bad about it. You know Grant, he feels insulted and injured and he's out for vengeance, but it does seem a shame for you to pay this money out of your own pocket. I know you can afford it, but why?"

To which March replied, "I know, but Grant feels he's been duped and he feels sore. And though I didn't start him off on this crazy track, yet I was with him in it, and it's a question of honor, you see. I have my code."

Flack returned shortly to Grant, who shouted, "By George, this Code is going to do overtime for us!"

The next "play" was to have reference to the Canadian contacts; the following one, to James Alexis, now a friend of Grant, and reported to be a friend of Yves Troland; and the third was to be an appeal to the Code.

All this took months, but in the end, March was unable to resist the long campaign of concert of the men, which he only partly understood, so that after eight months' labor, Grant was reimbursed by March to the extent of $10,300. The $500 given to the blondine Grant said he would leave with her, but in the end began plaguing March for that too. It took him another year to retrieve the near thousand dollars which remained, but he got it all. Flack at last went to March and said with sincerity, "It was unnecessary for you to give Grant that last five hundred dollars—I feel sure you paid it out of your own pocket because Grant howled so much. I should like to know how much this mad blonde adventure of his cost you personally."

March kept his Chinese face and murmured, "I have my code; it looked as though I took him for a ride."

Flack said enthusiastically, "It's my fault, perhaps; he's my friend, I introduced you in the first place. I didn't warn you he's crazy."

"You warned me he's crazy. I didn't get the signals right. And you must have warned him I was a moron. Or you should have if you do anything for that salary of yours."

"What salary?"

March laughed cheerlessly, "You're crazier than either of us. What are you jackaling around for a wolf like that for?"

"I love the guy: he's my brother."

"He's your ——." March poured out two glasses of whisky and put them on the desk. He eyed his and smiled slowly at Flack.

"He's a maverick: he's come a long way and he's got no code. The blondine has got him. I don't figure where you think you fit in in his scheme of things."

24

Barbara, now Grant's constant companion, had a strange medley of friends, floaters, promoters, "representatives," "agents," people who had once been in Hollywood or would go next month, or who had been in Berlin or Moscow, people whose political views were based on information, intimate, sound, personal from a "friend-of-mine" in Kiev, a friend-of-mine whose eyes were torn out by Bela Kun personally, a friend-of-mine in Lyons, France, brother-in-law in Lodz. Vociferously, insistently, persuasively, these intimates of history held forth in the White Bar and Manetti's and the Silver Beach at Grant's expense. They were busy all day about something mysterious, rarely disclosing their business addresses; they also did business at night. Some were customers' men getting orders in those haunts of boredom and perversity and small talent that get the curious on their quarterly jaunt from the suburbs and New Jersey. Some were shady business men, in the black market, full of schemes for evading currency and tax laws. Their women repeated their chatter, always with something missing, so that it sounded like talk in a madhouse. These men did business in bars, houses of ill-fame, and on the sidewalk in the fashionable district. Some had as their office a desk, an automobile, or a hotel bedroom. Yet they lived better than workers or middle-class people and were always seen in expensive restaurants. They traveled by plane and Pullman, at times had money. Among them were self-introduced majors and counts, an occasional General X and Lady Y: an international scum which declared itself well-born and excellently educated, rich, but just now out of luck, thanks to Hitler, or even farther back—the Soviets.

Grant, still a solid man and a newcomer, was sucked into this circling scum. They surrounded him with affection and filled his life. They were ready to serve him and Barb, his favorite, in any way. They killed his boredom by opening his eyes to practices he had never heard of. He smiled, blushed, and eagerly listened. Vice was understood; it was, to them, maturity. It was their life-blood; it gave them food.

In this setting, Grant and his blondine began to breathe air more impure, and yet to have a kind of suburban home-life together. They were a recognized couple. They had the same friends, resorted to the same eating places, and after the first two months when Grant was still busy with Flack on the "March

Operation," Grant and Barbara began to spend most of their evenings together. Sometimes, Miss Russell was there, and when she was there, they made up a quartet with James Alexis. He, at least, was no mean dubious character. He brought back to Grant the glitter of his former business life, true international commercial life and society. Alexis, an extremely corrupt old man, avid of depravity, laughed at Grant for his ignorance of variations in what Alexis called The Game. Grant was glad to degenerate. He felt a new sense of maturity, smiled at his former innocence. He had worked so hard, he thought, that he had grown almost old without knowing any fun. He often talked about his innocence, in their hours of flagrant vice. He was boundlessly flattered to be a partner of the rich Alexis in any undertaking. It now pleased him that Barb had been the mistress of Alexis.

Alexis astounded Grant. He was sixty-five, steel-gray with a wiry Vandyke beard and bloodshot, quick, gray eyes. He had, like Grant, risen from poverty, and now had begun to feel his age. He spent much of his time in gay company, though he was, like Grant, still scurrying from one capital to another, and even changing countries, pursuing interesting speculative lines of business, protecting his investments, and caring for his funds abroad. He had a wife and grown family somewhere, but lived the same life of bars, taxis, and bedrooms that Grant did. At the same time, his business knowledge, advice, and mental energy were remarkable. He and Grant discussed the stock market, and political news, every day in quick snatches in between meeting their women. As for the women, Alexis would take up with almost any woman, but he was Miss Russell's "friend."

During these months, Grant scarcely saw Flack except to employ him as a friendly go-between to Hugo March. The money had slowly come in. Grant had used the name of Alexis to frighten March about the alleged bribes to the Royal Canadian Mounted Police. This money, too, had come back. There had been no bribes.

Grant no longer wished to marry the blonde. On the contrary, he wished she would marry again, and so reduce his expenses. He realized that he had been in the grip of a furious, lascivious passion, and now had cooled down. He even regarded Barbara as rather a poor little thing, useful enough and suited to his tastes, one who would do anything, but poor enough, not the best kind of woman he had ever had. He began to laugh about her to his friends, and to say what a miracle longing was, it involved you consciously, of course, but unconsciously, too, with people you knew were no good. He and Alexis exchanged partners sometimes. Grant was pleased: he had beaten a costly weakness. And he chuckled to Flack, "She thinks I'm still in love with her. She thinks she can count on me. That partly explains the way she goes to work on me—thinks I'm still hers for the plucking." At other times it angered him that she was so obtuse about his dead passion. "Bloody 'ooman still thinks she can twist me around her finger. Well, I'm weaning her. I've got her down to forty dollars a week! From forty thousand dollars per annum to two thousand eighty dollars—good business, eh? And, you know, I think she's a bit in love with me now—maybe regrets what she's lost, eh? First time she ever found a sucker like me. Alexis is a night club man. Now her eyes are opened, she thought she was on plush for life, and she let me slip through her fingers. I would have married her, I was eating out of her hand, I knew what she was, too. Now, she's sorry. It's too late, though. She had me. Now she's lost me. I'm looking for a better woman. That's what I want. I got into her clutches. Not her fault. I take the blame, too. Now I know better. No more bloodsuckers. I'm going to get a girl with good taste, doesn't waste money, mustn't cost me above four thousand dollars a year, not that, a working girl is better, work half time; costs, say, only $1.40 extra? That's a fortune to a worker and you're doing her a favor; she can help out her mother or father. It's a poor family. You're their friend. Someone needs you. You go there and eat on Saturday, Sunday night, they don't ask questions, Mother cooks for you. Home food. And they go to trouble, oh-oh, my boy, they get in a chicken, some wine, oh-ho, my boy, that's the way to live, only the poor are generous. And she's grateful for one per cent of the money that bloodsucker wants. You're right, my boy; keep away from the spoiled girls, the parasites."

He became trivial, relating some of Barb's advantages, "I don't have to work out my sentence with Barb, but that girl is all sweetness, dripping with honey, no one ever knew me like Barb; but that's all over. I can't be a slave of weakness, can I?"

He confided in everyone. One day when he was repeating this, Flack was silent for a moment, and then broke out, "Don't you ever think of anyone but yourself, Robert? I've got troubles, now, and so has Edda. She's in despair. She wants to get married and she thinks you're wasting my time."

"She's got a boy friend?"

"She had, but something happened."

"Is that so, you don't say," cried Grant. "You mean she—well, well, that's bad. Sorry to hear that. Sorry, very sorry. She'll get over it, my boy. I should know. Love is my business, my part-time business. Look at this blondine affair. I thought last year she had me by the neck. She certainly had me by the heartstrings. And look at me now. A complete cure. I'm just paying her forty dollars—last week I got it down to twenty-five dollars—she's looking very blue this week—just paying it for old acquaintance. Easing her out of it. I got over it. Very sorry. Poor girl. Well, hope she didn't get into any trouble—eh? I mean emotional, of course. H'm. Love, you know, no knowing where it's going to lead you. Got to pay for it. It's a human relation. We forget that. It's a human relation, my boy. Even with that blondine. Somehow I feel she didn't get out of it so well. She certainly seems to love me now. Too late, eh? Bolt the gate after the horse has bolted. Well, she learned her lesson. Too late for her, though. As for me, I'm free, out of it—a free heart; and now I'm looking to lock it up again. But this time, a different sort. A working girl, some idea of values. You give this other one something constructive, she doesn't understand, only wants to sting you. What is the meaning of vision?—nothing to pay, it's mine, it's yours, we enjoy it together, it's democracy. She doesn't understand, only wants to know, 'What's my percentage?' I want to meet a non-profit-taking woman, understand me. Has some vision, some character, isn't a one-way woman."

He liked this, repeated it to everyone again, even when he went out with Alexis and the curiously self-announced "Brauner, Arthur," man of mixed breeds, and business without a business address, and friend of Barbara, a low-bred, cruel-looking man. Grant at times reproached her with the low company she now kept, said it would justify certain slanders he had heard about her, but she would only explain about any queer-looking individual, that, "He is Jim Alexis' friend, I can't offend Jim Alexis' friend"; but she seemed to find pleasure in the company of "Brauner, Arthur." When he fretted, "Who are these people? They have no money!" she would exclaim, "You are more snobbish than I am and I was brought up knowing nothing! You taught me to be a progressive, though I don't think friendship has anything to do with politics, but I try to see things your way and now you say, 'They are poor.' They speak my language, I can explain myself to them. You never listen to me."

She would say they were all "socialists" too, although in all the torment and fever of their lives, in all their hours of drunkenness, depression, and the love-fit, no one ever heard them talk about socialism, no one ever heard them mention anything but connections and money. There were not even the "Marxists" he had known in café society, they were something seedier, a swarm of parasites. He never believed that they were radicals, but it soothed his conscience to hear them flatter him, and the wicked Alexis, by saying so.

Sometimes he felt it intolerably shabby. The woman was strong and young, her ways were too much for him. But he said to himself, chuckling, "It is my vice," and he went on drinking deeply and greedily of this vice. If he did not have her, he felt he was getting old and that love was turning its back on him forever. In a fit of terror, he would cry to any one of the low company, "If that happened, I'd cut my throat, I'd have nothing to live for. I swear it."

He had to spend longer hours every day and much more money covering the ravages of his nights upon his great, healthy body. Meanwhile, Barb only got a little worse in complexion. She stayed in bed and only had her parties when she felt fit. She had other lovers and was able to keep everything from Grant. Grant worked in the mornings as hard as his age permitted him to and felt in the afternoon that he had done his work for the world, now he could enjoy himself, "And I don't even want to ask any questions: a man who's wandering in the desert and sees an oasis doesn't run to a chemist for an analysis of the water. He'll drink brackish water."

Grant had to go to Boston on business and found the house intolerable. He would never take an interest in Andrew: the woman had only conceived in order to tie him down. After having spoken scarcely a word to either of them, he hurried off to New York again, counting those hours all lost.

Barb found the air of town depressing and went away, with her mother, from time to time, for short holidays for which Grant paid. He was not sorry to see her go, but sought moral regeneration at these times. He spent his serious moments with Miss Livy Wright and other women not so bad as Barb, and his declarations of love and their responses gave him the illusion of freshness, innocence and even early youth at times. He had, in fact, retained vivid memories of his fresh adolescence and when he was not tired, in moments of real gaiety, with a woman who still believed in him somewhat, he was able to forget the foulness of his years. At these moments, during Barb's absences, he thought that one day he might reform. These dreams enabled him to pay Barb's bills without too much murmuring. He said, "It's worth it, it's worth it: it's a tonic not to see that 'ooman."

In February, 1943, Barb went to Florida with her mother and put up at a very chic hotel. She had taken with her a rather more expensive outfit than usual. When she had been away two weeks, her mother telegraphed Grant as follows:

BARBARA DOWNS MARRIED THIS MORNING TO CHURCHILL DOWNS THIRD, SURPRISE TO US, ALL VERY HAPPY. MARY JONES.

25

In the course of the day, Grant was able to discover that Downs had means, was forty-two years old, and had lived with his mother and a maiden sister in Riverdale until the day of his marriage with Barbara. He was an aircraft engineer and had recently moved from New York to Washington. Barbara had met him for the first time during this Florida trip. He was the man who figured in her photographs, a blond, tall, thin-featured man, smiling agreeably. Grant ran around to the Goodwins' and told them the news—they had it before him. He then gathered all his friends in the White Bar and told them the news. He ran to the Flacks' apartment and told how he had been deceived. She had once more, said he, married for alimony. One of these days she would tread on a scorpion, that was certain. He loved her, and she had deceived him. He had been going to marry her, divorce that so-and-so in Boston, and marry her, but she had not given him time—and how many times was this she had let him down? Why did he bother his head about her? He had other consolations. He had found a fine woman, the right one, and this time he gave a description of Livy Wright. He called up Miss Wright and begged her to come to town from Albany, where she was visiting—he had something special to say to her, having had a great shock and needing her understanding and help.

The voice came close to his ear, "Is it that yellow woman

again, that blondine? I bet it is. Don't bother lying to me, bully-boy. What did she do?"

"She got married and all the time that blond Capone has been living on my money. She went to Florida to get married on my money."

The woman at the other end laughed good-naturedly, "You don't know what a weight that is off my mind, if you want to call it that. I'll come to New York, bully-boy, and then you can tell me your sad story."

But he had to wait two days for her. In the meantime, the idea that the blonde had laughed at him, used him and despised him, bit into him like poison. He had no rest. He sought refuge with others. He felt poor and cheated. He told each one that his life was a wilderness with not one live plant in it but the woman before him. He spoke of marriage and love; he wept. Through talking of love and misfortune, he came to think of Mrs. Coppelius, whom he had not seen for months. He telephoned her, taxied to her hotel, and sat for a long time with her in the lobby, dined with her, tried to induce her to come upstairs with him, "While I put in a long-distance call to the mother, an old witch whom I'm perhaps wronging; I have had, at times, very sad letters from her, complaining of her daughter's ways."

Mrs. Coppelius told him that in his absence she had once more returned to her husband, but could not endure his gay infidelity. Said the husband, "You must take me as I am or live alone."

Mrs. Coppelius said to Grant, "You have been so kind to me, Robbie, that if it had not been for the few hours we spent together, I don't know what I should have been thinking of. I know you're not a marrying man: you are afraid women will hurt you. It's too late now. I can't even see into next week, there are clouds as thick as fog, it seems to me. I want to see through but I am choked with those clouds. I can't understand it. I don't think about it, but I think of you and I let it pour over me like a white sea, rushing at me and swallowing me up. But you are there, and save me. When I do that, I don't see the white wave and I don't think of despairing. I keep my mind fixed on you, stupidly, because at other times I look at buses and think, if I ran under suddenly, the driver wouldn't stop. Then I think of what he would feel and how he would have to go to court."

He grabbed her arm, plump, white beneath the short black sleeve, "Believe me, believe me, I know. Listen to me. I thought my heart was broken. I said to myself, 'Myra understands me.'

I've had a great shock. That 'ooman's a Capone. I want a shoulder I can cry on. I said to myself, 'Myra has had trouble. That is where I will find refuge. She's my oasis. Perhaps I've done wrong to her. I've neglected her.' I'm no good to myself or anyone. Who wants me? I said to myself, 'I'll make it up to Myra. When the war's over and Europe's at peace again, Myra and I will go there, we'll go to Rome or to my French farm—we'll go just where we please. Why do I bother myself with the other cattle? Myra has always been the woman for me. I don't know myself. I cheat myself. I put my hand in my own pocket. Myra's been hurt by her husband, I've been hurt by the cattle. . . . Now I want a mother, sister, and sweetheart. I'll give up business—business is closing down, the Liverpool Cotton Exchange is closing down, cotton is going to be harvested by machines, Russia's going to best us—new methods are coming—Government is going to control everything, no free market, no business—why worry? I'll go to Europe with Myra and build up something—we'll lead a constructive life.' "

She listened to his babble, kissed him, and gave him the consolation he looked for, the first time in many months. Before he went, once more flurried, anxious to get her gone, she kissed him on both cheeks, touched his hair and said, "I would have loved you, but I knew you had no patience with such a thing."

He protested, said he would telephone her, rushed her off, before the eleven o'clock newscast. As soon as she had gone, he turned on the radio and sat down with *The New Republic* while a sonorous male voice spoke in his ear. That done, he telephoned two young women to make appointments for the following afternoon, and wrote a letter to his wife to say that, as he had had a considerable shock in business, he would be unable to make the promised trip to Boston; but to see that the boy was warmly dressed as the weather was getting very cold; and to ask his teacher whether he was not lazy at school, or whether he needed a tutor. He asked after the boy's drawing lessons and requested the mother not to coddle the child, as he did not care for neurotics in the family.

He passed several days quite busily, telling his troubles over and over to all kinds of hangers-on and business friends, drank, ate, and made love more than usual, gluttonously "forgetting," as he put it. He had a surge of energy. He had a true story to tell, something to live for. As he now passed his life in a wilderness of lies, he enjoyed having something authentic to tell and to weep over. He burst in on their small lives with a great story. He thought it would make a good play. But he had no one to write it. The poet Burgess and David Flack had, at present, no money, and were too busy earning their bread. Flack, for example, was trying to sell a set of articles; Burgess did not even answer Grant's letters.

Grant said, "They live only for themselves."

The little dark-haired Myra Coppelius at once intrigued and bored him with the trouble she gave. She loved her husband and cried over him; she loved Grant and would not visit him. Grant told Betty Goodwin all about the affair, saying, "I ought to keep out of trouble, eh? But trouble attracts me. But she's a neurotic. Keeps me at arm's length. First visits me, then keeps me at arm's length; no logic to it. Now with you, there are not problems, it's a yes or no. You're a friend to a man, Goodwin doesn't know the bargain he's got. You understand me."

"Yes, I understand you. You don't understand me, perhaps."

"Look, do me a favor, let me confide in you, my dear good woman. Let's talk about me, I need consolation."

"Well, go on, tell me about Myra Coppelius, then."

"H'm, trouble ahead: change my course, eh? Steer for Livy, what's your recommendation?"

"To go to hell, for once, Robbie."

He burst out in a joyous laugh, throwing back his head, his sweet clear eyes gleaming, "Oh, ho, ho, for you I'd go to hell and never complain; and for the other 'ooman—too!"

He saw Myra Coppelius the day after this conversation. She bored him, spoke of her husband who once more invited her back, but laughing up his sleeve at her. She said, "What am I to do? I missed my way in life somehow."

Grant spoke hastily, "Cheer up, let me be your guide, you won't go wrong with me. Now you're a beautiful woman and you don't dress right. You want a nice apartment, a fur coat, some diamond bracelets, a new dress, you want a little car, then you'll find the right man, maybe it will be me. Eh? You get yourself a little car now and I'll pay for it, just to show I'm in earnest. I spent eighty thousand dollars on that cow, I can spend two or three thousand on you. Now you go shopping for a neat little secondhand car, you can go out in the country for the week end, take me, we'll see how we get on together: it'll be my earnest to you, I'm serious, I'm not like that husband of yours, get a beautiful woman and let her live in a one-room flat in a cheap hotel. I'll show you I'm different." He talked fast and almost involuntarily, sitting by her side and embracing her.

"I don't want a car, Robbie. What good is a car to me?"

"Look, my darling, I had a woman once, Laura, she twisted me round her little finger, but there was a reason and I'm looking for another Laura. You're the only one I ever saw made me think Fate had put her finger on me again, I saw you and I thought, That's the one, but you always had me baffled with this husband of yours, I love my husband you kept saying. Now what am I to do? Break up a marriage? Now, as an earnest, you get this little car, bring me along to approve it and I'll pay for it, we'll take little trips. I'll see how well you can drive first, though, got a wife and children depending on me—even if I get rid of them, can't leave them like that, go up in a puff of smoke on a Sunday on the Parkway!"

When he stopped, abstractedly running his hand along her arm, and looked broodingly into space, she said, "I can drive, very well, I have been driving since I was ten; if you mean it. But I don't know if you mean it."

"My darling, would I lie to you? What would I ask you to do a thing like that for? I give you my word, you buy a little second-hand car, I'll come over, approve it, and then we'll go out for week ends together and we'll find romance; I'll forget all those— 'oomen—you'll forget that husband. When the war is over, we'll go to Europe and try to build a new life, do something for someone who needs it. We'll take the car along. We can travel all over Europe, see some place and say, That's where we'll settle."

Myra Coppelius was startled by his proposition, at first doubtful, but taken by it, because it was so unusual. She said at last, "Oh, Robbie, if you mean it—"

He frowned. "Would I give my word and not do it? You don't know me. You get the car, and I'll see if you're serious. I don't want to start to get romantic about a woman who isn't serious. I don't even know you'll divorce your husband. I've got something to lose, too."

She was amazed, saying, "But you've changed completely, Robbie. It's a complete change of attitude."

"It was that blonde cow did it; I wasted too many years and too much money on a cheat like that. You have to save me from myself."

"I love you, Robbie. It would break me if you let me down now."

175

He smiled and began to glow, "You're a dangerous woman: you don't know what you do to me; if you want me you've only got to hold me."

All this conversation had been in a quiet bar where Myra felt at ease. She was so moved by him now, though, that she yielded to his fervor and went to his apartment for his "little tea and little chat." The preluding had taken some time and Grant, while in his flat, suddenly remembered that that night Livy Wright was coming to town again. He dismissed the dark little beauty hastily, muttering, "I hope I haven't hurt you, I want to be by myself, I want to think things over. I've got to adjust myself to this new life." And so he induced her to leave the place in time. But this evening, cold, very early spring, without snow or wind, Livy telephoned to say that she did not feel well enough to come to town; and he must wait a few days for her.

Grant decided to "celebrate his birthday" once more. Whenever he felt rebuffed by the world, he celebrated his birthday, when he became automatically the center of life. He called up several people and arranged a meeting in the Little Bar for an hour or two later. Without Livy, Mrs. Lawrence, or Mrs. Kent (now Mrs. Downs), he felt lost. The poor young women of his acquaintance were never invited to his expensive bars nor allowed to meet his better-living company. The Goodwins, of course, would be there with their lawyer Walker, now an intimate of his and with whom he was in on several deals.

He told them that it was really his birthday and a woman was giving him a car, as a gift, for love: at last he was really loved. She was a rich woman, said he, but he had insisted on a second-hand car. He made sure that this news reached Peter Hoag. In the evening, later, he telephoned Myra Coppelius and honied her, telling her, above all, not to forget the car, that was his pledge, that was the thing that was to bring them together. By that he would see if she was in earnest about remaking his life for him, "You buy one, get me to look it over and I'll give you a check."

The woman promised to do so as soon as she could; and he urged her, "Tomorrow, darling, tomorrow, I can't wait to take a ride with you."

"But you want me to shop around, don't you?"

"Oh, yes, but hurry, hurry, I can't wait to be happy, sweetie."

The following morning he received an express letter from the woman, a very small, scented, flowered card, telling him how much she loved him and signed only with her initials, M.C. He put it in his breast-pocket and kept taking it out, when no one was present, to read it again. He called up numerous girls this day, because he felt in bouncing health.

26

Grant meanwhile feared for his son Gilbert. The battle of Tunis was now raging and active war in the Pacific had begun. Gilbert himself kept asking for his removal to active service. Grant went often to Washington and made use of some of Peter Hoag's contacts. Luck favored him, for Gilbert was transferred at about this time to the Signal Corps in Washington Boulevard, in Culver City. Here he worked out continuities for instruction films and for the first time seemed enthusiastic. He saw a "great future" for these films after the war, not only for factories and schools but for teaching American techniques abroad. Grant was perfectly happy and went round celebrating. He now saw friends with the idea of getting Gilbert transferred to Astoria, New York; and in the meantime wrote Gilbert pleasant letters promising to put up money for him in these technical films after the war. For the time being he was himself interested in them.

Meanwhile, the crowd of parasites were ridiculing the old economical set of rooms he lived in in the hotel and urged him to live in better style. Black market days had begun. He bargained for a suite in the *Pickwick Hotel*, which he heard of through a friend of Miss Russell. It was a place in the middle Sixties, just off Fifth Avenue, east side, still fairly expensive and with an ornate bar, several approaches, anterooms and lobbies and with a restaurant. He settled for a rent of $245 monthly and reduced the cost to himself by offering the occasional use of room and bath to Walker, now a busy lawyer with the easy-money crowd. The room offered was to be Gilbert's room when he came to town.

Grant employed a respectable old English lady, Mrs. MacDonald, who, in return for good quarters and in consideration of his frequent absences and of her frailty, agreed to work for only $30 a month. He then made arrangements for Alfred Goodwin to use one of the spare bedrooms when he wanted to spend the night away from home, at a small rental. The apartment consisted of two sets of bedrooms and bathrooms, joined by a long hall inside the apartment, and separated by a large extravagantly furnished lounge or living room with a dining room across the hall

177

adjoining the kitchen. The place had been taken on a very long lease by a friend of James Alexis, a South American, who had gone to a Madison Avenue decorator and picked out anything that gleamed or was burnished, such as silks, metals, tortoise-shell, porcelain, glass, and put all this together in the apartment. Later, this rich bazaar was sublet to a variety of tenants.

The place was spacious, and Grant was at first very happy here. He had lost the blonde, he had begun a good life. He sometimes saw himself as living in this luxurious place for years and years, with Gilbert in the room at the end. He did not really intend Gilbert to go into films after the war. Gilbert had studied agriculture at Ohio State College and knew everything from the composition of soils to sowing by aeroplane and beekeeping; he showed a particular aptitude for beekeeping and had turned out six hundred pounds of honey in one month, more than anyone else in the college. Grant was enthusiastic enough about this to his friends, but what he was preserving in the young man was the long investment in his schooling and in his own hopes; he did not intend to have that investment go up in smoke on a battlefield. He had long ago drawn up his will, leaving the greater part to his elder son. He did not admire him, but he despised the younger boy and did not intend to let him touch his money till he, the younger, was about thirty-five. He then had to keep Gilbert by his side, to take hold of the estate when he died. He was obsessed with the idea that he would not live long. At the same time, during the war, he went on acquiring property abroad.

He had recently acquired a magnificent manor house in England from some British who had fled from that country thinking its day was done; he believed that the destruction of war meant high prices for what houses were left and a rosy future for construction as well as for all other businesses but armaments. The manor house had been worth about ten thousand pounds before the war, or as Grant put it "pre-Dunkirk." Grant had found out that there were plenty of hundred-pound notes in New York City at this time which could be bought for $175. Notes of this value could not be taken back to England, and said Grant to the "exiles," This is a long-term bet on England. You say it's through, I say I'll take a chance; it will look reasonable if I give you, say, eight thousand pounds post-Dunkirk for a property worth ten thousand pre-Dunkirk and I am going to pay you one dollar seventy-five cents a pound. He paid fourteen thousand dollars thus for the property and figured that as the pound would most likely

178

be inflated during the war, the price of the manor house would run up to thirty thousand pounds sterling. He at once offered the property to the Government for war-service and counted on getting rent and compensation for it during the war and on selling it immediately afterwards during the expected inflation.

With the same sort of prospects he had acquired a property, half farm, half manor, in the Bordeaux country, bought from some French refugees who despaired of their country's future; likewise had an option to the title of a fine set of farm buildings built into a close, and the large farm and orchard, yielding mixed farm produce and fruit and especially cheese, again acquired from French refugees, now largely established in New York. This farm was in Normandy in the rich Vallée d'Auge, a countryside he knew well, being near Le Havre, great cotton port in normal times. He had a house in Baden-Baden, got from a bankrupt friend of Laura's before the war, and a row of slum cottages in Dublin, having a high yield, and requiring little money spent upon repairs. The last he only mentioned in a roundabout way, in telling a romantic story of his mother's poverty, some remittance sent by him that arrived in wartime, to save an ousted family; and how a slum roof of his own was heaven to them, and such things; and money that had come to him, from a poor man, dying, because inspired perhaps by Heaven or Fate; he had saved this father's slum family, and such things; and then came out, the row of tenements in Dublin. He had a brownstone house in 124th Street, in New York, which he had acquired when he first knew the bridge was coming there; it was still little better than a flophouse, but he employed a poor relative there, of anarchist background, a woman spotlessly honest, to run it; and hoped for better. This house was rented out to various kinds of workers, mostly men and women living alone. The only drawback was that his relative the anarchist would often allow the rent to go into arrears for as much as six weeks, having an austere, lackadaisical humanity for these people. Nevertheless, he made a profit even out of this, telling his intimates (not those of pecuniary mind who would think him mad) how he ran a place somewhere in town for free souls and never asked the rent.

The house in Rome had been claimed entirely by Laura, who had society connections, to escape confiscation. She was Italian, her friendly ex-husband fascist. Laura would probably return it after the war, but might not. He fancied that if she turned out to be a spy or a collaborator of the fascists, through her previous sentimental and marriage connections, the house would be confiscated by the democratic conquerors and on his previous ambiguous title he could claim it. The slum houses always paid. The house in the St. Lawrence, which Edda called Hoot-Owl Hostel, which had caught his eye and upon which he had Spatchwood and others unknown to Spatchwood doing work, he might or might not buy. He had a simple, efficient system. He employed several persons upon each job, writing to each one an exhortation, a vague promise, and a denunciation of the others. Each one at once furiously set to work to do all he asked. One could not call it corruption. It was, in his mind, merely a technique for trying out situations to see if they were to his benefit.

If he had a financial or even moral loss in one of these small projections, he arranged to recoup it, financial and morally, through one of his other hangers-on. He knew he would have to pay something for the Spatchwood house, for he had written about several of the details himself, for example about the bronze bell which it had been his notion to hang in a small turret in the roof. The turret needed strengthening and the cost of a bronze bell with a bellrope to hang down through the house and into his bed chamber was more than he could have supposed. He had explained this curious bronze bell affair to Livy Wright, in a moment of confidence, when he had been promising to take her to the St. Lawrence house and live with her there, away from the world forever, by saying, "A private house is always dangerous, some crazy man could come around, envy you for your money, you never did him any harm, but go and argue with him; he'll hide and shoot you when you're least thinking of it—the middle of the night. He'll get in somehow. He's crazy. Their brains work twice as fast. I know it's all imagination, my dearest girl, but suppose it is my whim to have a bronze bell, then I have a bronze bell with a bellrope hanging near my ear."

And Livy had knocked the whole thing on the head by answering, "Like having a noose always hanging at your ear, not for me! But, Jesus, Robbie, you must be afraid of someone, to think of a thing like that."

"No, no, my dear girl, just a knowledge of human nature."

"I'm not going to any Spatchwood Coney Island, you can kiss me good-bye if that's your idea."

The feelings that had prompted him to think of the St. Lawrence house had passed away too. Now he was quite content in the *Pickwick Hotel*, and merely told Livy, who was now his closest friend, "Sell your business, my dearest woman, and come and live with me and be my love in the Pickwick: there's room for you and for me. We'll get married. I'm tired of gypsying, sweetie, you've converted me, I'll play a tune on my own hearthstone and I want a woman like you to hear it: that's all I want, a woman to whom my tune is always sweet."

What was lost in his nature, the good and tender, appeared when he said these things, his eye and cheek were clear and healthy, his red tender lips were inviting. Even Livy, turbulent and suspicious, believed in him. He was very pleased with this new line and repeated it to all his women, to Myra Coppelius too. He teased Mrs. Coppelius every day to buy her car and even sent her telegrams about it when he went to Philadelphia to visit Livy, or elsewhere, or to see a female correspondent of his in New Orleans. He sent weekly remittances to this woman, a woman of the lowest kind of life, called Nila, and to her mother. In return he received news that interested him about personalities in his old business city.

Meanwhile, through his long evenings, he briefly considered Livy and Myra Coppelius, in turn, as a new wife or wife-mistress. When he was bored with these brief images he turned to the Goodwins, the Flacks, others, and proposed sharing the place with them—Betty Goodwin, Edda Flack, wives and daughters of others, would live with him, see security and comfort him in return for shelter for their nearest and dearest. To them he said, "Perhaps I'm a born bachelor, a man has a headache, and who is there to give him an aspirin? I need a quiet home and decent friends around the table at night, and to listen, while I play my violin on my own hearth, eh?"

Then he would laugh magically, the spirit coming to him, stretch out his arms, throw his head around, manage to get an answering smile from his harassed audience. He would at once cry out, "Rejoice with me, we'll get out of town and breathe clean air. I'll fiddle a bit on my own hearthstone! We'll be happy. Let's be happy. No women. No life in bars, we'll study. We'll study agriculture, social construction, something that's good. I won't waste the few years left to me."

A little later, the same day, the next day, he would sing his gypsy pastoral to others: he never wrote it, but he would gladly invite occasional poor writers and poets introduced to him to write it, either as a play or a novel. Fascinated by his own *romancero* he imagined that when written it would sweep the country and make a fortune for them all." They all at first ate with wonder the humble bread given by the Maecenas to the poor, and for these he had another story of a glittering salon—in Rome, elsewhere, sometimes even with Laura there.

Meanwhile, Grant told Myra Coppelius that he had intended the *Pickwick Hotel* apartment for her, but that his boy would soon be visiting him and he wanted to break the affair to him gradually; the boy was devoted to his mother, an angel, a sweet woman and a perfect mother. Grant added, "In the meantime, the little car will be our guarantee; and as soon as I get the damn fool out of town, he's all right but the wrong end of a horse, I'll take to gypsying on my own hearthstone and we'll take week ends in the country in our little car."

Mrs. Coppelius bought the car, and as Grant urgently begged her to buy it in her own name for the moment, as he had momentary difficulty in releasing his funds, owing to his partner's unfortunate speculations in foreign markets, she managed to borrow the money for a part payment from two friends. It was only for two weeks at the outside, said Grant.

27

Gilbert came to town from the West Coast. He had changed, he knew women, and begged his father to take a companion for his lonely life. Gilbert said, "For instance, there was that Mrs. Kent. She was a lovely woman. I don't expect you to live without a single weakness, Dad."

Grant listened to all such remarks with an air of embarrassment, later roared with laughter as he repeated it to his friends, always nodding his head at the end and saying, "Good boy, though, good boy! But the wrong half of a horse. Good boy, though. No harm. Ha-ha. Thinks I'm a virgin. Wants to help me out."

At other times he wanted to punch the young man and restrained his considerable strength. Before any week was over, Gilbert would say in all companies, "Dad's trying to get rid of me and I'm not enjoying myself. All I can do is get drunk and all he can do is take a little stretch. I believe Dad stretches five hours a day, not to mention the evenings. Then he invites women for a little chat, he doesn't understand why he doesn't get women!"

And Grant, "Rubbish, thinking things out, lots of correspondence, don't understand my boy, shocks in business: don't care for night-life either, Presbyterian upbringing. Mother a millhand, your grandmother a millhand."

The intercourse of the two men was one of long desperate tedium broken by sudden quarrels. Grant's unreal conversation with his son was reduced to wise saws and his own romantic stand-bys, with an occasional jest full of common sense. The young man, of an upright, relentless nature, not yet forced, tried, hardened or corrupted, responded to the covert licentiousness of his father by fits of drunkenness. The older man feared drunkenness as he feared madness, ecstasy, fainting, sickness, solitude, death. At bottom, he dreaded Azrael, sign of a man who has not many years, the body's sure knowledge. The boy did not know it, yet found out his weakness and began to tease his father with it. When his father made him sit for hours in Manetti's or the White Bar without reason—for the young fellow still did not know that Grant was looking for women and cronies—he would drink himself into a fierce, hectoring, arrogant mood, in which he lost all shame and began to probe his father's character, talk about his age and worn-out looks, his friends and empty life.

He did not know that he was approaching those subjects which filled his father with terror. He only knew that then his father sat silent, swallowing everything, obedient, confused, yielding to him, and only at a certain moment (when an arrogant smile appeared in Gilbert's eyes and his father knew he thought he had won and was turning generous), then only, gruffly telling him to come along, that he needed a little walk in the fresh air. Gilbert, in whom the sensual life was developing slowly, liked to drink, but not to be drunk. He thought of himself as a gentleman and esthete. He would rise then with dignity, follow his father, and outside on the sidewalk, draw his father's arm through his: the good, manly son.

The father, to avoid the boredom of his son's company, and perhaps also to involve him in the low company he despised, now began to take Gilbert about with him, generally.

At the same time Gilbert had fallen in love, frankly, according to his nature, with Miss Celia Grimm, who was not more than two years older than himself. He became, in the course of a few months, sunny, generous, comradely with women, mature, open with men, and a frank radical, already smiling at his father's worn-out "socialist" sentimentality.

This unexpected result of Grant's introducing Gilbert to his real world was not clear to Grant, but he found the young fellow less human than ever. Then one or two accidental meetings and some gossip of the Goodwins', an ill-natured crack about his age, enlightened him. Gilbert's affair with Miss Grimm was of the most serious kind. Grant was thunderstruck. He resolved to get his son out of town and into something useful, if possible without waiting for the war to come to an end. Fortunately for his projects, Gilbert had fallen from a horse and injured his kneecap, and found himself discharged honorably toward the end of 1944. He threatened to re-enlist, tried to re-enlist, but was rejected. He spent a week or two in the apartment with his father, became unruly and vacuous and decided to get a job. He called his father's place "the zenana"—another hit in the dark which Grant did not care for—and wanted his father to move with him to another place, or let him live alone. The father would not permit this extra expense, pleaded poverty, and had to endure the detested idea of the boy roaming round town looking for a job. He quarreled bitterly with his son about this project of looking for a job. Unknown to him, Gilbert put an advertisement into the paper, supposing that this was all that was necessary. This was a great step for him, an act of courage. He was throwing himself naked on a world without connections. Gilbert received no replies. His father at once pointed out to him his defects in the business world: "What can you do? What do you know? What have you to offer? The labor market is a market like any other. You cannot go and say, 'Here I am, willing to work, but I don't know what at!' A laborer can do that, for he is strong like you are and has two hands and a set of muscles and he can carry things on his head, and does not ask for an accountant's salary. But for your sort of job you have to carry things in your head—something different! What do you know, Gilbert? Nothing! You're an abstraction and no abstraction is a commodity. Can you count—not much—" the father laughed ironically—"you can count your pennies, as you did when you were a child, you can put money into a bank account and draw a check on it, but you don't know the meaning of a check. What is a check? You don't know. Your handwriting is like a bit of secret writing. You can't typewrite, you don't know shorthand. Every little girl in the street knows these things and not you. You've been to war—so has everyone. My boy, do you know what you are? Grant's son—and that's your total stock in trade. I'll get one of my friends to try you out at something, as *Grant's son*."

Gilbert cried, "I'll go and work with my muscles, my head,

and my hands, as you say I won't get jobs from one of your friends except as *Grant's son!*"

"Even your muscles are nothing much."

"I'll do it."

"If I had any sense, I'd let you go out there some frosty morning, and shiver for a job in an employment office or at a factory gate—but I'm damned if I'll see you waste your time like that. I trained you in animal husbandry and chicken raising and I'll get an accountant for you, and a muscle-man for you, and you'll go out and look after my place in Jersey. That's what you'll do and nothing else."

The young man held out for several weeks, trying to land city jobs, but he saw his money in the bank getting lower, and he came to the conclusion that he had small ability and no training. He then tried two jobs with his father's friends, Goodwin and an acquaintance of Spatchwood, but could not obey, could not be less the spoiled boy, saw no reason to change his manners: "I am not going to sell furs after all, why should I adapt myself? Is there any moral value to keeping your temper under insults and in lying about merchandise? You don't know how Goodwin behaves in business, Dad."

The father now saw that he had only to await his hour; the ungifted young man, rendered more helpless by him, would soon capitulate. He now urged Goodwin to put up with the young fool's insults and tempers, in order to disgust him forever.

After Gilbert lost his job with the Goodwin fur firm (in which his father was a silent partner), he tried once more to get Grant to put money into educational films for after the war. He then went out to raise money himself, but without knowing where to go or how to get financing. He stood for two days, as the Christmas rush was approaching, in a department store, selling toy movie projectors. He was handsome and liked children. He made sales. But on the third day he came home and said to his father, "I have examined myself and tried myself out, no one can deny that; and I have written my findings down on two sheets of paper. The first tells what I thought about myself before I left the Army and just after, when I told you I intended to have a good time and see life and grope, and perhaps find— You remember I said to you that was my object and my right? The second sheet tells what I now think of my aptitudes and indeed general situation, now that I have tried to get a job and get financing for my film business. Underneath the second I have written a few lines about what I suppose to be my life pattern. Would you like to read them or shall I tell you?"

Grant, after casting his eye impatiently over the strangely written sheets, said, "No time—tell me, quicker—"

The son then, once more at ease, crossed his legs, spread out the sheets, and proceeded in his usual manner to analyze himself in stupefying detail. He found himself, in brief, a mediocre man who still hoped to have some place in society, but found nothing in himself to give out. He felt he should accept the first place offered to him, and unusually lucky to have a place carved out for him by his father. He concluded, "Don't think I accept your offer of a situation with joy or satisfaction! I detest the prospect and know I shall not be happy. But it will give me a few years to look around; and I am not, after all, obliged to do anything, am I? But I feel a debt to society, since I did not actually fight for society, if you understand me; so I shall at least undertake this drudgery as a kind of penance, or, if you will, because I haven't the guts to fight it out in the streets. I am an ordinary man, not even a malcontent or a roughneck; I am just a cypher or, as you put it, an abstraction. Perhaps this comes from the war or the scattering away of all ideas and aims by the war. I do not know. Perhaps I am just a function of a social situation. I do not know. But knowing all these things may be so and unable at present to face an empty life, I will go on your chicken farm. . . . I hope you will write at once to Manfred the manager, tell him to get up the accounts, and make arrangements about the Manfreds leaving. I don't like that woman and do not think she is clean. Please ask her to have the place cleaned; and tell her I shall be down on Saturday to make preliminary arrangements."

The father, startled at this, began to object, but the young fellow, having "thought this thing through," was not to be put off. Grant, who was expecting a visit from Livy Wright for the week end and did not trust this new son with Manfred, could only get the descent on Largo Farm, the chicken farm, put off for one week.

In the end, because of a new and more dangerous affair with the blondine, he was prevented from going.

It was hard to lure Gilbert away from the prey he had smelled out. Gilbert's natural inflexible rectitude, his only talent, had so far walked in the world unused; in the peculiar state of affairs at Largo Farm, he had found employment for it. The accounts were not only slightly at fault, but irrational, concealed; there were headings X and Y. There were signs of splits and handouts, things costing exactly three per cent more (one per cent, one per cent, and one per cent) than they should have, passing through three hands. Gilbert was not very good at arithmetic, but his rectitude itself served as an illumination and served him more than arithmetic. Gilbert had many angry sessions with his father, trying to point out to the old man, whom he now regarded as senile, how he was being robbed—"They take percentage after percentage—not a farmer roundabout but digs into your pocket." Grant flushed, raised his eyes to the ceiling, laughed somewhat, and looked at his son in a confused way and would say, "Let's go out for a Scotch-and-soda."

28

During the summer, Barbara Downs had come back to town and taken a flat in a fashionable street near the center. At first, things had been cool between Grant and his old flame, but presently they were daily companions, though Grant, at Barbara's request, concealed this new phase of the affair from their friends. They met at the Pickwick Hotel and once or twice they had run into Goodwin or Walker, one of Barb's lawyers, there, but both had promised to say nothing. Churchill Downs, a delicate, romantic man with old-fashioned ideas of housekeeping, would not have permitted Barbara to meet men outside the home. Grant once more opened accounts for Barbara and her crony, Miss Russell, at Manetti's, Paul's, and other small French-style restaurants where she was known. His friends missed him; he became absorbed, difficult at the office. He hurried from work and was up late every night. He began to drink too much again. Barbara, in order to meet him at night, pretended to be taking a course in some difficult language. She was very good at languages and did actually study a little on her own, to show that she was making progress. She seemed to have changed with this last marriage. Downs loved her, gave her fair housekeeping money, but was strict about accounts. Barbara would find it hard to get a divorce from him. She was already bored by the man, horrified at the prospect of sitting at the table with him at lunch and dinner. She told Grant simply that she could not tolerate the company of any one man, that Grant himself was the nearest she had come to a tolerable friend. With her husband she was obliged to conceal her real feelings, her experience, her genuine views of life. He did not allow any gossip in the house, believed she was injured but pure, and really disliked her reading novels and going to movies, but for her sake tolerated it. Barbara was quite able to please her husband and her mother-in-law, but had become very nervous with the strain of the long deception. She told Grant, "It is really not worth it; I only feel I am myself when with you!"

Grant not only paid for her many extra expenses, but became her moral support. With her he did not repeat so many of his saws, nor sing of his castles in Spain: they had the same intense, prolonged, profound interest in petty domestic details, in buying, comparing prices, changing cleaners, in backbiting, small profit-taking, bonus-getting, in discharging servants; they liked to talk about cures for colds, and change one drugstore for another to test the coffee, or the aspirin tablets. Either would go a mile to change a ten-cent plastic comb or forty blocks to get some rare herb at a backstreet herbalist. Besides this, Barbara was still very handsome, and Grant, in his best days, still looked the powerful, successful business man. Grant had begun spending big money again, on his beloved, but he had something to do: he was never at a loss. At times he said to her, "But what does he do, Downs? Does he wait at home for you?"

"Oh, he loves to listen to the radio and read a good book; he is a nice man: I have nothing to say against him. Only I don't get enough money; and he'll never let me go."

She could not stand the boredom and went off to Saratoga Springs, Grant sending her her extra expenses.

One day in November, 1943, Goodwin with Betty, drinking in the White Bar, and quarreling about the supply of sheepskins for fur, in the world, which Goodwin had oversold, declared to Grant, "You don't know about the supply of sheepskins because you don't know anything. I'll prove it. You don't know Barbara Downs is getting a divorce and you're a co-respondent. You'll stink to high heaven, you're a member of a syndicate and you don't know even that; and I'll prove it, here it is in an out-of-town gossip column, a blond, business man, eh?"

The unsuspecting husband, not a fool, as Barb had supposed (said Betty Goodwin), was given the alarm by one of Barb's own friends, it was thought, some jealous woman, blackmailing. This had all happened months ago, and while Barb had been amusing herself, the evidence had collected against her, even through the efforts of "Braun, Arthur," who had become her husband's friend. Goodwin shouted, "And while you were showing them the Land of Canaan, she showed them the milk and honey. Oh, boy—the Old Honeybear was asleep at the switch."

And the evidence had collected against her and the "syndicate" of co-respondents. Grant had seen Barb every day for tea and a chat at his apartment and did not know this. Barb did with him what she liked; and what about the others?

"And you, you telling us that she had fallen for you but too late—shabby old wolf, no one would buy you or sell you, but she did, for her business is rotten old skins and—"

Grant flushed and lowered his head; but his eyes blackened, for Goodwin was the blondine's friend and what did this attack mean? The man frothed on, vain and vile.

Grant said, "They have nothing on me, nothing on me. I've not been near the woman except for tea—she came up to my place on her way to the station, with all her bags and her little cat—she left the valises in the lobby, I told her not to—but she was on the way to Saratoga and it wasn't in this place, it was another, besides, that was months ago—and supposing she did— I always had a suite, that is not evidence enough, I know. No, no, they have nothing on me. Besides, perhaps it's just a rumor."

They told him much more. Her husband had left her. She was out of money. She would be "out on the street" . . . and would resort to anything. He went to the booth in the lobby and telephoned the woman, "Come back at once, Barb, I just heard some news that gave me a terrible shock. I must see you."

But she would not come till the following day and he left his guests after a short, irritable moment with them. All knew that he had telephoned her. He left them downstairs, went up in ill humor. After taking several glasses of brandy, he went to examining the linen closets, his suits and Gilbert's. The young man used the place when in town. Grant discovered a pair of pants with muddy cuffs, a pair of shoes that had some excuse for being sent to the mender's, a laundry list on which one sheet was marked as missing. Though it was nearly eleven, and Mrs. MacDonald had permission to retire at ten, he rushed through the silent, shining kitchen, and seeing a line of light under her door, knocked loudly. She came out in her dressing gown, her white hair in plaits. Her radio was still on. He dragged her out to the linen closet for an explanation about the missing sheet, then from closet to closet, fussing and complaining. She said at last, "But I think something has upset you, Mr. Grant, for you would not have me up like this unless you had something on your mind." Her voice trembled with weak emotion.

At these kind words, he changed his cry of "My good woman" into "You're pair-fectly right"—for he spoke a sort of Scottish with her—and sent her back to bed. He went into the young man's room, looked through his drawers, and set the letters and pencils in neat piles. He found an old notebook in which he had once pasted clippings about foreign cotton markets—a thing he had thrown away and Gilbert had kept. He glanced through a packet of letters from his wife to Gilbert—things he had never read and did not read now. But he noted their different tones. slavishly affectionate:

> Your poor little Dixie-mamma is very much alone but whenever I feel it too much I take a good nap, and this seems to make the time pass. I think of my Little-Bear and send you big hugs, big, big, big hugs from Middle-Bear. These last days have been so cold, there has been nothing to do but tuck up on the sofa and shut my eyes and sleep. Christmas is coming and I will see all my Dodos.
>
> Your loving Dixie-girl.

There were fifteen or sixteen letters, perhaps, almost identical; no turbulence, no reprimand, no plan appeared in them. Grant sat down and thought about his big affairs. His wife, first.

She was very pretty and very rich and—why not? The marriage improved his position. He was then building up his fortune. He had had no time to think about Dixie or his infant son, Gilbert. The thing had accomplished itself by the will of society, without protest from him. The grand affair with Laura had put an end to all his regrets: twelve years of misdemeanor had ended in this romance, his only moment of exaltation. Even so, he had proceeded with this foreign beauty with a business caution. When he received her letter, full of the passion, self-denying courtesy, and youthful recklessness of love, he had not replied to it. She had left her husband, a rich man, and mentioned Grant's name to him. She was, in Grant's view, ruining herself by losing a large regular income. Who would support her parents now? They had stripped themselves to give her a dowry, only part of which would remain with her. Grant did not reply to this letter. Laura had waited a week and wired: "Did you receive my letter? Telegraph."

Grant had not replied. After three weeks had passed, he had a note typed in his office,

Dear Madame Manganesi,
    A brief urgent business trip will bring me to Rome as soon as conditions permit. I shall stay at the Bristol where they know me. I have some financial matters to go over and am thinking of making certain investments in Rome; perhaps you and your husband would meet me for tea and could suggest the name of someone. I am looking forward to seeing you.

They had been lovers for several months at this time. All this caution resulted in this, that she had no documents against him. As soon as he saw Laura again, in a luxurious apartment she had taken and for which she had got money from her husband, against her estate, and had learned she would not be destitute, she had pleased him very much, and he had plunged almost wholeheartedly into that liaison which he later dinned into the heads of all his friends and leading mistresses.

He bought the house in Rome which Laura rented out in apartments, he and she sharing the revenues. He had, of course, as a daily affair, always betrayed Laura with poor street prostitutes, girls in the office, and temporary mistresses; but he had clung to the house and her.

The flighty, shamelessly licentious, curiously innocent and frank little woman sped from one "great love affair" to another, week after week. If she thought of suicide often, because she suffered and could not but come to the conclusion that life was futile, she would drown the feeling the next day by being "madly in love."

He had given her a number of bonds and some real estate, including a farm. In return Laura had signed over all claims to various family estates shortly to fall in in the childless, great Italian family. Some months later, he had gone to Rome from Boston, expressly to get control of this property again, alleging the danger of bankruptcy owing to immense commitments on the long side and the "advice of that fella David Flack." Laura had at once made over the property, bonds, and titles to save him, asking only for her own signatures back or for an I O U for the property returned. The next day, Grant had been nervously upset, had had a heart-attack and had clung to her, saying, "It was nothing but a glove, I swear, a glove. I saw it lying in the street. A strange woman. I picked it up. Don't let anyone in the door, my sweetie. It's the Maffia."

"What is it, what is it?" asked Laura.

"They're after me with the knife, the stiletto."

He rolled on the sofa with shut eyes, groaned. When the doorbell or the telephone rang, he started up, groaned and rushed into a clothes closet or the bathroom, shut the doors, locked them. He took headache powders, said, "I can't go out into the street, I only want the shelter of your arms, don't ask me to do any business, I beg you, sweetie," and then would burst out by himself into the streets "only to get a little fresh air," and return rather late, looking peculiarly unrefreshed. He would say, when she exclaimed about his looks and about his having been absent from her little party of friends of that evening, that he had had a terrible shock, had dreadful news, the person he had offended was someone high-placed, dangerous, unforgiving.

Thus he was able to leave Rome without giving her the papers she asked for, but said he would send them from the boat. They did not come from the boat, but there came a note, saying he would post them from New York. They did not come from New York; they never came, but in their place came pitiful notes, saying he had had so much trouble, he had had heart attacks, had taken this and that, and seen the doctor, had been in a taxi accident. In between these sicknesses, Laura asked for the papers once or twice, and then desisted, lost heart.

Some time after their breach, Grant, sensing war coming, persuaded Laura that what money she still held should be put into the U.S.A., which was in for a war boom, both before and after (and if) they entered the war. Laura knew his reputation for managing things in difficult situations and easily agreed, placing a considerable sum in American stocks and naming him a modified power of attorney. While she had the usage of the rich about property, the common sense, she managed to reason that though Grant had cheated her about the holdings before, he had a sort of argument in his favor which was that he had given her part of the property himself, and had shown so much good heart as to try to provide for her sick cousin. She meanwhile still held the house on the Pincian Hill, though jointly with Grant. She felt that Grant had perhaps merely tried to get back his equity, and knew that she had "cheated" on him, as he expressed her love vagaries.

In return for this power of attorney he agreed to reinstate her as fifty-one per cent shareholder in a concern called the Pincian

Associates. When Laura asked the reason for this redistribution of his holdings, he told her that new taxes, new currency difficulties, made it necessary. She only had a slight general feel of property, she could not calculate. At this time, nevertheless, she was a close friend of James Alexis, an international figure, and asked his advice about the whole matter. James Alexis agreed with Grant, and recommended her to follow his advice. He had then professed his great interest in the cotton business and desired to meet Grant. This was a flattering proposal for Grant, and Laura wrote to him about it, saying that she would be glad to introduce them on his next visit.

To this letter Grant made no reply. He wished to break with Laura and looked upon her letter as a woman's ruse. This fault in Laura made him very sulky. He marveled at her vices; he found her goodness of heart a true weakness, or a weak trickery.

When the war came, as he had foreseen, he used Laura's predated letter, acknowledging his title to her estate in the United States, thus it had long been American property. In the meantime, he trembled for the fate of his Italian property. As someone had once said to him that Laura, with so many German friends in Roman society, was never invited to the German Embassy and so must be a German agent, Grant had an excuse for making up a rumor that Laura was a spy and that he feared for her. He never wrote to her. He calculated that if by any chance the Germans won, he could depend on the vestiges of her love. If the Germans lost, he was safe, by having put her about as a spy. In either case he was more than compensated by control of the American part of her estate.

He had many other worries concerning his property in Europe. His managers and bailiffs had all fled, all having been liberals and even radicals. He liked to employ such people, having always found them loyal and rarely venal. He was fairly busy now, with his correspondence, as he interrogated all travelers, and sometimes had news of his properties. He had had very little misfortune. He was sagacious. Long ago he had given up hopes of a mercantile empire of his own. He felt the day was gone. He liked to battle on his own, and would never have consented to work as part of a monopoly or any private industry. Still, the notion of state control attracted him, and he was merchant enough to regret the waste he saw, and the mass-misery that competition and speculation brought into the production and distribution of clothing and other modest essentials. He loved these realities. It was not boredom alone that made him know in detail his, his son's, his wife's, Laura's, Livy Wright's possessions. It was also partly his industrious nature and the love of goods in their quality, the pleasure in six-threaded cottons, good Shetland wool, leather boots, high-yielding land, well-built houses.

The blondine had no notion of quality. She bought what was the fashion and expensive; she bought just as cheerfully rubbish and good workmanship. She disliked, if anything, materials which lasted long and showed too much handwork, as brocades, tapestries, heavy linens, and old laces. Besides, she bought more to bring business to one or two dealers she knew than to suit her own taste. She changed her lovers but not these dealers.

Barbara Downs naturally did not appear to herself as an adventuress, as Grant did not appear to himself as a lecher. Barbara, for example, believed that she was in the center of a kind of exchange of values: she was the broker. She knew a few laws, enough for her purpose, and for the rest she put nothing on paper, but her name to a marriage certificate. Her society was full of women like herself, who made connections, put people in the way of things, mentioned names, made love in the routine of business, and in return, received money in cash. All that she met could be paid for and was: she was therefore only a dealer. She surely believed that everything was for sale. With this tranquillity about her means of livelihood went a feeling of superiority. She had a right to live fairly well for she was intelligent. If she lived badly, she felt agony, and it was then that she sometimes lost her head and tried to make money in ways that she herself thought low, as blackmail. An affair like the Hugo March swindle, to keep her head high, she considered just revenge.

Lately, she had fallen lower. At first she had wanted to marry well; then to become the mistress of several rich men in turn. This failing, she proceeded naturally to prostitution. Her meeting with Grant had, in her own eyes, raised her in the world. She believed in the schemes she tried to involve men in, petty conspiracies in which she talked big about exchanges, blocked currencies, and political chances.

He spent the weeks until Christmas in anxiety and confusion over the Downs affair, and saw Mrs. Downs and the Goodwin cronies almost every day. Mr. Downs had cut off supplies, and Grant saw himself once more responsible for the blonde woman. At the end of the year, when Flack made up his accounts, he saw with dismay that he had three unexpected sources of loss, the new expenses for Mrs. Downs, some speculations by his partners and the cutting down of his profits on Largo Farm. Gilbert's ruthless honesty had reduced the farm to being self-supporting but not profitable. Grant realized that he must get the boy out of the farm and wrote to Gilbert, offering to finance him in technical films for which he thought him more capable. Gilbert was dogged, and it was hard to pry him loose from his prey. He remained implacable towards his cousin Upton, whom he considered a black-hearted, low-living scoundrel who had used his father's farm for black marketing. He reproached his father for his inexplicable tenderness towards Upton; and Grant always replied, "No family quarrels and no family feuds, my boy: that is the beginning of trouble; it invites bad luck." Grant, in the end, promised to engage a new manager, suitable to Gilbert, if Gilbert would return to the city and the film business.

Grant was furious with his partners and took this opportunity to refuse both junior men any further hope of the New Orleans business. The fact was he wanted to lose this business. He did not want to visit the city again, he smelled trouble with the celebrated cotton speculator with whom he had considered going into business, and with whom, in fact, he had participated in some small deals; and he believed he could, at this moment, sell his house and business there for a good profit. As to the expenses of love, he now told Mrs. Coppelius that he could not help her with the car, he thought she had acted rashly in taking an odd word of his, a sort of boyish enthusiasm, for gospel, and after all she had no written word from him. She must grow up, not believe in fairy princes, said he: she would be happier. In the meantime, she must make out as best she could; it was not his responsibility. In this way, he calculated, he saved the $2,365 the car had cost, and he could write this in to offset the blonde account. Mrs. Coppelius, who was genteel, hardly protested about the affair, she "gave two or three little squeaks" as he said to himself, when ambling round his apartment at night.

29

At the moment, he had only two serious affairs, that with the blonde and that with Livy. The talk of love had become a daily hunger with him, he was starving, never satisfied; and he needed the lavish affection and hopes of women; thus, he was obliged ever to talk bigger. But he was so hasty that all his women knew that he had little time for them, and Livy became very miserable, spoke of never seeing him again. She was a successful business woman, she saw through his roughly-sketched cajoleries. He went to Boston as usual for Christmas, and was dreadfully nervous there. He took no care of his person, not only from an established malice towards his wife, but because he wanted to be back in New York, in the beating heart of all his troubles. His wife showed him some drawings his young son Andrew had made. He picked them up, eyed them, threw them on the table and forgot them. The boy wept when he left the house. For a moment, going down the path towards his waiting car which was to take him back to New York, Grant hesitated: the boy had a heart, perhaps he was not a good father to him. But he hurried on, thinking if he went back he would have to listen to his wife's voice again, and anyhow children were but hungry, clamorous animals, until they became men; nothing more.

He had given no gifts in New York, nor sent any cards: he had given nothing in the hotel nor at the office, nor to his partners. He was determined to make up his losses. But he had sent a check of $50 to the mysterious woman in New Orleans who wrote to him every so often with personal news: to Nila.

When he returned to New York he found cards from all his female friends, some business friends, from the Flacks and a few of his other hangers-on; a pair of gloves from Gilbert, and a note from Nila, thanking him for the money, speaking of her mother, and ending with, "Hilbertson stays at home like a bear with a sore head: but everyone says he still speaks of getting you. What did you do to that guy anyway? He must be sensitive. I need $50 next week again; sorry. Yours lovingly, Nila."

Grant sent off a check for $35 and said his expenses had been high and he had sustained losses at the year's end.

Meanwhile, he was hurt that he had not received a card or gift from Myra Coppelius. He had hinted to her, at their last conversation, that she might make the car over to him as a Christmas gift, and that he might then make her a gift of some satisfactory sum; it was to avoid income-tax said he. Livy, too, had abstained from sending a Christmas gift. Grant felt lonely in his huge apartment. Everywhere people were visiting friends. He, because of his habit of going to Boston, was invited nowhere. He telephoned the Flacks but found them just about to go out to a party. Flack teased him, saying, "Go out to one of your bars, you Honeybear: they're all got up for New Year's. I'll see you on New Year's Eve.

And don't commit suicide, you nut; remember this is the time when everyone commits suicide. But remember, you nut, we love you, and we'll see you tomorrow if you're not too busy."

It was three days to New Year's Eve. He thought, "I must be loved this afternoon; I must make up for all my headaches," and he set out in a taxi to call upon Mrs. Coppelius, who lived in a hotel near 71st Street, West Side. When he reached the hotel lobby, he did not remark at all a preoccupation of the hotel servants, but he felt himself neglected. He wrapped on the counter with his malacca cane.

"Get me Mrs. Coppelius; room—" said he, and turned away toward the house phone. He heard someone calling, but it took him some time to know the clerk was hailing him.

"Are you a friend of the lady in room—?"

He eyed the fellow sharply, said in a low voice, "What's wrong? Anything wrong? Friend of hers said, no news lately, asked me to call in passing— My sister, Mrs. Goodwin," he mumbled.

They asked him, "Friends of hers? Do you know her friends?" For the price of two dollars, he heard the reason for this: the woman had jumped or fallen into the courtyard from the seventh floor just before his arrival.

"Are you a friend of hers? She may be able to say something."

"No, no, I never saw her—my wife asked me to give her a message, but—my wife knows more about her, I know nothing. My name's Flack. I'll get my wife. All she wants is a woman with her now."

He turned around and left the hotel briskly. He hailed a taxi and got home in a strange state, thinking without words, but what, he did not know. He was pale and trembled. Time passed. All he could think of was "I nearly met Azrael." He was late for his rendezvous at the Little Bar and found them all assembled there. He declared that he had caught a chill and must go home soon.

In the meantime he had thought out his chances. If the woman Coppelius had left a suicide note, she might have sent a message to him, and he would be questioned. She might have blamed him, though it was not his fault. Was she known as the doctor's wife at the hotel? Should he have given her husband's name and address? Had he been followed? After a few drinks, he felt stronger. Never once did he allow himself to think of the woman. It was a simple black-out in his mind. He thanked his luck that he had not mentioned Mrs. Coppelius to any of them recently. He went home very late to avoid telephone calls and left very early the next morning. By the evening, his confidence was restored. He had carefully gone through the newspapers and had not seen the suicide recorded. At first this worried him—would there be an inquiry? But in two days he breathed freer and was able to prepare a party at the Golden Tassel with his usual friends and Livy, who had come to town for the New Year season.

30

At night, when Mrs. MacDonald was in bed, Grant would walk up and down for some time thinking of his tangled affairs and trying to quiet his fears. He know that the blondine could and might get him into trouble. Well, he would run away, she would not get him in a trap. He did not feel well: he took a little brandy. He did not notice time passing, but when Gilbert came in, he would be cold, it would be some time after one o'clock. He would see the boy to bed and go to bed himself, but get up without rest. For the moment, he tried to make a friend of the boy. One morning, he heard the young man saying to Mrs. MacDonald, "Don't do it that way, I've got him eating out of my hand. I just speak my mind. He likes it because he must, and that's a rule with men. A man's truth is like armor. There's no way to get around it or through it."

"You are his son."

"Of two things, one, I'd like to see any fellow in the Army telling me to get dressed and where to put my drawers; to wash my socks. But why? I was a good officer. I was such a good officer as not to be too good an officer. I tempered my zeal with humanity or, you might say, caution. Imagine a sheet—is this the sheet?"

"That's a blessing; it is."

"I always lay my hands on lost things. Being no accountant, one day I found an error in Goodwin's annual bookkeeping. Everyone was looking for it, I found it. The accounts for Largo Farm need a palaeographer and a detective; but I'll see daylight there, too. I have a theory that people have an interest in keeping things muddled; there's a conspiracy of fraud. Not Dad, of course, he just never had my opportunities. It isn't the ability, it's the will and a certain eye. You could go out with a hogcaller, not find a straighter eye, and I say the Yanks have the straightest eyes."

"If I were you, I'd comb my hair, for it's not straight this minute."

When Grant came out to breakfast, this was done. Said the son, "I've heard you splashing and spouting for a bloody two hours in there, like a bloody porpoise."

The older man grinned, "Did you find the missing sheet with the scalloped hem?"

This led to a rediscussion of Gilbert's peculiar capacities. Grant let him talk, his anxious mind floating restfully on this vacuity. Presently he snapped his fingers: "Gilbert, I want you to meet Livy and Mrs. Lawrence at the Little Bar for me. I have an appointment with—" he muttered a name like "Rasselas." He went for his coat, "Stay here, rest a bit, come down for luncheon, we'll go to the Italian's, then you can go to the movies, and meet the women—"

"You would go to the Italian's—I hate the Italian's. Why? But I know why. It is because—"

"Come down, come down, we'll see—"

He rushed out.

Gilbert felt new strength since he had gone to the farm. He had acquired bad habits since his discharge from the Army; his waistband seemed a little tight. It was a bright morning, though cold. He decided as soon as he was dressed to walk all the way downtown to Hanover Square, to the Cotton Exchange. He stepped along, admiring the town. He took pleasure in thinking of the things he yet did not know. Everything that happened to him was different from his expectations and changed his views, even reversed them. With each new event he felt his hold on life firmer. At times he felt like gasping with the shock and the joy.

He loved Celia. This sound, strong, handsome, golden-skinned woman, by accident, was able to bring out in him a frank voluptuousness, which she satisfied. He did not notice the miles he was walking. Celia seemed to arise from him and floated beside him, golden, lying on her back among grasses.

He reached his father's offices much before he expected. The offices were on the ground floor, small, gloomy, sparely furnished but paneled in wood, and with a family air because the real living place of two old people, Grant and his secretary, who had been associated with him for twenty-five years. Miss Robbins was nearly fifty. Gilbert had known her for twenty years. For twelve years she had been his mother, sending him to boarding schools, meeting him at stations, counting his laundry, attending to all his wants, privately handing him a little change, finding places for him to stay in the holidays (quite often with Grant's favorites of the day), and sending letters to him. She had done it all without selfishness, as part of the duty of a good employee. She wrote for Grant the letters that no one else was allowed to see, and kept his accounts. Her low pay, common sense, and firmness of character had prevented her from ever loving him, ever admiring him; but she spoke about him to no one. She had conceived, also, no maternal feelings toward Gilbert, and she still believed that Mrs. Grant was as Grant described her to others, "—an angel, a wonderful wife and mother, a sweet, pure woman, an angel."

The light fell through a high, dirty window on Miss Robbins' yellow hair, which was piled high in the then fashion. Her hat with roses and her blue suède gloves lay on a steel filing cabinet in the corner. A dusty ray lighted up the blonde fur on her tweed coat with a dogtooth check. A lizardskin bag stood against the wall. Gilbert saw all this—a woman and kind—blonde woman. He smiled at Miss Robbins and pointed to the inner room.

"You'll have to wait a bit while the fit's on him," said Miss Robbins, and pointed to a chair. Grant was talking in the inner room, his voice hurried, clear, singing. The door stood open. He leaned against his desk with his back to Miss Robbins' office.

Gilbert sat down in the sunlight behind Miss Robbins. She turned about to say something, saw his shining hair and face, shook her head, and went back to her typing. From where he sat, Gilbert could not be seen by his father. Miss Robbins paused a moment over her typewriter before she went on with her letters. Her thoughts were a calm argument, "Gilbert is entirely a man now, let him know everything that comes his way." It had often come to her since Gilbert was eighteen that the youth was grown and could take care of himself, but she had continued to look after him. A moment ago it had come to her, but this time, with the force of the physical presence, that Gilbert was a man, and of an age that women marry. She knew what his new pleasantness meant, she knew him so well.

Grant talked continuously, urgently, into the phone, and at first Gilbert heard nothing, thinking once more automatically, Then she came away from the door and came toward me—what happened then?—there's a blank there—and after, I stood still a moment; I went toward her and put my hands— The incident unrolled itself before him, fixed forever in attitudes, unexpected sentences, silences, and the beauty of many absences. The past day and the present clung to each other. He thought, Then she put out her hand to the lamp— And one of those pauses came: what then? What then? He knew what came after. At this moment, he tried to shake off the enchantment and listened to his father's voice, which was saying, "Yes, darling, I am back in New York. I left about those muskrats that Goodwin had warehoused on a wrong certificate. Don't know the business. I'm very sorry, sweetie, couldn't get you the lambskins, got held up, all sold. I hardly had time to pack, go there, come back. Only a grip—well, you know, sweetie, I never take a train without having you to tea and a little chat, I don't like to be separated—"

To whom was he speaking, Gilbert thought, Livy or Mrs. Kent? Not his mother? The incident began again of itself in his head. "Then she came away from the door—" in the same words, the same vision. He forced himself to listen to his father's voice irritably asking the telephone girl for a number. . . . Then she put out her hand to the lamp. "You are so late," she said— He listened to his father, "My dear Barb, and now I hear from a third party there is a div—a private matter, and I know nothing of it. . . . From the Goodwins. . . . You told them two months ago, but not me. . . . But, sweetie, you told me you were busy all the time, I didn't see how I could get in touch with you, I thought you were trying to shake me. . . . But at four o'clock, Barb, darling, I met you and you told me nothing. Two hours later I hear this news and it was a terrible shock to me. . . . I'm very, very sorry, darling, but I couldn't get to Saratoga and besides you were very cold to me. . . . I have been very busy all the summer and needed consolation and— I'm sorry about the bank, darling, but I dropped fifteen thousand dollars last week, Sam did, I mean, and those muskrats were no good and Goodwin is head over heels in sheepskins, no good. I paid out five thousand dollars and there was the lawyer too. . . . I want to see you this afternoon and you must tell me all about it; it's not fair to leave me in the dark. . . . I'm not scared, sweetie. What can they say, I was your friend? That's no dishonor, is that wrong, I helped you when you were down and out—bah! those fellas have nothing on— I am not taking a run-out powder— I must see you, Barb; you're not fair to me. . . . Some hocus-pocus. I know you're not to blame; at the White Bar, darling, and don't bring Paula, I want to speak to you alone. I'm sure you are worried, darling—I'll see that there's money in the bank, Barb, tomorrow—good-bye, then—oh!"

It was evident that the woman kept plaguing him, for he went on, "You shouldn't have got an overdraft, I didn't make a deposit this month because—I know it's the fifteenth of the month—and Christmas coming—I'm twenty thousand behind at the moment! You remember that deal with that bloody Percival? Goodwin's mistake with the muskrats looks like it's going to be a big mistake, cost me four or five thousand at the beginning and now—and he's quarreled with his brother, who can get him in the jug if he wants to and I'm telling him, don't have any family quarrels, the family is made to stick together; and such fights cost money. Those are the fights I hate, darling, where love is involved—" He listened; proceeded in a languorous listening voice, "You must get another lawyer besides Walker—I don't like that fella—I know you're operating on a narrow margin, I am too, you know my expenses and how hard it is for me to get exchange through, but I'll look through my accounts tonight and try to give you a check tomorrow—I know you can't fight it without money—of course, fight it, that's my advice—fight it— get another lawyer, not Walker, he looks like a shyster—I'll be at Manetti's—by myself—don't worry about blondes, sweetie, I got one blonde on my hands, that's trouble—I don't mean that— of course, reverse the charges—good-bye, yes, I'll give you a check— good-bye—yes, I'll send you the gloves—good-bye—I know your lawyer's in Florida, reverse the charges—good-bye, sweetie!"

There was silence for a moment, in the friendly green-painted room, then Gilbert heard his father giving a telephone number. The sun streamed in. . . . Gilbert thought, I said, "Do you really like this tie?" and she came nearer and— He heard his father saying, "Wright's Agency? Miss Wright? Livy darling, when do you get in? How are you, darling? I miss you, sweetie! I wanted to go to Philadelphia right away after your sweet call the other night. I feel just the same about you, Livy. I met the right woman. You're the woman for me. . . . Never mind about the oasis. You'll be glad to be here, so will I. I couldn't be too busy—we'll make the wires hum—on Sunday? I had no one with me, I swear, Livy. If you heard a woman's voice, it was a cut-in. I'm very tired, pooped-out, no interest in women, but you. . . . I would lie to you, Livy, otherwise I'd feel like a schoolboy, but this time no need to. I lie when I have to, but this time, not. You know I don't say I don't like women when I don't have to. I'm a terrible liar but not to you. Well, Philadelphia doesn't give me a pickup; nowhere to go and no beautiful woman—I mean, except the one I have with me. Or perhaps it's the effect you have on me. . . . Barbara?"

His voice changed and went lower, "Bloody 'ooman—is there of course, got back from Saratoga only to plague me. She's getting a divorce. I heard some ugly rumors. I'm glad you brought it up. Livy, I must see my lawyer this evening. I'll meet you at ten o'clock at the White? I told you all that was through and now, by heavens, I have the proof. She thought she had me round her little finger, and now when she's lost me, she gets a divorce—I'll tell you. I gave you a true account of all that. Now she thinks she has me where she wants me. But let's forget her. Don't ever want to see the bloody 'ooman again. She went through my pockets and did me no good. Never loved me. She's not even dangerous any more. I'm easing her out—and she knows it and I think she's pulling something— Not me, sweetie. . . . Not now. . . . She was on the phone just now asking for some money. . . . I only heard yesterday that she's got into a mess and trying to drag me into it—though she can't, I'm pure, I swear it—wouldn't bathe in a muddied pool—I swear it—and this morning, she knows I know it—and she coolly asks me to pay into her bank account two thousand dollars to pay her lawyer— No sense and no manners, eh? . . . On the phone this morning, asking for money for her divorce! She took me for a ride. No sense and no manners and she's looking washed out too. Eh? . . ."

At the word "check" Miss Robbins had paused in her typing and written the words, "Mrs. Downs—check; at Manetti's to-night" in her notebook. Grant had gone into his gallopade, marking the end of a phone call, "I miss you, sweetie, you liven things up. Well, I can be quiet too. With the right woman—no, not cocktails. Not taking cocktails, not good for me, too. I like Sue, but too staid, eh? A bit old-fashioned, you're very modern, like me. You're like me; that's it, you're like me. Everyone here is anxious to see you. Told them all, that's the woman I should have known years ago. Gilbert thinks a lot of you. Boy has a lot of character, go by his opinion. He told me, 'Dad, that's the kind of woman who would understand you and put you straight.' Bit of a mentor with me. Means very well. Honest boy. He thinks a lot of your ability, too. Like me, he likes a fine woman. You're beautiful, too. I better watch my step. Better watch myself! Dangerous 'ooman—but you like me, sweetie? Don't you? Only a little? Don't believe it. Can't credit it. I know better. Made for each other, that's the word. Well—"

He listened and continued with immense bravura—"I always said, 'Livy, all I want is a woman'; and now it looks like I got her! Looking for her, I got into those messes, that's all. . . . Eh? That blonde cow? Don't laugh at me, Livy. I've been hurt too much by that blonde. Besides, that was so long ago I forgot her. She's through. She's not a nice woman, not like you. . . . Doesn't care for me, personally, always thinking of going through my pockets. . . . Do you know what she just asked me? Not to forget to keep the Coca-Cola bottles. . . . And she used to take the half-empty liquor bottles out of my closet so her girl friend could give parties when she was broke. . . . She takes trading-stamps, yes. She's a one-way girlie. Didn't remember my birthday. Well, wants too much, selfish. No way to get a man. Well—don't let's talk about her. . . . Gilbert will meet you five-thirty at the Ritz and I'll see you at ten at Manetti's; right?"

He did not put down the telephone but asked for another number and almost immediately said, "Miss Holloway, please? Hello, Katie! Yes, I'm in New York. Got in last night. Philadelphia is all right—"

Gilbert started and looked apprehensively at Miss Robbins, who, however, went on with her typing.

Gilbert's father chattered away, "When do I see you, sweetie, for a little tea, a little chat? I want to ask your advice about something that's bothering me! We'll have tea tomorrow sometime? My boy's here and I'm not altogether free. I'll be alone for a while tomorrow and I want cheering up. Had a bad time in Philadelphia, bloody 'ooman let me down. I want to see you, sweetie. . . . I mean it. Well, I got to be careful: your family might get the wrong impression. Like your mother, very fine woman. Never forget the dinner she made me. Wonderful cook. Can you cook like that? You have to if you want to get married some day. I can't tonight, dearie. Tired out with traveling. Train was late, didn't sleep all night, wishing I had asked you to meet me. Then I got here, lots of trouble, big surprises, big blows, blows below the belt, unpleasant things, quite a shock, that bloody blonde 'ooman, I told you. Thought she had me round her finger like a piece of string. Made a mistake for once. Tomorrow, four, at my place. The Pickwick—my housekeeper's there. I want to give you a little business for your store. Bring me ten pairs of nylons at two dollars. . . . But you can get them for me at two dollars, like last time, eh? Want them for my business friends' wives. Christmas coming, they all got their mouths hanging wide open. Surprising how you can get a hundred dollars' worth of business with a two-dollar pair of stockings. . . . The wives are cheaper than the husbands, my sweetie; take ten dollars apiece to buy a Christmas present for the husbands! . . . Don't say that, sweetie; we understand each other, we're friends—no, we're comrades. I'm a liar sometimes but I tell you when I am, and never to you. Why should I? I like you too much. I respect you. I rely on you, Katie, don't forget, ten pairs. Bye-bye."

He at once asked for another number. Gilbert glanced in astonishment at the muscular busy back of Miss Robbins, who went on typing, when they heard quite clearly, "Is Miss Sapper there? Hello, Violetta! Hello, sweetie, well, when you are free are you going to come and cheer me up, have tea, a little chat? I had a big shock, hit below the belt, and want to take your advice. A woman hurt me. I had a lot of shocks lately and I've been out of town and couldn't see you. There was no oasis in my desert; now I found you and I have an oasis. My wife hasn't any backbone, can't look out for herself, and is no good to me. But I have to go to Boston just the same. I regret it. Not like you. I'm very busy now, darling, tonight I've got to see a lawyer about getting rid of my business here—I want to settle down and have a good time with the right woman. Come to my place day after tomorrow. My housekeeper'll make us tea. Can't see you before, sweetie, because my son's here and I want him to have a good time. I respect him; want him to respect me. I don't mean the wrong thing. Wait till I get him settled out on the farm, then I'll see more of you. . . ."

Gilbert took out a vest-pocket notebook and wrote down Katie, Violetta (Miss Sapper). He had not finished when he heard his father speaking to another girl and he wrote within the next quarter-hour—Bernice, Janet, Helen.

Suddenly Robert Grant yelled savagely, "Miss Robbins!"

The woman with golden hair got up, went placidly toward the door. At the door, she turned and smiled at Gilbert. Grant said, "Someone there?"

"Gilbert!"

"Come in, come in, son."

The young man went in and sat down by his father's desk.

"You look well this morning, Gilbert."

"Wasn't that Mrs. Downs you were talking to before, Dad?"

The three old acquaintances looked at each other in silence for a long moment. Then Grant said, "Good God!"

He frowned, fiddled with the paperweight, began dictating, interrupted it to say quietly, "Well, son, it's no good pretending I'm a monk. I'm no angel and it clears the air if you know it."

"You don't know me, Dad. I—"

"Your mother's an angel, a perfect mother and wife, but I'm not good enough for her, that's all. And she never did me any good. Well—better go outside while I finish the letters, 'Dear Spatchwood, About the house on Owl Island, let him show me my signed order for the bronze bell.'—Flack will sign it, Miss Robbins."

He lowered at Miss Robbins and by the time he had finished his letters, was in a roaring temper. He yelled, "Get all those off before you go to lunch, don't delay."

Miss Robbins put her book down on her desk, sat and stared for a long while at the partition. Then she got up, put on her hat and coat. Grant looked at her through the glass, "Do those letters for me first, like a good woman."

"I think I need a little air, my head aches."

Grant looked at her queerly, and said in a low tone, "All right, all right—but get them off for me before three, like a good woman."

Miss Robbins said to Gilbert, "You don't know what he's like. I'd have resigned years ago, only that he's rarely here."

Gilbert looked genial, asked, "Is it new—with the women—?"

Miss Robbins let out a peal of laughter, and was restored to good humor, "It is time you knew your father: you don't know how he made your money nor how he wastes it. It's a shame how he wastes what we work so hard to make, that's all—but he would say it's his. I suppose it is."

Grant came to the door and looked at them suspiciously.

Miss Robbins went off to a cheap restaurant and Grant and Gilbert to "the Italian's."

31

There, Grant fell into a shallow, shameful strain and told Gilbert of his love affair with Laura and what he had done for her—the bonds, the farm, the house in Rome; how she had repaid him by public disgrace. Nothing she could give him would make up. About Mrs. Kent (Downs) he only said that he had liked her very much but she had turned out to have no character, which, with all her beauty, put him off; and then she had married, and now what could he do? But in order to pay him out, perhaps, she was now trying to frighten him "with a few innocent letters and photographs—and I don't want to paint her in colors too dark, perhaps she loves me and wants to get me back, but now it is too late," and so forth: "Livy Wright is a good woman and I like her well enough, but I don't want to give your mother any pain, she's an angel and I perhaps didn't always play the part of a good husband. I fell in love with Livy and thought she would make me three women in one. But she's very spendthrift and I don't want to make another serious mistake."

Then he chuckled and said perhaps he had been out once or twice with lovely women, who could blame him? Changing his note, he became romantic, serious, with clear open eyes and a fresh expression, and he declared, "I am your father and cannot tell tales out of school; but strange things happened to me, I suppose because I'm a romantic. If you believe in love, you find love. Only I never found it. But who knows—let me tell you a strange thing that happened. Once long ago, I was coming in a train from Naples to Rome and saw a beautiful girl in the train. I spoke to her and took her to lunch in Rome. She told me she was the mistress of a priest, she came from a wealthy family and had given up everything for him. But this fellow was a rascal, met too many women in his calling and she couldn't bear it. Now she was living alone in a pension. She gave me her address. But I did not go—I don't know why. I had Laura; and then I didn't know—the story was peculiar, perhaps I was afraid. One day I saw a woman in a restaurant like her and I thought, I'll go and see Mrs. Coppelius—that was her name—Maria—Coppelius—Signora—and the pension was called Pergolesi—there was a blonde girl there I knew once, in the same pension. I had a good impulse and went to see this Signora Maria Coppelius, and I went in and said, 'Is Signora Coppelius still living here?' And they said to me, 'What bad luck! An accident has just occurred!' It turned out that Mrs. Coppelius had just thrown herself out of the window of the fifth story into the courtyard. She died instantly. She did not leave any note and no one knew why it was, but it must have been that priest fellow."

Gilbert was surprised. He looked at his father, murmured, "What a shame!"

Grant added, "The anti-fascists commandeered a car from her, secondhand car she had paid for out of her own money. She never got it back. She couldn't afford it. Perhaps that helped. You see she had helped the anti-fascists and the Government was suspicious of her, and the anti-fascists, too, thought she was a *bonne bourgeoise,* no one trusted her."

Gilbert said, "She was a victim of our times, wasn't she? If you could have got there in time, you might have saved her."

Grant scowled thoughtfully. He tore a letter from his breast pocket and showed it to Gilbert, "What do you make of that, eh? Read it, give me your opinion."

He stared at the young man impatiently as he read, putting forth his hand to twitch it out of his fingers, restraining himself. He rolled back his head, stared, and snapped his finger for the waiter, "More wine!"

And to his son, "I'm enjoying myself; we'll have some fun. What do you think, eh?"

The son laughed, "I think she's fond of you!"

He tore the letter out of his son's hand and looked at it all through, without reading it, then, "I thought so myself. Interesting case. Never touched her! Interesting story. She was married two years ago, a bit on the late side, thirty-two, married a bachelor and I was invited to the wedding, had to send a present, didn't want to go, but went. Afterwards there was a reception and at the reception she said, 'Come and see us sometime for sherry.' I said yes. Why not? Never intended to go, wasn't attracted—nice-looking woman, but wasn't attracted. Married woman, wife of a friend. . . . Three months later I get an invitation and I walk in, see her in a tea gown, nice room, very comfortable, and she gives me sherry. I swear I did nothing, didn't even kiss her. She sat close to me and said I must come to lunch some day. What do you make of that? Love at first sight, can't be, eh? Don't believe in it. She invited me for lunch and he wasn't there, and then she wrote me these letters—read them all—have some wine, let's have a good time, for once—read them all—"

He pressed the letters into his son's hand. There were only three, short and vapid notes on small paper. The first began, "Dear Robert," the second, "Dearest Robert," and the third, "My Very Dear Robert," with suitable endings. The third, which once more mentioned the sherry parties, made Gilbert ask, "You only went once for sherry?"

"Oh, several times—but I took no notice."

The third letter was a bald appeal for affection, "I was so happy when I saw you at our first sherry party, and later, life took on a new meaning. When will I see you again? You said our sherry was very good. I got one even better for you; and now you have not been here for weeks. Did I say something to keep you away?"

Grant was saying gaily, "Eh? What do you say? She likes me?"

Gilbert discussed the affair at length, seeing how pleased his father was at each new suggestion. Grant ordered brandies and went on to further tales: a lovely widow, Gussie, all in black that he had taken to dinner but never touched, because her husband had fallen in the International Brigade; things of this sort.

Gilbert stared at his father, nodded and smiled. His thoughts were vague. He could not attend and yet did not wish them to fall back into his daze of the morning. The older man's face had become serious and its large blue caverns had appeared. Also his bronze beard was beginning to show and he had drunk too much: his eyeballs were white, bloodshot. He had a slenderly curved rosy mouth and smiled gently, Gilbert saw; what a nose! it was frilled and twitched with its peculiar thoughts. Could a man with such a nose—after all—be the frivolous but timid old fellow that Gilbert had till this moment supposed? Gilbert had put his father's affairs with women down as "wishful"; the father, sallow and drawn as he was with his immense searching, wide-flanged nose, charming mouth, and blue eyes which showed the whites beneath. A suspicion came to Gilbert and at once became a certainty—it was certain that his father went with women, perhaps one or two—perhaps Mrs. Kent? Perhaps "Violetta, Bernice, Helen—" But when he returned to his father's confessions, he heard something quite different.

"People said it was my fault, they said so, how did I know? The fella came to me here in New York and said, in New Orleans I promised to help him out, a friend of Laura's. He wanted five hundred dollars and he told me, 'If I don't get it I have nowhere to turn.' Told me some long story, I thought it was a tearjerker to get something out of me. He said I promised him aid at any time, to come to me. Not likely. He was with me for years. I paid him, eh? He said his wife was here and sick, he couldn't make good unless he had five hundred dollars. I told him, 'My dear friend, I knew you in Rome and there you were a successful business man. I would have helped you out whether I promised or not. Here it is wartime, exchanges are against me, my money is blocked, my hands are tied. Go fight City Hall! Don't blame me. You could have made your peace with Mussolini, there were no principles involved; you came to the U.S.A. because you thought gold grew in the gutters, I didn't invite you. I'm sorry, my dear fellow.' I turned him down. Next week he shoots himself! Is it my fault? Now people are going about saying it's my fault. Only a neurotic man would have depended on a last chance like that—six hundred dollars—can it make or break a man?"

"Six hundred, or five hundred dollars?"

"I don't remember—maybe I promised the poor fellow six hundred dollars—but that was in New Orleans and twenty years ago: they got too long memories! I'm not a refuge for the mentally and morally crippled."

"The man was a neurotic."

"A neurotic. Like Davie Flack. I'm quite fond of him, though I don't like his daughter, but he can't stick at anything. He's turned down job after job. He wants to hang round me, can't live out of my sight. I hear he turned down a good job in Cleveland and he can't go to Washington to work because he's a radical. Bad company for me. Mental and moral cripples. They think I have health, they think I have money, they think I have houses, they think I have farms and factories—so I have, my boy; but not for them! What claim have they on me?"

"I always said, Dad, you had the wrong people around you."

"Now, Gilbert, you'll look round a while and then you and I will go to Rome or to France when this war is over, and help to reconstruct the country. We won't live like neurotics, wasting our time and other people's. You leave it to me."

Grant drooped, pouted, and continued, "Now Mrs. Kent, misunderstanding, now she's angry with me, now she wants to go through my pockets. How can I marry her? I don't want her. She's beautiful but no character. I said to her, 'I'm looking for a woman with character.' She's taking her revenge. I had another shock this morning. This fella Spatchwood writes to me, sends me bills for services rendered. I asked him, look over this house on Owl Island, can I buy it or not, in what condition is it? He misunderstands, he gets in architects, plumbers, painters, he gets estimates, he gets plans drawn up, he probably thinks of living there himself—I don't know what possessed the fella— and now he's got it all ready and I get bills for seven hundred dollars. I got no exchange and I'm not indebted. Now Spatchwood is angry. I don't know the fella! He was a cotton speculator, and waited too long in Germany for his health. His grandmother was Jewish, his father British, and he came to Canada, but he's ruined now. I promised him two—three hundred dollars and asked him to do this little job for me. Now I find the bloody fool has let me in for seven hundred dollars and I don't want the house, it's like a menagerie, it's like the fun-castle. You have to put in a bell to tell the police when someone, some burglar, is climbing into your bedroom. No one would live in it. It's cold in winter. You and I, my boy, want the sun; we're going where the sun shines all the year round even if it's Chile or the Sahara! That's where we're going. No murder castles on the St. Lawrence. I tell a woman, 'Make me happy,' and she takes me seriously, she comes to visit me, I don't want that. I tell Hilbertson, 'Count on me for five hundred dollars,' and his brother comes and says, 'You're a murderer.' A man comes to me, 'I'm dying, my wife is starving, six hundred dollars will save me'—must I believe him? Once I had a little chat with him, said, 'If you're in trouble come to me, I don't mean after twenty years, for six hundred dollars.' He commits suicide. Everyone is looking for someone to blame. Say his wife or his brother-in-law blames me! I can't help myself. A man, Uzzazuzz, wants my blood, he's crazy, he comes to me in Owl Island, he says, 'There's a man with a big house, bags of money, and I'm going crazy for five hundred dollars, I'll hold him up'—a hijacker. No good, I'm all alone. I pull a bell, too late. Christmas! He's got a rope round my ear. Ugh! What do I want with that Chamber of Horrors? I wrote to Spatchwood, 'Pay it out of your own pocket or let them sue you, it's not my affair.' He has no letter from me. Let him go in partnership with Davie Flack. They take advantage of me. If you misunderstood me, it's no fault of mine. I'm not interested in the place. I say, don't pay two, three hundred dollars when there's no business. Sell the house if you can, I'm out of it. That was last week. He sends me letters, he says—no matter what he says, he's a ruined man and he's neurotic too. I have other things to think of. Spatchwood's invested in the Murder Castle—a man without five cents to his name—he lives in a cold-water flat in Ottawa. I say, 'Smell it out, act for me, think of my interests,' and he tries to involve me—probably wanted to have an interest in it himself; and the whole correspondence was written by David Flack, I am not a party to it. Flack had his hand out, too. Wanted to live there himself, with Edda. Wanted to live on Largo Farm, too. Let him pay for his own dream castles. Probably seven hundred dollars will bankrupt that couple of cripples."

He frowned and suddenly gave a frank laugh like a halloo.

He patted Gilbert on the arm, "I can't help laughing—oh, he-he-he—he lives in a cold-water flat in Ottawa in winter and has to buy his heating himself and he can't go out with you because you're giving him food and he can't buy food for you—he-he-he—and now he's got big ideas and because Davie Flack wrote him some letters with a bit of conversation we had once, he's gone ahead and had carpenters and engineers and architects draw up plans for a Victorian mansion in the St. Lawrence—a house not built on sand but on water—eh? He-heh-he—a neurotic, eh? My boy—a neurotic. If it was a good proposition he could show it to me, I could say yes or no. But going ahead—eh? What do you think? Give me your advice! You've seen men in the Army. Megalomia—eh? Megalo-mania, something wrong, eh? Some mental disease, eh? Bad 'ooman, eh? Then he writes to me, 'Dear Grant, My mother in New York wants to send me dollars, will you arrange for the transfer?' Was I born yesterday? I told him, 'No, no, don't know what your engagements are, my boy—' Why get involved? I don't know what's behind. Perhaps he's angry, no reason by megalomia. Cut a loss, cut a loss. If you have to ask 'Why?' don't do it. A poor man is a liability, he has ideas, no money, he's got to stick you, no way out of poverty but sticking someone, eh? He eats, that costs, he drinks, that costs, he coughs, that costs, you must pay because you know him; he divorces, he wants to borrow, he has a sweetheart, he wants cheap perfume, he breathes, it's your air he wants.

"For argument's sake, you're both in a bomb shelter, you've both got to breathe, would he spare you? A poor man costs money. So out with Spatchwood; sue Flack, I'll tell him, but you won't get anything. Calm yourself and perhaps next year we'll have a little business up there, I'll tell him. I don't like that. Thought he was my friend. I wrote to him, 'I'll have nothing to do with it, make your own arrangements'; I've had enough of him. A poor man is neurotic, has delusions of grandeur. I said, 'The prices they quote are way above the market, they probably think you have to get a kickback.' I wrote to them, 'Make me a fair price and I'll see, take it off your hands, but I don't know Spatchwood except as a friend, he's irresponsible.' Thought this way I'd get them frightened and we'd both be better off—Spatchwood, for he can't pay, be glad to see the thing settled, between you and me; and I, I might take on the house as a proposition. Well, Spatchwood didn't know but he went to lawyers, but they said, 'Show your claim, naturally.' No sense, no manners, no business sense. He was once a friend of Laura, that—mur-mur—lady—murmr—Rome—she said to me once, 'Look after him, he's poor.' But she doesn't know human nature, kind, good woman. Sends me people, wants to get me back. Nothing doing; I got hurt too much. I learned a lesson.

"If I cheated a little, my boy, I learned a lesson. I need you, my boy. You see, I need you. You'll run the day-old chicks. Get rid of Upton, sentimental, fool ideas about women, runs around, don't like a libertine, signs things with his own name, irresponsible. Excuse me, my boy. I made mistakes, but I regret them. I'll fix it up a bit, go over the accounts like you say, very surprised to hear Upton made deals with neighbors and black-marketeers, very shocked, we'll clean it up, we'll run a clean business. Never trusted Upton—man wants to get mixed up with a girl, says it's his farm, weak, my boy, no character— In a year or two we'll see what you can do. Never mind them films—no gate-crashers in the film business, wouldn't risk my money. Stick to bees."

The young man answered equably, "Yes, yes," and was thinking.

32

Later, when he was left alone, Gilbert found it hard to piece together the conversation, put it down to his father's light-mindedness. He met Livy Wright at the Ritz at five and desired to tell her about Celia and how he loved her; but out of chastity and prudence did not. He had instead a long, tranquil talk with Livy about his father, who now needed organization; how he would not feel bitterness or shame at a divorce, but wanted a divorce for his parents and should not feel bad at seeing Livy his father's second wife. He referred meanwhile to many things he supposed Livy knew, and was surprised to see her surprise. He painted a full-length portrait of The Great Affair (Laura) and how Grant, still all to be made over, had been enchanted by her: "Dad always says, 'She walked all round me and made a magic circle; she made me a pervert, a gentleman and jealous—' "

Grant had told everyone he was going to marry the woman, a rich woman, a sweet wife, and would have become a Roman for the tiny dark-haired belle.

Livy shifted continually during this recital and at length burst out furiously, "So he was in love with her."

"Yes, he says she taught him what love was. Poor Dad."

"Did she? I don't see the results of much education."

Gilbert laughed.

Livy cried, "He must have been a terrible hick if she taught him anything, from what I see."

"She was elegant, of a good family, very rich—"

"That must have been it; he appears to have nothing but rich women to fall madly in love with."

"Mrs. Kent, now, is not rich; if she has anything now, which I doubt, for she's always asking Dad for ten dollars, it's because he gave it to her, that's a weakness of his, but shows he's not entirely angling after money. He wanted to build her up, it's the constructive side of his character. He wanted to see what she could make of herself. He gave her a little money to go to Hollywood—"

"Not forty thousand dollars?"

Gilbert looked shocked, "The house in Rome cost forty thousand dollars."

"It's a figure he's fond of and it's worth keeping in mind. But why did he leave Laura if she was so fatal?"

"He did not want to. But she betrayed him too often. Even at the end he wrote to her, 'Take me back'; she didn't even answer. It was her coldness in the end."

"But he doesn't look like the sort of man, to me, who would put up with a woman cheating."

"It took him years. He never knew where he was."

"He's not fond of her now, he's through with her," said Livy.

"Who knows? But I rather think it's his entanglement with her affairs, the money question. Money goes where money is, money yearns where money is."

"You're right. He doesn't come out of it too well! But if she's got his money, why doesn't he make her give it back?"

"He's very kindhearted. It's a kind of regret, expressed in money, an obligation. He choked back his feelings—she sneered at his social origin. It took him five, nearly six years to leave; it's the story of a passion."

"But why—why? If she was such a crook?"

"She got up early in the morning, looking very sweet and pretty, to make breakfast for him. He never had that kind of attention."

"And what did your mother think of all that," she said nervously, in a lower voice.

"I don't know. I was too young."

He paused and said, "You have no idea, Dad says, what Laura did for him. He said he was a wild man, a bear, like we see now, only much worse, he was younger then, uncontrollable, in-toler-rable, as he says. She made him a gentleman and his entire attitude toward society changed. She handled him with silk gloves, she had a silk rein. She made him exercise, go out in the fresh air. . . . She made him read poetry, think! She made him sit up late at night with people he couldn't stand, but who were people of culture. She taught him Italian—"

"He doesn't know Italian!"

"Yes, he gets all his letters from her in Italian. She taught him when and how to drink apéritifs, wines, and brandies. But he still doesn't drink much. She made a contribution, as he says."

Livy's tone changed, her eyes sparkled, "He doesn't drink? I don't know much but I know that he came to—see me once before work in the morning and when he asked me what he would bring, I said two bottles of brandy. It was on a bet; but he did it; and we drank it. Since we're being so frank—"

Gilbert looked seriously at Livy and thought for a moment; then, "I suppose none of us knows him too well."

"But your mother is satisfied with all this?"

"Mother has always been very rich and I've come to think it's a mistake. It makes people indolent and they seem to have no sense of reality. They trust their wealth to bring them every-thing—no hands, no sense of smell, no eyes! I am sure Mother does not know. I am telling you because—"

He looked at Livy again and stopped. But Livy grinned and seized his arm, "You're swell, Gilbert! You are a tonic for me. I don't want to live in any dream world either. Tell me more about this Laura. What else did she do for him?"

"She ordered the dishes he liked, even before he himself knew he wanted them. He'd come home from work grumpy, tired, not wanting to eat, and she would have made something for him with her own hands and when he saw it, he'd call out, 'That's just what I needed but I didn't know it.'"

"What a romance!" cried Livy sarcastically.

"Even if she was ill, she was there in a fresh dress, smiling, with perfume on her hair and handkerchief. She drove him into the country every week end, to her farm to get fresh eggs and milk, and she drove like a demon. He used to say, 'You're such a tiny thing and you drive like an ace.' Although she is a society woman, she sewed on buttons, darned his socks—and if he had one of his headaches she gave him powders and got a basin for his feet. She washed his feet!"

Livy shook her large handbag and plunged her hands into it, getting out one thing after another, tossing her head and saying miserably, "And he liked that coddling? It doesn't seem like him! It must have been a home away from home. Surely your mother noticed those things about him, when he changed?"

"You know, I don't believe, now that you mention it, that Mother ever noticed anything in her life."

"Well, why did your father marry her!" inquired Livy savagely.

Gilbert started; then answered, "She was beautiful, young and —very innocent; very sweet. She was famous for her beauty."

Livy's voice became more strident, she twitched more than ever, "He never told me any of those things; he never told me they were all rich society women! She owned a house? And a farm? And your mother owns houses and a farm?"

"Yes; I am going to own the farm."

"But they all own houses. And Mrs. Kent—"

"That is not the same."

"So you say," she said rudely.

"And he left her for her corrupt ways? And Mrs. Kent's corrupt ways?"

"But it is not the same with Mrs. Kent."

Livy cried out, "Your old man likes them corrupt, too. He's corrupt himself. Why should he have told you all that? Doesn't he introduce you all round, to all these pills and pikers, and these pickpockets he's with day and night? Don't you know them all? You don't know the company you're keeping, fair youth. Low company! That's his idea, to get you into it. Isn't it? I see through that bully-boy, though he's not transparent. . . . Very well, I'll get up early in the morning—I'll buy a house, I'll wear perfume on my handkerchiefs, I'll—"

She howled with laughter, "I won't wash his feet!" she shouted.

People in the soft, sophisticated, and depraved mid-Manhattan set which at that moment filled the bar turned, and turned back. But Livy, like a breeze at a suburban corner, blowing, turning and hooting, kept up, "I'll take your offer, fair youth. I'll take on the bully-boy. And why did he leave this Laura? She had everything, then."

"He just says, she broke his heart, she wounded him too much."

Livy looked at him with big eyes, but dubiously, "She broke his heart. He loved her, then? But why? Did he really love her

216

then? Why, when she was such a crook! For her house and her farm?"

Gilbert looked at her with surprise, "Don't ask me to explain it. One day he moved to the hotel. He waited for days. She phoned to say, 'Where will I send your clothes?' That was all. He waited for her to say, 'Come back.' But she didn't. That broke his heart. And at that moment she was having a furious affair with a pro-fascist. He couldn't stand it. It wounded him when she knew he was a liberal and anti-Hitler."

Livy, tying and untying a knot in her handkerchief, looked intently at him, and seemed puzzled, "Did that really mean so much to him? I don't know. He keeps funny company for such a radical. I don't seem to know him. And this Laura—she knew all society."

· "She still knows everybody. He says she knew all the wrong people too, the Hitler gang, she was, perhaps, an agent."

"She went everywhere—all the nobs—and he lived in that society five years? In Rome. And he speaks Italian. She made him dishes. You know he never told me that? He told me lies, and he said, 'I tell you lies but I'll tell you when I'm telling the truth.' But he always said he was telling the truth. Then he would say, 'Beware of me, I'm a liar, when I get warmed up, when I admire a woman I say anything.' I didn't mind. I thought I could follow him somehow through the mess of lies. I thought I was getting a ground-plan of the whole thing. But he told me lies and he left out all the romance and all the interesting bits. Now I know nothing. No one knows anything about that bright boy, do they? What a bright boy is the bully-boy. The man who lies most says he lies."

Gilbert said, "I wouldn't say that Dad exactly lies, he cuts his cloth to suit his company, and in a way that's good manners."

"He mixed with people in embassies. He let me think that an ordinary punk like me, from Pennsylvania and New Jersey, could carry him off. He's not a squareshooter. He's a rattlesnake; he rattles and says, 'I'm a crook, I'm a liar.' I'll tell the bully-boy what I think of him. 'Take your hat and umbrella out of my hallway,' I'll say to him. 'I don't know people in embassies. You had a woman who had everything'—she drove like the wind, and I expect to get him to stay in my back yard. Off with his head! Out with the bully-boy! We're through. Oh, why isn't he here, the bright boy, so that I can tell him, 'We're through, sonny. It was a long time meeting you and it's a short bad time since.' "

Gilbert looked at her with concern, and said, "Livy, he sent me here to meet you. I know he's breaking with Mrs. Kent and I know he's broken with Laura. What does it matter? He told me you were his woman."

She burst out laughing, "His 'ooman, his 'ooman!"

At this moment, Grant himself appeared beside them, with Mrs. Lawrence. He appeared busy and natural and the woman unusually soft and modest. Grant kissed Livy noisily, sat down beside her, and said his lawyer's appointment had been cut, and he had just met Mrs. Lawrence. Mrs. Lawrence said that just as she was leaving the business place down near 20th Street, someone had come in who had to tell everyone about her sinus and its many various cures.

"Doesn't that always happen to you at closing time?" Livy laughed noisily. "I hope you haven't been playing puss-in-the-corner with the bully-boy. Take him? Take him with a trading-stamp! I'm through with him. I have no houses and I have no pearl necklaces or ruby tiaras."

Grant looked at Gilbert and Livy and his face became grave. He pressed them to drinks. Livy sputtered with laughter and called out, "You're in the ashcan, sonny. Who was that man I saw you with last night? That wasn't a man, that was Robbie Grant."

"Now, Livy," he said, soothing her, leaning forward and delicately offering a cigarette and a match. He looked half puzzled, shot amused glances at one and the other. He did not look at Mrs. Lawrence at all.

"How can we be through, when we haven't even started," he said, looking at Gilbert, and making a sign to the young woman.

She called, blowing smoke across the table, "You're starting behind the eight-ball with me. Let the cloud be thick." She pressed the smoke together with her hands. "I don't want to see that big face in my dreams any more. 'Take, O take those lips away.' To hell with it. I'll cut a loss, bully-boy."

He laughed, and glancing now at the other two, very brightly, "Come and hug me and you'll squeeze a profit out of me, yet."

"Maybe I will and if I do look out, I'll squeeze you to death. I'd love to see you the victim of a first-class murder mystery. Hasn't any of your dates chased you with a revolver in her hand-bag? Hasn't anyone sent you anonymous letters telling you what she thinks of you? Hasn't anyone set a big bulldog on you? Oh, it hasn't happened yet, but it will happen here! Someone will

218

soap your stairs. You'll land on a big rock at the bottom, the way you're going."

Gilbert, offended at this, was surprised to see how gladly his father received it. His father took it as a compliment. He was blushing, his eyes shone, and his head doddled like a water lily when a rowboat passes. Said he eagerly, "What way? What way?"

"You're not looking for the exit yet. You're looking pale under the suntan, though. You're afraid of the last trump coming too soon. I bet you take all those washes in the morning to wash away your sins. But though you've got a whole day to work in, you don't get any farther. The liar is more than skin deep. He lies most who says he lies. You say you lie; is Epaminondas the Cretan a liar?"

"Why, Livy, what is the matter with you?" said Gilbert anxiously, for he could now see he had told her too much.

She laughed, smoked, and seemed in a good humor, but she went on in a lower tone, "I know his weak spots. He's afraid to be sick and he's afraid to die. He's afraid to die and he's afraid to lose his money. He won't go near a cemetery or a funeral home or a headstone factory. 'Azrael,' he says, 'I nearly met Azrael.' Perhaps he sent customers to Azrael. Perhaps he ordered his casket already. Say that frightened him! He won't look at a funeral and he passes the other side of the street to avoid a blind man or a beggar, and a widow and an orphan. I know my bully-boy."

Grant, who was very angry, did not know how to extricate himself. "I don't know why she's angry with me."

"I'm not angry with you. You have to be involved with someone to be angry with them. I'm indifferent to you."

She turned to Mrs. Lawrence, "I bet you've heard all his lines, Sue! Have you heard this one—"

"My lines?"

"His lines?" said Mrs. Lawrence and Gilbert simultaneously.

Mrs. Lawrence looked steadily at them as if in fright. "His lines! You mean—"

Grant was serious. His eyes fixed themselves on Gilbert and wavered.

Livy said, "It's my birthday today. I'm lonely and away from home, and I want to celebrate."

Grant cried instantly, "It's your birthday? Let's celebrate."

He snapped his fingers for the waiter, "Some champagne, it's the lady's birthday."

Livy shrieked with laughter, but sobered up and said mildly, "That's his line."

"That?" said Mrs. Lawrence, in wonder.

"It certainly is."

"You mean Robbie says that when it's not his birthday?" asked Mrs. Lawrence.

"There's little harm in that," said Gilbert, laughing and blushing.

Grant was blushing and frowning.

Livy said quietly and earnestly to Grant, "My life has been a desert and when I met you I found an oasis."

Grant smiled, and Mrs. Lawrence looked steadily at them without moving. Grant said, taking Livy's hand, "Do you really mean that, Livy?"

"That's his line," said Livy.

Gilbert laughed. Livy continued, holding Grant's hand fast, kissing him and pulling him toward her, with her arm in his arm, "I had a terrible shock just now, Robert, and I need consolation."

"Was it something Gilbert told you?" asked Grant.

Livy held on to his hand, "Let's have a little chat and a little tea together tomorrow, I want to consult you."

Grant looked at her queerly, but not injuriously. The others did not laugh. Livy said, "Do you mind coming upstairs with me for a minute? I'm expecting a long-distance telephone call."

Gilbert said, "You mean that's a line?" He looked at his father; and laughed a little.

Livy said, "I've got everything; all I want is a woman."

At this she burst out laughing in his face and Grant laughed. He hugged her and cried, "What's wrong with it? What's wrong with it? I make a play for 'em. I'm only looking for the right woman. I'm only asking 'em, Reform me. Go to Europe, Rome, France, after the war. Build up something, constructive. A woman's always constructive; and I want one. I've been a bad boy in my time, and now I want to reform. I should have been different under a different system. Listen, sweetheart darling—"

He turned to Livy and pulled her by both hands toward him, "I like you. I fell for you the first time I saw you. Let's have some fun. Do me a favor. Don't give me any trouble. Don't hurt me."

"All right, old man of the sea. You can do it better than I can."

Mrs. Lawrence spoke up, "You mean he says those things to—many people?"

Livy said, "Not many people, dear, many women. Good God, the way we talk before your son. I like Gilbert. He has character. Sue—he's a box of tricks. Don't play with the latch. The jack in the box will spit out in your eye. I'll box him up, though, I think. Be careful, Livy, he knows more than you. He lies most who says he lies. Livy, you better watch your step. The bully-boy's a K.O. champ. Watch out for that sideswipe, and here comes the haymaker. And out goes I."

She laughed, and grabbed Grant, leaning toward him with her lowcut dress, "You baffle me! I don't know how to approach you! You make me nervous. I'm a neurasthenic when I'm with you."

Grant laughed, "That's not like you, Livy."

"But it's very like you, bully-boy. And that, Sue, is another of his sweetheart posies. Love is not blind. Gilbert gave me permission to try to kidnap you and I will. I'm not afraid. I'm a guerrilla fighter. Watch out for me, you haymaker."

They were all cheerful again, except Mrs. Lawrence, who had, as usual, retired into a piteous silence, leaning out of the circle, her large eyes sorrowing in her veil.

Livy said, "Are you laughing at me, Robbie? Do you mind my telling them your sweetheart posies?"

He fixed her wisely with his eyes, "Well, if you know them, you know them, then you can use them! And so can I! But let Gilbert just walk down Lover's Lane, but not to the end. Let's go somewhere! Never mind my lines. I take them up and show 'em my etchings. That's all. I show 'em the pretty pictures, but they deserve it, eh? Neurotics! Looking for Canaan. I show 'em the Land of Milk and Honey. Not my fault if I persuade 'em. Eh? Do I look like a half-wit? I deceive no one who doesn't ask to be taken in and sold for tripe."

He burst out laughing, sat with an arm round each woman. "All's fair in love. *Caveat emptor.*"

"What does that mean?" asked Mrs. Lawrence.

"Beware of the dog," said Grant, with an innocent gaiety. Gilbert laughed. Grant said, gathering them all, with a gesture, into his arms, "Let's ring up my Polish friend, Karolyi, let's go somewhere, have a good time. We'll go over to his place, Hotel Benevento. I got a play he's writing for me, *All I Want Is a Woman.* Let's go and hear our play! He's nearly finished the dialogue. Going to be a smash-hit. Our names in lights on Broadway. All our names. Let you all in on it. You all brought me luck. And my name'll be on the program. You'll see my name with five—or six stars! Walter Winchell. A smash-hit, sensation of the year. Sell to Hollywood for three million dollars."

He gave a great laugh; then, energetically, "Wait till I get started; I'll show them some new tricks. I can sell anything. But what we got, it's a marvel, it's a marvel, a smash-hit." He sidled toward Mrs. Lawrence, put his hand on her lap, grinned at her, and poked his nose into her veil, "I'll wipe the rest of them off Broadway. Roy Rodgers, Mamoulian, Cole Porter, Orson Welles —they'll be trembling when they eat their breakfast: 'What's that Grant fella got up his sleeve today?' We'll be a sensation. Our names in lights, Karolyi, Grant—" he cried, looking round in a jolly rascally manner, winking at them—"wait till my novels come out—*All I Want Is a Woman*. Best-seller, a million copies, cover the bookstores, Brentano's, Macmillan's, you'll go up Fifth Avenue and just see *All I Want Is a Woman* by Robert O. Grant. H'm! Eh? How do you like it? I'll throw a big party, we'll all have a good time, the day it comes out. Advance, four hundred thousand. I'll show 'em how to sell it, if I have to buy a pushcart and hire a lot of fellas and set them at the corner of Fourteenth Street and Fifty-seventh Street and Thirty-fourth Street, Beaver Street, and outside every Longchamps in town."

"Bully-boy, bully-boy," said Livy.

Grant turned his back to Livy and seized Mrs. Lawrence's arm, patted her plump hand, now gloved, "Eh? Eh, Sue? What do you say? All any man wants is a woman, and every woman thinks she can be that woman. That gets them, eh? Then you have a constructive story, beautiful woman, she has talent, she's a success, and she says, 'I'd rather come home and fry you two eggs and bacon in the morning.' He says, 'No, no, go on with your career. No for you and no for me. You recover my investment.' She says, 'I'm a success, but I'm going to give it up. I want to bring you an aspirin when you have a headache, I want to get up in the morning and pour out your coffee.' Eh?"

"It has general appeal," said Mrs. Lawrence.

Grant looked round triumphantly at the circle and murmured to Mrs. Lawrence, "Don't understand it at all, a fine woman like you, not married again. You got me turned round like a spinning-top. You got me where you want me. But I'm afraid of you. You put me off. Even on the telephone I'm afraid of you. You're a lady. You make me neurotic. You keep me at a distance."

He bent closer, speaking into her veil, "Come on, give me some encouragement. Don't hold me off that way."

She began to glow and charm covered her again, like a sea animal which opens its colors and fringes to the tide. Her large eyes swam under the veil. "I'm afraid of you too," she said.

Grant pressed forward, "What have you got? What do you do to me? Eh? Tell me! Don't keep me at arm's length. You've got charm. You're dangerous. You keep the boys away. Don't do that to me. I'm afraid of you."

"That's all right, that's a good one," said Livy, licking her lips, and staring at them.

"I mean it," said Grant, turning round.

"You always mean it."

He burst out laughing and released Mrs. Lawrence. He leaned back, crossed his arms, surveying them with a genial eye, "I always mean it when I say it—afterwards, I don't know. I get carried away."

"One of these days you'll hit the wrong woman," said Livy.

"There is no wrong woman," said Grant.

Mrs. Lawrence had retired again and watched them resentfully from her shadow.

"Let's go, we'll call on Karolyi, make him go over his scenes. Wonderful situations, that fella doesn't work but he has the stuff in him. Let's go. I want your opinion. It'll be a smash-hit, believe me. Five stars, our names in lights on Broadway. Wipe the floor with Cole Porter, Roy Rodgers—"

"Richard Rodgers," said Gilbert, laughing.

"Don't get Karolyi, he'll sting you for a meal," said Livy.

"Want your opinion, he won't sting me for nothing," declared Grant.

Livy got up.

Grant took her by the arm, "Come, darling, I want your opinion. You're a business woman. A woman is never negative. She sees the human side. Let's have some fun. Do you love me? Eh? You're not laughing at me? You love me?"

He led her off ahead of the others and stopped at the head of the broad stairs, lined with palms, to kiss her. The others followed; Livy leaned heavily on Grant.

33

At the top of the stairs, Gilbert touched his father on the arm, "Let's get Karolyi, he's poor, he needs the dinner, and he won't sting you, I'll see to that. And let's get Celia Grimm, I know she's at home this evening—I happened to see her at Manetti's yesterday."

The father half turned his head, "I don't want the 'ooman. She's no good, no fun. I want fun. She likes colored people; I don't like mixed drinks. It's neurotic. Don't want her. Let's get Betty and Alf Goodwin."

The son planted himself in front of his father and said, "I don't agree with you. I think Miss Grimm is good company, and if we pick up Karolyi, we'll need another woman. Besides, she's an amateur actress. She knows theater."

Grant looked at his son in astonishment, "I didn't know that."

He took his son by the arm, led him in front a bit, leaving the women to straggle after them. He said, "Took the bloody 'ooman out a few times, bought her dinners, took her to Café Society, thinking I'd get in cheap, and I had to pay for ten people—and I didn't make any progress. Four, five times—that's all I give a woman. Didn't even kiss me. I don't throw good money after bad. The installment system's my system. A bit down and they deliver the goods. I don't like to be taken for a ride. Forget her. No good, my advice. We'll get Betty Goodwin—or—Mrs. Kent. I know a fine little widow, her husband fought in Spain."

He looked up into the face of his son, and saw nothing there. He took his son's arm with bonhomie, and led him ahead, "But let's get another woman, you're right, I'm sick of these cows. Let's get Betty. She's theater. She can talk to Karolyi. Never understand what the fella is talking about. She'll amuse him. Eh? List'n, my boy, wait till you hear the play—we'll make a smash hit, names in lights along Broadway and sell to Hollywood. We'll sell the damn farm and the day-old chicks and go to Rome or Lake Como. You can write sonnets, serenade some Italian girl. We'll have our day in the sun. We'll leave your mother behind, she's no good to me, and I'll get me a real woman, not these cattle, and we'll have a good time. You can walk down Lover's Lane and later you'll get a woman to marry. You can live where you like, I got places everywhere. I'll get them back when the war's over. To him that hath shall be given; that's true. We'll float on the tide, whichever way it turns. Don't worry, my boy. Trust me."

Gilbert tried to shake his father's arm from him. The father, his great face thrust forward, haggard suddenly, like an old gossip, said hurriedly to the young man, "I showed them my etchings and they were satisfied. Let's duck after we've given them dinner. I want to spend the evening with you. Take a little stretch, hear the news, no damn cows."

The young man shook his arm from his father's. Grant looked curiously up into the young face, and began to gabble, beset by a sudden need. He had never had anything but hangers-on. His wife had never known anything of him. Swindlers and prostitutes had received all his confessions. He had never dared to show his ragged, rotted side to his honest friends, whom he kept in one closet of his acquaintance, for the sake of his self-respect. He had been much surprised at Gilbert's calm attitude before the revelations of this afternoon and supposed him now "broken in," perhaps an accomplished petty lecher. He chuckled suddenly in a senile way, such as Gilbert had never heard, clutched his son's arm, and chattered, "I thought over what you said about the letters, the sherry woman, you're quite right, her husband disappointed her. Must be. You're always right. You've got an instinct. So she fell in love with me! But what can I do about it? Never meddle with a married woman. On that you can depend; I'm strict about my friends' wives. Nothing to be done. He-he. I get into enough jams as it is. I'm a romantic, my boy, must be a bit of the gypsy in me, or Spanish blood, eh, what do you think? Doesn't look as if it's in you, though. Well, a maverick, maybe. Listen to this, I need your advice. The other day I met a girl at Betty's. She has a lot of people around I don't like, talking unpatriotic. I say to her, 'What do you want with them? What do you get out of it?' She says, 'You're a snob.' I say, 'Not at all, I'm a democrat, but it pulls down my morale to associate with certain types.' This girl came from Cleveland—so she said, left her husband; some story, I didn't inquire, not interested. But good-looking girl. We went down in the elevator together and I—I perhaps gave her a little serenade. She says to me, 'Come uptown with me to my hotel, Seventy-first Street, till I change and we can dine and dance. I go. Why not? I do anything once. When I get inside the door, I put my arms round her, kiss her, she draws back and says, 'I want to talk to you about the financial reconstruction of Germany after the war. I have worked out the reorganization of India and now you can help me with Germany.' . . . Crazy!'

He slapped his thigh, 'Did you ever hear anything like that? I said, 'Come, my dear, we'll leave all that to the men in Washington, we've got something else to think about, love.' I thought perhaps she was fooling. She says, 'You're very kind, Mr. Grant, but I think we ought to do something for the world.' I'm thunderstruck. She gives me a drink and I sit down. She goes into the bedroom and I think—shall I follow her? First time I ever got into such a thing. Perhaps she's clean crazy and she's waiting for me with a gun. Presently she comes out, only her slip on, but stockings, slippers, and her bracelets and two little brown bows in her hair. She sits down and says, 'I think we should put a wall around Germany. I think we should put a brass or steel wall around Germany and then go inside and reorganize their finances. Shut them off from mankind for fifty or a hundred years, until they've forgotten about the rest of the world.' Eh? Clean crazy. I was a bit nervous by that time and I said, 'Never mind about steel walls, sweetie, let's think about us.' I kissed her and tried to make a bit of progress. But she pushed me away and said, 'I like you very much but I feel that we ought to purify the world, not think of our own egos.' I was turned to stone, my boy. I thought, Here I am, shut up with a madwoman. I looked for the door; and picked up my hat. She said, 'Yes, let's go out, dine and dance.' She went inside and presently came out in a nice black dancing dress, long, with black shoes, but no stockings. I danced with her and she told me she never wore anything under a long dress, it wasn't necessary. Dress is only for decency, isn't it? I didn't know what to make of her. Then she wanted to go to a late show. She had to go home and change again! She said her sister was coming from Cleveland and she might be there already. I didn't mind waiting in the lobby; I was afraid. When she came down, a man followed her out of the elevator, and I went up quick and said, 'Let's go.' In the movies I found out she had nothing on under the dress, we were very tight-packed. I took her home and she smiled at some man outside the hotel, a friend, I thought. He followed her in and she started to smile at him. I took him aside and I said, 'Don't go with her, be careful, she's crazy.' Something wrong. I let her go upstairs. What do you make of it, eh? I know her address."

The young man walked a few steps with his father, then stopped and said in a stranger's voice, "You're in terrible danger, you don't seem to know anything. I'm afraid for you."

Grant said eagerly, "You think I was in danger, crazy, eh? Might have had a revolver?"

The son sighed but did not manage to say anything. He turned toward the women and drew them to the curb, where he signaled a taxi. In the taxi he said, "I tell you what, let's get the Flacks."

"No, no."

"Yes, I want them."

"It's a good idea," Grant burst out. He put his arms through the women's arms. The young man faced him. He said sentimentally, "I need friends. I need consolation. You can take my word, I never did harm to a single human being. Sometimes, though, fate takes a hand. Women weren't always kind to me. I don't pretend I'm always a success. One Christmas I stayed in New York, I had business, had to see—" he mumbled a name like Sam-Positive. He leaned forward and patted the boy's arm, 'There's nothing wrong in the story. Shows how fate can walk in the door. Dangerous, living alone. I was invited to the Delafields', but later on, and there I was waiting alone in my place when the phone rang and it was a woman's voice. She said, 'I'm Lisbeth,' a woman I met at a theater once, someone introduced me, maybe I serenaded her, I don't remember. She said, 'I'm all alone for Christmas and I'm coming over to see you, otherwise, I'll throw myself out the window.' I tried to put her off, but nothing doing, so I said, 'All right, I'm invited out, so you can come over for a drink.' That was my big mistake."

He caressed his jowl and said, "You never know. She said on the phone, she only wanted to see me for a minute, she loved me. She said she loved me. Maybe I had had tea with her. I don't remember. Naturally, I let her come. When she came I saw she had a little valise. 'What's that for?—I'm going out later.' She said, 'I'm going on somewhere.' She was a beautiful woman, but looked a bit —drinking, I thought. I gave her a drink and when I saw her sitting around, I said I had to dress. I went in and locked the door!"

Everyone laughed, but Grant proceeded gravely, "No joking matter. When I came out, she ran to the window sill and put one foot on it and she said, 'If you leave me, I'll throw myself out.' Well, I tried to telephone. She wouldn't let me telephone. So—you know— I did my best—thinking she just needed a little affection; then I said, 'Now you must go, my dear girl'; and she ran to the window again. She said, 'I'll throw myself out.' I said, 'Go ahead.' On my word of honor, I never thought she would do it! She threw herself out. I looked for my key and overcoat and picked up all her clothes and threw them out the window after her. I started to go quietly out of my door when I heard a sound, I looked and saw her coming up the fire escape, just her head and shoulders, with a bundle of clothes in her arm! She was coming in again!"

He stopped and laughed. "Imagine my astonishment! An apparition! Resurrected already. I thought, they got American efficiency now. I ran out the door, leaving it open. I didn't come home all night. Naturally next morning she was not there. I looked out the window, and I saw there was a kind of cage round the fire escape. She had only fallen one floor. Of course, she knew about it, she must have gone and looked—maybe she knew the apartment house! A narrow escape anyhow for me, eh? Maybe I gave her a song and dance once—" he acknowledged dolefully, nodding his head, and patting the women on the knees. "It just shows the seed doesn't always fall on barren ground. Neurotic! Supposing she had hurt herself. She was going to commit suicide, but she came back to me with her skirt on her shoulder. Suppose she had made a mistake, but still had a few minutes to live, and mentioned my name! It's dangerous. I want to find the right woman. Get settled. No crazy people!"

When he got out of the taxi, Livy took his arm and leaned heavily on him, while Mrs. Lawrence, after a few minutes of silence, began murmuring maternally to Gilbert, "Is that a friend of yours, Miss Grimm? Haven't I met her somewhere?

34

They had reached the midtown hotel where lived Karel Karolyi, Polish playwright famous in Berlin, Vienna, London, who had fled from Hitler's régime at the last possible moment. He had overstayed his time, for his revenues and property left in Europe were considerable. Now he had lived for several years, by the courtesy of friends, alone in one room, here, there, and everywhere, dreaming of American millions, looking for a sponsor or an "angel," and writing as he could. The floor on which Karolyi lived was composed of small parlor-bedrooms, rented mostly to musicians, continuity writers, divorced men stripped by large alimony grants, peddling promoters, and successful street women. At this time, after some years of war, there was not a hotel nor an apartment house in town which had not this assortment of the half-poor and the fringe-people of Manhattan. The girls made a quick turnover, paid their rent; no one cared to harass members of the armed forces when they paid visits to "friends." For the time being the rascality and the skimmers were accepted. Everyone scooped greedily in the great cream pot of war. All criminals drove their trades in the open, carried their banknotes from store to bank, and loaded their women with precious stones and furs. The town reeked of easy, greasy "dough."

Karolyi was in. They saw him first against the smutty green carpet in a boxlike entry. He was a tall, dark, agreeably neat-boned townsman of about fifty, agitated, dressed with Paris taste. He went in behind the women, running his long nervous hands down their backs and buttocks with rapid electric strokes. He brought his hands up again, caressing the midline of the backs, with a delicate pressure. He was then introduced to the women and began gazing with indifferent penetration at them, slightly smiling. Grant, who had just noticed seriously the etchings on the pale green wall, tried to place the women on Karolyi's divan, but the playwright sat them both on the long piano stool, so that they could observe these several erotic drypoints, which were of the thighs of naked women placed in defenseless attitudes. Through the thin steel and concrete walls of the skyscraper they heard, on the right, a violinist practicing the Paganini variations; on the left, the feigned ecstasies of two bought girls at their trade. The playwright, indicating the drypoints, said with elegant candor, "Rodin, you know; do you like them?"

His eyes honestly admired the women. Mrs. Lawrence looked out the window. Gilbert said, "Dad always says, 'Show them the etchings,' when he means, 'Give them an outline,' but I didn't know anyone really had etchings; I thought it was a joke."

Grant frowned solemnly.

Livy said, "I think they're foul; I would give a nickel a dozen—"

Karolyi became anxious, said very rapidly, "They're supposed to be very good, not vulgar. I can't afford better at present, my darling lady, in Cracow it is quite different, I have sanguines, a whole cabinet, you would appreciate that; all over Europe, dear lady, but here, I cannot afford Rops, Fragonard—as well as you, I am aware —Fragonard—Goya—Picasso—I should gladly—I am not a—I beg you, I apologize—"

He looked at the women as if in despair.

Grant broke in crossly, "Read us Act One, Scene One, *All I Want Is a Woman*, that'll sweep them off their feet, a smash-hit, no need to open in Philadelphia, go on, my boy, read, my dear boy—do me a favor, I brought the girls to hear it."

"Yes, I am ready."

Karolyi seated himself haughtily on a chair. Grant bustled up, said to the women, "Not there, not there, sit on the divan," and got them away from the etchings. Karolyi, after a slight bow, himself sat upon the piano stool, pulled a folder off the top of the piano, and began to read. He had not got beyond the third interchange when Grant began to shout, "Where's the dialogue, no dialogue, got to fill it in, eh? What's this, just an outline, eh?"

"It's all right," said Livy.

"All right, eh? Like it? Wonderful, my luck. A smash-hit. I bring luck. What do you think, Livy? You brought me luck. My play's going to knock them sideways. Nothing like it ever seen. My name in five stars, Karolyi's too, electric lights. We'll celebrate the first night, go to the Silver Beach. You all brought me luck, give you a participation. Oh, boy, there won't be no echoes in our theater. Attracts everyone, girls, men, *Dream Girl*, every girl wants to be a dream girl, every boy wants one. Packed to the doors, no standing room, don't have to pay the clack. No free list. People coming on from Jersey to celebrate their golden wedding, I got the woman I wanted. This boy's got something, eh? Listen, but it needs filling in. No dialogue."

He begged Karolyi to go on, but shook his head about the dialogue. Written like that, the whole thing would be eaten up in five minutes, no play there. Karolyi began again swiftly, pregnantly mumbling the first scene. The others were attentive, and Grant, eying them, saw them pleased, jingled a handful of coins in his pocket, and before the second page was ended, called out, "What's your opinion? My play's going to be a five-star success. A headliner, Burns Mantle, John Macy Brown, Richard Junior, Louis Crownberger, Winchell, Winchell—a headliner, give them a cocktail party, free passes. We'll have five road companies too. Believe me, I'm lucky. You're lucky too, Livy."

Gilbert whispered to him. The older man mastered himself, stared, said, "Come on, now, let's have Scene Two: that's for the shipwreck, Karel, that last scene reminds me of *Roses in the Dust*, that Broadway hit, good thing, who knows, get the money out of the pockets twice for the same thing, ha-ha, once a sure-fire, twice a sure-fire—good, good—" he looked at Gilbert—"that favorite of years ago. Human nature doesn't change. But this is original, we did it; Karel and I. Listen, go on, Scene Two. Shipwreck very original, taken out of Shakespeare, only modern. Got to base it on something you know went. If it was a hit, then it'll be a hit now; human nature doesn't change. Different frills, that's all."

He was frowning at Karolyi, who had put down the folder. He was trying to talk him back into his seat.

"I copy nothing," said Karolyi.

"Good, good, my friend, a smash-hit, we like it. They'll lap it up. Let them start a plagiary suit! Good publicity. Everyone say,

'What is this thing, just like *Roses in the Dust*, so good, they got to sue for it!' The talk of Broadway. Go on, Karel."

Karolyi said, "I read no more. You have mine honor wounded. . . . Steal-thief! You said a steal. Karel Karolyi is not a juke box. *Was sind Sie* but a moneybags? *Je ne sais trop pourquoi je vous explique tout ça. Je ne serai votre Pérou. Sortez!* 'Raus! *Chacal! Requin! Ein schrechliche bourgeois parasitaire!* Smashit on the Broadway! *Was haben Sie geschrieben?* Sing, sing, I pray you! One note from this magnificent *herrliche gosier. C'est fini. Was für a schande! Ich bin jetzt a pockpick; asseyez-vous, Mesdames, Messieurs, que je vous contrefais un morceau de La Biche, Racine, Lessing, Checkov, tout ce que vous pourriez imaginer. N'importe qui—tout.*—I steal! Tell me, magnificent gentleman, as you are, whether I would know you in Berlin—in *Warczawa, Wien? Je suis mille fois plus riche que vous.* I pay *zwei hundert gulden monatlich* to my mother in Amsterdam. I do not profit by the difficulties, *het is wel te verstaan.* Even *zo* in Russia, *le chacal, qui rôde, qui vole les artistes, le voilà, n'est connu de personne.* Pardon, magnificent gentleman, I was a major. *Majoors, luftenant-kolonels en kolonels zijn hooger officieren. Ich bin reserve-officier à l'heure qu'il est. Wien me dorlotait.* I was not proud, why an artist works always. He works in silence, his life passes in a small room, no one knows him. He is a prisoner. Who shut him up? *Son génie. Qu'est-ce que c'est le génie? C'est l'instinct comme les—ces petits animaux—les cobayes?—de se suicider par le travail.* I send two hundred guilder and here I work and the magnificent gentleman has not as yet paid *un sou!* Smashit, he tell me, on the Broadway, I give you *vierzig, fünfzig tausend* dollars. I send my money to Amsterdam—I wait. *Droeve workelijkheid! Bien sûr que je mange à mon faim.* I get up at five in the morning, never later, when *schlaft die ganze Welt.* . . . I walk by the streets. *Ne parlez pas si fort, cela les rend nerveux. On appelle ça genus irritabile. Is hier geen levende ziel te zien.* Money is the sinews of war.

"*Quel temps intolérable, je suis mouillé jusqu'aux os!* He doesn't give me back my coat, and I cannot wear a dairty one. I walk, I walk, how can I work when no one is up, *parce qu'il faut que je clâme, vox clamanti. Je ne veux nuire à personne. Ah-ha-ha! il se croit malin,* he's a moneybags too tight sew up, nothing leaks out. *Un sou, ich werf en l'air:* smashit on the Broadway with one *sou.* Go with me, go with me, meet someone, I tell you publisher, projucer put up, I give nothing, so say the magnificent gentleman.

His pocket sings, not he. *Je vous jetterai dehors*, but I have honor, *il n'y a pas d'espagnol aussi fier que Karel Karolyi! Ah, quelle malchance!* I went in a ship that went from port to port, nowhere to land. *Endlich*, come I here. I wait three years, then meet I the magnificent gentleman. He tells me, You steal! *Je vous chasse! Charlatano!* For the ladies I will read. For you, I do not wish. I prefer not. Go and I read all for the beautiful, honored ladies."

Suddenly this macaroni poured from his mouth, rolling like quicksilver, at first fiery and then faster and faster, until the ear caught little but the cadences of a sinewy voice speaking for itself, a discourse, nonsensical but oddly composed, in fact, little but a piece of music *extempore* rushing out of the mouth.

The women, who had begun by smiling, heard him through to the end, while Grant moved uncomfortably, smiling shyly at his friends. He tried to put in from time to time, with, "Now, Karolyi, now let's get on, very sorry, misunderstanding"—and he frowned and jingled when Karolyi referred to the money he had proposed to put up for the play. Karolyi opened his mouth again, and a new mournful strain was heard, in which occasional small phrases hung together:

"André my poor typist, I pay *seulement quarante dollars, est-ce assez!* He is poor, he must eat. *Was macht er* in Westport? *Das weiss ich nicht, dans une grande maison sonore il m'a raconté, avec deux enfants. Il a tous les reçus Madame,* and what must I tell him? I cannot say, *'Je n'ai pas moi-même le sou, André!'* I engaged him. He does his work. I say, 'Monsieur Grant has not pay me yet. *Il doit souffrir.'* I need only two hundred dollars in all, *et puis fini, c'est la fin. Est-ce qu'il n'a pas de parole,* the magnificent gentleman! *C'est un businessman connu.* What must I do? Ollyvood, we can sell for five hundred thousand dollars, my name is known; or I publish itself. . . . But the typist, André, comes tomorrow and puts his hand out, 'You owe me twenty dollars; where is it?' You promised it today. . . . I am a man of honor."

He told a long anecdote about his affairs in Europe, at the same extraordinary speed; it sounded like a wild ballad sung. He came back to the question of André the typist in the great echoing house, and now sat down on the piano stool and with his hands stretched on the keyboard but still, he turned and said, "*Tausende* pounds sterling, guilders, francs—more than forty thousand dollars, pyramiding—and my collection of old silver worth one million *zloty. Häuser in Warczawa,* on the *Marczalskaya, dieser endroit ist bei mir sehr geliebt, auch ein schloss*—is it possible I have not twenty dollars to give him, and save mine honor?"

Livy said impatiently, "Let's hear the scene. Aren't you men ashamed, brawling like children?"

Karolyi said, "*Gnädige Frau, Pardon, Sie verstehen nicht!*"

Grant said, "I'm going to pay when I see I have something. Why can't I have my play? Do me a favor—I never said you stole anything."

"Shadow money produces shadow scenes. But I do not write shadows. When I come to Ollyvood, they will find out. One million dollars—and I will form a corporation my own, in Radio City—"

"Read, Karolyi," said Livy.

"I read for you only, *Gnädige Damen*," said Karolyi, and they heard a few vague words, when "What do you think of my scene, eh?" cried Grant, leaning toward them. Karolyi took no notice of him but read through to the end. Grant kept crying out, all his stock phrases, about their success and "my scene," and the ladies, whom Karolyi's vibrant voice, full of an alien chant, had moved, broke into applause. Karolyi listened for a moment, his face rapt, but he broke in on them as if he had not heard. He began another weird declamation about his chances, his finances, and the misery of his typist who would come tomorrow and must return empty-handed, and into which they suddenly heard come a phrase of excitement, lonely fever, "The honored ladies heard my scene and said, 'Karel, this is a enchanting, you are a spellbinder, when women hear this, they will faint with pleasure and throw you flowers.' Only let me kiss the feet of these tenderhearted women who understand me. 'I understand you,' she said, the dark young American lady, and this thing will be a hit on the Broadway and you will be a millionaire again in dollars. You will have masses of gold, handfuls of dollars. You have guilders, francs, marks, zloty and lire in Europe, and a thousand pounds sterling: magnificent, wonderful, and original. And it is a serenade from beginning to end, she told me, the charming, gracious woman, Mrs. Livy. They were swept off their feet, these New York ladies and cried out to me with tears in their eyes, 'This will be an unprecedented success and you will be invited at once to Ollyvood.' *Katinka* was not a success the other night, it had a cold reception. This is excellent news, this is good news for us. They do not want that any more but here, my play, *The Subway Princess*—"

"What's that?" cried Grant.

"My plot, *The Subway Princess*."

Grant flew out of his seat, scarlet with rage, and shouted that the name of his play was *All I Want Is a Woman*.

Another violent scene followed, at the end of which they all went out, Karolyi bowing to the ladies but remaining watchful, brooding. Grant grumbled all the way to the restaurant, "The fellow's a nut, can't have him along. It'll be a smash-hit. It's the nervous strain. Don't you think it'll make us a million dollars? Do you think he's written anything, though? It's a skeleton, it's all in his head, eh? I promised him a few dollars, but I don't pay till I see something. He's been five months on the play and I haven't seen a line. I expected to see it produced long ago. I heard him improvise but I didn't see anything on paper. Damn fella just sat down and copied from other hits maybe. But it'll be a grand success when we—" and so forth for the evening.

Meanwhile, Livy had paid great attention to Gilbert, and had probed her own memory for details of Laura. She said disconsolately once, while the father was talking for the hundredth time about his "hit," "Yes, but she's got the house. When the war's over he'll go back to her if only to get the goods. I don't know what I'm wasting my time on."

When they left, late in the evening, she assumed her best manners, and invited them all for the second evening following, "I haven't much time in town, the next one is on me, and I want you all together, and why not ask Karel Karolyi? I like him. He's completely nuts, with him 'meshuggah is trumps,' but I like him, I love him."

Grant agreed to this, "Tell him to bring the script—got to see more on paper—just a few words, do me a favor, that isn't dialogue, he tells me—André—I don't need no typist yet—he can type the two-three words himself."

When they had taken the women home, Grant, like a madman, went back to this theme, adding to Gilbert, "Karolyi—seven-fifteen yesterday on my doorstep asking for twenty dollars for the typist. I don't know where I stand. And this morning he telephoned Miss Robbins and David Flack. All the day on the telephone—he sings in my ears twenty dollars, and the receipts from the typist. I have three receipts but where is the dialogue? Neurotics, you got to see the stuff on paper. He can chirp like a canary, but we can't take that to a producer. Not so mad as that."

He retold the anecdote many times and found Gilbert in

agreement with him. But Gilbert went farther and asked his father to get out of the whole affair. If he had not put any money into it, then he had no investment to recover, and he was well shut of it. Let Karolyi sell his play, in skeleton, to someone, or to Hollywood. If his father had money, free cash, let him put it into educational films.

"We're not play-peddlers; it's business I don't understand, people I can't handle."

35

The next evening about nine-thirty o'clock, Grant, who was entertaining the blondine in his apartment, was roused by a telephone call from the head waiter of Manetti's restaurant. This man asked Grant what to do about the foreigner who was waiting for him at the restaurant. He had been there since a quarter to seven and insisted that he had an appointment with Mr. Grant and some ladies, so could not go. At the same time he refused to dine, since he was invited to dinner by Grant.

Grant shouted, "Throw the fella out, I've no appointment," and banged down the phone. He frowned, thinking of three or four who were goading him at the moment, schemers whom he had promised money, and discouraged after reflection. He said as much to the blondine, and grumbled, "I'll make a clean sweep of those fellas, cost me money, don't work."

At this moment the telephone rang and Grant heard Karolyi on the phone, strangely descanting from the Tower of Babel with his sudden laughs, names never heard before, intimate interpolations, "You know, as you said to me, honored sir, my honorable and distinguished friend, believe me, never, I say to myself, would you humiliate me, you are a man of honor and respected in the business world—"

Grant listened to this for some ten minutes, whole passages in unknown languages, perhaps Polish, perhaps Rumanian, perhaps Czech. He then passed the telephone to Mrs. Downs who listened for a while, making nothing of it, except that it was about his play, his lost craftsmanship, all given up for success and successfully, a moneymaker, he; into it all came the theme of money, money, money like a lost voice. She heard it in all his languages—money and its denominations, the names of currencies, the conditions of exchanges, and how it was that money was blocked now by the Nazis, and how hard it was for people in those warring countries to eat, though he kept his word as a man of honor, and thus it came back, money and honor, and how of his own circumstances he said nothing. Still he trusted with his hand on his heart, said he, to the honor of his true friend, Grant. At the end of a few minutes the blondine softly put down the telephone.

"Do you make out his gibberish?" asked Grant.

"He wants money."

"Let him talk his shirttail from his pants, he'll get nothing from me, to the devil with him, let his teeth chatter, if he won't give me my dialogue. He can eat my doorstep, he can eat his typewriter keys, he'll get nothing out of me till I get my dialogue, to hell with his receipts, not till I get my ideas on paper! Let the typist starve to death—and his children, too. I'll get my words on paper."

But scarcely were the words out of Grant's mouth when the phone rang again. Again it was the frenzied man, his monologue starting in the middle of a sentence as if he had gone on speaking since the blondine had cut him off. Now he had gone farther along with a freshet of German, saying that several famous publishers had agreements from him and he had an agent, but he wished to stand by his friend Grant, for he was a man of honor and he had this night conceived a new scene for the "masterpiece" which would annihilate all their enemies and make them the crowned kings of drama in this country, *My Narrow Paradise* the better name, or *My Dream Girl*; and if anyone could crowd Grant and Karolyi from the profession after this, such a marvel would never have been seen. Let him expect the script, it was supernaturally beautiful, but only let him give the twenty dollars for the wretched typist who lived in the country for poverty's sake and came to town today like a beggar with his hand out. He, Karolyi, his honor torn from him, he standing in the shreds of his honor, had nothing to give to the man of the promised sum. What must he do? The typist, André, would be there tomorrow, having stayed in town in Karolyi's flat, not having the fare to return home; but he needed the twenty dollars. If Karolyi came round early to Grant in the morning would he get the twenty dollars, or would he wait upon his friend Grant in the office, or at any time, but of course, lunch or dinnertime, in order to give him the receipts again and to get the twenty dollars? Grant would be satisfied, pleased, enchanted with *My Narrow Paradise*. He ended suddenly, "Then it is all settled, I come tomorrow at ten in the office for the twenty dollars."

"Bring a good dialogue and a finished play to suit me and you'll get the twenty dollars."

Grant cut him off in the midst of the next phrase. His mad harping fell away into silence. Grant took the receiver off the hook.

The blondine said, "I don't believe he's written one complete scene; he's crazy."

Grant said, furiously, "I've paid him eighty dollars for his typist; if he hasn't paid it out I'll sue him, I'll get it back. I've waited five months and paid him eighty dollars! I know he's behind in his hotel bill. He gets nothing till he's got something to show. I'll have him thrown out and seize his clothes. He has a silk scarf of mine, French, Charvet. He can't play me for a sucker. My play should have been produced long ago. I want to get my profit."

"What do you want to fool round with these people for? They're only trying to pluck you. They laugh at you behind your back. They think you're an angel. You watch out or they'll take you over. I wouldn't touch any of them, your friends. I can't see why you have such friends, not one of them has a cent. Why do they have you for a friend? They flatter you so they can get something out of you. Spatchwood trying to get your house on Owl Island. You're naïve. Someone flatters you and you take them out to dinner. Last month you took the Flacks out to dinner three times: what for? What do they do for you?"

Grant put out his hand, "Now, sweetie, I got to do something for them, for old sake's sake. He's no good, he hasn't worked for years, and she's a cold, unattractive sort of girl, I don't like her, and she laughs at me behind my back—"

He began to flush and said in a harder tone, "To hell with them —you're right—why do I waste my time? I invited them everywhere and they backbite. I gave them free passes to my house in Canada, and in France, and in Rome—and I talk too much, I told them too much, now they take advantage of me. They want to live on me. Why the hell should I keep them? I didn't work for anybody but myself. The boys and that bastard in Boston are fixed up for life. Let's have a good time, sweetie—a short life and a merry one and all for ourselves. Who cares for us? Let's forget that crowd of parasites, you're right, sweetie. Just you and me, eh?"

He thought for a while and continued furiously, "Flack wrote four scenarios for me and I haven't sold one of them. To hell with Flack. He'll get nothing out of me. Twenty per cent, I told him, he'll wait till I sell them. I'm not a Christmas tree, there for the plucking!"

"It makes me angry to think what you've spent on them! You're soft, you're downy! What did it get you? You listen to anyone who asks for a ten-dollar check. You made your money the hard way, let them. You watch out for them. They'll suck your blood, all those ten-dollar-check friends of yours. Do they care for you? This picture she drew of you, with a long nose and a fat belly—that's what they really think. They're laughing at you, and you're naïve. I wouldn't give them a sandwich or pay for a cup of coffee for any of them."

Grant demurred, a little frightened by this picture. But he patted her hand and murmured, "I'm softhearted, I can't be tough, I can't be tough," and as he was expecting a call, he put the receiver back on the stand.

Instantly the phone rang, and Grant picked it up, anxious that Mrs. Downs should not hear the female voice he expected. He only heard the voice of Karolyi, like a sharp hill river now in the rapids:

"—together and must protect ourselves. Not only will there be radio and movie rights—but we will sweep the world and in South Africa—we have this office in Radio City—and Australia, wherever you like, I was played in Sydney, Capetown, last year—and now in Melbourne I am playing—twenty dollars only you understand, my dear, and in Amsterdam at this moment—and at the Savoy, London—and in all these places, they're only waiting for Hitler to go, and they will play me again, you understand, my dear, what is there to lose? But he must not wake up tomorrow and I with my word in shreds, send him away empty-handed. Guilders, florins, Belgian francs, Swiss francs, and even blocked rubles—I have all those, in mountains heaps, I have only to go to Europe after the war and I am much richer than the magnificent gentleman who is a miserable, cheap, big miser, stinking with avarice, a moth-eaten rotten old skin full of money and ready to burst. I assure you, my dear, I am but midway of my career and when I go to Ollyvood you and I will be rich, my dear. Yes, I will be, as you say, at your office tomorrow at eleven, but it will be better for me to call upon you earlier at your hotel—no time is too early, I rise at five and walk about the streets, not a sound, everyone sleeps, and I am walking in the park—then I have a cup of coffee, not more, and go back to the hotel and write all day, you understand. My friend Mr. Grant, a rich broker on the Cotton Exchange, will give me five hundred dollars, but then I will pay this twenty dollars and he speaks to me of such a wretched sum of money, but money—"

Grant turned to the blondine, "It's him again. He's mad. I'm afraid of the fellow."

"Send him to me, I'll finish his little game."

Grant laughed, shut down; then picked up the phone, and called the hotel desk, where he left a message that he was not to be disturbed in the morning, if anyone called. He then rang Karolyi's hotel and left a message for Karolyi to call upon Mrs. Downs in the morning at eleven, to receive the twenty dollars.

"That'll fetch him," said he.

"I don't want him at my place, you know my husband is having me watched."

"Wait for him in the lobby," he said, eying her with irritation.

The unfortunate dramatist rang at the door of Mrs. Downs's apartment at eight in the morning, was admitted at nine. He told her he had already visited Mr. Flack at seven. He was sleeping. He had thought of visiting the secretary, Miss Robbins, a kind woman, but had not done so since she lived alone and he might disturb her. He kissed the hand of Mrs. Downs and offered her, in a piece of tissue paper, a single red rose, superb in form and fresh. He also had, under his arm, his script. The blonde, who had never brusqued a new male acquaintance, forgave him for his early visit. Her face was the flooring for a ballet of little agreeable artificial smiles. She turned her face toward him wherever he went, as he walked up and down talking; she seemed to dote upon him.

He suddenly took the script from the table, snatching it from under the hand he had just kissed. Rushing to the window, he began reciting with extraordinary passion. Sometimes he stopped declaiming and his voice with its broken surging *parlando* went on, explaining his own past successes, reminiscent, and passionate for new success, with such an elaborate sustained yearning that her hair stood on end. She became serious and said, "If only you could act it to people, it would sweep the country."

I cannot recite English—my accent—"

"Yes, we must have someone known—"

But he did not wait for any compliments, only raised his dark eyes, brilliant with preoccupation, to her, and without seeing her, went on with his intricate plans for their wealth and success—immense, worldwide, when the war was over—money, money everywhere and castles, houses, properties, all to be returned by the beaten fascists, tossing the speeches out of him like smoke, himself glinting and trembling and crying, "Dear Madame, O, *gnädige Dame*—" and then he stopped. His trembling hand lit a cigarette, his eyes were now peculiar as unclosed buds in a northern spring. He said, "And where shall we go? Let us find the Russian Tea Room—no, no, Manetti's, is it—tonight we meet together and fête our success, is it you, Madame? Grant has invited me and I will bring the script. You have seen the script and you will tell him, Karolyi never lies."

And out came one of his long explanations, with foreign phrases madly tripping over their foreign neighbors, jostling their way, panting out of his mouth, so that he hardly waited to draw breath, yet in fact, orchestrated his phrases before they were said and sent them out, poured them so frenziedly without sense but with such form and sound and with a throat so full of inner agony, that his whole speech was very moving and like new music full of a sense that she could make out. It had the form of music and no form of speech. Then the blondine who, naturally, had in spite of all her lust and avarice a great love for men, drew closer and became more attentive to this man who never looked at her nor answered her questions. At length she deduced that a party was being given at Manetti's that evening to which Karolyi thought she had been invited and at which Grant and some "charming honored ladies" would be. She even grasped that Karolyi thought he had been assigned to her as escort, Grant being partner to another "charming honored lady," who thought the world of Karolyi's genius. At first she said she was not going there, but seeing a sudden darkness, even despair, on his face, she said, "Go there and you will find them there. Perhaps I will come if my headache is better."

He remarked, "My breakfast is very light, only a cup of coffee, but for lunch I dine very well, soup, a steak, salad, a dessert, coffee, and a liqueur, there is an excellent place on Sixth Avenue where I go, indeed I eat very well—and I am not accustomed to receiving checks from ladies, though many wish to support my genius. In Europe, there is no such thing as the 'angel,' a bad system— I kiss your hand, Madame." Then picking up his script, bowing, kissing her hand, but still absorbed and without actually looking at her, he turned from the door.

36

The blondine experienced a very strange sensation in her body, as if her heart had leaped, but it was such a long time since she had loved a man that she did not realize what this was. Almost at once, she began thinking furiously of the money the dark agitated creature demanded, and that she had saved the $20, and of the party which was being given, by Grant, without her, to the hangers-on who were spittling after his checkbook. She thought of Karolyi for several moments poignantly. She despised and detested his beggardom! She despised it more than the pocket-love of others. He seemed to her more of an enemy to Grant's money, and yet with a greater incapacity. She envisioned for a moment the end of the war—she knew it was true that Karolyi had once had a large fortune and owned estates, and that the Nazis had confiscated them. She had seen the script. Suppose the drama succeeded? She wished to go back to Europe, where life was more amusing and professional mistresses could reign. But a natural hatred of poverty put an end to this momentary dream. She asked herself if Karolyi were not mad. If so—they could—she thought of a scheme to put before Grant. Let them see the typist, let them have the copy! Then her anger turned against Grant. The previous evening she had told him all her troubles. Her husband, Downs, whom she had supposed a gentleman, had done an ungentlemanly thing. He had had her followed, and now had photographs of damning scenes. In some of these scenes, said the blondine, Grant figured.

"But how, but how?" Grant had kept on saying, puzzled and disturbed at this betrayal. He had thrown himself into an armchair and stared blackly at her, trying to review the occasions on which he might have compromised himself. The photographs were in the possession of her lawyer Walker; and she believed Walker was in love with her. She believed that, with a small sum in addition, she could get those photographs which were perhaps photomontages, but involved Grant. Grant fought back, "I myself can pay for photomontages, the boot will be on the other foot. Let Alexis pay."

"And there was a recording apparatus installed, and I thought him so inexperienced. He is furious with me. I cannot handle him."

"How could such a thing have happened without your knowledge, Barbara?"

"Why should I be suspicious? The guilty are suspicious. I had no idea Churchill was so hypocritical, pretending to be so inexperienced. Now he feels himself an aggrieved party and he is out for our scalps."

"How did it happen that you told all this to the Goodwins first? I felt very embarrassed. I go to the Goodwins and they spring this on me. I was terribly upset. I expected you to have some confidence in me; further, I am very much involved if he had—photo—montages. What proof just the same that it is me? It might be James Alexis."

She had said with savage coldness, "It is no compliment to me to see you sitting there writhing inwardly, and figuring out how you can slide out of this."

"Why shouldn't I writhe inwardly? He's a blackmailer. Don't you see that? And this lawyer, Walker—what's he doing in it? You say you can buy him off for some amount? That's blackmail. And I don't like Alexis's leavings, taking the rap for Alexis."

"That's hardly the light in which to view it. This lawyer's hard up, he likes me, and for me he will do something."

"They have nothing against me. It's a frame-up. I'll do nothing. I never forgot March gave you five hundred dollars. . . ."

"You're afraid for your wife and sons, you're afraid for the money your wife has."

He had turned on her. "To hell with my wife and sons, I'll do what I like; I'll have you if I like. Let them know the worst. But no one will blackmail me. She won't divorce me; she'd rather do anything than divorce me. Don't flatter yourself. You'll get no divorce from her. You won't corral me so easily. As for the boys— let them mind their own business. I'll not arrange my life to suit them. They don't like me. Too bad. I've got them tied up in a bundle in my pocket—" and he made a terrific gesture of squeezing something together and tying it round the neck.

He stared angrily at her, "But I won't let anyone blackmail me. And I won't pay a cent. If he thinks he's an injured party, let them get money out of those that injured him. If you've done that to him, I'll tell him it's Alexis."

She said in an ordinary tone, "Downs is going round town asking people to burst out crying over his injuries. His heart injuries. He asked me, 'What will my mother think when she knows this? This is a very terrible thing.' Poor man. We must get up a subscription for him, I thought. It's my opinion that any heart-wounds of that sort can be healed with a hundred-dollar bill, and if he has been stabbed a lot of times as he says, then perhaps five or six thousand dollars will heal him. Then he can go away and rest with his dear mother and not think any more of the terrible woman he got in with. After all, I am a young woman, and I cannot allow him to ruin me. It is better to buy him off. It is extraordinary how you can always buy off these romantic heart-afflictions. Or else it is just a strange coincidence that you give an honest, injured party five or six thousand dollars, and then, somehow, he sees new horizons."

Grant had opened angry eyes upon her and fixed her, "You want me to put up five or six thousand dollars? Get it from the others."

"What others? There are no others."

"The syndicate mentioned in the indictment."

"What indictment? You mean the complaint? There are five or six others. Only five or six thousand dollars. I know that Downs lost money in the market, and now he is trying to realize on his wife. His mother told him I was too great an expense, and now she has pushed him to make money through me. You see he does not think he is blackmailing, or a pimp. It is an idea that came to him that he must be paid, the world owes him five or six thousand dollars to bandage his honor, because he once or twice saw me in the street or in Manetti's with a man."

"With me? What does that prove?"

"As I say, it doesn't prove a damn thing. I said to Churchill, 'What will your poor mother feel when she sees your name in the paper, Downs vs. Downs, and you claim that you were made ridiculous by Alexis and Grant, Inc. You are being ridiculous now. I am of unblemished character and I will bring character witnesses.' "

Grant laughed mildly and said, "Oh, we must be careful, think this thing out. Of course they have nothing on me—but he is a child, if he feels himself the injured party, he'll try to vindicate his rights, if you can put a poultice on them—but I have no money free, you know how I stand with the exchanges—you know how short I have been lately—"

She had cried, "Don't cry poverty to me—I think I have had astonishing forbearance—you have abused me. You promised to marry me. I marry someone. What do you do? You seduced the wife of a man. There is such a thing as normal expectation. You let me see you were pleased enough to get me on his payroll so I should weigh less on yours, and I made no complaint when I saw your meanness getting the better of you week after week, while all the time my expenses were the same and our relations were the same—I kept him from any suspicion—you had all the protection and all the pleasure—I was the lonely, poor, anguished person. I know very well how you treat your friends. Don't I know what you do for all those mangy dogs you have round you, sniffing after your money? You promise them a pension and pie in the sky, like you promised me. Let's speak plain. But you pay them in peanuts like you pay me and all the time they have the exceptional compliment and pleasure of your company! They are paid off with a fat Christmas bonus too, you think, with an *œuf à la russe*, a cocktail. But I am not taken by the same trick twice. You can't wriggle out of this. You must stand by me."

"Sweetie, I'm not trying to wriggle out of anything. Let's look at this sanely. You are married to a man who, whether he knows it or not, is a blackmailer. Perhaps he's right. I don't know, I don't say. I don't know if he has proofs or not. He has nothing on me. That's my story and I stick to it. Photomontage—perhaps; nothing else. We'll face this together. Depend on me. As for five or six—ridiculous—if you've been making a little whoopee with someone with that much money to throw down the sink, you must go to him, but with me, my dear girl, you have the wrong number."

Thus he had exposed his present defense. She had only observed his disquiet about the "photomontage." She, meanwhile, had thought out her own situation and had seen that she had had a great mistake in marrying a naïve man. The best thing would be for her to marry Grant, whom she disliked and was tired of, but whom she knew she could manage, in his old age. She had to bring the thing into the open. In doing this she would be pulling against her counsel, Walker, and Goodwin's friends, Goodwin himself, for all these expected that Grant would put up a good round sum. It was regarded not only as a good joke, but as sound business and a mild way of soothing Downs. Goodwin had yesterday afternoon offered to settle the whole thing to everyone's satisfaction, by talking horse-sense into Downs. He would make the following proposition: That Grant should pay for the Reno divorce and lawyers and for the agreed-upon alimony; but the alimony would be "severance pay" to Downs, whose business was in a bad way and who would certainly be glad of the money. Goodwin was quite confident, "Walker has already been to Downs's lawyer, Smitt, and Smitt was not too cold."

The blondine, who was in debt and overdrawn, sat for some time thinking over Grant's defense and his attitude to her, and then reached out in her memory and considered what pressure she could bring to bear on Grant, or what use she could make of the few friends of his she knew outside the Goodwin circle. She felt very bitter against Grant and wanted to fling the blame for her whole spoiled life on him. She knew she was not a black-mailer but an injured woman, followed by bad luck, who was trying to get a portion of her rights and expectations from a malicious miser. The thought of the heavy weight of money lying in his banks, and of the properties abroad in his name, made her think more keenly of how desperate she was for a mere living. He was a hard nut to crack.

She decided to go to Manetti's that evening, not to make any trouble, but to watch Grant and see what company he might be keeping at the moment. If she worried the thing over for several days, with Goodwin and two lawyers working for her, and with them sought some business arrangement with her husband who might be got off, she would be able to get out of this mess. It came to her more forcibly what she would lose if this affair were whistled away. She was really thirty-seven. She had to get a marriage or a large sum of money out of it. She began thinking whom she could ask to write certain letters for her. She thought, I do no harm to the wives, for I open their eyes to what kind of a man they have got; and if I shake the basket hard enough one of those hard nuts will fall out and crack open his bank account. She lined up the men to whom she might reasonably apply for help, men to whom she had given consolation. She saw them in bright, hard light against a white sheet as in a police line-up. She arraigned them and thought each was guilty. The one nearest to her was Grant, then a French immigrant antiquary who had done well during the war folly, Murvieux, James Alexis, Hugo March, the rest were poor men, "love affairs." She could get very little out of Alexis, with whom she had private arrangements. There was only the distant possibility that in a few more years he might take up with her; but never in a satisfactory way. He would ask her to live obscurely and without a name or any amusement on an orchard he had bought in Spain, if the monarchy came back.

She had a luncheon appointment with Goodwin and Walker; she sat down to sketch out the letter which she would have sent to the wives. One of them would perhaps bring it out into the open. She thought about her project as she wrote. Would it be better to wait a while? To drag it nearer and nearer to the daylight herself—and yet be able to control the moment of exposure?

After the interview with Grant she had found herself very depressed and had lost heart at the difficulties that hung upon her like a monstrous obesity. It seemed to her the lawyers and the Goodwins, who wanted her to stick Grant with the divorce, for malicious fun, were pushing her toward some disaster. Her husband's lawyer had indicated, said Walker, that he would not be satisfied under ten thousand dollars. She did not believe she could get this sum even from Grant, and by the time it reached her husband would there be enough left to satisfy him and his mother and would there be a cent for her? Besides, the lawyer had told her she must work to show that she had a means of livelihood, better away from her cronies.

At the last moment, a distrust of the Goodwins came to her: what was their interest in it all? In this friendless state she went with her mother to Manetti's and through a screen of pot-plants observed Livy's dinner party. The old woman's pestilential suggestions, envious, venal, filled her ears until late into the night. She sent the anonymous letters.

37

The next day she attacked Grant by telephone and in two rendezvous, in a height of sordid and jealous passion. She was ready to listen to any plot against Grant. Grant met her, for example, twice in the White Bar, but would not allow her to meet him at home. He seemed agitated and alien, over the phone, "You have me, sweetie, if no else stands by you, only don't come here. I'm packing. I had a letter from my wife and she's anxious about me—a bit dubious too, perhaps. Don't blame her. I'm going to Cuba. Bit of business—Sam Positive—I have been very anxious about what you told me, darling, and about those photomontages. My wife's telegram is very puzzling too."

She seized this opportunity, "It would not surprise me if my husband, that inexperienced man who is forty-five years old but is pure as a newborn child, and so must make the rest of us pay for it, if he sent a letter to your wife. He is calling everyone to witness how innocent he is and what kind of a woman I am, that is as he says. He said men like you should not be loose in society, that you ruined the lives of innocent women, meaning, of course, your poor wife. It was very touching. He said an ex-

246

ample should be made of you so that you would not be able to hold up your head. I told him that if he had remained guaranteed pure by the Pure Food Act, at forty-five, it was a miracle. He threatened me and your family life, injecting his poison in the most fantastic, unexpected, unnatural places. Who is the wrongdoer, I said, you, or me, if you do such a thing as to write to innocent, ignorant people like Grant's wife?"

Grant muttered humbly, "What you say worries me very much, darling; and about those letters, if he is behaving like a madman and writing all over the country, we must stop them. Make him bring his proofs into court or settle the whole thing out of court, but not allow him to run amok. This is very serious. You can't do anything with a man who's running amok. It's shoot him or tie him up. We're innocent, sweetie. I've just been kind to you because you're one of a large circle of friends and we have friends in common, and we all went out together on parties, it is hard to show harm in that. I suppose a man and a woman can have tea together without injuring the marriage bond, without having irregular designs on a contract. It is not actionable. They haven't a case, sweetie. I helped you out—"

"Oh, you've been marvelous," she said icily.

"I did my best for you."

"Excuse me, while I dry up my tears on that subject. Pardon me, Robert, you have been very cruel to me and I don't know what to make of it. You are simply backing out of it and leaving me in the lurch. I got your note this morning and it made me furious, explaining why I was not in on the party last night. What a pity Mother and I ran into you as you were leaving with your gay party. You told everyone about the situation I am in. I heard you, otherwise should not have believed it, but not a word about your own part in it. 'The blonde got into some trouble. Do me a favor and see if she's there, I don't want to run into her.' What a pity I have good ears, not my own. You don't suppose I have friends, do you? I give big tips and I have friends. Walls have ears. I turned to you for help. You try to turn tail and run, leaving me to face the pack. It wouldn't be a wonder if I went out for revenge. It will be useless to pretend that we had tea together. Churchill was making inquiries behind my back and you confided in every stray dog in town. We had a long intimacy and no one would believe it, even if it is true, that we met about two hundred times, a lot of them in your flat, and you only kissed my

247

hand, and gave me a rose, like Karel Karolyi. Not with your reputation. Not with your unblemished character! Ha-ha. You try and call character witnesses. Will anyone believe it was tea? Where will the gull be found to think it was friendship? It was a friendship between a married man and woman. Under the circumstances they are entitled to think what they like. It was criminal if custom makes it so, even without the photographs and letters, the telegrams and cards from florists."

"You kept those?"

"I'm a collector."

"I'll pay the lawyer to get you off, that's all, and it's only because I don't like to see a decent woman friend of mine—perhaps the photographs are of a different fellow altogether."

"I thought you said photomontage?"

He started to bully, "I don't want to hear any more about it. He's scaring you. That sawny wouldn't go through with it. Perhaps he knows something else you haven't told me."

"An accident happened for which I was not responsible. Churchill has been crazy, insane, and following me for months. He had a detective—in a car outside my apartment house! I had no home life. I had to join a bridge club to get out a bit. Then I took singing lessons, just to get out. I went to work looking after a friend's baby as a sitter—"

"As a sitter—" he said, concerned.

"It was to show what I did with my evenings. I have plenty of character witnesses. He opened my mail. I had to take a box. He counted my money—what did you do with the fifteen cents? My life was an agony. I was in a house of detention. He found I had no one keeping me—"

"Eh?"

"Keeping company with me."

"I know, I know, darling," rumbled Grant cheerlessly.

"And you, like the rest, suspect me; you leave me in the lurch when I most need a friend. There you are at base headquarters, while I'm in the firing line. I didn't get the check yesterday or this morning."

Grant at once went into action. "Look, sweetie, I have no dollars at the moment, I had several big shocks financially. Goodwin lost all that money in wolf, Poynter needed three thousand dollars for his lawyers to get him out of jail, I paid Walker five hundred dollars for you—my partner, damn fool, dropped fifteen thousand dollars—I'll be in the hole at the year-end, don't like that.

I'm sorry. My funds are tied up abroad, can't get a cent out. Just pay my hotel bill and keep my family."

"You surprised and disappointed me last time I saw you. You told me you would go to Boston and see your wife and come back and stand by me, and you're still here. And in your note this morning, signed by your secretary, you say for three weeks. You say you have to go to Cuba—how am I to live? What will happen if it gets to the newspapers? All those head waiters sell to the gossips. I have no money to buy those newshounds and Churchill has!"

"You can go and see the lawyer and do anything you please, tell him he'll be paid. The lawyer can go the limit to protect you and get Downs cooled off. But I don't want to pay Downs. Does he want to pimp? Besides, why should I? What does it look like? Them photos are photomontage. Those letters are forged. That fella's crazy, he'd make up anything."

Her voice was acid: "Look, darling, we can both be very inconsiderate and unkind; or we can both be considerate and make the best of an unfortunate mistake, an accident. The latter course is by far the wiser one—especially for you. A woman is always in an unfortunate situation. People have dirty minds. You have been most indiscreet. You talk loud and big; everyone in the restaurant the other night could have heard you if they had listened. Walls have ears, too. No one would believe your teatime story. They only have to bribe the elevator boy or the doorman in your hotel. Or Mrs. MacDonald, and they'll make up some story to please the gossip columns. And I frankly have been stupid. I looked upon you as my friend and was indiscreet. You made a solemn promise to me and you backed out of it."

He laughed suddenly and clearly, "My dear girl, you're a married woman! I'm married. I could make no solemn promise. If I made it, it wasn't solemn—you can't go into court with that."

"Oh, I know your horseplay and cheap calculations. But I went out on a limb for you; I compromised myself, a married woman, and no one would exculpate you. You have not an unblemished reputation, you either. Just let the gossip columnists get hold of your name once and you'll hear a horse-laugh from here to the Battery. Let us be serious. The fact is that neither of us can afford to stand on ceremony. We are in this together and in deep."

"Just let your husband try to get money out of me, we can get him for extortion, intimidation, blackmail, compounding a felony, everything," said Grant.

"I don't want to be dragged through the mud to save you a few dollars; and if I am held up to ridicule, so you will be."

"Don't exaggerate the situation, you're nervous," said he nervously.

"I wouldn't dream of exaggerating the situation. I couldn't exaggerate the situation. My life is an agony. But I have no time to think about myself. My needs are too urgent. I can't pay the rent. I shall be dispossessed. I can't confide in Mother. It would kill her. Even Downs can't pay the rent, he's a dope and a dupe and he's broke. You are asking my sympathy for your forty-thousand-dollar loss and other losses, and telling me you must leave me to be crucified, to run after your wife when I find out she has one hundred thousand dollars and more in her own name. What does she need your sympathy and support for? So I can only think of my own small losses which must make you laugh in your sleeve. What an imbecile getting excited about five hundred dollars, about being put out on the sidewalk, and going back to pavement-pounding! How small it all seems to you, that a person can cut their throat for what to you is petty cash that you spend in two evenings at even your cheap cabarets! You cannot make up forty thousand dollars by the year-end, good, but five hundred dollars would be peanuts to you. I am tired of your horseplay, my dear Robert. Five hundred dollars is very small for my present needs, and I only say that because that would keep me from the gutter.

"You know, Robbie, there is such a thing as normal expectations. We have no written agreement, but you owe me a good deal. If a man ruins a woman's reputation, breaks up her marriage, it does not look very good for him in the public eye. He can hardly go back to his wife and children and say, 'Respect me, my hands are clean, my conscience, too, my head is high.' No, he must say, 'Do what I say, don't do what I do.' Your wife, who is a child, would never stand for what Churchill threatens. If a man doesn't intend to make reparation and he breaks up a woman's marriage, and breaks up his own marriage, what will a jury think of him? Perhaps he is not in cause, but even in the State of New York do you know it is unlawful to commit adultery? You did not know that? Well, you would not come into court with clean hands. Then I know your line of defense, which would be broken down by a clever lawyer in two minutes and you would have committed perjury, contempt of court as well. And the court would see that you abuse a woman, break up her marriage, make promises

250

to her, and then allow her to be crucified—this will not impress the jury or the newspapers."

"The jury—the newspapers—" he expostulated.

"You have got Churchill roused. He is an honest man who never knew there was anything wrong. The majority of the jury will be just like him, men in moderate circumstances who would not like their wives to be seduced away on a bargain basis, by a rich Don Juan—such men hate Don Juans: you won't stand a chance—"

He murmured, "Good God, I am not going to trial—"

"Naturally, Churchill would see you were called as a —— Listen to me, don't interrupt. Your happiness and mine depend on it: we are just as if we were married, we're one in this. You know that even a small amount of money can seem very, very important to men like those who will be in the jury. And if they heard that I sought assistance from someone who had led me to believe that he sought understanding and help and had had a shock, and needed consolation; and that he promised her something for the future, and did not scruple to break up her marriage, and that he was unhappy at home and took every kind of comfort from her, and that he was, relatively, to the men in the jury, very rich—well, will they cry their eyes out about forty thousand dollars and three thousand dollars—if you could bring in such dealings before their eyes without compromising your whole life? Yet, they will say, when this woman, who has been a real friend to him, asks for a little loan and a little help, especially a woman who can show she is working honestly at a job, and has taken night jobs as a sitter for a few dollars—and a photographer's model, dressed, anything respectable—and he never so much as sends a Valentine—and if this rich person has got this poor woman, the sitter, this so-called criminal, this unfortunate, into this very situation himself, forcing her to work as a sitter—what will the members of the jury and the press think of such a person, so very much richer relatively than themselves?

"I will tell you, Robbie, what they will say. They will say, 'Here is a man-about-town who took a woman and used her for what he wanted, lied to her, and left her in the lurch when he saw a bit of danger to himself; he was playing with matches, he started a fire, and then ran off yelling for the hook-and-ladder crew, leaving her to get burnt up. He turned tail and left her without a roof over her head when he has ten or twelve roofs over his, and some in enemy country; and when her husband gets into a bad temper and gets suspicious because of his ignorance of the world, then this man runs off to the West Indies, or to dear wifie.' What a sweet picture! 'Here is a hunted, unfortunate woman,' they will say, 'and the man does not take any consequences of his own acts, who says he is only a friend and does not behave like any friend in the whole world.' A rich man throwing away thousands in cabarets, and paying two hundred and forty-five dollars monthly for a place to bring women, and corrupting a fine, respectable old woman, his housekeeper, does not appeal very much to a jury which can hardly pay its own rent. Don't forget it is not a crime, it is only natural for a woman to see a rich man friend helping her out a bit when her bills are behind-hand: that is not a crime or a felony. That is not grand larceny or arson, or extortion. A man goes to a friend and says, 'Please help me out this month and I will pay you back.' The rich man says, 'No, I can't give you fifty dollars.' People say he's a miser. A woman can say the same—my husband is inexperienced and suspicious, please help me out, I'm a little rash and I ran up bills. I like to dress nicely and the fashion changes so often. Is a woman worse than a man? Yes, she is, but she is more unfortunate in the eyes of a jury, too. And they say, he is a miser and he is an extortioner. He paid her with a rope around her neck. They say, 'She was perhaps a bad girl, but not mean, she did something for this man, he threw himself upon her sympathy'; they think she is weak, perhaps not one hundred per cent unblemished, but they like a good time themselves, and they think, Must the man get off scot-free if he has a good time too?

"They will think it is a very common, very old game, like a soldier who goes to a woman's room and does what he likes and when she is not looking, slits her stocking and takes the money from it. You know men boast of a thing like that; and you will boast of what you robbed me of—my reputation, my marriage—but it will not seem as good to others as it seems to you. They think, There has been some wrongdoing, perhaps, but the woman alone should not be the one to pay. You will be subpoenaed and nothing you can say will do you any good, for it doesn't look good from any angle. That is the only reason I say, Robbie, looking the thing over from your point of view and with your best interests at heart, you had better think over what Walker and Smitt propose to you; what it will be I don't know. . . ."

All this was on the telephone. Grant listened intently to all; and here interrupted Mrs. Downs.

Grant said, "I won't pay; only a man of the lowest character would ask it. You've been talked into this, it isn't like you. You don't know what you're saying. I know you, sweetie, and I have confidence in you. I want to meet you and have a little chat with you about this. We can't leave this for others to poke their fingers into. But believe me, for me to pay anything would be a confession of guilt—and from his side—"

The woman's voice changed: it broke in with a crying sound, sharp, "At nine-thirty a.m. I was awakened by the landlord's agent asking for the rent. I must pay the rent. I gave them his address; he was not to be found. Churchill, I mean. I told them I expected the money in the morning's mail. They watched me while I opened it. Imagine what a state I was in! I told them I would go down to my broker's and get it. They let me go out. Will they let me go in? I told them it was certainly today or tomorrow. They already gave me three months' grace. They are not bad to me in this housing crisis. Yet they are anxious now to get me out. I cannot even have an old friend up for tea. Churchill has been making too many inquiries. They have found out where I work as interpreter. I get thirty-five dollars a week. They know I cannot pay my rent on that. They do not care about honest work. They want their money. Very proper. If you have no money a dog is better than you, says the *calypso*. They keep calling for their pound of flesh, you see, it is in the bond. But no doubt you had a very pleasant evening last night and slept well and had a pleasant morning getting in your money and dictating to your secretary, and crying over the forty thousand dollars you lost which only leaves you your last one million, eight hundred and ninety-seven, six hundred and three dollars to eat on this week. I know you are making a profit in the U. S. A. of one thousand dollars a week, on an average, and you only work part-time now, because you don't want to pay in the higher brackets. Who are you fooling? I am in bad trouble and there is no one behind me. My own friends turn and rend me—"

"Look, sweetie, I'll send you a check as soon as ever I can. I am not responsible for your rent, and I don't want to pay it, especially now. I am not trying to get you into trouble, I want to help you. I want you to meet me in the White Bar at four o'clock, and we'll go into all this. I think you have raked up a mare's-nest. I think you are seeing things that are not there. You are nervous and excited. This husband of yours has nothing on us, sweetie. But don't try to bother me, don't try to threaten me, it is not like you, sweetie—and I don't like to hear it, it doesn't sound like you. We'll work out a for-r-mula that will stop him dead in his tracks. I expect a long-distance call, darling. I'll call you back."

She said swiftly, "I was so agitated yesterday that I did not go to work, I went to the movies with Mother and went shopping and bought a few things and I sent the bill on to you. You owe me something for all the mental agony I have gone through. But let me have the check. I could not stay in the apartment anyhow, it has too many unpleasant memories and it appears in those photographs—"

"Photomontages—"

"I stayed overnight with Paula and I feel better; but now Goodwin and Smitt have upset me and I must consult with you."

"I thought you said the landlord awakened you at nine-thirty."

"It was Karolyi let in by the landlord: he knocked at the door then—I went home early to get my mail with the check. But in the mail was a letter from Mother, she had just got wind of the affair. It is all around town and she cannot, naturally, understand. She is in a terrible state. But she says, 'I am sure Mr. Grant will give you the right advice and I do not see what you have to worry about, as you are innocent. But you must try to get Mr. Downs put away.'"

"Are there any grounds for that? I'd like to see that."

"With money you can do anything—almost."

"That would be a good way out. Put him away for only a month and then you can always say—if you have grounds—that is, swear out he's of unsound mind."

"Mother was worrying because I do not send her money as formerly. She made a hole in her savings and changed the furniture around in her apartment and could not get her teeth fixed. And I put her off from month to month, and now in this letter she says, 'I suspect you are in low water financially, but Mr. Grant will give you good advice.'"

"Mother is right—so I will—so I will—so meet me at the—"

"I had to cry with you about your losses of two thousand dollars, three thousand dollars, and all the time these months I have been thinking—twenty dollars. A dollar fifty I owe for a pair of shoes I can't get from the shoe repairer, fifty cents a quarter of a pound of ham! That doesn't look as if I have a bad reputation, does it? As if I get money from outsiders? But this has made me a cynic, Robbie. I have no more faith. That was one thing I had, faith and confidence in myself. I believed there was some good in every man, now I don't. There is more faith and loyalty in crooks and thieves like 'Braun, Arthur,' than in business men. I have the chance of a job in Cleveland, I'll send Mother to a milk farm in the country. You can imagine what this exile will mean to cosmopolitans like us, but I will do it to retrieve my situation. I shall pay off my small debts. Let him pursue me there. But send me first the check for five hundred dollars so I can begin to retrieve my situation."

"I'm strapped now, dearie, but when I can get a few dollars out of the Argentine—"

"And I don't know where to turn, for he is going crazy; he says he will call the men's wives, send letters to them, signed with his name, so that they will know everything, drag it into the open."

At last he was able to put down the receiver, after telling her to be sure to be at the White Bar—that he would bring her some money. In the meantime, she had said that she proposed to move into his apartment if she was put out of her own. He begged her to do nothing rash, their interests being the same.

38

Trembling, flushed, and out of breath, he left the office at once and took a taxi uptown to the Flacks' apartment. They were now living in a three-story fire trap on Sixth Avenue near the women's jail. It was a house in the middle of a row of mid-nineteenth-century houses with antiques, grocery and clothing stores on the street level. Grant had seen the place once only, and had never gone back. Inside it was all of dry, rotting wood and would make good kindling one night or other. As Grant saw it now, troubled as he was, he felt the as yet unborn flames licking his skin.

The Flacks had an apartment opening on the street and on a view of back yards. The bathroom, yellow ocher, with rusty fittings, opened on the staircase. The rooms, large originally, had been divided up by frail partitions. There was a kitchen with a ventilating shaft against the wall. He asked them for some food and a cup of coffee, and plunging his hands in his pockets, his face anxious, he told them, in modest fragments, some of his story and his present danger, "Dangerous 'ooman, never would ha' believed it of her—"

"Anyone but you can see she is a rattlesnake. But now is no time for post-mortems. You have to leave town."

He was anxious, lining up the reasons why he should go and

255

why he should stay to watch the affair. "Someone is poisoning her; she is terribly nervous, and someone is driving her on."

They discussed this—the husband, Goodwin; who then?

"No, Goodwin came to me first and told me the story; he's on my side—our side."

Grant could not leave town because he could not go home to pack, nor cook up an excuse for "the boy" Gilbert, because that woman wanted to move right in with him. He had an engagement with her at the White Bar, but he knew 'her ways, she might go up to the apartment.

"And there must be a detective or a bought employee in the lobby—even the elevator boy! You only gave him cigarettes for Christmas," said Flack.

He sat in a chair with a Mexican rug over his knees, his face flabby and yellow in the street daylight. Supposing himself in excellent health, because gay and garrulous, he had not been near a doctor for years, and had been overcome by an incurable though not painful disease. He was now unable to do regular work, but still could write free-lance articles.

Grant, in his terror, was without resources. He listened to Flack childishly and agreed to do everything that was suggested. It was arranged that Grant should occupy for several nights an apartment belonging to Hugo March, rented by March & Company by the year in an uptown hotel, for the convenience of out-of-town clients. Flack would go to Grant's office, dispatch his business, bring letters that needed Grant's attention, go to Grant's apartment, warn Gilbert, and bring all necessary things. He would buy Grant a ticket to Bermuda or Havana, just as they decided by the afternoon. Meanwhile Grant must stay hid in Flack's place—there the blondine would certainly never find him. Let the blondine wait in the White Bar for her check; that would keep her occupied while Flack did his part. Flack would see Hugo March, some more dependable lawyer than Walker, and send a letter to Mrs. Grant.

Said Flack, "And while I am gone, you stay here, you big noise, and don't take a taxi to any of your haunts: you're as secretive as a mastodon."

Grant blushed, giggled, and began looking round hungrily, "Have you got anything to eat, Edda? Where is it—? I'll take her out to lunch."

"You stay where you are or I'll desert you, you restless bumblebee. You stay put. And don't annoy Edda with sentimental details of your romances—she's just recovering from an affair which was pretty serious; she doesn't want to have your nosegays thrown in her face."

"A fella—eh?" He began to smile, he was already at home.

"Yes, and shut up about it. Forget your *Decameron*." Flack grinned, then burst out laughing with pride, "Edda's a passionate type of girl and she doesn't know too much about your sidestepping and minueting, and I'm glad of it. So just keep the lid on; boil inside if you must."

Smiling from ear to ear, Grant, much flattered, sat back in his chair, noted one or two details of the place, found the poverty displeasing, frowned, "Well, leave it to me, trust me. Can't understand Downs. Such a stodgy sort."

"He loved her, she was an angel, remember."

"Well, she's an angel, but a black angel—"

He instantly regretted having said that, but the pleasant flavor lingered on his tongue. He laughed, confessed, "It's a syndicate, they put me down for ten thousand dollars. She told me he couldn't raise two thousand dollars if he moved heaven or earth. He's honest, so he's got no credit. It's his first stroke of business. He doesn't know it but he's auctioning her off, who will pay most for my second-hand furniture, including my wife? I'm first," he laughed, and repeated it, then—"Murvieux, antiquary, second; drug-wholesaler, third; James Alexis finished fourth in the love-nest stakes. Ho-ho-ho. Call it a shakedown if you like, life is never dull with the blonde. Ho-ho-ho. Maybe I deserve it, but deserve it or not—I don't pay. Can't be me, so it must be Murvieux or Alexis. He doesn't pay, I don't pay. Alexis. Looks like it must be Alexis."

Flack went out to telephone Hugo March about the apartment. He came back to say it was fixed up and he would go to March's to get the key, and bring Grant any necessary letters. He went away warning Grant again not to leave the apartment. At this moment Edda brought in some sandwiches and red wine for Grant. Flack left.

Grant ate heartily, taking two sandwiches at a time, and draining the glass at a draught. Then he fixed his moist and penetrating eye upon Edda and looked her over. She had changed a bit, for the better, he supposed. She looked as if she had been through something. He knew by Flack's hint that she had had a lover. He cleaned up the plate, drank another glass of wine, and shaking his head, said merrily, "I'm looking for romance, for a woman, and I get a harpy; how do you explain that? Not a good picker. Never could pick a woman. I trust them; I take them on faith. A woman can be beautiful but she has no character. 'You're nice to look at,' I say, 'but you have no character, it's not good enough.' "

Edda burst out laughing, "This is where I came in, Robbie. Don't hand out your bromides, please. I've got other bromides singing in my ears."

She picked up the plates and the napkin from his knee, brushing some crumbs from his waistcoat, "Watch out—you only have one suit till Dad collects your things."

She began clinking things in the kitchen.

Left alone he began shifting, stretching his neck, and looking at his address book. He had intended to meet the blondine that afternoon and now he had no idea how to fill in the time, either now or afterwards. He would sneak away if he could and meet her. To spend evenings shut up in March's hotel room: one evening? He could at least telephone Livy, or send a telegram. He began to think about the woman in the kitchen. It pleased him that she, who had always been priggish, sharp, had uncorseted her feelings. She was now, for him, a woman. When she came back he looked her up and down with his head held on one side. She had brought him another plate of sandwiches. Putting them in pairs, he soon swept this plate clean too.

"You're a good cook, good cook—"

She sat down beside him. He saw her manicured nails. She had frizzled her black hair round her head. Her young neck had three deep creases although it was quite slender. She had a dun skin. He whipped out his crocodileskin notecase, half opened it, showing the large bills, and pushed it toward her below the table, rubbing her calf gently. He gave her a soft, knowing, inquisitive look and nodded slightly. She drew her legs away, said in a domineering voice, "What is the matter, Robert, are you looking for somewhere to leave your money? There's no shelf under the table," and as she said the senseless phrase, kicked slightly with her foot and brust out laughing. Not quite sure, he hesitated a moment.

"Put it back, Robbie; you'll lose it."

He put it back and half muttered, "After what you've been through, it's unique to be so Presbyterian."

Without offense, she picked up the plate, washed it, and came back to sit with him, moving her chair. He began to tell her his stock romances, the Spanish woman in black, and so forth.

He broke off in the middle and eyed his watch. He began to

258

walk up and down, seeing nothing, "Must tell Davie about the shagreen case, the hatbox, remind me, will you? Make a note."

She sat there. He turned round, "Make a note, do me a favor, make a note."

"I'll remember."

"Why must you be so stiff, Edda? It's not—" he remembered. He laughed, "You were always very Presbyterian."

He strode about, "Look, my dear girl, just do me a favor and make a note. I'm very disturbed, had a great shock. Trusted the bloody 'ooman. Now she tries to take me for a ride, rope me like a steer."

Edda complied at last. He began rapidly, "Shoe trees, shoe covers, leather-jack, pair of pigskin riding gloves, leather belt with silver, the hatbox I left at the tailor, the glasses in the shagreen case, pound of margarine, two tins cocoa, Nescafé, ask the optician for my collar case, ask the maid to find two gold studs locked in a little silver box, mouthwash—" and so on, for half an hour, changing his mind about suits, enumerating his shoes—"and get the sports shoes mended, I can't go away without the sports shoes, and if there's no key to the pigskin, get a key, and tell Mrs. Mac-Donald to get the carpenter to fit new keys if they don't work—"

"What is this—the tailor has the hatbox, the hatter has the collarbox—"

"The optician has the collar case," he corrected, seeing nothing amusing in it. He frowned at her and implored her to try to keep the list correct. He continued, "The carpenter, Jones, telephone him at once, and ask if the missing sheet is returned. Keep all telephone calls, bring the linen shoe covers and the shoe trees, get a pair of laces—" and so on; he shouted three times, "Bring all the keys he can find, and there's a package, an envelope on top of the wardrobe, an umbrella in the bathroom, and give the laundry. Look in all the pockets for my spectacles in the shagreen case, and if there aren't any they're lost; go to the optician and get new spectacles, twenty dollars, and if there's no shagreen case, get a new shagreen case. Get new ones anyhow, I might break them or lose them. And bring my sun lamp—"

"It's like the night before Christmas."

"Do me a favor, my dear girl, make a note, just as it comes to me."

He took several turns and muttered rapidly, "Unlock the closet in the corridor and bring the liquor here, but leave the Coca-Cola bottles, and the milk bottles; I keep them for the blonde, it's her hobby. Bring the Nescafé. Don't leave anything in the closet."

When Edda got tired and threw down the pencil with a childish laugh, he said urgently, "Look, Edda darling, you're like my Little Sister, you're sacred to me, we can live together for years, I'd never think of touching you, I respect you and I know you're such a bloody Presbyterian—it's good for me. It's what I want, sister and friend and nice girl too, all in one. Do this for me. It's for us all. We'll take over that house in Rome from that bloody 'ooman hurt me so much, she's a fascist anyway, and we'll do just as we please. Good for Davie, too, he needs it, needs to be free from worry. Now write, make a note please, my dear girl."

He went on. Then he broke this off too, to become nervous and wonder why Flack did not return. He began to soften toward Mrs. Downs, "Don't like her waiting there. Let her wait. I paid a lot for the cow but she's worth it. She had me round her finger. Didn't know how to keep me. Now she's trying strong-arm methods. Perhaps she thinks I let her down. Maybe I did. Where's Flack?"

Presently he said, "She made me need her and I like it. She's got the honeypot and I'm the honeybear."

The young woman listened to him curiously. He was pleased, "I paid a lot for the 'ooman; but she was worth it."

He became restless, "She gave me good value, but now I'm through with her: she outstayed her welcome."

"I'm not so sure," said the girl.

He was pleased. He began to rave, sitting opposite her and spitting out his stand-bys, his *romancero*, with a tender, sweet expression. They heard Flack coming up the stairs. He sprang to his feet and rushed out on the landing.

Flack said, "Everything is going to be all right."

The Hugo March apartment was in a quiet hotel near Central Park and just off the Park, east side. In it professional people and business men lived the year round. It was near all Grant's haunts and in the heart of the most fashionable district, where he daily took his walks. Flack, who feared for him, warned him a hundred times about walking out and going to the St. Regis, to the Chatham, to the Ritz, to the White Bar, to Manetti's, to Charles, Pommes Soufflées.

"Hide your head for shame, for once, you bum."

"Trust me!"

39

They all took a taxi uptown to the place. The apartment looked on the street, and on a light-well, and contained a large bedroom and a sitting room, connected by a pretty corridor full of windows, and leading into bathroom and kitchenette. Numerous tall old-fashioned wall closets opened into the rooms and corridors. This pleased Grant, who ran about opening and sniffing. As soon as he had sent Flack and Edda out, with orders to go to his apartment and begin to pack, he telephoned Miss Robbins, Miss Livy Wright, Betty Goodwin, and two or three of his young female acquaintance, giving them his address and making appointments with them.

"If I have to lurk here in a hideaway, I got to keep myself amused; otherwise, I'll start running out and advertising myself everywhere."

He laughed to himself and began peering into the cupboards once more. He found some salt, coffee, and canned milk in the kitchen—a profit. In one of the drawers was a small enameled pillcase about one inch square. He liked this and pocketed it. He looked under the chest of drawers and wardrobe, puffing and flushing, and found one or two things which he examined and discarded. After this, he found the wait intolerable and telephoned Mrs. MacDonald at his apartment to find out if the Flacks were there with Miss Robbins, packing, and to tell her to get Jones, the carpenter, to come for any locks that stuck. He then called each one to the phone in turn to give fresh instructions, always the same. Flack yelled, "I told you to lie low and not even to telephone, you lummocks. How do you know the switchboard girl isn't the one who's watching you?"

He grumbled and rang off. But after a moment he called again, saying, "I know her, I took her to tea. She wouldn't. Do me a favor and bring the first load here at once, I want to see what you've packed. I'm the only one who knows what I want. Take a taxi, two taxis. I want you all to come."

When he telephoned again, Flack had left with some valises in a taxi. Grant at once commanded Miss Robbins to proceed to the new hotel, in a taxi, to receive his instructions. The two taxis arrived at the same time, for Flack had thought to take a roundabout route via Grand Central to fool possible pursuers, while Miss Robbins, in a hurry to appease him, went direct. Grant at once tore open the three valises Flack had brought and raged about, "If you don't know how to pack the stuff, get the hotel valet, he knows! Go back, give him the three pairs of pants to press that are lying on the bench, and get them from him and tell him to sort out my—"

He wanted to telephone his apartment to give instructions to Mrs. MacDonald. Flack said, "If you telephone again, I wash my hands of you; I leave you; get out of it your own way."

"I can manage the affair myself. It was you got me into all this mess."

"I'd like to know how, you idiot."

"If it hadn't been for you I would have seen the 'ooman and fixed it all up with her. Now she's angry with me and she's probably gone to her lawyer. God damn it, you put me off, I know the technique, I know the cow—get out of here and let me unpack. Everything's missing. Where are the white silk socks? Who packed the bags?"

"I threw the stuff in. I didn't pack."

"You didn't put in one thing I asked for! Where's the list?"

He took the telephone and rang up his apartment, angrily shaking off Flack and roaring at Mrs. MacDonald, "Not there, unpack that—" and so forth. He ordered Edda to come at once, bringing his umbrella out of the bathroom with her, also a pair of cuff links and his "leather-jack." She must take a taxi. He then spoke to Mrs. MacDonald, ordered her to be at this new address first thing in the morning, eight o'clock, and to bring with her Jones, the carpenter, in a taxi, to try the keys. He shouted across the phone, to Flack, "Where's the hatbox? Did you get the spectacles? Did you look in all the pockets? I told you to get the collarbox! The hatbox is at the tailor's—goddamn it all, no one listens, I have to organize everything."

He returned to the phone, "I wasn't speaking to you, Mrs. MacDonald, my dear, good woman, but to the bloody fool—to someone else. Ring the carpenter tonight or go and see him. Tell Miss Flack to come at once with the umbrella, if she can't find it—perhaps I lent it to Goodwin, to buy me another this evening, before the stores close. . . . I know it isn't raining, my good woman, but it will rain sometime. Get Miss Flack—Edda, look in the upper top drawer right hand of the—" and so forth. The telephone call, interrupted by objurgations and commands to the miserable pair unpacking his valises, lasted twenty minutes. Triumphantly, he jammed down the receiver and strode toward them, parted them, pushed them away with his hands, and knelt down by the first open valise. He took each thing out and looked at it, began piling things in heaps according to a system of the moment. He grumbled, "Nothing here, what do I want with that damn stuff? Nothing here I wanted."

Flack showed him the list. He pushed it aside, "No one does what I want! Nothing here—where are the shoe covers? Can I travel without shoe covers? Where are the shoe trees? There were three tins of shoe polish, one half empty—"

He pushed the stuff aside that he had just piled and ranged into the cases: "God damn it, Flack, why can't you do a thing I ask!"

Flack bit his thumb and looked at Grant with anger.

Grant at once said, "Oh, ho, sorry, sorry, but you know I'm glad you both came, help me. We'll settle in the country, Flack, Edda and you will have a quiet life when this rumpus is over. We'll get back that farm in France and grow French beans, we'll go to Rome and live on the Pinchem when it's not too hot, there's always a breeze there, nice house, have servants, Edda won't have to work any more, recover, get back her color, not so Presbyterian, or we'll go when we want to Pontresina, she can skate, get a young man, anything you like—only bear with me now, my dear boy. The blonde got my blood up, I don't know where I am. Stand by me now, my dear boy. I'm not a bad fellow, but don't bother me now. Did you send that bloody fool Gilbert away for a week? All day, whatever I say, he drags in Celia Grimm. I'm afraid he got in with that bloody woman, she's no good, went native. I took her out three times and not even a kiss. She's not a squareshooter. I don't spend money on a woman for nothing, to be made a fool of. Sorry to see him get in with a woman of that type. She'll skin him and leave him high and dry, no morals, no sense of responsibility, no sense of reality. I told him, 'I know that girl, look out for her, she's not straight.' The young jackass laughed. By God, if she got her claws into him, she's making a mistake. I got a woman away from him before, I'll do it again. Money talks and what the devil—I can do it without money; but why should I? Money talks faster than I do."

He laughed, "I said, 'There's a fresh wind today,' and he comes in with, 'Celia Grimm says that she loves a fresh wind, it's good for her skin.' She's got her hooks into him, eh? I'll take her out, give her a good time. I found out he bought her a couple of Scotch-and-sodas. Ho-ho. A college boy. Let him stay with old Mr. Wright in Philadelphia; Livy owes me something. I wasn't so bad to her. And if she leads him astray—ho—I should worry, as long as he doesn't tell me all day long, 'Negroes dance better than white people.' Do me a favor, my boy, and go back to the hotel and look for the leather-jack; I can't understand why you didn't find that plaited leather belt with the Mexican silver clasp, it's in the night stand."

As soon as he had dispatched these two, Mrs. MacDonald arrived, with some keys, and he entertained her for half an hour with instructions for the morning, meanwhile telephoning to the blondine to meet him downstairs in the Awning Bar, but to tell no one. He also cautioned Mrs. MacDonald about telling anyone of his movements or of his present rendezvous. He laughed, "Flack thinks he's my wet nurse. Got to have a bit of freedom, or I'll tear down the house."

As the blonde could not meet him till ten-thirty, he kept Mrs. MacDonald by him, occasionally telephoning the other apartment to find out how things were getting along, and arguing with Flack, who eventually took his daughter out to dinner and refused to see Grant until the next morning. Flack said crossly, "And I give you my word, Robbie, if you don't give up all your doings with this lowdown crook, this blonde woman, a thief and a harlot, I'll not do another stroke for you at any time, not even for your farm and your house on the Pincian."

Grant let out a grand, musical laugh, "Don't worry, my boy, don't worry, my boy, you love me too much, you think too much of me, go out to dinner, I swear before God I won't see the 'ooman again, not in my life, I swear it to you by all that's holy. And tell Edda too, I wouldn't associate with a woman like that, I know, though I've done some bad things, perhaps, that she's not in the same class, and that now that you and I are going to live together in the same house in the St. Lawrence, I'll never go near a woman like that again, she's reformed me, tell Edda. By God, what I like about her is she's so Presbyterian. But she doesn't know enough, doesn't understand the blonde. The blonde's innocent, only not her style, that's all."

When he put down the telephone, Mrs. MacDonald said to him, "Mr. Grant, it is your own affair, but it surprises me to hear you so untruthful."

He bellowed with laughter, smacked his knee, and going up to the old woman, kissed her on the forehead, "Allow me, my dear good woman, that is what I would do if you were my own mother. I don't deserve a mother like you and indeed I didn't

264

have such a one. But I want you to watch over me, I'm not the best of men, though my heart is in the right place. You and I are going to stay together. You'll come with me everywhere. You'll be my housekeeper at Largo Farm, for my boy and me. It will be good for your latter days, see the old country once again, eh? Because you're a good influence over me and you come out with it—a good woman's honest tongue, with a little mustard on it, has set many a man straight."

"Indeed, I like to believe you and I do believe you have a good heart."

Grant puttered about and said deprecatingly, glancing at the old woman, "It's all over, I swear. I've lied often, but not about this; I lie because it's a quick exit. If I lie, I say I lie, sooner or later. But I've had my lesson. My mother told me never to lie and I know she had to meet the hard knocks."

Having said this, he fell silent and thought it over. He began defending the woman to himself, and then he came out with it, "But the husband put her up to it, that I'd swear on the Bible. It's not like her. I don't want to say she's more sinned against than sinning—"

"Well, you're perfectly right to be charitable, Mr. Grant."

"—who would think a Presbyterian like that, a church deacon who maybe goes to bed in his Sunday-best, loved her, he said, thought the world of her, never met that kind of a woman, he said, would turn against her like that? Is that love? It shows stupidity, it shows a small mind. You don't turn against a woman, you say, The fault is mine, *mea culpa*.' That's my idea. I'm no angel, but when I do a wrong thing with a woman I don't blame her. I made a mistake, that's all. I don't know what she thinks of me either."

"Shall I repack these shirts, Mr. Grant?"

He immediately passed into a great state of excitement, "What can I do without the shoe covers? Why can't they do as I ask?"

"You can very well wait till the morning for your shoe covers, and I must go home soon; it is nearly ten o'clock."

Grant went round the valises and the apartment, repeating sadly, wisely, comically, shrewdly, pensively, boyishly, and even to the accompaniment of a bizarre and gay *pas seul*, "What will I do? I can't pack my things without the shoe covers; shoes are a great packing problem—" and he would come close to her (as she bent over his things, sorting them out, picking out a few soiled things), and start an examination into the nature and kinds and uses of shoe trees and the laxity of so-called friends of indolent character, and of the natural interest of a true friend in his friend's shoe trees and shoe covers, and of the lasting question of keeping the creases out of his seventeen pairs of shoes; and a forensic statement in which a considerable number of that week's events as recorded in the *New York Times*, the *New Statesman* and *Nation*, the *New Republic*, and the *Manchester Guardian*, were rounded up, added up, and cut down to the period of his missing shoe covers. Then, to amuse the old woman who wanted to go home to bed, he started a small jesting vein, about the wits of certain persons who were brilliant enough to turn out any number of predictions about the ups and downs of the stock exchange, and were fairly dependable on the exchange, and even wrote articles for the *New Republic* and *Collier's*, but had so little sense of humanity, so little realism, that they could not lay their hands on shoe covers when requested urgently by a friend who surely merited their attention, just as a favor.

"That's the trouble with men like that, impractical, surely there's nothing more simple and everyday than shoe covers! How can I get to Havana without my shoe covers?"

And thus working himself up to a fury, coloring with resentment, and down to a drizzle of sorrow and longing about the shoe covers, he came to the end of the corridor and shouted to Mrs. MacDonald, asking if she had not some old shoe covers, and after rummaging among the things she had just arranged, came out with an old shirt of Gilbert's, put in there by mistake and holding it out to her, cried, "Do me a favor, my good, dear woman, and cut this up tonight, you hear me, make a patron, cut them out tonight before you go to bed, then you'll remember and sew them up for me tomorrow morning and bring them over, eh? Just for once, please."

She had tears in her eyes, her hands shook as she stood holding the big striped shirt, and she said, "It's indeed a great pity to cut up this good shirt, Gilbert could use it."

He came forward, twinkling, smiling, blushing like a boy, looking into her eyes and took her hands through the shirt, "Do it for me, like a good, dear woman, make a little patron, cut out the shoe covers and sew them for me with your own needle and thread. You have needle and thread, haven't you? It will give me a great pleasure to see your stitching in it and I'll think, Mrs. MacDonald did this thing for me, when I asked it. I have to go away but that big apartment will be home to me, for I'll think,

Mrs. MacDonald is there, and it'll be the first home I had since I left my mother. You and I are going to be together for years. The other women are no good to me, I confess to you, you see, what I want is a mother and a housekeeper who'll do me some little kindness when I ask it. You have your little home with me and you make the place like a home."

"But, Mr. Grant, you can buy shoe covers in the stores, three pairs for a dollar ten."

He pressed her hands, looked into the shirt, "I'll say to myself, they were made for me by the needle and thread of a fine honest woman and that woman's in my apartment at this moment, until I come home. Do me this one favor."

"I'm sure I don't know what to say to you, to tell you, there's no need for such sewing."

"You'll do it for me, then, like a good woman."

At this, he brusquely changed manner, got a piece of brown paper out of a drawer, pushed it into her hands, said, "Take it for the patron and wrap the shoe covers in it. Well, go home now, come again in the morning with the carpenter."

He had the door open for her, before she had her package wrapped. He met the blondine downstairs with a mischievous joy. To begin with, he felt himself well concealed; and he did not tell her he was going to Havana, he said he had changed his mind. He grinned to think how he had fooled Flack and Mrs. MacDonald, and also how he was fooling Mrs. Downs. He could handle his own affairs best.

He listened to all the blondine had to say. She was neither more nor less than the bearer of an offer from her husband. If Grant would pay for the divorce and costs and compensation, the whole thing would be dropped; and she had brought with her a weekly newspaper in which their affair was hinted at in a startling way. Her husband was out for blood and had told everyone. She and Walker and Goodwin and others had managed to talk him over. The whole thing would cost twelve thousand dollars at the least: that or an eruption into the daily press with full details and all the names.

"But the others?" said Grant, evilly.

"I am only thinking of you, darling. What will people say when they see your name with Alexis and Mr. Exe? I am only thinking of our credit. I tell you he's run amok."

Grant prolonged the discussion, going with her into every possible detail. He felt at ease with her. They arranged another meeting for the next afternoon. When he left her, he thought, "In this way I fool her; my technique is the right one."

40

At eight in the morning he telephoned the store downstairs from the Flacks, which he had noted down in his address book, a white-wood furniture store. He asked them to call down Edda or David. While he waited, he thought about the furniture store. He could get them to make an estimate for his package-home scheme, which he wanted to promote in Europe after the war to replace the houses bombed and put to fire. He would telephone his editor friend, Bernard Robison, right away after the Flack call. Robison's publishing house was backed by Mrs. Burthen, a beautiful society woman, with millions. He would get an appointment with the beauty and tell her there was a question of paper mills. There would be a paper shortage after the war. The only thing would be to get up a combine of small publishing firms like Burthen's, and plant them in or adjacent to great forests, say in Canada, Scandinavia, or Siberia. No transport, no paper shortage. He'd put Robison out of business, oust Mr. Burthen, take over Mrs. Burthen, use her capital. The tree turned into a cheap edition overnight. Paper would be a splendidly profitable shortage after the war; and his idea for not so much a monopoly as a pulp empire would give good paper cheap, also promote education. What about the same thing for "boxed houses," "package houses," "too many dictionaries, too few houses," "house of the month.". . . Surely Edda was up by this? When she came to the phone, he said politely, "I hope I didn't wake you. Listen, my dear girl, tell David to go straight to the apartment and look for those things he missed last night. I want the missing shoe covers and tell him to bring all the keys. The carpenter is coming here this morning. First thing of all, go to the tailor for the hatbox and get the collarbox from the optician. Get a new shagreen case. . . . Now you have a white-wood store downstairs, they must make keyholes in things, and have cheap keys, eh? Ask them what to do about getting keys made cheap, not copied, made. See if you can buy from them an assortment of any keys they have lying about the place, just see what they want for them, don't buy them right off. See what sort of keys you can get in Woolworth's. Then you bring the keys here like a good girl.

Also ask the furniture place if they have not a bandsaw, they could cut some shoe trees for me."

"Shoe trees!"

He mumbled, "War scarcities, shoe trees very rare, I don't mind putting up with some without springs just for the time being till after the war, see they're coming back but not yet, wartime measure: ask them, my dear girl, ask them, I'll give you the sizes on a piece of paper. Ask them if they have a bandsaw."

"You can get cheap shoe trees, I saw them in Stern's yesterday."

"Ask down there, you're downstairs now, do me this favor. The fella must have a bandsaw. What am I to do? I told the carpenter to be here at eight o'clock, and it's nearly nine."

She must look round the workshop while she was down there, and see if they had any bits of wood lying round that they didn't want. Waste wood, was worth nothing, they wouldn't sell that kind of stuff for kindling. She could pay them for the work on the bandsaw, the wood was waste—or better, buy the waste wood from them, if she saw it lying round their workshop, and bring it up to him, in a taxi, in a taxi, of course, and he would give it to the carpenter, give the shoe plans to the carpenter and let him make shoe trees out of it, easiest thing in the world. What had he to do but turn on the bandsaw? He liked this new word and began to build schemes and save money round the very notion of "bandsaw."

"I'll go and buy you some shoe trees, make you a present of them," said Edda.

"No, no, no. Let the fella make 'em. I did him enough favors, gave him business, I'm letting him fix the keys for me. One good turn deserves another. I'll pay him the electric power cost on the bandsaw. All these chairborne officers bought them up—"

The storm-center now shifted from the shoe trees to the carpenter and then to the keys, last of all to David Flack, who must proceed immediately to the other apartment.

When Flack arrived at the Pickwick, Miss Robbins had been there an hour. Mrs. MacDonald was sitting on a chair sewing together shoe covers with old woman's big stitches. She trembled and complained in a high rasping voice, "And today Mr. Goodwin telephones me and tells me that last night Mr. Grant sublet this apartment to him and his wife and sister-in-law, and I must work for two young women. I don't want to leave but I can't help myself. I haven't the strength."

Flack started, "But last night, Robert promised me that Edda and I could stay here while he was away, and while we looked around for another place. He said—"

Flack burst out laughing—"The old fraud—why do I believe in Robbie any more? He said, when he came back, we would live here and try out what living in common would be like."

He kept on chuckling, then his eyes grew large and he said sorrowfully, "What the devil makes him say things like that? He doesn't need the rent. Why must he sublet?"

"They will have to fight it out with Walker and his parents," said Miss Robbins. She told them that Grant had long ago promised the apartment to the lawyer Walker for two hundred dollars monthly.

The three, with Gilbert, who had just risen and not yet gone to visit the Wrights in Philadelphia (in fact, he declined to be boarded out at his age, he said easily), had assembled by eleven o'clock in the morning the following:

Three pigskin valises, which, packed, one man could not lift;

Four old suitcases, one dispatch case, and one hatbox—all leather;

One old-fashioned opera-hatbox, the one from the tailor's, locked;

One shoe packer; one traveling sun lamp; one medicine case;

One collar case, from the optician's, locked, and two old shagreen spectacle cases;

Several pieces of airplane luggage; four coats; a package of liquor out of the closet; several packets with coffee, tea, and other groceries.

Grant, somewhat intimidated by Flack's ill humor, had not dared to telephone them at the apartment; but the carpenter called twice, and indicated that Grant had been at him half the morning. Presently, a messenger came with a note from Grant to Flack, "Come over here immediately. Let Miss Robbins follow! Call at the carpenter's on the way; and bring the hatbox and the collar case and Jones with you."

Flack had not left the apartment when Grant was on the phone, asking if he had left, raging because he had not. Miss Robbins must come at once with the valises in three taxis, with Gilbert and Mrs. MacDonald, "In no matter what condition—"

"I don't understand you, Mr. Grant; they're in perfect health, better than yourself this morning!"

"Eh? Eh? Bring the valises in no matter what condition and stop at the carpenter's on the way and see if his assistant has left."

"Mr. Flack's gone for him!"

"Do me a favor, my dear girl—"

A quarter of an hour later, the doorman at the Pickwick, having hailed three taxis and seen the valises, et cetera, stowed away, had no difficulty in hearing to what address they all were being transported.

At the door of the hotel Grant met them. He was pacing up and down without a hat, and eying the passers-by furiously. As soon as the taxis drove up he rushed at them, opened a door, and began dragging the valises from them, shouting at the same time, "Did you find the umbrella? Why the hell didn't you bring the umbrella? Mrs. MacDonald, did you bring the shoe covers? Goddamn it, Miss Robbins, why didn't you bring the carpenter's boy? Where's the boy? I told that fella to come here at once. Have I got to wait here all day to get a lock open? Where are my rubbers?"

By this time, he had got all the stuff onto the sidewalk with the assistance of Gilbert and the taxi drivers, and he now rudely snapped his fingers at the doorman, "Pay them off!"

Picking up the two heaviest pigskin cases, he shouldered the others aside and swung these into the lobby. A bellboy and a porter, who ran forward, could not move the cases. Grant saw this and took charge of all the heavy stuff, running up and down in the elevator, giving orders in the lobby and on the landing, and in his sitting room, for a moment busy and content. He had not yet greeted anyone there and ignored Flack, who kept asking him where to stow the things. His eyes were concentrated on the valises. His huge, smooth muscles were at work. He puffed, and occasionally uttered remarks like, "If that fella don't come by —get the bandsaw man—can't make out how you overlooked the rubbers—fourteen keys, not one fits that lock—"

Somewhat calmed by his exertions and by the impressive mess of property in which he stood, he concluded with a mild reproof to Flack and Miss Robbins, "Can't understand how you could have overlooked the umbrella!"

Then he settled down to a more humane sort of discussion, striving to open their eyes to the seriousness of his luggage, with a few brief comments about the blonde and other personalities.

271

He went on, deeply absorbed, delighted that his life had reached this boiling-point. What was the true situation with the blonde and her husband and Alexis? He doubted about the gigolo and the coiffeur. The husband had run amok. But if there were other men, he felt very gloomy indeed. Did he want to bathe in a muddied pool? Would he drink from a fouled well? Would he eat oysters from a bay where sewers opened? Supposing Mrs. Downs were a crook—he was himself partly to blame; but supposing she were not, then there was someone making suggestions to her, and it was much more serious. Who could it be?

"It's that bragging Goodwin," said Flack.

"Nonsense, my dear man, perfectly ridiculous! He put me on to it first."

"That's why he's guilty. You know the rule with an anonymous letter—suspect the first person who visits you after you receive it!"

"Im-possible. Don't let me hear any more of it."

"I'm tired of your insults, Grant!"

"Now, my dear fellow, I apologize, sorry, very sorry, bear with me."

He became pathetic. Who was working against him behind the scenes and for why? He had been a guardian angel to the bloody 'ooman. She had nothing on him, that he swore, as he would never swear to his mother. He took Mrs. MacDonald's hand and kissed her wedding ring. No-thing! He babbled on, as he tried the keys one after the other, kneeling in front of them, and snapping his fingers, lifting his eyes to them, asking for this and that, insisting upon their attendance, stopping in his narrative if anyone absented himself for a moment. He dropped clues, lifted masks, showed his tracks, all through his discourse, and then seeing what he had done, doubled back on himself, made false scents, artfully mixed in incompatibles, but not with any true idea of dodging them, but of keeping their minds intent on himself and his romantic situation. He did not care what they saw as long as they kept looking and wondering at him. He felt all kinds of rich emotions, a sentimental innocence, in the pleasure of showing himself to them as a creature they had never dreamed of—more sorrowful, wickeder, gayer, more romantic, more lecherous, more bewildered.

The plot or conspiracy of his affair with Mrs. Downs was not just a straight relationship of give and take, I'm lonely and you console me, he explained to them, but a network of events, a country of shifting sands. It was something new in life for them.

If they listened it would be instructive for them, he said. It was, let us say, like a war map, with front lines and back lines and strategic retreats and lines of communications and hidden depots, of spies and forces and even—he laughed—a hospital case or two, and a bit of battle surgery; that too. There was the question of supply, of general strategy: of not wearing out your strength, and not extending yourself too far. With the blonde it was even like a business. It was a pity the damn woman had not gone into business, but she had a lovely body, "I'm among friends—she—the boat goes into harbor, it's a sweet harbor—that's the secret of the woman—"

As he went on, names came up of old acquaintances of his, proved scoundrels and promoters, that Grant had sworn were cast out long ago, but who now appeared in this great Blonde Network, as giving him advice, introducing him to lawyers, running between him and the blonde and the husband and the Goodwins and Delafield and innumerable strange people. When Flack questioned him about these dead, suddenly revived, Grant fumbled a bit but said it was an accident, only the other day the said rascal walked into the White Bar, and it happened he knew James Alexis—and in short, Grant now had him working as a footrunner, or an expendable, or a trench-digger in his great campaign with the blondine. Indeed, the very frauds, cheats, homeless swindlers, blackmailers and income-tax delators, Mann-law provocatrices, these café beggars who fancied themselves as Azevs, these international Counts and Majors, who never could sail for their own native lands—these were, it appeared, rather the ones Grant was employing, and had all along employed in his dealings with the blonde, and in his most secret and daring work. They were the proper ones to take trips in disguised planes to survey the enemy territory. If they told on him to the blonde, they also told on the blonde to him, said Grant, laughing wickedly, and he could do more with his knowledge than she! But just as they were viewing with open mouths this huge landscape and a kind of skirmishing with the blonde that had gone on for years, in undeclared war, the picture dwindled and became—the layout of a love nest taken by the pinhead eye of a newfangled movie camera in someone's buttonhole. How else could anyone have taken pictures of the blonde and others in incorrect relations? He stoutly cried, "But I am not involved as is Alexis, only I ask myself how could they have any evidence? She's a very smart woman, and he's very smart."

Said Flack, "She fixed it with Downs."

"Im-possible, believe me, my boy, I've been sold up and down the river, but not by that 'ooman. I know her inside out. Better than that husband. If I found it was her, I'd soap her stairs."

"But since you're not involved—"

"You're perfectly correct. But what about photomontage?"

"You know yourself you were always suspicious of her."

"Yes, never went near her place. I thought, Walls have ears."

Gilbert heard all this with a morose expression. Grant noticed this, went up, clapped him on the arm, and roared, "It'll work out as a blessing in disguise! Trust me. I'm through with her. It's a blessing in disguise. What do you say, Edda? A blessing in disguise. We'll get rid of this mess, and when I come back to New York we'll pack up our traps and we'll go out to Largo Farm, sell day-old chicks."

He did not notice Gilbert's surprise. He continued with his usual promises for the future.

Seeing that they were all trying to get away, he got up from the floor, saying, "We can't do anything till the carpenter's boy comes and Mrs. MacDonald finishes the shoe covers. Let's have Karel Karolyi and tell him to bring the play."

"What are you here for, you're in hiding," said Flack.

He protested that Karel, that crazy man, didn't know where he was living, or what street or—skip the details—even what country.

"He knows the address of twenty dollars," said Flack.

Grant frowned, "Let him come over, and show us my play."

He telephoned the hotel and found that Karolyi had not been in overnight. Grant paced up and down, simulating immense anger and disturbance, so that they would not leave him. He began to pour out his notions about the "drama."

"I don't know what you want to be an angel for," said Gilbert disagreeably.

"I don't put in a cent more than the one hundred and eighty dollars I've put in the kitty! I told him I'd put up the money. See if the others put up. Then I'll put up. It'll be a four-star smash-hit, it'll be the talk of Broadway, we'll be rich overnight, a gold mine—"

He called the desk angrily, suddenly breaking this off, "No calls for me yet? I can't understand it."

He told them he was expecting "Gabriel Bitkoff from Jigago, and Sam Positive."

"That can't be his name!"

He mumbled. He kept them there waiting, though he expected calls from the blonde and from Miss Livy Wright at any moment. At last the blonde called. He ran into the other room and murmured hotly, then thinking that he heard the line click and that someone was listening in the other room or downstairs, he said, "Don't think the line's free. Wait till the play is produced, and you won't be sorry you went in with me. You'll get a big cut, I'll let you in first, Goodwin's friends are going to put in forty thousand dollars, and Karolyi has a friend with fifty thousand dollars; I myself will wait and see how they're coming along, I don't want to be an angel, but we'll get one hundred thousand dollars easy, and you'll get a cut, you're in this with me, so don't worry about money. It's going to be a gold mine and you get your claim first, I found the field, you're my partner. You cut in and the rest have got to wait till I get my money back and a good profit and then they can get whatever comes to them in equity, I'll take it to arbitration, but we're in this together. I talk my head off, they only listen for a profit. *Caveat emptor.* But you are my partner. I have to see you downstairs sometime today, in the lobby. I'll call you in an hour. Good-bye," and he cut her off. The phone at once rang again, and he said into it, "I'll meet you downstairs in the lobby at half-past six. Wait in the inside room near the restaurant, near the mirror."

Livy's voice said, "Have you gone in for table-turning? How did you know it was me? Or did I cut in on another dame?"

"No—got to meet you downstairs tomorrow at six-thirty, tomorrow, can you get in? Must consult you about my play. I'll call you back."

He came rushing out to his friends and servants with a merry expression, "Got them both at once, Gabriel Bitkoff and Sam Positive."

"Positive can't be his name."

"Got to call Uzzazuzz, expressed interest—they're going to put in forty thousand dollars each if they like the play. I've got to get ahold of Karolyi, seems a bit of a bungler. Think he'll make good? Misses the point."

He gave them another frenzied monologue, praising "my dialogue" and "my smash-hit," "The public is buying everything that costs money—they're in a good mood, they'll haggle over fifteen-cent ice cream with no cream in it maybe, but that's only to soothe their consciences; so they can go ahead and pay out twenty-dollar cover-charges, seven dollars for a seat at a bum show, and twenty-five dollars for a seat at the opera. But that's old stuff. Wait till they take it to the safe-deposit. We'll all be rich. When I get started, they won't know they ever heard Billy Rose's name, we'll go to Hollywood and start our own company, no Poverty Row, no B. Films; and in two years—"

He came to the end of this pleasant fever suddenly, "Where's that damn Pole, that crazy welsher? Davie, you go and find him and bring him here. I paid out one hundred and eighty dollars and I want my play. I got some beautiful situations, I gave him wonderful dialogue, it's the real thing, why write about a lot of Green Valleys and Green Corn, all green, I got a smash-hit and that double-Dutchman hasn't even written them down; I give the ideas and I sell, he's only got to take notes. He gives me a dialogue, it's a skeleton—can't get people in to pay seven-fifty with only a skeleton, 'Yes,' 'No,' 'Is that so?' He took my one hundred and eighty dollars for that kind of dialogue. Say he was wonderful in Europe, made millions, can't figure it out, perhaps fell on his head somewhere, on the way here."

41

Flack dispatched, he begged Mrs. MacDonald to make him some lunch, while Edda was to sit down and make notes of a brilliant idea he had for a new play, *The Rainbow Girl*. He begged Gilbert to listen to the story which had come to him last night and to give his opinion. It was a true story, realism. He had once met a beautiful girl, all in black, in a transcontinental train and he serenaded her: figured she'd had a little trouble, would be glad of a friend. He said to her, "Don't wear black, wear the colors of the rainbow, for hope. I'll bring you hope." She told him a terrible story about going to Hollywood to try her luck because she took beautiful stills, and about being given the runaround—she showed him photographs, nothing on, had to be that way, they insisted, swimsuit, nice figure, unnecessary he thought it, terrible story, and was only employed by a gangster agency for wild parties and director would say, "Send up a pretty girl at four-thirty, no time to look around," and they would send her and they said, "You must sleep with everyone, someone will make good," but she didn't get a job, poor girl, terrible story, terrible story. Well, he wouldn't go into details. As she told, she burst into tears. He was touched. Perhaps he serenaded her. He went with her to New York and fell in love with her, wanted to make her forget. He went on with warm, muted voice, "Perhaps I went too far, I swear by all that's holy I never meant to harm her, one day she fell out a window—just as I came into the hotel with a message from her sister, and to take her out, cheer her up. In a way, it was a blessing in disguise, because I'm susceptible and perhaps I would have harmed her. But I was saved from that, nothing to reproach myself with. I can give you more experiences. We want to fix it up a bit, gay, lighthearted, no funeral urns, modern, no tears, no lilies, we extract the gloom and put in the honey: that's our formula, what do you think of it?"

Struck by this formula, Grant said it over and over, burning with his power and glory to be, "We'll be famous! We must put in something about reconstructing Greece, America's generosity, and salvaging the yellow East. The U.S.A. is going to have to compete with the European movie houses after the war and they don't want boom-boom, bang-bang, war stuff, *Wings over the Pacific, Green Valleys, Green Corn*, mine-boys, no interest, they want reconstruction; lots of honey. Western civilization has to be reconstructed if it's going to stand as a barricade against Russia—that's the idea they want—ask me, I'm a socialist, I know. We'll sell them what they want, eh? Why not? Reconstruct Western Europe, bring democracy to Asia, make them a barricade, American style, against Russian terrorism. Don't impose but give them the American week end! No work, no police at your front door, but the American week end! Meanwhile, they won't know what they're getting! We won't do no harm."

"Let's put in the suicide, a blessing in disguise," said Edda.

"It's my own experience, reality, my dear girl, nothing uncalled for, nothing cynical. We'll see how it goes. All collaborate, participate: democratic production, eh? A new plan."

She put down the book in which she had made some notes and began walking about the room. She stopped in front of Grant and said very high, "Why the hell should you pension Dad and me? Unless you're crazy or a philanthropist or an angel! But you got me because I had an ulterior motive. Dad is very sick. He doesn't know he's very sick. And I thought it would be good for him to live on a farm. That's why I hung on to you all this time. You know the time I asked you, 'Can I see Mrs. Grant? I don't want to go out to a family farm, a strange girl, without seeing your wife. It looks so queer.' You said, 'Yes.' That was a showdown and you came up to meet it. I was impressed. I believed in you then. So I hung on another ten months! Now I see I'm a fool. I don't blame you, I blame myself. . . . No more fairy tales. You sung me a serenade. I'm a working girl."

Miss Robbins looked gloomily at her. Gilbert listened closely.

Grant puffed out energetically, "Stand by me, my girl, till we get this play through and write down these notes for me. We're partners in this. It's a masterpiece, a work of art, also it'll be a smash-hit. Truth and honey is money. Your troubles will be over. You can go away with Flack to Florida, to the mountains, to the West Coast, wherever he should go. You won't have to worry about me. It's a work of art, it's a true story, a heart story, it's touching and romantic. We'll get up a kitty from those bozos and we'll all get our expenses out of it."

"It's junk. Where's my hat? I'm going out to get a job."

"It's superb, it's a unique story, it's fresh, beautiful, it's art," cried Grant.

"It's garbage," said Edda.

Gilbert interposed, "Why are you doing it then?"

"For money! Only Robert has to go through his act." She laughed, sat down and crossed her legs.

Grant frowned at her, "Nonsense, nonsense, it'll be a sensation. Look, here's twenty dollars."

"I'll take it."

Grant put it back in his pocketbook and said quickly, "We'll get Karolyi and the typist to help make up a kitty and we'll pay you out of the kitty. Will that satisfy you? I admit you ought to get something. I paid 'em some money, now they can make up a kitty; this is a co-op, eh? We'll form a co-op. They can pay you out of the co-op kitty. Now make a note for me, like a good girl. I was in the West End Hotel, and I saw a young woman—"

Edda burst out laughing and said nothing.

"What's the matter, what's the matter?"

"I can't afford to support a shoestring promoter. I thought you were rich."

He did not understand her at all and began to dislike her. He watched her as if she had been a barking dog, but when she started to go to the door, he rushed to her, seized both arms, laughed, cried, kissed her, called her Little Sister, kept her.

Eventually, the carpenter's boy came; and Grant permitted several of his listeners to leave. He spent some interesting hours with Jones trying the locks. This carpenter had become his handyman. He was like many handymen, a good-natured, unselfish man, absorbed chiefly by the casual problems of his business. Grant got on well with him, put on several representations for him, of Ford, Will, the Money-Egotist, the Genial Capitalist, and sandwiched his boyhood socialism in between. The carpenter did not care much about money, even though he had a family to support, and allowed Grant to take a few dollars off every bill, on one pretext or another. He fixed all the locks but one, and promised to get several keys made. Grant made a great scene over the lock not fixed, but looked lugubrious when the carpenter moved off, saying he would find a locksmith. Grant muttered, "You could do it, my dear boy, if you worked a little longer."

As soon as the carpenter had gone, he forced Mrs. MacDonald to call up several locksmiths in succession, and get "estimates" for the fixing of the lock. Each was informed that he had to come to the hotel as Grant would not allow the valise out of his sight.

"But there is no reason whatever for your obstinacy," said Mrs. MacDonald.

"My dear good woman—"

"Well, you will pay through the nose."

"I don't think Jones put his mind to it. Call Jones and I'll speak to him."

When all these had gone, he had lunch with his son, telling him a romantic story of his relations with Mrs. Downs which in no way fitted his previous mischievous play-acting. After he had dismissed the inexperienced young man, he had several conferences with Miss Robbins (about certain mysterious affairs known only to him and to her), with the Goodwins, and last with the blonde lady, downstairs in the lobby. There, Mrs. Downs told him that Churchill was "out for blood" and would hear of no settlement, the case was going to the courts and would be on the calendar next week. There was nothing that could be done. He and she were in this together for better or for worse.

He left Mrs. Downs and sent for his son. There, without telling him that he had met Mrs. Downs, he began an accusation, "She does not know my hideout, thank God, and I swear before God, I shall never see the —— again. She led me by the nose. I thought I was in love with her and she thought she would go through my pockets. I had my head in the air, she bewitched me, she turned me head over heels, and I thought her so innocent. If you knew the innocent picture she made— I should not say this, but perhaps I was not always as I should have been, but without any thought of harm, I swear, I was carried away. I saw her, by lamplight, on the fresh linen, with her blonde hair uncoiled and a white cat there, a picture of innocence, asleep, with a rosy cheek and hardly breathing, like that princess, the 'Sleeping Beauty,' I kissed her forehead and up there woke a rascal and a criminal."

As he warmed up, he began to twinkle and blush, his eyes growing big, the corners of his handsome mouth turned down.

"She bought me at one corner and sold me at the next. Can you believe it of an old merchant like me? But now it is too late. She lost me."

He listened to a few moral remarks of his son, sat down near him, sideways, leaning on the table, and began another of his stories, secret things, but turning them as well as he could with his rough imagination, to his advantage, as he thought; he said intermittently, "Your mother is an angel. Perhaps I would have been better if I had stayed at home and been a good boy—but I don't think so, ha-ha, I don't think so. It isn't for you, but I'm not the same man. . . . I knew a girl, Celia Grimm, I took her out several times and I got nothing for it, not even a kiss. It isn't correct, I thought, but perhaps she's a Presbyterian. Then I find she is always going listening to the Negroes sing. She's a pervert, going native. Don't waste your time on her, my boy, I went out with her. I could give you tips. There's a secret to everything. Now there's a man upstairs in the Pickwick, an old Greek, and I, one day, am sitting in the lobby, waiting for Delafield, when I see several girls ask for him, not all at the same time, one after the other. What is this secret? I ask. I knew several of the girls. After they made his acquaintance, they never even had tea with me. What is his secret? I ask him and he tells me. He thinks of them, too! Imagine. Not for me, I said. I don't need that for my pleasure. I'm not a pervert. I don't believe in it. I've been in one or two wild parties, just got led into it, but I didn't enjoy it, didn't like to refuse."

He laughed pridefully and mentioned a few of his exploits. "I get led on. But not you."

"Are the Flacks going to live on Largo Farm?"

"I don't mind them coming down for a week end once or twice."

"You promised them to live there."

"It's mine to do what I like with it."

"Then they're not going on it?"

"Do you think I can be a Christmas tree to everyone? Let them work!"

Grant returned to his romance.

After several hours of this, with the vague idea of getting his son's sympathy, of confiding in someone who could never leave him, and even of debauching the young man a bit, bringing his kin nearer to him, Grant sent Gilbert home to the Pickwick and went to bed. He tossed, worrying about Mrs. Downs. He tried to see what scheme she had up her sleeve. The best thing was certainly for him to fly, yet he hated to leave her free to act. Life had nothing else of interest to offer him. He had been asleep only about ten minutes when the telephone rang.

It was two o'clock. At first he could not understand the voice at all, one he had never heard, and in a language he had never heard, the whole thing like gibberish in a dream, an effect of flying clouds late on a lonely night. There was a sort of laughing and crying in foreign tongues, and from time to time Grant, who had a gift for spoken language, picked up three or four words out of the babble-fit. The voice went out at a great rate, at terrific speed sometimes, over four hundred words a minute, as Grant guessed, laughing and pleading always but for what, he did not catch. Now he knew it was Karolyi. He heard the words, in German— "and in koronas and lev and lei and rubles, and Swiss francs you can exchange—my dear sir, my dear beloved Robbie—" and the voice ran on once more.

"Speak German or French," said Grant.

The voice broke into a torrent of speech in German but blacked out once more into what was perhaps Polish, with suddenly in English, "You understand the magnificent gentleman has no exchange."

"What's the matter? You woke me up. I tried to get you all day, Karel. Where's the script?"

"I have it, a tremendous success, an unprecedented success, will sweep them into the Atlantic, always, a wonderful success, played in Paris, London and Berlin, a multimillionaire, though the exchanges have fallen and I don't—kroner, gulden, six hundred thousand—I'm very famous, I assure you, there I do not go to publishers, not I, but they come begging, pleading and praying, asking, 'Karolyi, have you nothing for me?' But given a chance, I will conquer here, too, I do not beg and pray in my turn, I say, I can show you all—" The voice of Karolyi, about things incomprehensible, drifted on furiously, "I am more than ready, I assure

281

you, and I have a fine actor to read it. But bring several ladies with good taste, I beg you—and Mrs. Downs promised me likewise that Mr. March would bring me ten thousand dollars—work is not a torture for me, but I must eat, though I had an excellent dinner, to begin with there is the typist—early tomorrow morning—"

Grant said firmly, "Come to my place tomorrow morning at eleven and bring the script. If you have something to show I will let my partners Positive and Bitkoff know and I will give you the money for the typist. If there are three copies—I pay for them—if not, no soap. I don't pay for nothing."

The voice started again and Grant hung up. When he heard the telephone again, he listened for a moment and hung up. Karolyi's telephone bill was $40 monthly; he sat at home, played solitaire, and telephoned. Grant did not believe there was any finished play.

Grant was up, shaved, and half-dressed when Karolyi called upon him the next morning at seven-fifteen. It was very cold. Karolyi was well-dressed and with clean clothes, though himself far from fresh, and unshaven. He had with him a small package. This package, undone, proved to be the script, written in an elegant small fast hand, one copy only. Karolyi had put on his name, *The Subway Princess*. Grant grabbed it, held it tight between his powerful hands, weighed it, spun the leaves to see the quantity of writing, peered critically at the words on page one. He sent for coffee for two and sat down, keeping the script in his hands. He was deeply gratified. He believed he had created a "drama." But, suspicious, ignorant, and a hardened merchant, he began by quarreling, at first about the title. It must not be *The Subway Princess*, which would attract no one, but one of two sure-fire titles created by himself.

Grant could see the poor, rakish, sick fellow had been up all night and he suspected that Karolyi had fabricated the play overnight, just reeled it off, to get $20. He turned the things in his hands, working himself into a pet, observed some short phrases like "Is that so?" and pages not entirely filled. He screamed, "It seems to me there are holes in the play—you haven't finished it. You can't present a thing like that to a producer. There are hardly any words in the dialogue! Where's the dialogue? This is only a skeleton. I pay nothing until I get a complete play. No skeletons. I want good work and I want it finished. Take this back and fill in the words."

He threw the script on the table, though very loath to let it go from him. Karolyi, his hands hovering and trembling, picked it up, opened it eagerly, and began to show Grant the dialogue, saying as he went through it, "This will be a smashit; this will bring us a million dollars—"

He began to rave again— "South Africa, Australia, all the British Empire and in Europe where my name is enough to sell, I do not have to go down on my knees—"

Savagely Grant said, disturbed somewhat in mind, "Let me have the whole thing or nothing—and then, my boy, the whole world will be round our pushcart; but the whole thing or nothing! And I want three copies. Tell the typist he's a swindler. I said three copies and you got nothing. I been swindled; I got nothing. And I don't pay another cent till I see what I want."

He went on with a formidable frown, and began to push Karolyi out of the apartment, saying, "Let me see the thing in two days; see if you can finish it by then and three copies."

"But the typist—the typist—to town no more—he cannot—"

"Then you ring up David Flack and tell him to tell his daughter to make three copies; we'll get up a kitty, we'll all put in and pay her out of the kitty. I won't pay for a phantom typist. I see nothing— Tell Flack, go to Flack, tell him to hurry up, get it done—I paid and I got nothing—"

He strode up and down, feeling injured. He telephoned Miss Robbins, telling her to pay no money to Karolyi, who might come yelping round the office, with his script, "Don't believe him, it's a try-on."

42

Mrs. MacDonald paid him a visit very early, crying, saying she had been obliged to make breakfast and do the shoes for the Walkers, not mentioning Gilbert, whom she did not count; and that the housekeeping was beyond her at her age, this was never in the bargain, full-time servants were getting at least $125 per month. Grant was cozy and charming, taking her by both hands, leading her to a chair, sitting her in it, "Only for a few days, my dear woman, stand by me till I get settled; you know I'm being hounded and pursued, I've my back against the wall; and then I'll be back again and they'll be out, only a few days, patience, my dear woman. Then, when spring comes, you will come with Gilbert and me, just the two of us, two bachelors, out to Largo Farm, and you will be housekeeper there, your word will be law.

Is that to your liking? This is a surprise I am keeping in my sleeve for you, but why not tell it now? So stand by me, my dear, you are like a mother to me and I need a mother and friend now. They are yelping round me, my back is to the wall, I want a good woman. When spring comes we will go to Largo Farm and live there for the rest of our lives and your word will be law. I'll get you a servant, Gilbert will be my farmer, a cozy little family. Two bachelors, eh—is that to your taste? There was a time when two bachelors would have kept you awake at nights, but now you will be our mother."

"Is it really so, you are not fooling me, Mr. Grant?"

"On my word of honor, as soon as spring comes—Largo Farm —you will have fresh-killed chicken and someone to cook it for you, you will only count the sheets, see none are missing. There. . . . Will you go back and put up with the Walkers for only a few days? Will you?"

The old woman mournfully went back, saying that she feared with the best will in the world she could not manage for two men and two women, and he must or they must get her a woman to help. Laughing and promising nothing and at the end asking after Jones, and beginning to chew his lips because she had not brought the telephone messages, he let her go.

When he was alone again, he got the old-fashioned leather hatbox, the locked one, which had been all night on top of the wardrobe, and put it on the polished oval table in the center of the room. He looked at it several times and pulled at the lock. He spread out all his keys on the table, about thirty-five in all, and after sorting out about eleven smaller ones, he began to try them systematically. He was going through them a second time, with a serious, contented air, when the hotel desk telephoned him to ask if a lady could come up. He said to send her up, supposing it to be Edda Flack. When he flung the door open, he saw, however, Livy Wright.

"I've come to have breakfast with you, like Laura," she announced.

She looked fresh and brilliant, her black hair piled in a braided crown. Her business dress, cut low in the bodice, was of silk shirred all over in two-inch bands, tight in the waist and very short. She had steel-studded buckles on her high-heeled shoes and long black kid gloves. She threw her black astrakhan coat on the sofa, with an enormous handbag in calf and gold. She had a wide bracelet of brilliants, much perfume, and no color in her cheeks but a dark red lipstick which brought out the darkness of her eyes.

"I've come for breakfast, darling," and she smacked her lips on his lips. They stood smiling, holding hands, while Grant ran his eyes over her freshly powdered skin and wondered about her visit. He closed the door and said, "I'll get up some more coffee."

She vociferated, "What are you in your dressing gown for? I thought you got up at daybreak to get washed and dusted and scented and lotioned—"

In passing round the room, she fixed on the hatbox, "What the hell's that? Looks as if it came out of the ark!"

"That's a hatbox."

"Oh, that's a hatbox. Surprise, surprise. What's in the hatbox? Not hats, of course. Probably the missing shoe trees."

She pulled at the cover, "It's locked. Have you been dancing a war-dance round it? Go and put a morning coat on, or your business coat, Robbie, I don't want to see you round the apartment in the morning in your dressing gown. Don't jingle your money, my darling. It's not good manners. Ring for breakfast, now, darling; and let us sit down in a decent way, like a married couple. The place looks like Grand Central—are you going somewhere? I suppose it's that damned blonde. Are you moving, or just moving in? Don't you skip without letting me know, old boy! Come, now, telephone for coffee and telephone Mrs. MacDonald, and I'll help her put your things in order. We must put these things off in the corridor somewhere. You look like a line-up of refugees at the Polish border. Station Six of the Jewish Underground. Or pengo billionaires unpacking enough pengos to get a sandwich and a cup of coffee. . . . What the hell do you have pigskin for? It's an invitation to the customs officers to rip out the linings and see what diamonds you're bootlegging. No wonder the women try to take you over. You look like a walking checkbook. I'll have to improve you a bit, old joker. You look like a god-damned Christmas tree. Now, Robbie, I found out that that Laura of yours on what you call the Pinchem Hill used to get up with the lark to look after you and if that's what you want, son, I'm going to do it too. I'll even wash your feet, if you like, like a blessed Magdalen, or Martha, or whatever you like, if you want that—you name it, and it's yours. I'm a big gambler because I have nothing to lose. So here I am and I'll come round every morning to be at breakfast with you, and get you off to work."

Grant made oyster eyes and listened to this mad address, first with astonishment, then with a wide smile, and then seriously. He kissed the woman, hugged her furiously, then went to telephone. All the time he kept smiling to himself and casting glances at Livy, who was rubbing her hand over the thick leather top of the hatbox and tugging at the lock.

Now Gilbert arrived with a candid morning air and kissed Livy, then breakfast arrived for all three, and Livy bounced the hatbox off the table, and sent the waiter for a cloth, meanwhile making sallies at the two Grant men. She continued, "Why must you wash so much, Robbie? Are you washing away your sins? You want me around to see you sleep tighter and have fewer sins. These bachelor days are no good for you. You won't stay the course if you get up at five to wash. What on earth do you do all that time? When I came, he had on his dressing gown only, and his hair wet. The place must look like a Turkish bath. I'll put a stop to that, when we're married, or even if we have a trial marriage. Excuse me, Gilbert, I know you're friendly to that. That's our bargain, isn't it? Your father made that Grant bargain with me. Try first, then no disappointment after. Is that so, Robbie? A Grant bargain."

He looked straight at her, arched his neck, eyed Gilbert, and came back to her. All the time she was pouring out coffee, putting in cream and sugar, shouting at Gilbert, "Don't do it that way, but this way," pouncing upon spoons and knives, quarreling with the amount of sugar, cream, and coffee given, with the quality of the coffee and its strength; and all robust and serious as a fishwife. When the cups were passed, she heckled still, with, "Robbie, you take too much sugar, think of your figure and think about diabetes, you're likely to get it," and, "I hate this kind of tablecloth, I like fine linen and old lace, and I'll never allow a tablecloth cornerwise in our home, that's a hotel mannerism, we've got to change many things in your way of life, haven't we? Ah, in general I'll have to clean up after you, the mess you've made of your life."

She rose noisily from her chair, once, to throw her arms round Grant. Bending over him she became warm; sparkling, she declared she loved him and was a blessing, not in disguise—"Leave it to me, bully-boy! There's no disguise on me!"

Grant hardly said a word, listening to her shouting, with his head slightly to the side, a faint confused smile on his face. She kept on prancing and making caracoles like a wild black pony. Bored, he at last pulled out his watch, when she cried, "You needn't look, you've got all the time in the world, all day. You're in hiding, aren't you? No blondine to come here, no little tea, little chat, eh? Leave your timetable to me, darling, and you won't have to go to Bermuda or Havana—which it was, I don't know, your stories vary like hell. If you go out, I'll send Gilbert out first to scout around and then I'll hail you a taxi and hustle you into it. But you've got nowhere to go. You just sit here quiet and behave like an invalid, which you are, a moral invalid, a moral leper— let this be your leprosarium, bully-boy, I award myself the job of keeper. I'll leave Gilbert here in charge and I'll go off to my business and be back with you when the sun goes down."

She rushed to the telephone and ordered the waiter to return for the trays. When she came back, Grant had picked up the hatbox and put it in the middle of a side table.

"Is that the hatbox?" asked Gilbert.

"That is *the* hatbox. Isn't he sweet, paddling round with a hatbox? Is there a head in it? No hats, I'm sure. He has fifty-three hats, and probably in the hatbox he keeps his old watches; because the hatbox was at the optician's."

"The tailor's," muttered Grant. He had begun trying keys again. The telephone rang, Livy sprang to it and announced that Mrs. MacDonald and Miss Robbins were on the way up, "Quite a levee!"

"I want the carpenter," he said savagely. He went down on his knees before a valise, with a key he had just picked out, "This fits one lock and not the other, the carpenter must find me another. I told him to bring all the old keys in his workshop."

"Why not the locksmith?" said Gilbert.

"At the corner of every street is a man who'll make you keys," said Livy.

"I don't want them," yelled Grant.

"I wouldn't want to sit at breakfast opposite that temper; you go ahead and find some doormat to try that on," cried Livy.

"All this turmoil about a key is just an example," began Gilbert.

"—of living alone and we're going to put a stop to that," cried Livy.

Grant turned round and grinned, "The trouble with me, sweetie, is you know I'm lonely. I live the life of a bachelor, get into bad moods, and so I fall for the wrong women, fall easy."

"Easy and often, too often for me; here's your hatbox and

where's your hurry—don't bother me; I don't want any drill sergeants."

"Don't talk like that, I need you, Livy, I need your common sense; the world's a desert to me and you're my oasis. The well was dry, then you came along and filled it."

"Fell into it, you mean; I heard that before somewhere. Where was it? It was here, you fraud, bully-boy. I know your salesline. Get a new fall line. Ha!"

He laughed and pushed his bust forward, "I mean it, lovely woman, good companion, common sense, business woman, own property, not trying to go through my pockets, own opinions, understands me, consoles me—in your own way. Now this bloody 'ooman—in Jigago—I never would have believed it, I came to her like a little boy, I was looking for a wife, a sweetheart, and a sister, and she only thinks of drawing blood, a bloodsucker." He hesitated and flushed slightly, giving Livy time to put in a shout, then he continued, "Trouble is, her husband's a mean man, small nature, and all these months he's pretended to live at home but not paying bills or speaking to her and she had to come crying to me to borrow a little money, not much—and it looks bad she says, or he says. Finally, he took a room and watched her with a detective—sitting in a car outside her apartment house. That shows a very small nature. He even had the newspapers delivered in his hotel, and wouldn't let her read the newspapers! She had to come to me for the rent and to patch her shoes—she even asked me to keep my Coca-Cola bottles so she could return them and get the money—"

Livy whooped, "That's the meanest collector I ever heard of—and you stood for that?"

Said Grant stoutly, "She told me she needed a pair of gloves, I bought them. Why not? You know one time I was sweet on her, but she gave me some of my presents back. And she carries my Coca-Cola bottles away in a shopping bag—shows she's honest."

His laughed betrayed him. Livy fumed, "Does she carry off your old shoes too? You think she's cute."

"Well, Livy, I admit I liked the woman, thought she was high-class, had character. Thought she had me round her little finger and cost me a forchun—and I didn't mind it—I was naïve, I admit it—don't want to lie to you, it's no use—I liked it—but when she started playing double-treble, selling me short because there was a lot of me lying around ready to pick up, so she thought—I didn't want it. It takes two to make a bargain. You got to have the supply. She made a mistake. She's a cash-register type. Came to my place every day in a taxi and never had the money even for the tip and her friend Paula too. Told my doorman to pay. How does that look? I warned him; then next time I didn't pay him, told him, 'I told you not to.' Next time she was stuck; had to phone upstairs. That taught her a lesson. And then when she was going away to Reno, she comes there on the way to the station with her bags all packed and marked for Reno. I sent her away; and I paid for the ticket, then someone tells me, the Mann Act and I don't know what else. She didn't know what she was doing. Used to having fellows looking after her. She's innocent that way. Never looks ahead. I gave her the money for her ticket, she changed her mind, and then I have to go and pay all over again! Muddled, but a cash-register type and a one-way girl too. Never gave me but one tie in her life. She has a dentist, a White Russian, she says, 'Give the poor fellow a bit of business.' I send Gilbert to him and give her the money for the bill. She doesn't pay. Says she has something urgent that day. I have to pay all over again. But she drives a hard bargain. Should have been in business or a diplomat. She knows men and she's no fool. Says she saves money for me. Ha-ha! Then she writes to me, 'Only a boor and a peasant haggles over money, or a Jew or a Syrian. You stick at every penny. Perhaps you have Jewish blood. But I forget what they say about the Scots. Am I to pay your bills for you? I cannot spare you a penny, I am poor.'"

"For your money you get value," said Livy.

"Of course I had to pay the fellow," said Grant.

"What fellow?"

"The doctor."

"It was a dentist a minute ago."

He laughed, "I couldn't track her down; you try to." He paused, evidently reviewing some events.

Livy said, "Well, go on, you behaved like a worm and she got you into a mess. Serves you right. If you mix up with bought women. I don't have to be bought. I give myself, and then I give something else too. I'm generous. I'm an extravert. I don't hang on to money. I don't need laxatives for my purse. Take me. Forget that woman. Don't keep harping on her. You don't see her any more."

He looked up from the valise he was delving in, "Couldn't have believed it, you know; she looked like a real lady. And she loves her mother, doesn't want her to know anything wrong. It shows a very nice side to her nature."

"A stage mother—they've all got them. I've got a father," said Livy over her shoulder.

Grant made an impatient gesture and bawled out to Mrs. MacDonald, "Ring up the carpenter and the Flacks. I want Flack here. If the girl's at work then I can't help it."

"Look, about the Swiss watches," cried Livy, turning about-face.

"Yes?"

"I got you five dozen very cheap."

"Is that so? How much?" He turned on his heels.

"Five dozen Tavannes, eighty dollars basis."

"That's not bad," he said, turning back to her.

"If the lot suits you, I can get twenty dozen at the same. Through the same party, a friend of my brother-in-law."

"Done, I'll take it," he said, turning back to his trying of keys.

"Don't stick me with them." He took no notice.

"I'll bring them tomorrow with the invoice."

"All right, all right."

"I have to leave you for a while because I'm negotiating the purchase of two houses in Montague Street, Brooklyn Heights. They belonged to our family before, but my father had no business sense and allowed them to pass to an uncle who sold them off. One was valued at forty-four thousand dollars and can now be got for twenty-one thousand dollars. I can make an arrangement. It's in excellent condition, oak panels, a private elevator, all the floors arranged for small apartments, plenty of electric light and hot water. The revenue from rents is four hundred and five dollars monthly plus rent of a two-story garage in the end of the garden which I am reconditioning, with an apartment above, ninety dollars, makes four hundred and ninety-five dollars monthly, plus a basement now used by the owner as a sort of table d'hôte for the tenants, which I'm turning into an apartment, with use of garden, an additional fifty-five dollars, say—it has to be lower although it is an entire floor, because it is a basement, rather dark, and there is the boiler room there, five hundred and fifty dollars monthly. My taxes will be five hundred and ninety dollars, mortgage payments four per cent on twelve thousand dollars, four hundred and eighty dollars plus two hundred dollars for amortization. In five years the house will be mine, if I raise the rents a bit by black-market arrangements, which anyone will accept. There is a house on the street not quite the same condition, fifteen thousand dollars and needs about ten thousand dollars on improvements, the garage turned into a small house in the garden. I am buying the two of them tomorrow."

"Ah, they've accepted your conditions," he said, turning round and eying her sharply.

"Of course, tomorrow I sign the papers. I'm going to have houses, too. I got a lot of business done this week before I went to the factory, and for some time I've been thinking, Why pay rent for my father and young brother and for myself? I save the rent and get their rents. I've always a roof over my head. I'll fix the place up as a home elegantly, there'll be two floors I'll keep for myself, if I want them, if I marry, I'll have one. Father and my brother will have the other, or a smaller one."

"A smaller one," he said, screwing back his head and eying a lock.

"In a few days I'll be a landlord, and pay myself back in three years. I've heard of a small estate up in the country, in the borsch belt, which has gone to seed. The owner is away at the war and doesn't want it, and I can get it for the taxes, a farm with barns, fifteen hundred dollars. It's on a mountainside, with no road to it, but they're going to build a road to it. This will do for my family and me in the summer. It's at an elevation of eighteen hundred feet. You can grow all vegetables in spring."

"Where will you get the money for all this?" he asked cautiously.

"My family will lend me some to get back the family property. I'll use my savings and my business is solid, I'll pay out of that."

"You're pyramiding, aren't you? I don't like that."

"Don't worry about me, Robert. I want to show you I've got everything you can ask for."

"I'll wait till I see, you got to show me," he laughed, wagging his great head at her.

"I'll show you the deeds, you'll see everything."

He laughed maliciously, remarked, "Well, I'm glad you've got something to depend on, the boom won't go on forever."

She said, "So I own a house, two, two houses, and a farm. Now you know another woman who owns a house and a farm, two in one, I put my cards on the table. Gilbert's mother owns a farm, I own a farm. Laura made a contribution. I make a contribution."

Grant grinned, "Well, I'm glad of it, but don't get into deep water over me, sweetie. You know me, I'm an eel, I can't help sliding out from under, that's the way I get about. I wouldn't want to be the ruin of you. We have our bargain, if it doesn't work, no recriminations, gentleman's agreement, eh? He-he-he! You're a high style of woman, my sort of woman, you got character, and I wouldn't want to have you on my conscience if you went bankrupt."

She said, "I know what the score is."

He turned his back to her, suddenly shouting to Mrs. MacDonald for the parcel of shoe covers. Livy flounced bravely and cried, "Now I've got to see my lawyer, go to the factory, and I'll be back at two-thirty. Be good."

As she put on her coat and powdered her face, she watched Miss Robbins making out a laundry list, in an adjacent room. Without lowering her voice, she said to Grant, "And another thing I have to reform in you is your secretary. You let any girl with a temper run you. I wouldn't trust anyone the way you trust that woman. I don't like the way she dresses, I don't like the way she talks to you, I don't like the way you confide in her. She signs your checks, doesn't she? Is that good business? You're soft as a marshmallow, you're soft as a rotten tire, I'll see about that when I come back. One of these days I'll take you over, my bully-boy. I'd let no one get at my bank balance, old top. I'll get you a young woman out of high school, doesn't know her nose from her elbow, and I'll train her and I'll look after your private affairs myself. I never saw such a messer and such an amateur, for a business man."

Grant looked up at her from his heels, and laughed, winking at Gilbert. She continued, "One of these days you'll get taken over, you'll see. You trusted this Laura and bought her a house and she lets you down. You're getting out of business. You're retired, you're getting soft. I'm still making money. I got to manage strikes and salesmen, and sell my goods. 'Im different. You're an old-timer, you're out of the running. You don't know what it's like today. I'd get rid of that woman and get rid of her fast. Get a youngster, too—an ugly one."

When she left, Grant called them together, Mrs. MacDonald, Miss Robbins, and Gilbert, and asked softly, "What do you think of her? She's got character? She wants to take me over, buy me out, eh? She's making a proposition, what do you think of that? Two houses and a farm. She hasn't got a bean, I know her finances, I looked her up. But what do you think of it? I'm quoted higher today than yesterday; the farm came into it, because of the

chicken farm! Eh? What a girl! That's what I need—maybe!" And
he went off into a splendid carillon, slapping his bent knee and
exclaiming about Livy's aggressiveness, ending with, "But she
likes me, eh, she must like me, what do you think? Maybe I
showed her the pretty pictures a bit; maybe I put in a few ara-
besques, serenaded her—but she's a fine woman; and I didn't always tell her the truth, maybe; but at the time I meant it. Can't
help myself, like to please a pretty woman. A serenade costs nothing and look at the results. Now she's out to lassoo me. Oh, boy!"

He said to Gilbert, "And she wants your farm too, son! He-he-he.
I give them full details—they fancy they see the figures in my bank
account, maybe they think they're in my will! Ha-ha-ha. I'll give
them my house on the Pinchem every day. Stay with me a month,
a year, two years—ha! Why not? I don't mean to cheat 'em. I
swear it. It just comes out of my mouth and they think I have to
stand by it. Is there anything down on paper? Believe me, my
boy, anything down on paper, signed, sealed, and witnessed, if
anything is dubious and I got to take it to arbitration and the
judgment goes against me, I pay. If I can't get the judgment reversed. Ha-ha!"

He looked thoughtfully at his work and continued at once, "She
bought the watches herself and she's taking a loss, but let her!
I'll make it up to her some way. I'll see. I'll see how she shapes
up. Got to lead her on a bit to see what's in her. I liked her last
month a lot, told her we might get together. Don't like her so
much now. She disappointed me. Don't like this bullying, this
screaming. Not used to it. I like a lady. But I'll give her a chance.
Maybe I wasn't quite aboveboard with her. Sang her a song and
dance. H'm. . . . Why isn't Flack here with the collar case? Ring
him, Miss Robbins. What did that bloody 'ooman want to come
here for breakfast for? I like my breakfast alone. Miss Robbins is
not used to seeing women around me in the morning. I don't want
women looking in my papers. To hell with her, she's out, she
talked herself off my payroll. I do what I like! She can buy a
hundred houses on a shoestring and I'll see her in bankruptcy next
month and give a horse-laugh. She can't buy me with her ten
cents. Listen, Gilbert, Mrs. MacDonald, don't leave me alone
with her! Mrs. MacDonald isn't used to seeing women promoting
me at breakfast time. You don't understand, my good woman;
neither do I. You'll go to Largo Farm, Mrs. MacDonald, and
mother Gilbert and me: no Xantippe! Not a nice way to behave.
Not a lady. I never had a woman in my office. Miss Robbins is

my confidential— Never had women to breakfast! Livy got the wrong idea. Always called her my sister, treated her as a sister, respected her, never laid a finger on her. Where'd she get the idea? Thinks she can buy me with a shoestring. . . . Ha! She'll ruin herself! Let her! Ha! Bloody fool! Gilbert, go and get me the key of the desk in my bedroom."

Taking advantage of Gilbert's absence, Miss Robbins approached and said, "I don't think you ought to let Gilbert see your private life like this. Why don't you send him to the country as you said? It isn't fair to him."

"Gilbert! Forty of him wouldn't make one of me! To hell with him! Let him see! D'you think I give two cents for what he thinks? Let him know the worst! He eats out of my hand for a farm, like the rest of 'em, doesn't he? I can buy and sell them all! You're the only decent one, Miss Robbins, you and Mrs. MacDonald. Let him see me at my worst. Let him find out where his money came from! If he doesn't like where it came from, let the *schlemihl* go and make his own."

"Shh! He'll hear—I brought the boy up."

"Let him bloody well hear. What do I care for the Gilberts? He and she and the youngster can take my medicine and like it. I saw Livy's father. I sang him a sweet song. I'll marry your daughter when I'm free. The old man thought he was on Easy Street. The old woman brought me a turkey. What's it to me? They want my money! Let them try and get it. My object is to keep it. That's all there is between us. Pull bear, pull baker. That damn blonde woman is worth the whole pack. I don't care if she's all they say she is, she's more to me than the whole pack. Let him hear! I've got to hold my tongue for a clerk in my office?—that's all he can do, if that! I'll speak my mind when I like and if he don't like it, let him starve. He'll do what I say, or starve. He's Grant's son. Let him sink in shame, let him have the mud from my wheels. He stole my woman, he's not so good. He'll get my money; he'll take it."

He ended in a terrific roar, which echoed through the apartment. Gilbert must have heard everything. Now Grant stamped up and down for a while as he cooled. At last he said in a quiet voice, as his son entered, "Gilbert! Well, you've seen me at my worst, best thing, blessing in disguise. We have to understand each other. I'm no angel."

Gilbert said, "What you said is true! I made up my accounts

with myself, the black and the red as you say, and I am Grant's son. I couldn't earn my living. I must swallow my pride. Pride is ignorance. And very often honor is just another word for a neat income: I don't have to black shoes, I'm honorable. But when I have your money, I'll bring honor into it."

Grant gave him a stern look, "The money will have the same stamp. Oblige me by trying that desk key in the hatbox. Your mother was always too good for me. Sweet woman. Probably my fault we didn't get along. An angel. But, my boy—he-he!—between you and me, it's hard to live with an angel. You're turning it in the wrong direction. You didn't get shaved this morning, and look, you've nicked your cheek twice, from yesterday. Very dangerous, go and put rubbing alcohol on it. No, it doesn't work. Now put the key back in the drawer, no, put it in the left-hand corner of the uppermost drawer in the bureau. Gilbert, come back—"

The young man re-entered with the key still in his hand. Grant grumbled, "I want you to follow my instructions. You actually left the door key on the desk that time in Jigago! Can't understand it."

Gilbert left the room while his father kept shouting at him. Miss Robbins said, "This key does not fit the hatbox, that's certain."

He grumbled, "But it fits something! Should have bought keys in Woolworth's. Go to the man on the corner, buy up his odd keys. No foresight. That's it! This fits! You should have said to yourself, 'If this key doesn't fit the hatbox or the trunk, it will fit something,' and brought along every key you could find at home."

"Why can't you have a locksmith or valise man and fit the lock?"

"God damn it, don't put me off, I do things my way."

Presently Edda and Flack arrived and he had them all fitting keys in the locks, muttering meanwhile against the carpenter. Flack said, "Today he has to carpent, perhaps. Stop rumbling like Vesuvius."

"Can't get anything done! No one listens to me! Why didn't you lock the kitchen closet?"

Flack screamed at him, "I did lock the kitchen closet, also the closet with your precious Scotch and brandy."

"Quite right, you're quite right, but what I can't understand is why you didn't bring your own valise keys so I could try them. You and Edda must have plenty. You should have brought 'em along! There you see, my boy, the difference between a dawdler's, a scribbler's brain, and the brain of a Scotsman who made his own way in the world, forget nothing, leave nothing to chance. The literary brain thinks, it may not fit, it may; romance. I won't bother with it. I'll leave it on the desk in Jigago!"

"What?"

"It don't matter if I can't open the hatbox, I'll leave it to chance. This is the way you don't earn money, Flack. I made money in business by thinking about details. Why don't you go home, my boy, take a taxi and get me your keys? Edda, you do it."

"One more word and I'll throw the key ring out the window!"

"Do me a favor and try those keys again on the hatbox! Don't get shirty, my boy, try and help me. I need consolation, I don't want to be put off."

"I told you, Robbie, they don't fit. If you had half an eye, and any kind of an observation, you'd see what kind of a key your hatbox needs, a small English-style key, it's an English hatbox. This key is a large trunk key and this a small closet key, and doesn't fit anything here. This is a jewel-case key and this key—"

"Try them all again, I want to see it done, oblige me by trying— Here, Gilbert!"

Gilbert said, "Now this hatbox and key turmoil is an example of—"

"What was the example of leaving the key lying on the desk in Jigago? Could you open the door with it? No. Could I find it when I expected it in the right-hand corner of the collar drawer? No. Could a thief get it, or the maid pick it up and put it in her pocket? Yes. Now did you put that key in the upper left-hand corner—?"

"Fuss, fuss, you're like an old woman," said Gilbert, trying the keys.

"If you were a socialist as you pretend, you'd leave the trunks open," said Flack.

"What? Never!" declared Grant, wagging his head prodigiously. He grinned, "Must a socialist turn out his pockets and say, 'Rob me'? No, sir. Must socialist mean Nitwit? I believe in socialism and when it comes I'll be in line to give up my property. If you look down at the end of the line, and look at the last man, that'll be me with my titles and bonds. And I'll be the first one on the Committee for Compensation of Landlords; and if we're dispersed, I'll present a petition to the Government if I'm not in arrears for taxes; and if all else fails, I'll retire to Switzerland and live on my Swiss funds. Yet I'm a socialist. I won't fight for the fascists; but I won't fight for the socialists. If I buy and deliver guns for reactionaries, I'll see they get lost and go to *Guerrilleros*. I won't join the anti-Soviet committee, but I won't either send my luggage away without keys. . . . Now this key might fit anything?"

"Oh, it might fit the secret archives, the desk of your friend in the F.B.I., and we'll get the file on Mrs. Downs," said Flack.

"Not such a joke, not such a joke!"

"And you'd be arrested as a spy! And have to go to Leavenworth with Al Capone."

"Al Capone made his own money at any rate. He wasn't a cop. I wish I knew which key it was."

"What key?"

"The key the bee-expert here left on the desk in Jigago. It might have been the hatbox key."

"You know it was the desk key, Dad."

"It might have fitted the hatbox. I've got it, I've got it!" he cried. He rushed around, holding them by the shoulders, and then pushing things aside as he looked for something, "Where's the collarbox? The key's in the collarbox. Where's the collarbox, Flack?"

Flack became hysterical, "I told you I put it inside the desk, as you said, and locked the desk!"

Grant shook his fist, "That's better, that's good! A key locked up inside a locked desk! You knew I'd want it, god damn it all. You put me off, I've got no time to lose. Where is the key to the locked desk?"

"That's the one you gave to Gilbert."

"Where is it? Where is it?"

"In the upper left top-hand corner of—the upper left-hand top corner of—you know where it is!"

"Get it! Don't leave it lying on the desk like you did in Jigago, an example of the agricultural brain, a key that could open anything—"

"I'm on strike," said Flack.

"A literary brain says, 'Leave the valises open, it doesn't matter if things get lost and people steal your goods and you arrive in Havana without socks'; a beekeeper's brain says, 'Leave the key lying round, it's of no value, what does it matter?'—you leave the barn doors open, too, on the farm; let the cattle and horses stray out and Mr. Knight gets them, what does it matter?—leave the incubation houses open. Let them black-market thieves come with the trucks in the night and steal the chickens, what does it matter? So Upton let them come in the daytime; what's the difference? It doesn't matter. Because neither of you never made a sou for yourselves in your life. But I know the value of money and the value of keys. My entire life is under lock and key. It's here—" he said, putting his hand on the top of the old-fashioned leather hatbox. He picked the hatbox up, weighed it in his big fist, and shook it at them, showing that it was heavy, "It's here, in here under lock and key, everything! No Land of Canaan, no lead you up my garden, no etchings—property, property, money, money, money! And where is the key? You lost the key! The key's in the collarbox locked up in a desk, and the desk key is—"

Gilbert said, "Here it is. What are you waving the hatbox in my face for?"

"Here, here—" said his father and stopped with a grim smile. He took the desk key.

"Where is the collarbox?"

Flack told him and refused to get it for him.

"Mrs. MacDonald, my dear good woman, you're my only friend, kindly take this key and—a woman's instinct is for housekeeping and keeping things under lock and key! But don't try to open the collarbox, I've got the key to that here," and he slid a finger into his vest pocket and produced a small key. He cried triumphantly, "Not a literary brain, not an agricultural brain—" He turned the little key in the collar case, where it stuck. After wrestling with it for a few moments, he looked thunderstruck and exclaimed in a high voice, "It isn't the key! I know, for I remember the key—what key is that? Here's a key—it opens something! Keep it, never mind. It opens something. Keep it. Miss Robbins, try all these little keys. Mrs. MacDonald, please go through these other keys again on that other lock."

"Go call a locksmith," muttered Flack.

"No locksmith! Send for the carpenter!"

"Send to the druggist for a pair of patent-leather shoes," said Gilbert.

"What good is a key lying on a desk on a table—it fits something, someone will find out what it fits," said Grant, passing him with a threatening frown.

Miss Robbins said, "If you think he wouldn't send to the druggist for shoes: he gets his liquor there, he thinks it's cheaper."

43

At length Jones, the carpenter, arrived and managed to fix the obstinate lock and was sent away, with a warning that he must be there at nine on the next day. Grant then suddenly began to dismiss them severally, Flack to get a " 'sports-jack' with a ribbed collar, not the one with the leather collar"; Miss Robbins with Flack, to hunt for a very particular envelope containing photographs of the blonde, which no one but they must see; Mrs. Mac-Donald to go home and receive telephone messages; and Gilbert to go to the newsreels for a couple of hours. Grant said, "I got to take an aspirin and rest."

Gilbert went out of the front door, took out his notebook, consulted his *balance-sheet of self-analysis*, hesitated some time, walking up and down the landing, and then quietly re-entered the apartment. He heard his father inside, talking on the telephone, "I am not showing temper, sweetheart, and I am very sorry you have money troubles, I will do the best I can, but I can't get exchange and you can't get blood from a stone. I don't want to leave you in disgrace, and I don't see why you should have to go to a psychoanalyst. I'll send you a check for Walker as soon as I can. I haven't seen Walker! I've been very generous to you, sweetie, and I know you are strong, physically all right and mentally all right. You just need a couple of sleeping tablets, which I'll send round to you— or meet me down in the Awning Bar at seven-thirty. Send Goodwin round to me tonight at nine-thirty here and I'll go into the question of your expenses. I don't want you to be put out on the street. Don't exaggerate. You're the romantic, Barb, not me, you're the one living in a dream world. I am very much horrified by what you tell me and I must think it all over. It shades extortion, it looks like blackmail—I'm very much shocked and depressed. You can imagine, darling, that I am not feeling very happy."

Gilbert listened for some time to his father's expostulation, and idly picked up the little key which had not fitted the collar case and which lay on top of the hatbox. He put it into the keyhole; it turned and opened. He lifted the lid, looked in, and had turned toward his father's room to call out when that door shut with a great bang, as if it had been kicked shut. The conversation droned on inaudibly behind the door.

Gilbert started to open the hatbox again, instead slid the key into his own vest pocket, and looking about, saw on the dresser shelf some bottles of wine and Scotch whisky that Flack had brought from the other apartment. He quickly drank down two glasses of Scotch, sat down, yawned, and tried to stretch in either armchair. Valises, paper, and clothes had been piled on the long brocaded reclining couch standing by the wall. Gilbert started to clear these off and once more changed his mind, meticulously replacing the valises and clothes in their exact positions. He stretched out behind these, instead, against the wall, and in a few minutes fell asleep.

Meantime, Grant had finished with the blondine and telephoned Livy, asking her not to return till five. He had to go out and was going to lock the place up. This done, he threw himself on the bed, rested for a few minutes, took an aspirin, went and washed and came back into the sitting room in his shirt sleeves with his spectacles on, to read the paper. He sat near the window and did not observe the young man sleeping.

After he had read the paper for half an hour, he went to the phone again and said tranquilly, "I am expecting some messengers and a typist: three young women—send them up." He went back to the window and began to skim through the pages of a magazine. He looked very different now, like a benevolent small storekeeper airing himself at home on Sunday. He had a contented expression and made no noise at all, being extremely smooth and light in his movements, when he had no one to impress.

Someone knocked. He took his time at opening the door, then he said, briefly, "Come in, Violetta? Where's Janet? I phoned her to come at two-thirty, too."

Violetta was about twenty-two, with handsome long legs, a fresh skin, pink cheeks, very pretty, and somewhat shy. She wore a plain brown street coat with a blue dress, a small hat with a veil. She was ill at ease and advanced into the room with hesitation, looking about her and at Grant, without a word.

"I expected you, Violetta, about half an hour ago, but a good thing you didn't come. Sit down over there."

The girl sat down facing him and the window, about twelve feet away. After an expert look at the lower part of her body, Grant took up his paper and went on reading. The girl said nothing and sat without fidgeting. After some time, he looked at her over his avuncular spectacles, said, "I'll wait till Janet comes," and went back to his reading.

Presently the girl said, "Perhaps I ought to go?"

"Did Janet say she was coming? Then wait for her."

They resumed the first pose. After a quarter of an hour, there was another knocking. Grant thrust down his paper, peered at the girl over his spectacles, and padded over to the door. He had kicked off his slippers, showing holes in both socks. He opened the door as before, saying briefly, "Come in, come in."

This visitor was a thin-faced, oldish girl with a work-tired skin and brown hair. She wore a very cheap brown fur coat and a silk dress low-cut over a shapeless full bosom. She wore a pair of plush earpieces and a gold cross on a chain. Her thin shoes left wet patches on the French gray carpet, showing where the holes were. She greeted Violetta and chattered with her a little, then sat down on the seat that Grant pointed out to her, pointing with his finger, without a word, and looking strongly at her over the tops of his spectacles. He went on reading, coughed, looked at them, went on reading. The girls chattered quietly a little; then the newcomer said, "Are you really going away tomorrow, Robbie?"

He looked at her as before, "Did you bring the things? Where's the bill? Let me see."

She handed him the package she had brought.

He pounced on it, unwrapped it, went through the contents, grumbling at things he supposed were missing and later found; and checked over the bill. It bore the name of a pharmacist from far uptown, in a poor district. Janet was a housewife who sometimes ran messages for the pharmacist.

Grant said, "All right, come into the other room, Violetta; I want to give you a message for Delafield."

The young girl looked as if she were about to refuse, but changed her mind and with embarrassment followed the man into the inner room. He shut the door. While they were shut up in the room, came a third knocking at the door, which Janet answered when it was repeated.

The third visitor was a woman of thirty or more, in poor winter clothes, with sloppy hair but alert, dark business eyes, a flushed skin ruined by late hours. She also had a parcel with her.

"Hello, Katia! He's inside."

"He's going away? I brought him three dozen pairs of nylon, at two dollars a pair; I suppose he's taking them."

"He's going to Havana, I think."

"I'll get him to pay me today."

"I would."

The door opened within, and Grant and the girl came out.

Grant, when he saw the new girl, cocked his head and said without greeting: "Did you bring the stockings?"

"Yes! So you're leaving us," she said, with a dusty, beaten bravado.

"Friend of Murray's doing a big business in Havana, Sam—Positive," he said, swaggering to the window, and sitting down with his newspaper.

"Not doctor's orders?" said the newcomer, Katia, sympathetically.

He gave her a look, frowned, and went back to his newspaper. The first young girl came back quietly and stood near the door. After a minute he coughed, raised his eyes, went back to the paper, looked up again, got up, putting his fist into his pocket.

"No need to wait, Violetta," he said amiably. He accompanied the girl to the door and there kissed her, clasped her arm, and gave her a five-dollar bill, saying, "Buy yourself a blouse." Then he padded back to the window and sat down, looking the other girls over pensively. He murmured, as he eyed them, "How's your brother, Katia? You let me down, my girl, last week; and now you're late. I hope you brought the stockings. I need them for my business friends. Got to go on a business trip to—"

He took up the paper, glanced at it, and dropped it. He looked out the window, jingled his money. Then he looked back at Katia and laughed, "What's the matter, Katia? You don't look well today." He got up and walked near and round the seated women, looking them over negligently, then he blurted out, "Janet, you needn't wait, I'll send a check to the pharmacy—tomorrow. How's your father? I'm going away for a while, I won't see you, sweetie, come inside, I want to say a few words to you."

He repeated the previous maneuver, except that this time he merely half-closed the door and could be heard whispering to the woman. In a few minutes he came out, as before, swaggering, rolling his head, looking blackly before him. He stood near the door and when the woman came out, he seized her by her thin arm, marshaled her to the door, with a couple of bills in his hand, and pushed her out with these, muttering, "I'll send you a postcard. Good-bye. I'll call you when I come back, think of me, sweetie."

He shut the door and came back with a satisfied but serious expression. He motioned Katia to an easy chair, standing by the window, "Let's see the stockings. Not seconds, are they? Show them to me! How much?"

"You know the price."

"Now, do me a favor, oblige me, my dear good girl, and show them to me. Why can't I see them?"

She undid the packet and showed him the stockings. He scarcely examined them. She sat with them in her lap, and leaning forward toward him, her face in the unflattering street light, she began, "When are you coming back, Bertie, dear? I had a letter from my mother this week and from my husband in Vichy. If I could get to the south of France like you promised, I could either wait there till it is over, or get through the occupied zone. No one has anything against me. We were always anti-Soviet. I could get through to Vichy, or where my mother is. You say your Rome manager is in Bordeaux now, you just had a cable, so won't you write to him, Bertie, as you said, and help me before you go away? I waited more than two years already on your promise. You said your word was your bond. That's all I ask. I'm sick of work here and the black market is going to close up soon, I know that. I don't want to get a job or be unemployed, and I'm not a citizen, they'll throw me out if I'm unemployed, and where will I go?"

"You should have become a citizen. Not nice, here nine years and not a citizen, you can't blame them," said Bertie.

"But why would I, when you promised five years ago that you'd do something for me and it's two years since you heard from your manager the first time and told me he'd make all arrangements? I was waiting on you, Bertie."

Robert turned the conversation for a few minutes on to some common acquaintance called Reverend Blank, apparently an acquaintance of all these three girls and others known to Katia and Robert, and to the gentleman's housekeeping arrangements, "You mean Mrs. Taylor is doing the house for him now—ho-ho-ho!"

The two went into some scandalous details, whispering eagerly by the window. Grant held his hand on the woman's shoulder and bent closer, chuckling with his insatiable curiosity. She cut this off abruptly and asked for the payment of her bill. Grant told her he would send a check from Havana, but she insisted upon payment now, "Besides, I'm sick of work and want to go to Sun Valley for a change."

"How are you going to get out there? Have you got enough money?"

"Oh, I'll hitchhike. I can always find someone to buy me dinner."

"You need more than dinner."

"Oh, I'm used to hitchhiking."

"Well, I'll send you your check, look after yourself, my good girl."

"And what about France, Bert? You know you promised right in the beginning to help me over there, with your connections."

He laughed, "Your memory's too good, my girl. You know if I had to help to Europe everyone I'd promised, I'd be bankrupt. They'd skin me alive to get to Europe, I can't help it if they take me at my word. They've not got anything on paper and have I got to watch every word? Other people can talk and not have to pay through the nose for every word! But the moment I open my mouth, people act on it. I should have been a statesman, a Mussolini, good grief! Look, my dear woman, I can't pay the passage of half the U.S.A. to Europe. I can't have a thousand people under one roof in my house on the Pinchem Hill. You aren't reasonable and no one is. I'm no fairy godmother. I'm goodhearted, that's my only weakness. I get interested in my friends and I promise things. You can't blame me, I do it in the excitement of the moment. That's the way I am. Sue me! I'm a Presbyterian, my dear woman. I don't like to see people hanging round with their tongues hanging out. They don't show any character. You might call me the punishment of God. Not of God, but of fate. I promise and then nothing happens! That's life, isn't it? It happened to me. Take your medicine, my dear girl. You delayed too long. I like to see girls with character and I thought you had character. You ought to have gone over long ago. . . . I thought you had character when I saw you making your way with that little store—fine, fine, very good. 'That girl's got character,' I said; 'she may not be the Queen of Sheba but she has character.'"

"Oh, can it, Bertie. You promised to put up money for the store, and you never gave me a cent for it."

"I'm generous, I can say that, and you managed all right? I should have helped you out if you'd needed it. You didn't. I admired that. You're a fine little woman. Now, I've got someone coming at five-thirty. Sam Positive from Jigago, law case, so I got no more time."

"Well, pay me the stockings at any rate, but in my humble opinion, Bertie, you're a welsher and always will be."

"Oh, welsher—you know me, little girl. You know I'm not a schoolboy. *Caveat emptor.* I don't pretend to be an angel. I'd say it shows a poor sort of character if anyone tries to pin me down to a promise when I'm excited, interested in them, feeling generous. That means you're trying to take a bonus out of fun, consolation, friendship, doesn't it? Now I like a girl to love me for myself. I call that character."

He jingled his coins, paid her half her money, and led her to the door. At the door he fondled her and pushed her out, with a five-dollar bill, saying, "Now don't go off to Sun Valley unless you have enough money; you don't want to behave like a tramp, girlie. I'll telephone you when I get back."

Grant banged the door, heaved a sigh, and picked up the keys. Gilbert rose up behind his back, hearing the clinking, came forward to the table. His father stepped back a pace and stood sturdily looking up at him. Gilbert withdrew his two fingers from his pocket, with the small key, and put it on top of the hatbox, "I found your key. Then I had a drink and lay down on your couch. I fell fast asleep; probably snored. I thought I heard voices and woke up."

"There were some girls here. Why didn't you get up and announce yourself? I would have introduced you." ,

"I should have looked like a blamed fool, coming out of the valises."

His father burst into a shout of laughter. He flushed and bent merrily to the hatbox, then waved his son away and toted the hatbox to the bedroom. When he came padding back he was thoughtful. He explained that Violetta was a typist that he was going to engage to write his autobiography—he had had to put it off for months, but when he came back he would make notes and let Flack write it up for him.

"It will be a best-seller, my boy. It'll make us all rich. Nothing like this trash, *Green Corn Valley*, *My Son Is My Undoing*, nothing like that, best-seller to beat all the records, we'll keep going for years, and constructive, nothing unnecessary like *Gone with the Wind*: no sex. Then we'll go into the one-dollar book distribution business, tie up with some chain store, or radio network, and we'll be the vanguard of the book monopolies."

"That's a good idea!"

"Katia's a good girl, she gets me all the black-market nylons I want. She's a good girl, but a character weakness, not too honest, not too clean—morally, you know—and doesn't like to work. Works five months and then spends seven months bumming round the country."

"Wish I could do that, how does she do it?"

"Yes, yes, very weak character. White Russian, too, and family in Vichy, don't want you to meet her. You wouldn't like her. Janet's one of Delafield's girl friends. I don't inquire. I know nothing; but not a very good character. The trouble with these girls, my boy, is that I like them, I want to like them, I need a friend, and I'm fond of women, I'm a democrat, poor girl workers, I respect them; but when I look closer, I see they're not very careful. Not very clean morally. Then they all want something."

He took up the paper and began skimming the pages, threw it down, walked round the room, then sat by the writing desk. He put on his spectacles, glanced through a letter and threw it at Gilbert, "Read that. Tell me what you make of it. Read it aloud, I want to make up my mind."

Gilbert read,

Dear Bert,

This is to tell you that Maxwell and I are in Florida where we have opened a boarding house and hope to make some money before the winter is over. Maxwell is well. We went in with my brother who has already made a good profit in the grocery and frozen foods business down here. . . .

"Never mind, never mind, it's from Flora Hopkins," said the father impatiently, his eyes wandering.

He said after a moment, "I went on a couple of parties with Violetta, no reason for her to hang herself round my neck. She looks like a nice girl, you can't credit it. Would you believe"— he supplied his son with some details of the parties; then coming to attention—"I saved that woman's life, Flora Hopkins and her imbecile of a husband's life. He went bankrupt, owed me money, owed everybody money, also he had cheated—taken money out of the till. She came to me crying, 'Do something, Maxwell will cut his throat.' Would have, too. A weakling. I consoled her and sent a message to Maxwell, 'I won't get after you and I'll speak to the others.' I lost two thousand, seven hundred dollars. I said, 'Never mind it, wipe it off the slate!' She came crying to me three times. . . . Looks as if he's doing well, eh? Think I'll get it back? Listen, I got a letter here, see what you think of it. Give me your opinion.

Dear Flora,

I am glad to hear you have gone to Florida and are doing so well, the same being true of your brother. It is past the

Christmas season, when I had many expenses and had some shocks when I made up my yearly accounts and saw that I had taken quite a beating on several items, so that I could very well do with the payment of some outstanding debts. You will remember how close we were and that I had the advantage of doing you a little favor when Maxwell was thinking of putting an end to his days. I got you out of that spot. Can you send me a check for $1,000 to reimburse me in part for the debt of those days, that is, $2,700? You can pay me the rest later, as I suppose you have some financial future down there. My regards to Maxwell and tell him I am glad he is a different man economically and morally from those days when he thought of cutting his throat. Kindest regards to you both, and love to the children,

Yours, etc.

Eh? H'm? To the point?"

"It's too mean, it's raw!"

"Raw? Try and ask for money in a polite way! You don't get it. It's my money. I saved her life, she would have been a widow begging her bread, but I said, 'Wipe it off the slate.' They owe it to me. He's alive because of me. He can pay one thousand dollars for his own life—and cash. I want the balance in notes. Eh?"

While they were wrangling over this, with Grant thinking up saltier and rougher expressions "to scare them, that fellow's afraid of his shadow—mention death to him and he'll weep tears of blood, he won't even go to see a sick child, he thinks it's a trick of the Grim Reaper to catch him—" while this was going on, with Grant bubbling over in fresh laughter, the desk called him to tell him that Mrs. Downs was below. His eyes began to shine, and he waved his arm energetically at his son. He said, "Send her up."

Then he did several paces and a fantastic minuet, rushed in for his coat, and came out, slicking down his hair.

"I'm delighted you're here, my boy. You'll hear everything. She is blackmailing, the bloody 'ooman."

This caused him to burst out into a yell of laughter. He pushed his son into the bedroom and said, "Sit there behind the door and you will hear a peach of a line. That bloody 'ooman's got them all licked for sheer brass and by God—"

He heard the elevator stop at his floor and pushed the young man down the corridor, following him and whispering energetically that he must be his witness. He must take notes.

307

44

Mrs. Downs wore a beaver coat that Grant had never seen, with a little fur toque, a platinum and diamond pin. She wore several bracelets, of which two had come from Grant, and a small pair of fur-rimmed boots.

Grant gave her a stare, "You look like a duchess today. You don't look like hard times."

"You look as if you're going on a long trip."

Grant walked round her, in surprise, "Isn't that one of Goodwin's?"

She threw the coat on a chair.

"That's window-dressing. Alfred said a jury doesn't ask, 'Where did she get the clothes?' but, 'Is she attractive?' He lent me the coat."

"What jury?"

"Oh, my dear Robert, please don't torture me; I have enough on my mind. You know well enough what jury, unless you have lost your memory, which would be out of character. The case Downs *vs.* Downs is on the calendar, and will come up in ten days if we don't do something to stop that man. Knowing this, Alfred advised me to make a last plea to Walker to see Churchill's lawyer and try for a settlement. Alfred said, 'I am sure Robert is just as anxious to avoid publicity as you are; you can depend on him backing any settlement agreement you make.' I agreed with this, knowing what you stood to lose, Robert. I wore this outfit to Walker's to look like money and it worked. I would advise you not to make any wisecracks, but to listen to what I have got to say. I know you're hard-headed; and you are anxious for a settlement out of court. . . . It is no extortion, no illegal action as you suggested on the telephone, Robbie, very incorrectly, but any payment you made would be, from Churchill's point of view, in satisfaction of breach of a contract. True, I breached the contract, but you were my accomplice and I have no money that is not Churchill's. Furthermore, you owe it to me, since on account of you, I have not received any allowance from Churchill for the past three months."

"As to that, my good woman, you must sue him for that," said Grant.

"Don't call me my good woman. The point is to reach amicable settlement without trial, I think. Many cases are settled out of court and there is no extortion in those cases, as you suggested.

Now I should like to show you, Robbie, that during these few years you have associated with me as a friend, you have broken the law about nineteen times; for example, you are liable under the Mann law, adultery and fornication are punishable in the State of New York, you aided a fraud when you paid my fare to Reno and expenses there, for I was evading the New York State law on divorce. I am only referring to the man-and-woman aspect of our relations—"

"Blackmail!" said Grant in angry agitation.

"You are vindictive and stupid. I am on your side and all you can do is to say blackmail and extortion. We have been in business together and we have done no differently from anyone who made money. But the law does not pity those who are caught and say, 'Go in peace, my son,' because others are criminals too. No, it is you who have to bear the punishment for the other black sheep. Now don't take that tone, Robert, for we will get nowhere. Also, let us discuss this in a business matter: let us leave out personalities and accusations and try to see it in an impartial manner, as outsiders would see it."

"I'm damned if every outsider wouldn't see it as blackmail and your husband as a pimp."

"Yes, throw your bombs, let them burst in my hair, and when you are finished, I will go on with what I have to say."

"For God's sake, then, say what you have to say."

"For God's sake! I am afraid that God has nothing to do with the matter. We have both been guilty, Robert, and I am trying to pull us out of the mud but you do nothing but attempt to escape the consequences in flight, leaving me to bear all the disgrace. My position is very, very serious, most unenviable, but particularly because Churchill acted as no gentleman would, and sneaked and spied on me, set detectives on me when I was unsuspecting, and so by mere surveillance got me once in a compromising situation by no fault of my own. I never expected such treatment at the hands of a gentleman. Gentlemen are overestimated, that is my experience. Photographs were taken of this situation and others. Alfred, Walker, and Churchill's lawyer have seen these photographs. It is not the sort of thing they would care to let a woman look at; and not the sort of thing you would care to look at, Robert."

"Shh! Never mind about the photomontages—" said he.

"Very well, but don't be so glib, the truth of one set of photographs, accidental, lying, lends color to others."

"You mean color photographs?" he said in alarm.

"Now, why will I be called to defend myself in this case? Because only one set of facts have been presented, but they are Churchill's side of the case. I need a lot of money to present mine and I see no possibility of raising that money; therefore what will go before the jury in this case which is now on the calendar will be his, not mine, not yours. Such an action, whether successful or a failure, can only result in ruin for me and you, and of course will make Churchill ridiculous, but he has run amok and does not care about that. We all have our own lives to lead, we have to protect our privacy and the sanctity of our own soul. We are only human beings and we are facing a mad bull, a Hitler who would tear down everything to satisfy a private vengeance. Therefore, I think we had better settle the whole thing as quickly as possible before our dirty linen is dragged into public."

"They've got nothing on me! If I were you I'd get a look at the photographs. You could have a look at them, very cheap; or get Walker to describe them to you. You say Goodwin's seen them?"

He paced up and down.

"It seems this 'Brauner, Arthur' showed Churchill how to install a dictaphone, and Churchill did not hesitate to stoop to use it."

"How long was it installed before you knew?"

"How do I know? Churchill's counsel has it and he is very mean."

"What can Churchill hope to get—financially?"

"He hopes it will be so bad that someone will stop the case."

"Someone—me? Or the others—"

"Whoever is in the photographs. And the dictaphone records."

"That's not liberty or democracy, to allow the use of such methods," said Grant.

"That's what I say, Robert; but we are dealing with a very fascist sort of man. Churchill has only enough brains to be a fascist. Now I have talked this over and I believe that if he were offered fifteen thousand dollars, plus the expenses to Reno, and my future assured, he would settle. It is no use saying it is extortion, he feels he has been wounded, and in law a breached contract and other injuries are allowed money satisfaction. He would be only acting as a wronged man in suggesting it, and sincere in accepting it. He would even be intelligent, to accept it rather than go through an expensive, shameful lawsuit which would expose me

310

and other people. He has a human side. He feels it would be better for all parties. Think, he is in a good legal position, but he prefers to settle."

·"He won't get a penny out of me," roared Grant.

"Then we will go into court and you will further be guilty of perjury. You always quibble, even when people say 'Good day.'"

"You're acting for Downs," said Grant.

"No. He has counsel, he has no need of me. I am acting for us all. I do not wish there to be a trial. Think of what would happen to me! I have never been in any trouble."

"When I met you—that wasn't trouble?"

"No. That was bad luck."

"H'm. I advise you to try to make some sort of settlement, of course, but the figure is preposterous. No one would pay it. What about Alexis?"

"Naturally, I will ask him too. But he says he is not guilty—like you, Robert."

"The chief thing is to get a look at those records they say they have."

"Also there is testimony from his detectives and hotel people."

"The photographs are the main thing. Get a look at them. I'd pay to get them into my hands."

"They're worth fifteen thousand dollars," she said, and got up and walked about.

"Am I as good as that?" he said with a sudden laugh. He looked at her for a moment, then began softly, "Why should he get it? The man's got no character to act as a pimp for his own wife. Why divide the spoils? Or you and I will divide it, that means you get half and no one else knows. We don't want any transactions with strangers."

"I've got to get a divorce and pay my lawyers and provide for the future. My salad days are gone. I want to return to normal life."

"Where is—the other fella—X?"

She hesitated.

Grant said, "He's not here, he ran out on you. He told me he was going to California and then to Mexico! That's it, he's not here. He won't be back for three years!"

She said, "I wouldn't know."

"Every king looks the same on a postage stamp, every man looks the same at the back of his head—even if he's tonsured, and X has a hair-comb like me. Oh-ho-ho. Why didn't I think of it before? He thought he had me cornered and he just chased me out onto the broad rolling plains—oh-ho! Does he think I'm going to put my finger in my eye and answer to a charge of adultery, am I going to be a co-respondent when they're a hundred washing their feet in the public fountain in the public square? Grab one boy, haul him up by the neck to the magistrate. All right, but not me. Oh-ho-ho. You got to see them, Barb. If it isn't surely me—and them voices, oh-ho-ho! Under certain circumstances, for example, at Echo Point and in a tunnel, and in swimming under water men's voices all sound the same and on those machines too, on the phone, on the radio, who can tell? You can't tell your own brother! No, sir! I'm out. That's out. I'm not a schoolboy. Blackmail. I'll sue him for blackmail. He sent a woman to me, his wife, for blackmail. He used his wife as an instrument and agent and provocateur of blackmail. He's the one that's going on the stand, he's the one will be disgraced. Oh, Churchill Downs, you're a respectable man and have a standing in society, but you're no better than a fascist blackguard when it comes to a woman, for you use women as your innocent agents for blackmail! The woman does not know what she is doing. She parrots something she heard in the mouths of crooked lawyers and fools like Goodwin and her own husband, who taught her and led her into crime and used her weakness for crime. Is that a pretty picture? That's a prettier picture than the photomontage. No, my dear girl, I won't run out on you, I'll stay and see it through. And I'll charge —blackmail, extortion, pressure, threats, stress, strain, using the mails for fraud. If I have nineteen charges, he'll have twenty-one. Don't trouble yourself, my dear woman, I'll say, 'I gave her money when she was down and out, I asked no questions. I was her friend. What is he? He turns a respectable woman into a gun moll' I'll say, 'When I knew her she was living a dubious sort of life. I asked no questions, but treated her as a sister and gave her something to eat. When he married her according to the law, he turned her into an extortioner: this respectable man, this magnificent gentleman—' "

He paused. Then he whirled round, with his arms spread out, and gave way to an excess of gaiety.

The blonde woman said acidly, "You won't get out of it that way. It is going to be a hard business for all of us. He hangs on like a bulldog. He has his teeth in me and he will get them in you. I recommend you to think over his offer; after all, he is being fair to you in even thinking of it."

"It shows how hysterical he is to ask fifteen thousand dollars for
—what I had—"

"I do not think you will make a very good witness. I am trying
to put this from your own point of view. I want to see you come
out of it safe and sound."

"I won't appear."

.5

As he walked up and down, once more troubled, the telephone
rang and Grant, answering, said sharply, "Mrs. Grant? I don't
know a Mrs. Grant."

He listened and said, "I have no wife named Mrs. Gr—" There
was a pause, he put his hand over the mouthpiece and said softly,
"Mrs. Grant? It can't be Mary? Good God!"

He said into the phone, "Ask her to wait a few minutes. Eh?"

He slapped down the receiver and said, "She's coming up! Gilbert!"

Gilbert came out of the bedroom. He said earnestly, "Dad, I
asked Mother to come. I thought things had got into a tangle
you couldn't untie."

Grant looked at them for a second, seized his hat and stick, and
rushed to the door, saying, "You got yourself in it—get yourself
out of it," and leaving the door open, he rushed to the staircase.

The blonde woman recovered herself, sat down, and began making up her face. Gilbert thoughtlessly closed the door, looked at
Mrs. Downs with a great air of rectitude, even pleasure, "I didn't
mean to get you into a thing like this, or Mother either."

"I can take care of myself, my dear boy. I am thirty-five years
old. One sees a lot in thirty-five years. But what will you say
to Little Dixie?"

The young man started.

"Your mother is very rich, isn't she? She can keep herself?"

The young man looked indignantly at Mrs. Downs. The elevator stopped at their floor and he opened the door. The woman
said, "I know everything—Gilbert—everything—remember."

Gilbert welcomed his mother. She was a dumpy, handsome
woman with dark eyes and plain white hair cut short. She wore
a rich fur coat, black coat and skirt and white silk blouse, and
wore plain shoes. She took in the disorder, the woman sitting in
the basket chair, said with cold, mincing delicacy to her son,
"Who is this lady?"

Gilbert hesitated. The blonde woman looked inquiringly at

313

him, while Mrs. Grant went forward and looked long at the valises. Gilbert introduced the women now. Mrs. Downs brought out her card case and handed a card to Mrs. Grant, saying, "I am waiting for your husband. I found him out."

"I thought your father was in," said Mrs. Grant, stiffly.

"No—he went out to try to get some keys."

"Is he coming home?"

"No, he is going to Havana."

"How long has he lived here?" She was now looking bitterly at the other woman.

"He has only been here about four days, four days."

"Why did he move here if he is going to Havana?" she asked, again with her eyes on the woman.

"The other place was too big, he sublet it to the Walkers."

"Who are the Walkers?"

"Didn't you meet Alfred Goodwin last year? His lawyer."

"Your father does not see fit to introduce me to his friends. I live at home, a cabbage wife, I see no one and no one comes to see me, my dear Gilbert, and you know this."

"Alfred Goodwin has a fur business and Father is his silent partner."

"I know nothing of all this." She turned to the blonde and looked directly at her.

The blonde woman had become very gracious. She said, "I am a volunteer worker for the British War Relief Society, and I called for Bundles for Britain, you know. I should be so sorry to intrude; but your son told me I might wait a few minutes, as he expects Mr. Grant back at any moment. It was, I think, for some old shirts," and she indicated the pile of shirts and socks on the bed.

The wife at once went to the bed and fingered one or two of the neckbands.

"These shirts seem in perfectly good shape. Why is your father throwing them away?" she said very acidly to her son.

"I didn't know he was, Mother."

"It seems to me no one knows what your father does, where he goes, or even who he is," said the wife. She sat down and looked at the visitor, who made no move, but said pleasantly, "The weather is very tiring, isn't it?"

"Very!"

"There is nothing so fatiguing as the end of winter. The season is nearly over. people are tired of going to the theater and to

314

parties, and one only wants to stay at home and rest. I feel quite exhausted but I feel obliged to keep my promise, you know. I feel it is our duty to help the British, who have put up such a brave struggle, and are an example to us all for their courage. I have some English blood myself, that is perhaps prejudice. What do you think?"

"Oh, the British—naturally, we should help them."

"Oh, we are cousins under the skin, after all, aren't we? There is the tie of language, and we all hate Hitler. Are you interested in war work?"

"Well, I—I go to the Red Cross meetings. I am not very good at anything, but my fingers are my best part, I suppose. I am not very good at figure work, not artistic, but I used to try to draw and it still stays with me. And so I have nimble fingers, I roll bandages quite well."

"Oh, I think this war has changed us all completely. Even though we are exhausted at the end of the day with social and domestic duties, we feel we must sacrifice a few ounces of energy for the British. They are so much worse off than we. Think, they get only one egg a month. I feel quite ashamed. But I must feed my family. I cannot resist giving them the best when I can get it. I think it is a woman's duty to do her best for her husband. Every mother feels that."

The wife had slumped into a somber mood; she murmured, "I'm afraid I don't do all I should. I hate housekeeping and cooking. But I feel it is a wife's duty to bring down the expenses. I keep my housekeeping accounts very close. I have no head for figures and so this takes all my time. I get so tired with it all that I cannot keep up my painting. Then my son, my other son, Andrew, is a very tiring child. I want to take him to a neurologist, but my husband won't hear of it. I think he is neglecting Andrew in more ways than one. You see, Mrs. Downs, my husband is never at home. He spends his time away from me in New York."

"Ah? You live out of town, Mrs. Grant?"

"In Boston. I like it there. I met my husband there and we made our home there. But my husband prefers New York. He prefers to live like this. I suppose some men ought not to get married."

The blonde coughed politely. The wife said after a moment, "Do you know this hotel?"

"No. I have been here once or twice for Bundles for Britain,

315

but I have never stayed here. Naturally, we have our own home, I do not care for hotel life."

"It seems a funny sort of hotel to me. It's so dark, the rooms are so small, and I cannot understand how anyone could live in this disorder. And downstairs they run things in a haphazard sort of way, they pay no attention to you and say anything. They told me my husband was here, then they said he did not know anyone named Grant. Then they said to wait in the lobby. I resolved to come up and see for myself."

Mrs. Downs said, "It's unbearable. You would think they ran the hotels for their own convenience. We do not count. But when it comes to tips, they are there with smiles. They are very fond of you, then, when it is too late; and your bags are going out the door. I only give tips when I have had service."

The wife gazed at the bags with an anxious eye. The blonde said, "One is so embarrassed in a hotel lobby. They look you over, you must stand there like a salesman or even worse. I hardly know why I make these visits when I should so much rather be in my own home. But I feel I must make some little sacrifice for Britain."

The wife bit her lip and looked at the luggage. "He has not put any labels on yet. I wonder if he is really going?"

"Am I intruding?" asked the blonde.

The wife looked, hesitated, then said coolly, "Why should you make an extra trip? It is so fatiguing. I cannot prevent Robert from throwing his clothes out of the window, I know very well. Please do not feel you are in the way. Gilbert, please don't sit there, looking as if you were going to a funeral. Go and do something. Pick up some of that mess. Do you know which are the shirts? If you do, pack them up for this lady."

"As far as I can see these shirts are in good order and Dad would be mad to give them away."

"You know that neither you nor I can influence your father. Won't you do what I ask at least?"

"But—" Gilbert got up, threw a furious look at the blonde, blushed, and went down the corridor, where he began opening drawers and closets.

"It's a very tiring trip from Boston."

"I am awfully tired. Why, that's my father's old hatbox! Why does Robert carry round that antediluvian thing? He can't let go of anything, but he suddenly gets into a mood and gives away perfectly good shirts."

"Men are very hard to understand. My first husband was so good to me that I had to think of nothing, I did not have to understand him. I became impractical, I signed checks without funds. He left me a widow and for three years I had nothing but misfortune, my life was very tragic because I knew nothing of men or business, you see. Then I met my second husband and we married. But I am afraid my first husband spoiled me for others. I do not understand Churchill and I am afraid he leaves me much alone, perhaps my own fault, though I do not feel it is. A woman never knows what is expected of her. Men make so many demands, and are so strong, though they are children. It is no wonder we get tired. Then they are surprised when we need more rest."

"Naturally, everyone has troubles. It is only to be expected. But in general I try to be brave and not to think of myself at all. When anything comes along at all upsetting, I take a little more rest."

"You are quite right, Mrs. Grant. I always get my beauty sleep for one thing. Then I think breakfast in bed gives you peace of mind for the entire day. I have servants, I do not need to get my husband's breakfast. I often ask myself whether I should go on with this war work, for one sees so many women getting fatigued-looking and harassed, and cosmetics, and face-lifting, and new hairdos don't really do anything for you. Beauty is more than skin-deep; one must sleep, that is the only recipe I know. I had it from my mother: she always said to me as a child and still does, 'Sleep, my darling, and you will always have a clear skin.' "

"Yes; but people do not want you to sleep. They do not care how anxious they make you or what burdens they impose on you. My husband never thinks of what trouble he brings upon me. He leaves everything on my shoulders and so it has been since Gilbert was small."

"Oh, this is not agreeable. But I see you are very brave, I can see you are a woman of exceptional character. This costs you so much unnecessary effort; it is a pity. Yet, they told me, Mr. Grant is such a kind man."

"Who told you that?"

"My friends, the Goodwins, Betty Goodwin is such a darling, and she told me that they had a friend very much interested in helping Britain, a man with British blood in his veins; and they gave me this address. I confess that at first I thought I had made a mistake. But your son, such a fine young man, told me his father would return shortly."

"Don't you feel embarrassed visiting men in hotels? I should find it quite impossible, I'm afraid."

"Oh, no, no; you see I knew Mr. Gilbert was here. I telephoned first to make an appointment, and at that moment Mr. Grant was here, too. But it seems there is some difficulty about the valises—the keys—" she laughed and shook her head whimsically at Mrs. Grant.

"Why isn't he at work, I wonder?"

"I understand he has only gone round the corner. I have much to do but I have so little time I cannot make two trips. And my heart bleeds for the poor British youngsters, the dear little babies—you see, when we cannot use the shirts, we cut them up for dresses or little shirts."

"Cut them up!" said the wife, shocked.

"But I see Mr. Grant has cut some of them up to make shoe covers," said the blonde, pointing to some shoes standing on the couch in shirting covers.

"He must be mad. I am afraid Robert ought to go to a psychoanalyst."

"Men have their little fads, they are not mad. But for us it is so difficult to understand."

At this moment, Gilbert came back with some odd things in his hands, "I don't dare give any of these things away, or I would. But Dad makes such a blamed fuss about every collarbutton."

"Gilbert! I am afraid there is something the matter with your father. Mrs. Downs just showed me the shoe covers made out of good shirting; and look, there is the shirt he cut it from."

Said Mrs. Downs, "Why, it is like paper dolls. I should be anxious, myself. How can a woman face such things?"

"Darling—you can't imagine how tired your Bunny-mother is. Darling, I am exhausted, and the waiter on the train was so rude to me. They expect such large tips nowadays; they are not at all grateful for a human attitude. What is the use of our being so fair-minded to the Negroes, when they only take advantage of us? I find it impossible to face life these days, with everyone so forgetful of what is required. I am all by myself, no one visits me, and so I was forced to visit your father. But we are strangers. Yes, Mrs. Downs, you must know we are complete strangers. I am in the apartment of a stranger, just as you are. I have not even come to ask for shirts. These are not my shirts, I cannot give you these shirts. They are not mine. This is my son, and that is all that is mine here."

"You are completely exhausted, Mrs. Grant. You should lie down a little. I have an excellent sort of pill here, better than aspirin, no effect on the heart. I am sorry to say it is German, but I understand they have been here since before the war. Do take one. I must be going. I can only wait five minutes more, for I have an appointment for tea. You should go inside and take a little rest."

The wife said, "Help me up, Little Bear. Come in with me and take off your Dixie's shoes. I want you to tuck me in just like you used to do. Help me, Gilbert darling. Take my hat off. There! You don't mind if I leave you, Mrs. Downs? No, I never take tablets. I sleep quite naturally. I have a little trick. I just keep my eyes shut and curl up like a child and make my mind a blank and—I am fast asleep."

She went into the corridor dragging her son by the arm and saying, "You didn't call me Bunny once."

"I will then, rest if you want to, darling Bunny."

"You didn't call me Dixie once."

"Mother!"

"No, no."

"There, Dixie, then, Dixie, let me take off your shoes."

"Dixie so-o tired. Gilbert!"

"Yes, Mother."

"Bunny very tired! Put Bunny to sleep."

"Ye-es, Bunny—there you are. There!"

She suddenly said querulously, "The doctor told me, nothing but rest, only rest— Wake me when your father comes in. Gilbert!"

"Yes, Dixie?"

"Don't give that woman any shirts till I've seen your father. It's disgraceful. Waste in wartime! He must be mad."

"She's going now, Mother."

"Little Bear?"

"Yes, Middle Bear?"

"Sit with Mother for a while. It's years since I saw you, darling."

"But Mrs. Downs—"

"Mrs. Downs can sit there, like a frozen carved image, or she can go. You're not crazy about her, are you? Do something to oblige Middle Bear."

46

When he returned, Mrs. Downs was sitting under the lamp, reading the comic strips.

"My mother is asleep. Are you going to wait for my father?"

"You're an honest man; you have a good character. You behaved very well. I am obliged to you. You might have made a fuss, helped no one, injured all parties. It would have been theatrical and less than ethical. But you did not. I was delighted to see you did not want to play Harry the Sleuth, the great exposer of crime! It shows you have grown up, you are mature, and you know the ways of the world. You may not understand all personal arrangements but you respect your ignorance. You don't think you're Superman, like Robert Grant."

"You have no right to speak to me in this sarcastic way. I only did it from the most natural motives; and because I was cornered. It went against the grain to deceive my mother. Everyone deceives her. I will not keep quiet later."

"I cannot discuss things that might be considered by some a little irregular. I shall wait for your father. I am a reputable person, not an underworld character. I am more to your father than your mother is, as she herself says, 'I am a stranger,' she says. Your father promised to marry me; but I should not like to have it on my conscience that I let her know that or of the close friendship between your father and myself. I sacrificed my feelings and my pride to save your mother any shocks. I trust you will do the same. What benefit will it be for her to know? Your father has enough to explain without explaining me. Don't you think so? Or do you think that once he had explained his leaving your mother to take a jaunt to Havana, he must next explain that it is on account of me, that I am getting sued for divorce by my husband and that your father is implicated? I am trying to get your father to settle this out of court, so that no one will be hurt. Think of your little brother. He is a neurotic, sensitive child. Think of how he will feel if he hears about his father from the little boys in the street. 'Your father—so-and-so—' and they will laugh, and point the finger at him. Do you wish to injure not only me and your father—that is perhaps indifferent to you, for you are a young righteous crusader, crusading of course entirely for yourself without reference to the feelings of others—but do you wish to injure your little brother and your mother? She is lonely now. She is nervous. Life is too much for her. She has a weak character. How will she feel when her brother-in-law and father and her neighbors say, 'What a dreadful scandal, poor Bunny! But did he really become involved with another woman that he loved so deeply? Those letters they published in the paper must have made you feel very miserable, poor Dixie.' Ha!

"Perhaps this is nothing to you. I am an older woman and I think more of your mother than you do. Believe me, I would not marry your father now; I am quite documented upon his character. So there is nothing to worry about, and as I do not like to leave unhappiness behind me, where I have passed—I made up my mind to persuade your father, at all costs, and with any technique, not to brazen it out. Do you know what he wants to do, this magnificent gentleman? He wants to drag all our names in the mud and injure your mother's reputation and peace of mind for life, out of vanity. And your youth? My situation I do not speak of. It is pitiable. Through kindheartedness, affection, innocence I was trapped. I know a woman should not be so careless. I take my medicine. Let us skip that. By a great stretch of the imagination, puritans, who are good at that, might say I was guilty, but I am certainly not guilty vis-à-vis your father. He promised everything and then backed out. A bargain was made and he broke his side. I am in a tragic position and worn out by a series of disappointments. I have no luck with men and have been cheated over and over again. You are an honorable man. You would not cheat a woman. Or you might have promised to marry a woman and backed out. It happens. Men change their minds. Yet I am not like other women, I go into the daily battle with men, I meet them on their own terms, I ask no quarter, but I sometimes give it, because I am a woman. You see I try to make a living as a business woman, I do not sit at home on a cushy chair and read a book. I don't hang round the house and sleep on a sofa, while a servant gets me a cup of coffee. I do exactly what your father does. I get my commissions; I live on percentages. It is a difficult business. Did you ever try to sell a shoestring tie, let alone a piece of land, or bond, or an insurance policy, or a load of raw furs? I am sure you would find it hard to sell those trashy brooches the girls are snatching out of the peddler's hands nowadays. I advise you, Gilbert, to hold your hand and hold your tongue until I have seen your father. You must remember that if I were not so kind, I could upset the apple-cart right away by going in there and shaking that woman awake and saying, 'I am your husband's friend, and he has promised to marry me.' Eh? What do you say to that? What could you do?"

"I don't understand you, Mrs. Downs, and I know this is very serious; I don't say you've not been injured; this is justice. I don't know what to do. If I did, I'd do it."

"I have always liked you, Gilbert, and you liked me. I am not less than human. I am doing this for you more than for Robert, who merits nothing good from me. Perhaps you think your father is innocent, pure, with spotless character, a scholar and a gentleman, a very gallant gentleman, no doubt."

"I was not thinking that."

"But you think I am much more guilty. A woman is worse than a man."

"I do not think that. That is against my principles."

"I know your mother is having a bitter struggle. It is not easy for a woman to find herself virtually without a husband and then to come and find the husband is intending to leave the country. I do not want to add to her worries. I would even do something to help her. Especially as I know that Robert has other fish in his big frying pan, isn't that so? It isn't really I who am the sinner, not I alone? This situation is very tragic for me. Am I the only woman Robert has ever known? I looked to him for companionship and comfort, I am no longer a young woman, I am thirty-five, and this relationship of ours has been broken into—first by myself, who married honestly and intended to do the right thing, and then by your father, who begged me to leave my husband. There are other things—I know your father has other women friends! You yourself have met them. Can you say to your mother, 'This is a bad woman, but my father has other friends, ladies, who are better suited to him? I have met them and like them.' Can you say that?"

Gilbert said, "You are quite right. This is not blackmail, but the truth. And Dad by his complaisance, by his idea of showing life to me—because I am sure he is a very naïve man underneath—himself got me into this hole. I am glad you showed it to me. I should have behaved like a cad—and I should have done infinite harm. But what is there to do now? I am an honest man. I don't see what an honest man can do in this situation. I don't really know what your motives are, but I don't trust Dad, either; and I analyze it this way: I don't know enough about life. You are not at fault. I am at fault. I was a good officer, they said. Probably I couldn't have have helped one of the men to write a letter home to his wife. I have never been married. It's a different kind of life. It kind of hits you in the nose when you see it for the first time. I thought what you said to Dad was a bold attempt at intimidation; now I think perhaps you were trying to do the right thing in a situation where there was no right thing. Even my mother, I know, might have done more. She sleeps, poor Dixie! She should not sleep. My father took the initiative, that I admit. And my poor mother is guilty of the most extraordinary laxity and sleepiness and dullness there ever was, probably, in a married woman. I don't say you are to blame—"

"Gilbert—do you know what is in that hatbox?—I am sure you know very little about your father."

"That old thing? Not hats, of course—"

At this moment the telephone rang, and the desk announced that Miss Livy Wright was coming up. Gilbert did not say anything, but went to the curtains. Looking down sadly to the street, he was surprised to see his father's unmistakable figure under the awnings on the other side of the street. His father walked up and down and boldly eyed all the women from head to foot, continuing his pacing. Occasionally, he stopped to stare after a woman.

The apartment door rang.

Livy flung her arms round Gilbert and kissed him lustily, "Hello, big boy! You've put on three ounces at least. Watch that waistline! Civilian life doesn't suit you. You look morose. How is the educational movie game? Did you get the old tightwad—?"

She had taken her arms away from the boy and saw the other woman. "Oh, Lord, I didn't realize you had company—shooting my mouth off—behaving like a sister to you—"

"Mrs. Downs—Miss Livy Wright."

To Gilbert's surprise, the women showed no emotion, but acted the lady.

"Are you waiting for Mr. Grant, or are you a friend of Gilbert's?" asked Livy.

"I'm collecting old clothes for Bundles for Britain."

"You expect to get some from Robert Grant? He wouldn't give a torn tambourine to the Salvation Army! He collected squeezed-out toothpaste tubes from *me*. I had to save them for him. Some dame, friend of his, wanted them. If you prize one pair of old torn pants from—h'm—pair of cotton socks he bought in a subway and wore into holes, from Robert Grant, Esquire, I'll give you a punched nickel."

"Livy," said Gilbert.

323

"Well, it's true, big boy, isn't it? You know the old hyena. We love him, but we know him. Mrs. Downs may as well not waste any more of her valuable time on your old tube-collector. He's the original Scrooge. He's got suntan and rosy cheeks, he's a bully-boy, but he's not the prince of bighearted jakes. Ma'am, excuse the freedom of speech, but you are wasting your time. He wouldn't give away—h'm—he keeps the parings of his nails, I can show you the drawer, the upper left-hand drawer in his tallboy, with the key of the collarbox. You won't get the moving picture of a Coca-Cola bottle top. He keeps them too, for some dame, same one, I guess. Must be same type of chiseler. To have and to hold is on Robert Grant's pocketbook. God bless you, man of means, I say, you can't make money by throwing purses out the window to the hydra-handed mob. I'll tell you his type of patriotism: if they didn't give him a free ride in a Constellation or a free peck at an Army hostess, he paid taxes for nothing. It butters him no waffles.

"It's useless, my dear; you must take your business elsewhere. If you came to my place, I'd give you a couple of old hats, barrelfuls of old clothes. Lavish is the word for Livy. I want, I buy. If I'm in a big game, I bid high. I'm in a big game now, the stakes are the bully-boy; I'm not in his class yet but I'll be there. I'll have houses, I'll be in the ninety per cent bracket. And even now, I get a hell of a kick out of looking at Robert Grant holding on to his millions and hearing the Doomsday Book of his great estates in Spain. Ma'am, he'll end up like Queen Victoria with a museum full of old petticoats. Don't forget they're all bundles in Britain and there's a lot of the British in him. That's his rag-picking side. They're all wearing politics over there that have been musty since Queen Anne; and he's an ardent supporter of 'British scientific evolutionary socialism, no bones broken, but if I have to give bundles for Britain, you'll find me at the end of the queue.' So now you know where you stand, if you didn't know already. You won't get half a shoe cover from old Grant."

"And you defend his old shirts very well," said the blondine.

"Why not, what the heck? And a man is as he is, you can't change him much though I'll do my darndest, when he's my forget-me-not."

"Are you a close friend of Mr. Grant?"

Gilbert, horrified, advanced toward them, which both women observed severely. Livy said, "You might call it that. You've got to be a friend of Robert to stand for him at all. You have to love him, not to hate him."

"Do you live here?"

"No, I'm from the sticks, I live at present in Philadelphia. I'm in real estate. I come up to town to go on wild parties— ha-ha!—with Robbie. Sit round half the evening talking about Winsome Churchill and Major Elstree—I mean—British evolutionary socialism, better than the Continent with those reds— Do you know Mr. Grant?"

"Yes, I met him abroad years ago."

"On the Continent, ha? In France? Not in Rome?"

"Yes, I met him in society there; and in Rome. I have a house in Rome. On the Pincian Hill."

"Must be quite a colony there! Are there a lot of houses on that hill?"

"Naturally!"

"H'm. Is it fashionable, airy, a nice quarter?"

"Oh, yes, yes."

"I have been invited there to live: a friend of mine has a house there."

Gilbert, standing at the window, turned round in surprise. Livy continued, tossing her head, "My friend and I have a cheese farm in Normandy, also, and we may pass six months of the year there. Gilbert will send us day-old chicks by airmail. Or he sends the eggs on and they hatch on the way. I forget the technique. I should make the place pay. I'm a very good manager. I should like country life. I worked hard enough in business. But I'm going to keep my two houses here, too. I just bought two houses in Montague Street, Brooklyn."

"Brooklyn!"

"Why not?"

"That's a coincidence! My friend Mr. Grant told me yesterday that he was buying two houses on Montague Street!"

"Well, well, did he! Well, the old so-and-so! He makes good time, he has his eye on the ball. Ha-ha-ha! I bet those are my houses! When you were in that house in Rome did you ever meet a Roman society woman called Laura—Manganesi? Is that it, Gilbert? Grant's not been friendly with his wife for—"

"Oh, hush, you don't know—" said Gilbert suddenly. He came away from the window. He had just observed his father walking round the corner of the block with a young woman, and toward the hotel bar downstairs.

"I don't know what? I want to find out about this Roman bitch for good and all. This Laura had a house on the Pincian Hill! It must be densely overpopulated, two-thirds of the Italian nation."

"Father had a house on the Pincian," began Gilbert.

"That makes four," cried Livy; then, "Is it the American quarter? To hell with it—it sounds noisy."

She got up, pulled off her hat, and went over to the valises, "The big boy hasn't got his laundry sorted out yet. Don't sit there with yer tongue hanging out for the big boy's laundry, Mrs. Downs. Britain could sink in mud before Robert Grant, son of Lancashire and Paisley, sent one cotton shirt or Paisley shawl to —— And where's the hatbox? I just love that. I am longing to be here at the opening of the hatbox. Here's his ration book. He has extra sugar stamps—"

She walked up and down, counting the stamps, "I can make some preserves, he doesn't need sugar in a hotel—"

Mrs. Downs said icily, "Mr. Grant gives all his sugar stamps to me."

"To you—what the?—Oh, well, I'm sorry. He ought to divide them up. Does he bring you tea and marmalade too? What a guy! A pinch of sugar and a pennyworth of tea, eh? Old style Briton, he is. I see you're—in on the game—not worth it. Fair words butter no parsnips. Who the heck wants buttered parsnips? Or any kind of parsnips? What are parsnips? So the sugar stamps are your territory. What else do you take in? Meat coupons? Don't you get enough at home? I buy black market; sorry, but I can't help it. I help the war effort other ways—what other ways? Search me! I buy bonds, I'm forced to, for the business. That's enough. And if you come out to my place or send someone out with a hand cart, I'll give you a bundle of old bras and girdles, and God knows what— Can you get face tissues? That's something I miss. What's the good of saying you can do without face tissues because they had a civil war in Spain? That's what Grant says. Crazy argument. In the old days they didn't wear clothes, either. I'm not hardhearted—it's a mess!"

At this moment the door to the bedroom opened and Mrs. Grant came out, looking very neat and mild. Livy stared and cried, "Gilbert, who in creation is that?"

Mrs. Grant was carrying the hatbox. She stared indignantly at Mrs. Downs, and with ladylike coldness at the black-haired hoyden. She put the hatbox on the center table.

"This is my mother! Mother, this is Miss Livy Wright."

"So pleased! I heard voices and thought that your father had come back."

"Oh, I don't think he'll be back for some time."

"Why not? They could send the keys up! Do you think you should wait, Mrs. Downs?"

"The apartment seems to be a bit overcrowded," said Livy, who had been staring insistently at Mrs. Grant. "Like the Pincian Hill and the chicken farm! And the cheese farm in Normandy."

Mrs. Downs said, "But I should not dream of living in such places. I intend to spend my summers on the Lago di Como; and in winter we shall go to Pontresina, St. Moritz."

"Does everyone do the same thing in Europe?"

Mrs. Grant picked up the ration book and said, "Gilbert, your father has not used his sugar stamps. That is a good thing. I can make some preserves. He just throws them away, I suppose."

"No, he gives them to Mrs. Downs."

"What for?" said Mrs. Grant, suspiciously.

"To make preserves for Britain," said Mrs. Downs.

"Oh-ho-ho, that's the best yet!" said Livy.

"But I thought you didn't know my husband."

"Only through the Goodwins."

Livy said, "What, do you know the Goodwins, too?"

"They're my closest friends—perhaps."

"Have you ever seen—" she looked at Mrs. Grant and then went on brusquely—"this woman, a blonde, who is in trouble, a perfect so-and-so, she seems to me, he calls her a swindler, a cheat, fraud, and bought woman? Do you know her? Everyone seems to stick by her. I can't understand it."

Mrs. Downs answered, "I know her; but she's not like that. She's a really nice woman who has had a lot of misfortune, but she lives modestly and earns her own living. She has had bad luck, but she has plenty of courage and in equity she should collect damages, not the husband."

"You speak like her lawyer."

"I could be. I know all about it, all—more than I can tell you."

"I can't believe it. It doesn't sound like her! What he says about her is fantastic—but he seems to like—men that age seem to like bad women and cheats and rotters. I'd like to see her and make up my mind. But I know enough! It's disgraceful! Well, are you staying long in New York, Mrs. Grant?"

"I don't know," said the wife through close lips, looking aside.

"Well, I'm blowing, and give my love to Mrs. Barbara Kent, your dear friend, and tell her I think she's a rattlesnake."

Livy looked at the woman sharply, started to laugh, and while she was putting on her things, looked back and forth at the woman, then said, "You're not Mrs. Barbara Kent, by any chance, are you?"

The blonde did not answer.

"You have the hair knot, you have the hat, by God, that's the kind of hat!" Livy laughed roughly. "I see there is only one house on the Pincian Hill. It's quite a lonely spot, after all, perhaps. I'm blowin'. Gilbert, I'll telephone your sweet papa tomorrow or the next day. I'll be downstairs tomorrow as arranged at six-thirty to see about this business of Swiss watches. Tell him I can arrange for a hundred dozen: and some to go to Venezuela and some to Chile. And tell him I fixed up the three-way affair with the Argentine and Switzerland. Will you remember? Good-bye, ladies."

"Good-bye! Your father is a long time at the locksmith. I think you should go and fetch him," said Mrs. Grant.

"Mother, let me take you out to dinner; Father will not be in till midnight."

"Why didn't you say so before?"

"I only just recalled!"

"And will Mrs. Downs stay here?"

"Oh, no! I must come back."

47

When the blonde woman had gone, Mrs. Grant said, "This is very tiring. Where are you taking me to dinner, Gilbert? And where am I to sleep?"

Gilbert said angrily, "Did you like those women, Mother?"

"Gilbert, don't bother me now. Of course I didn't like them. I thought the first was a lady, but I am not sure; and the other screamed her lungs out, like a fishwife. I can see as well as you that they are hanging round your father, for of course I do not believe that Mrs. Downs only met him once. But it is a boring subject, and I prefer not to discuss it."

"But, Mother, don't you want to do something? It seems to me either you are married or not married. It is a question of personal honor. You are such a sweet woman, Mother dear, an

328

angel, but there's Dad, too. A man cannot live alone. You must think of him, too."

"I should not worry about it. Most things are better left unsaid."

"But this lofty attitude, Mother, is actually wrong, because you are encouraging Dad to lead a life of his own. One could not blame him if—" he waved his hand—"the woman sees him alone! A man can get into messes."

"I should not bother my head about that if I were you, Gilbert. There is absolutely nothing to worry about. If those women run after your father, I do not want to think about it. It destroys my peace of mind. I love my tranquillity. I can only manage to get proper rest by ignoring many things, my dear boy, though if I liked to think about it, like other people, my life would seem a real tragedy, an agony, a pure waste. But I think discretion is the better part of valor."

"What will you do if some woman gets hold of Father? Mother, you shut your eyes to the consequences of a man's living alone."

"There are many things in life I prefer to shut my eyes to. You will find that after a while they go away, they go up in smoke. These things are not important. I am philosophical. We are such stuff as dreams are made of and our little life is rounded with a sleep."

"If you will not see, Mother—that it is wrong—"

She laughed, a high, clear tinkle, like the tinkle of china in a large room. She put her hand on her son's sleeve and laughed girlishly. She clutched his sleeve and put her handkerchief to her mouth. Then seeing his indignant look, her merriment went down and she said, "My dear, I know your father! He's a very dull, quiet man, with no initiative. When he comes home, the rare times he does, I get quite tired of seeing him sitting around, moping in a chair with nothing to say. He eats anything that's put before him and never asserts himself. He doesn't even speak in the right tone to the servants, but in such a subdued way that I'm quite ashamed. I am always simply exhausted when Robert is about. He goes out for the papers and comes back. Then, almost at once he wants to go to sleep. He sleeps half the time. If we go out to visit Uncle Bernard or Grandfather, or my friends, he sits there for two hours without opening his mouth, and then if he's asked a question point-blank, he just grumbles, 'Yes, yes,' as if it hurt him to get it out. I am not at all proud of my husband.

If they ask him what he does in New York, he says, 'I read the paper and go to bed early.'

"I assure you his visits are not very pleasant for me, but I must insist on seeing him sometimes, for Andrew's sake. I think if in the beginning I had pushed him a bit he would have gone farther and made more money, I have plenty of backbone, I have all the will power there is between the two of us—but why should I? I told him once, 'I could push you into something,' but I cannot push a man; it is for him to take the initiative. But your father has no enterprise, and so I gave it up as a bad job. My life has not been as quiet and humdrum as you suppose."

Gilbert looked at his mother, dumfounded.

She continued, "Yes, I know what you are going to say, what Aunt Martha says, that I should have done more, but he is a dead weight round my neck. I was so happy and contented as a girl, and imagined I should be well looked after when I married. Everyone said Robert had promise and talent, but I have never seen a spark of fire since we married—the first couple of years, of course. He soon slumped down into the house-slippers style, just as so many men do. If I had married a brilliant, lively man with character and will power, I should have been much happier. I could have done something myself. I should not have minded—even perhaps not really minded—if he had not been thoroughly honest, a bit of a charming rascal, for it does seem strange that honest people like your father are so dull and mousy."

"Mother, that's not a bit like Father really is—"

"You don't know. You never lived at home. You were always at school. Another thing I disapproved of. But he said children made too much noise in the house. That's another thing, he's so neurotic. He should be psychoanalyzed, I think. He is always afraid he has an enemy in Boston. As soon as he comes, he wants to go, because he says someone is going to get him, he has a feeling in his spine."

"Does he tell you why?"

"He won't answer the door or the telephone, but runs into the bathroom and puts his head in the clothes bag!"

"The laundry bag?"

"And, Gilbert, I feel a man should be spick-and-span, and your father goes everywhere with a two days' beard and never changes his shirt—all through the Christmas season. If you knew the humiliations that man gives me. His table manners are shocking —he eats with his fingers and sucks up his soup."

"Mother, he never does that, never! Father has excellent manners."

"Don't idealize your father. I need someone to understand me and what I have gone through all these years. If I had married a man of good education and breeding, who looked after himself—Your father—I hate to say it—doesn't even wash—and has dirty hands at table—and he eats raw onions—oh, it is a shame to tell you, but you must know sometime."

"I never heard such a story in my life."

"You see, you don't know what I go through. I simply sleep all day both before your father comes and after he goes away. It upsets me so."

"Raw onions? The laundry bag?"

She said coldly, "I should not perhaps say this to you—but you realize he is a stranger to me: I have not had a husband for years."

She turned away.

"I know he rarely goes home, Mother. That is what I am talking about."

"How can you understand? Many years ago, when he was about thirty-three, your father got into a taxi accident. The other occupant of the taxi, a Mr. Delafield, by a miracle escaped injury; his eye glasses were broken, that was all. But your father was disabled for life in that way—that way—so that we became strangers."

"Oh—I—he told you?"

"He was obliged to tell me himself. I was too young and innocent. I did not know the whole story—what it meant to my life." She put her hand to her face.

"Oh, it's—look, let's go to dinner. Dad will be up soon, perhaps, and I don't want to meet him just now."

"Why not? I upset you? Let's go to a nice quiet place and you'll feel better. I blame myself, but it is time you knew something about life."

"You will never know as much about life as I know at this moment," said Gilbert, impressively.

48

Some hours later, Gilbert was sitting on a folding cot that the hotel had brought for him, in the disorderly sitting room of his father's apartment. He had just come back from taking his mother

331

to the Pickwick, where—after some slight argument with the Walkers, who had already moved in—she had, for the night, Gilbert's old room. Robert Grant, in a very good frame of mind, with a cheerful eye, was pouring out for his son a large dose of Scotch whisky and saying, "But no more, Gilbert. Three is enough, so late."

The son rudely held out his hand and gripped the glass. He scratched his shoe gloomily. At last he took up, "Now this question of the hatbox, as I was saying—"

"All right, my boy, all right. Leave the hatbox alone. You said your say. Leave it to the morning. Get your sleep."

"Oh, you're as bad as Mother with your eternal sleep-sleep."

The father looked at him in a lively manner and in a minute reprimanded him for speaking so of his mother: "—an angel, a good mother, a sweet wife."

"Cut the comedy," said Gilbert.

"You're drunk."

"I know everything about you—I'll never know any more about life than I know now. There can't be any more to learn."

"Who told you everything—about me?"

"Mother—about the laundry bag—"

"The laundry bag?"

"About the raw onions, about the whiskers, the accident in the taxi—"

"The taxi accident? Which one?"

"Long ago—with Delafield—"

"Oh, Lord! Did she tell you that? Some women will blab anything. Oh-ho-ho! That's ripe, eh? That's choice. What do you think of it, eh? You know that was unnecessary. She was not right. Women are coarser than men."

"At home you are a dull and unclean old man; here with your favorites, and in low company, with stock-exchange runners, you use cosmetics. But with honest and respectable people, with whom you could count, you must show your worst side. It's incomprehensible."

"That's what it seems to you," said the older man, indulgently.

"The truth of you is what I just heard. I thought you had glitter, I was taken in by your glamor, I saw you throwing money around. I've just discovered the other side. I feel I've been a child."

"You've had a shock."

"I'm the son of a woman with sleeping sickness and a man

who puts on greasepaint to show better under the street lamp with whores."

"What does this mean?" Grant said dangerously.

"I saw you just now in the street—while Mother was here and your favorites were here—waiting—and then—I saw everything. And then this story about the taxi—everything is rotten!"

"You're drunk, son. Look!"

He picked up and shook the hatbox. "Put down your glass!" The young man did so, sulking.

Grant said, genially, "This is an old hatbox! It came from Benjamin Bungay, your grandfather, who built the firm of Bacon and Bungay. Look at the workmanship! The leather is as solid as iron. This was for one of those old-fashioned tophats like— Lincoln wore. You've seen that?"

"And what's in it—an old-fashioned tophat, a relic from the court of Queen Victoria?"

"A man pulls a rabbit out of a hat—on the stage. I wear greasepaint, you say. You mean suntan; you say that's wrong. You have ideas about right and wrong which are childish. If I wear greasepaint and I don't look an old man, I am not an old man. You are childish. You'll wear greasepaint one day—some sort. You'll smear up your conscience, I know you. You're like Benjamin Bungay and your mother. Ha-ha. I do too. Is it wrong? Ten years ago, you did not know there was any right or wrong. Now every day you make a fresh decision: this is right, that is wrong. You have the mania of making decisions. Even your mother never makes any. You think you're an adult— You will only be an adult when you have no more such decisions to make, when you have forgotten the questions. Yes-no, yes-no, is that a man of action! This is a British hatbox and like the old-time British, it is a solid hatbox and they don't make their equal today. Also, it isn't necessary. That isn't right or wrong; it's the way things are. Now, my dear boy, you haven't the slightest idea how things are."

"I learned enough today to last me a lifetime."

"You learned nothing today. But you will not go to bed this evening—without learning—everything I can teach you. You're a different man from myself."

"It's because you're an old man and I'm young."

The father frowned, but his face cleared and a kind of tender merriment swam into it. The sun rose on it. He said, "You know, Abe Lincoln had a big hat, and Steve Douglas had a little hat. Abe Lincoln used his hat for carrying his papers. Gettysburg

Address—was in his head, then in his hat. Campaign against Douglas was in his hat. Then in the box. I got nothing from nobody. Your mother married under a separation agreement. All I have was in my head—then in my hatbox! Ha-ha!"

He unlocked the hatbox, opened it, and stood looking into it for a minute, with an intent, speculative expression. The young man started to rise.

Grant shouted, "You'll stay where you are. You'll see—"

He got out a wad of papers and he began searching through them. They were in no sort of order. Letters, photographs, telegrams, bills, were mixed with stock receipts and titles to real estate and with lawyers' letters. Grant held out a paper which he seized upon in the first pile, "That is my list of holdings! David Flack's handwriting. You can believe him. He got it up the other day."

Before the young man could glance at the three typed pages, Grant tore it out of his hands and folded it, adding: "I always carry a big position, something to think about, mostly conservative, because I'm not a natural bear. They bring me in upswings eighty-five thousand dollars net, yearly. Last year, that fella Flack, he's a bear, gave me the wrong advice, I dropped three thousand dollars at the year-end, no presents, had to go to Boston for Christmas. There's the title to the Boston house, not ours, the one your Aunt Sally lives in; that's the house I own in Brookline, I built it myself. I made the plans myself, intended to live there at first, but didn't get on with your mother's relatives. Never mind. See this, 'With reference to the property at No. 29 —— Street,' Jigago that is—don't read it, just look, date March 25, 1945—yesterday—what business am I in? How did I make my money? You want to get some of it for your comic-strip film business—how do I make the money you want to get hold of?"

"In cotton?"

"In cotton, he says—in cotton, like a summer shirt— Here! Plaquet and Grant, Cotton Brokers, Jigago; Bungay and Grant, Ltd., Liverpool; Filatures Grant, Lyon, France; Grant, Cotton Dealers, Genoa, Milan, Cotton Union (Georgia) Inc.; Grant & Co., Rio de Janeiro—Grant, Grant, Grant, me, me, me—us! In Jigago, two hundred thousand dollars; in Liverpool eighty thousand pounds sterling, fully paid up; in Lyon five hundred thousand prewar francs; in Genoa and Milan, five million lire; in Cotton Union, eighty-five thousand dollars; in New York, fifty thousand dollars with Samson; in New Bedford, a little firm, ten thousand dollars. Here are the agreements for you and Andrew—twenty-five thousand dollars upon arriving at the age of twenty-five, subject to, of course—subject to our agreement, you will get yours in three months; we have to agree. Andrew has to wait a little, not a business type too. The farm in Pennsylvania, valued—thirty-three thousand dollars; the farm in Normandy, valued one hundred and eighty thousand gold francs; here's the fur business—never mind that—raw furs, St. Louis—sorry I ever touched it, that fella Goodwin is a plague, a blackmailer; that Delafield never did me any good, all a mistake. I dropped three thousand dollars last month; had to pay it, too, he quarreled with his brother, no good. No business sense, never quarrel with a member of your family in business. Your mother began with forty thousand dollars which I never touched, not a penny, marriage agreement; no sense to it, but there it is. An estate in Rome worth fifty thousand dollars (he mumbled a name) and a farm in the *campagna* if I can ever get it back, don't belong to her, I O U's: those are subsidiary, the house in Rome, a place in Liverpool, small rows of houses, Dublin, never mind, just sentiment, those are baked beans, not interesting. You needn't worry your head.

"Now, I ask of you only that you put your hand to the plow and help me a bit—I have no one but you and it's going to be Grant & Grant, no nephew, no cousin, no women, no chiselers, no Flacks—let them sleep easy, thinking they're going to get a chip! Not they! They love me for myself or not at all. I'll be gone before your brother grows up and he's neurotic anyway. I'll see it never goes out of our hands. Let your mother stick to the Bungay money: that's the way she arranged it when we got married. Didn't like it, right away. Well—probably was a left-handed compliment, in a way. All that—my boy—an empire, a bit scattered now; but that's because the war scatters empires, but this is too little for them to bother about. I exist under the fascists, the Nazis. Someone holds on to it for me. Di Giorgio hid in the mountains two years, and holds on to my property for me, has my titles. Loyalty, eh? So he holds on to it for you, if it's yours. Not one empire will stand up after this war, not even mine, perhaps, though. That's why I want you to stick to the day-old chicks, too. A hedge. Always must have a hedge. No gambling. If you gamble you must be ready to cut your throat. That's impractical! You can stay alive too, and not pay the fella. I'm an old man and dirty, huh? Have dirty nails, eat raw onions, eh? I live my own life and I have no use for any Bungay or Bacon or any other name living. You are nearly my sole heir. That Andrew will perhaps never live to grow up. Can't say, all things told, I'd be sorry. A neurotic. The entire forchun, the Grant Estates, will go to you. You'll think of me, at any rate. Think of me on my birthday. But now you must work for it—fair enough, eh? Never mind how I do my hair in Boston, or whether I put on a clean shirt Christmas Day. Keep your nose pointed to the essentials. Ha-ha—raw onion—oh-ha-ha—and she told you about the laundry bag—oh—"

"But you don't know how Mother feels—"

"Oh-ho—I don't know? If she had had a man with talent, she would have done uncommonly well—eh?"

He went off into a series of laughs.

The young man said, "But aren't you throwing your money away? Is that businesslike? Aren't you throwing away thousands and thousands every year? And why are the farms so scattered? Why don't you buy a row of houses like Benjamin Bungay, not one here, one there, one in Rome?"

Grant became engaging, "Let me throw it away! It's mine. Why, my dear boy, why should I leave even you a cent? We have no such law here. I could leave you a pauper and even Upton would have a better claim to the chicken farm; and you sue for it! I could leave it to old maids and old dogs and cats—to my little pay-girls, Janet, Katia, all the rest—I could leave it to your brother, or your mother, or your grandfather, or the Flacks or Mrs. Mac-Donald, old servants, if I wanted to. It's mine. I can throw it out the window and go bankrupt, and give it to Livy Wright or Mrs. Downs, or use it for toilet paper and throw it down the drain— if I want to. It is mine! I made it! I can lose it! Do you know what that means? In your terms? In my terms too? I can lose it— but I won't!"

He put a hand on the shoulder of his tipsy son and smiled radiantly, almost innocently, "Don't worry! But I want you to run the farm, no movie-educational films; show me what you can do. The investment's already there—no new investment. Your cousin Upton is writing very nasty letters, has something of the black-mailer, surprises me very much, don't want the guy around, must get rid of him, need someone to protect me, only a Grant, that's my motto, from now on, only a Grant. All I've got in this world; no bloody 'ooman, want to shake you down, want to promote you. You think you know the way of the world? Wait till you get to my age, the way of the world will be clear—but I don't want you to make the mistakes, and then you're not the same type—you're

336

my son, don't have to, since I blazed the trail. I'll tell you the way of the world: the money don't belong to the do-nothings, they get it, it's deeded to them, trust funds, protected, sewed up, no good, the constructive boys get it anyway, you can't be like your mother. Slept her life through. She's blind, like all do-nothings. You learn when you have to fight someone for a profit. If someone had handed you caviar on a shovel you could remain blind all your life. You're not going to inherit yours the soft way—not for you, not for you, for it, for the money—and then, I don't give a damn if you do get it that way, I'll arrange so there are no loopholes, no booby-traps—there has to be one exception—and then, mark you, I don't care if you go to pieces when I'm gone—but wait till I'm gone and don't tell me I need a hair restorer now, damn you, like the other day." He laughed.

Gilbert flushed and started to speak.

Grant hesitated, frowned, "I'm joking, that's a joke. If I weren't sure you wouldn't waste a cent, I wouldn't let you stick your nose inside the farm—and you won't yet, inside the hatbox! Ha-ha. I don't want any ne'er-do-well, I don't want an artist, can't count, no good. You can only get on yourself on five thousand dollars next year if I'm not satisfied—the rest will be doled out to you if you don't make good. I'll explain to you my reason for everything—I'll be fair. Everyone has to learn. I'll teach you the signboards. Then you must learn to drive: and avoid the hairpin bends and the closed roads and the dead-ends."

He waved his arms, went about chuckling, daintily avoided the stuff on the floor, then suddenly gave it a kick, saying, "I'll get the damn Walkers out, only pay two hundred dollars, why the hell did I? And they want me to get rid of Mrs. MacDonald: she's too old, can't work. No heart, no sentiment. Don't like them." He stood still, his arms akimbo, faced the boy, sagged his head in his collar, said, with rolling eye, "You must not analyze the way you do in public, not even at all—it must be instinct. Train yourself to listen to instinct. Instinct is always right because before we had brains we had to have instinct, so it must be right—no wrong switches. No analysis in public. Doesn't look smart. If you know already, you don't analyze. If you know something, you don't tell others.

"Listen—but with all this, you must have a frank, open, gay nature, laugh. No dirty jokes, nothing unnecessary. That's for barroom types. Gangsters don't trust any new man talks dirty. Sign of bad business. Natural gaiety, that's the word. Anyone, if he thinks about it, can show natural gaiety. Then, it's a good concealer. People expect you to be worried. You don't want to bring out in people the public prosecutor, the detective, and the tax collector: three parts of human nature. Have a human streak and people trust you. Don't talk dirty, people think you are simple. Another thing—have some weakness, like sinus, or you can't speak straight, or you got a headache every night, must take headache-cure, everyone wants to give you a remedy, takes an interest in you. Nothing like—nothing wrong—no gonorrhea—no paralysis in the uzzazuzz, so they can laugh at you—something simple—tooth-ache, bursitis—nothing like ulcers, you got to take an operation, something they can all help you—what harm, it brings out the good. Then another thing, if you see people want something, promise it to them: they'll never get it anyway, very likely, and so what harm do you do? People pray to God, did it since the Year One, and does God send parcels-post? There are cinders in Europe that once were one million innocents, and does that stop people from believing in God? Why should you worry? You're not like God. They don't expect it; also, you don't burn up anyone in an incinerator. God's credit is good, too, eh? Better than yours or mine.

"Have a human streak and people will be your friends; I got lots of friends and it costs me nothing; and a man must have friends to get things done. No lone wolf. Then about this weakness, you must have. You must have a vice too, some sort of vice, even like taking snuff, it makes people laugh. They are sorry for you; they think you will come to a bad end and they let you pick their pocket—I don't mean that, but I mean they go into partnership with you. People like it. Then you must go in it in a big, naïve way, so people like it and no one can catch you by your vice, though they come up to you with that idea—that idea and a proposition. They can't catch you by your vice, if it's a big one. A man with a cellar full of whisky, you can't buy his partner-ship with an old-fashioned! Not with a bottle of whisky. Not with a case of whisky. You got to make him partner in a distillery. Do you think anyone could catch me with a woman—or a woman could catch me? Pardon me—my boy—I respect your mother, but I don't want you to see things through a glass darkly like she does —all right for a woman, but not for you. You think I am wasting money? It is common sense. Waste money where it is least needed, not where it is needed, never where it is needed. Never give to the poor, nor to begging friends. This is a bottomless pit. Any need is

338

a bottomless pit. Also they hate you. They hate you anyway, because you have it. They hate you at the end, because the need is always there. For argument's sake, a man has cancer, you pay the first operation. Then his family must be supported, also a nurse. Then there's another operation. More nurse, nursing home, so on to the end. Then there's the funeral. Then the widow and orphans, don't touch it in the first place—a bottomless pit. He can bankrupt you, that pauper; and at the end, you'll be a bastard. I don't care if it's your father, your mother, your father-in-law, your brother, or your best friend. Remember, a poor man is a bottomless pit. Don't give him a letter of recommendation, don't bring him into the country, you might find out he is mad and you have to pay for him in a sanitarium; don't witness papers, don't say you know him, don't sign, don't sign—there was something wrong, I knew, when I heard Hugo March built a house for his friends. Something wrong, I'd like to smell it out. Don't buy him a cup of coffee unless he gives you advice worth a hundred times the price of a coffee.

"To give money away, or financial support, is no good; you can give free advice, no one takes it. Then, you must work, but work for years as if you were a stevedore, for at last the vice of being able to buy things will be catching up with you; but—ha-ha—that's not for you! You must work like a man on a chain gang. Why do they have chain gangs? Not for fun. Not for punishment. For contractor's profit. You too must be on a chain gang, for your own profit. You can loaf on time, not on money. Money is not to be loafed on. It takes a holiday too. Money is going down. Money is going out. In fifty years money will not be the fashion: and it is a good thing—for the world. Also, I won't be here. But you might be. Because we are not in that paradise of coupons and ration stamps yet.

"Money is an art. People are going to lose that art as they lost the art of stained-glass windows. It's not going to be any use at all. So you won't get anyone else to tell you what to do. It'll be too late. Now, get this note—don't take any advice about money from people who didn't make any money themselves. Give them a cup of coffee, listen to them, promise them, show them the etchings, but all the time listen for the music of the Scotch piano, that's the cash register; and if it seems to ring up No Sale, watch him, he took out of the till, he's all right. There's a dollar bill in every man: he's born with it but he doesn't know where it is. You must find out. You can't say, 'What's in it for me?' though:

that's vulgar, that's cheap. You must say: 'What's in it for money?' Money is a jealous mistress. If you want money you must want only money. Now, I'm not a moneyman, I'm only doing my best to put you on the right track. But I must tell you the one secret of life, there is only one: *everything* is a jealous mistress, everything is terribly possessive, and, by God, we want to be terribly possessed if we want to get somewhere—and we want to be terribly possessed—anyhow; or what is life?"

He was serene. He plunged his hands in his pockets and continued presently: "I know so much I don't know how to get it out. It's there, but not in words. The real things you know—you can't put them into words. But I want to, for once. No for-r-mulas; no slugs. I made plenty of mistakes. I'm your construction engineer, you're my conservation engineer. I'll see you up there in the observation tower, everything spick-and-span, and I'll pull myself up short and I'll say, 'He's an example to you, not a big money-maker, but an example. He respects my property, what I did.' What happens when money, property, falls into the hands of widows, children, favorites, sisters, divorced wives? You do the best you can for them, but you can't leave them brains in your will. Your brains die too. Too bad. It is no longer personal property. If it doesn't belong to your son, it belongs to no one. It belongs to the insurance company and the stock exchange when the trustee puts the money in stocks, and the Government for taxes, and to fancy schools and colleges, and to dressmakers, not to you or yours. Not for me. No widows and orphans. It is not wealth, it does not represent anything, it does not produce wealth. It is a fiction, floating money, the first five thousand dollars you find floating downstream on a grindstone. Nothing at all. And I worked my life out for nothing at all, on a grindstone, in a river? I don't believe in money that has no owner. Comes a crash—it disappears up the chimney and the next thing you know, Government has it, Du Pont has it, no one has it. Swallowed up by the corporations. You can't track that bit of money that once was produced with hand and brain and, by God, nights without sleep, headaches, through all the holding companies and corporations—suddenly, it's nowhere, in the middle of the desert, you must take a train two days to the office of the company—on Prince Edward Island, in Madagascar. Taxes, lawyers—a farm can't thrive divided up even between two, or given to a bank or a lawyer to operate, or a woman sleeping all the time. She'd sell it to buy an embroidered bedspread, a doctor to hold her hand, a dream-doctor. Banks don't run farms. Banks can't run your property. Banks don't understand property. Property is personal and can only be run by one person, and I swear to you, no matter how dumb you may be at the beginning, if you have property and stick to it—you learn a lot. No bank, no lawyer, no official can beat you. You go into that room, thinking, I'm coming here to hold on to my property—and no one can cheat you, no one can make a better deal. Property teaches you all you need to know. So I have no fear for you, once you know you're the one. You will know—but not yet—

"Now about the stock exchange. It's a casino. I go into it. I play around with two or three thousand dollars—it's a vice. It keeps me out of mischief. I don't try to pay the gas bill out of it. On the stock exchange there is only one rule: if you're a natural bear you'll make money in a bear market; if you're a natural bull, you'll make money in any bull market. Now I'm a natural bull, because I'm constructive, but I don't know what you are; and it's likely you should keep out of it altogether and you're better off. It's a casino. Don't fool yourself like those guys on padded seats in brokers' offices. 'I run the country with my money,' those chimpanzees think; 'why don't the workers stop striking and get to work and support me on this fat cushion?' No, sir, workers don't need me at all and they don't need you, either. I sit on my pants and I run the country—no, sir. Don't get that idea and you'll keep your money. You'll find out the workers don't even need any money at all. Forget it. If I can make a pair of shoes, do I need a fella sitting on a cushion seat in a brokers' office? No, sir. Forget it.

"Then, don't work hard to make money. You're not a money type. I know that's contrary to others' advice, but it's my advice; it's immoral to work to make money. There's something unlucky in it. You got to work for the work. You got to work on a farm, for the farm—then it makes money. You work and expect hens to lay eggs for the money—I don't know why, but the day-old chicks die on the way over. It's a sort of superstition. You got to be superstitious. You lose a woman if you think about her all the time and never look at another woman. You lose money if you look at it all the time; got to love someone else too.

"Then, this is easy for you, you have to be fine, delicate, not a vulgarian, I'm very delicate. Not come out with it. Unnecessary. Now that's Livy's fault, it's indelicate to put all your cards on the table, foolish too. No one wants it, your opponent wants to think too.

"John Stuart Mills and Albert Spencer said, if you gave a penny to a blind beggar, you destroyed the foundations of society, or to a man who plays *Il Trovatore* on the hurdy-gurdy, you destroy the foundations of art and artists; that's a serious thought. I'm a laissez-faire. You can't patch up all the holes in the social fabric. Got to wait for socialism, best thing is to fight for socialism, not aggressive; constructive, scientific socialism, no bones broken, respect for constructive people, laissez-faire, individual effort.

"Now these 'oomen, I was always looking for a woman, not my fault, question of temperament, your mo— h'm—I swear I should have preferred a great romance, always looked for it, oasis in the desert, thrown money out the window, something you can't pay for, believe me, love can't be bought. But you look, now you find the right woman, there is actual physical sharing, you want to give her everything, not even share, undress yourself as a man of property too—very natural, no good, very human—now it is wrong to taste another human, but if you love, you go completely crazy, not healthy, you don't taste, you want to marry, throw away your whole life, not healthy, give away all your money—now you have to watch out for that, you might meet the right woman, very dangerous, a man would give thirty thousand dollars, say, for that, boat rides into the right harbor, eh? Got to watch out, conquer your weakness for a 'ooman. Now, I meet a few women for tea and a little chat, nothing wrong, I swear by all that's holy, your mo— H'm—but they protect him, worth the money—he might be running around, romantic, looking for an oasis. He said, 'I'll give up everything for you, take my money, I'll marry you.' Now this 'ooman might be, say, a Communist, she'd say, give it to the Party or give it to the Negroes, say, she had gone native, now you wouldn't know that; it's a romance, you love her, you do everything she says. Now that's very dangerous. A man would give forty thousand dollars for that, so why not ten dollars to the Party? Natural, human. I see the human side. Now, if you taste women, I don't say it's right, but you got to watch out for your romantic nature; she isn't romantic—in a love-affair always someone loves better than the other—it's the man because he can throw away the money; then it's better to taste women, because you don't upset anything, you watch your step. You think, She can't be worth all that. I'm not in favor of sophistication, mind. Now unless you know what to do and keep your money free, why it's better not to meddle in something you have no talent for and my experience is, a lot of women have a talent for money—you

342

are romantic and you give them five thousand dollars. Now, you're romantic at present, and I don't go near where the flesh is raw.

"Now, let us talk about the present organization of society, for that is something your friends talk about, especially all the women at present. This dividing people into poverty and wealth is insane and *will pass*, no good counting on it. I am angry whenever I see some parasite like Delafield or Goodwin get inflated and say otherwise. I say to them, 'You're inflated because every moron nowadays is making money, and like you; must have a nation full of warblers singing O *Sole Mio* with throaty baritones before you can get a Caruso, so you must have a nation full of financial geniuses to get one real one; why, you're just the male chorus, but you don't know it, you all think you're the one who fills in the holes in Caruso's singing.' Now there's a boom, that is Caruso, and so they are all great singers.

"Every idiot who last year was trying to get a job tipping over garbage cans and couldn't make it, this year, he has a safe-deposit box, and he carries it there in valises; and next year or two, he'll be getting strained eyes looking for a dropped nickel or a cigarette butt on the sidewalk, but he doesn't know it—but today, like Goodwin, he's a Napoleon of finance, a Mussolini. Now don't listen to those boomtime men. They are carried on the wave and they say, 'Look how I roll and shake the beach!' But listen to me: what you see now will not be here in fifty years. Now, it's a question, can you ride every wave and not think you are the big organ saying boom-boom, or are you a man to go and sit in his orchard and say, 'I'll just grow cabbages whatever happens'? Now, they won't expropriate your cabbages, but you have to think if you want to spend fifty years waiting for the time when you'll congratulate yourself because you have a home-grown cabbage soup.

"I know my answer—if I were twenty or twenty-five, I'd go to the Soviet Union and say, 'Make me a Commissar'; I'd make a good general, and I'd make a good Commissar for Textiles, and I can grow red, blue, yellow cotton. But it's too late. So I recommend you to be a socialist, no fascist, because they have long memories and them fascists have no sense, burn up everything, produce nothing. You at least can produce cabbages. Produce cabbages if you can't do anything else. Be constructive. That's my idea. You will know how to farm. Never mind educational films. Cabbages never change. People always can eat cole-slaw, cabbage and corn-beef. Never invest in anything where the technical changes can rot your dollars: that's God-given for monopolies. Don't be a pioneer; monopolies grow rich off pioneers. This money world maybe goes on for your lifetime. Maybe I made a mistake. Then I have provided for Communism too, and given you an occupation suitable for it. Andrew is an artist; an artist looks like a nut but survives somehow, can live in an attic and live off cabbage soup, and next year, he buries them all, he's a best-seller; no trouble: doesn't need money. He doesn't need property, he pulls it out of the air and beats the exchanges, no blocked currency up there. Not you.

"Property is a woman, remember. Think of property every morning when you get up, otherwise she'll run around in the daytime, and talk to the butcher boy. There is no law against it. They kidnap property every day, no law against it, it's legal. Property is a woman. You do not leave a woman you want with your neighbor or your best friend or your cousin, for she becomes the woman of your cousin or best friend. If he doesn't try to steal her, no credit to her. She's there to be stolen. The whole thing in a nutshell. Now I don't say woman to mean woman. A woman with property acts like a man. In property there are no sexes. You can meet a rich woman but she is tougher than a man because she is angry: you see property in her; she wants to be liked for herself. Like me, too. Don't blame her. Human nature always writes a brief and makes a plea, but it don't win very often, property wins; and human nature doesn't like that.

"Like being married, property gives you a special viewpoint. You understand the law and society. One must manage property, though, and have a title to it, and have to fight for it, and have invested in it. You go with a woman and it is—one dollar, ten dollars, and good-bye: you don't understand women. You marry a woman, buy her a house, install her—you live with her maybe five years—then you understand women. Now never mind that. You don't like my friends. I want to expose my views to you. Don't discourage crooks and yes-men and people trying to get your money. Take a woman, does she get mad with men who are trying to make her? It's her business, it's human nature, and it's a compliment. Lead them on. There's nothing to pay. They don't expect a dividend: they only hope. Maybe sometime they'll do you some favor, and you can do them some favor. If not, what do you lose?

"Never go into the thing unless you want to: if you want to, go into it even if it looks bad. Don't go into it, if it looks reasonable and yet you hate it. Don't go into it with friends, only with

344

people who don't like you. Friends are a different sort, or they wouldn't like you; the others are in the same game, your competitors, so they smelled it out, and are right. Only your competitors can show you your game.

"Now, a question of law. In property, anyone who wins is right. It must be so, the law is for property, because it is real.

"Never be cynical. Remember the human factor. Cynicism looks bad and is the mark of a small man who will end in the poorhouse, because he is sneering before he gets anywhere. Affirmation is the right note. Some monkeys, Flack told me, collect blue chips. So it isn't wrong, not opposed to human nature. We are now going away from blue chips. We are leaving the monkeys. But there's a lot of blue-chip monkeys still with us. But while it lasts, my blue-chips monkey is your friend and no sense taking up with the widows and orphans and blind beggars and Negro Congresses. Get your property into your hand first and then see if you wish to give handouts. Handouts is the other end of the world. Wait till you get there. When you have your money, you can give it away, not before. You look in the subway, I see the man who gives to the beggar or the collector is always the poorest dressed. That's a symbol, a warning. If you let someone else take it away from you for any reason whatsoever—for any reason— you'll die in a doorway one winter's night. That's the first thing to remember.

"All property in one sense originates with you; even if you didn't get it, I got it for you. All hangers-on try to make you think you cheated it out of them because they're suddenly a group, the poor people. All right. I'm not against it. It's their racket. If you believe them, it's your fault, and they deserve their dividend. But remember you don't owe it to them. They have this feeling: that they put some idea into the kitty and some money came out and you didn't divide up. They're right, but that's hard luck.

"You ought to get it in your head that you were trained to live in a society which doesn't exist, because no society is the same between yesterday and tomorrow. You have to live by your wits even if you inherit a million dollars. Keep awake. No romances, no going native. The monopolies grabbed the money and so there isn't much money any more, the unions got big pay but there's not much money any more, people pay big prices and they have safe-deposits and they wear diamond cufflinks and they pay twenty-five dollars for the opera—but still there isn't much money any more. I can't prove it, but I feel it—keep your money, keep my money, because there isn't much money at all, and though they can look at me like a sideshow because I have only a million-some dollars, it still counts, it's money; but money that is in billions and in monopolies isn't money at all, because the people have none, and money is democratic, everyone has to have some or there's none at all. Money that's one price in a country and three prices in three countries outside, isn't currency any more. It's a sign there are earthquakes. And that's the reason I got all those farms and houses, everywhere—you can go anywhere and you can eat for money. Money isn't money when it's pesetas in Spain but paper in France, and francs in France but paper in the U.S.A. And an American can take it out of England but not a Briton, and you can take it into Belgium only if the customs is looking the other way and if I can't pay my rent in the U.S.A., although I'm a millionaire in Capetown, and if Karolyi, who has a million kronen somewhere, can't buy a sandwich here—there isn't any money any more. So you were born rich and I made you rich, but you have to watch your step because it isn't like being born a rich boy, you're born a tightrope walker. But property still speaks a general language, and it'll be our refuge, when they're yelling, "Bread and a roof." They'll take one roof, we'll still have a roof. I want you to learn who you are and where you're going, because I worked for it; but, my dear boy, that's the only reason I have—that—and that I'm giving you a forchun."

"Well, Dad, look, I've said some terrible things, I didn't know, I didn't know what I was saying, I hardly know my way about, I think I'm drunk, too—"

"And you can't do anything without a philosophy. You can't be a good French-polisher, or a good shoemaker, or locksmith, without philosophy; any sort will do."

"You'll do me for a philosopher. Dad, I have to hit the hay, I'm crazy to sleep. I guess I drank too many this time."

"You didn't hear a word I said. Well, too bad—you'll get the money anyhow—unless—"

"Why don't you keep all this in a safe-deposit vault? Everyone does!"

"One day they say it's a national emergency, they say there are too many black marketeers not paying income-tax and they open the boxes by decree: that's philosophy. The Governments used to keep their promises, now they're Committees of Public Safety. By accident one of my papers will stick to his fingers."

"What good will it do him?"

"You don't know how some men found their forchun!"

"Blackmail—but how?"

"But you will get nowhere if you persist in having no theory, no philosophy, even beekeeping. It surprises me that you got four hundred pounds of honey in one month without a philosophy. For that is what distinguishes the big moneymaker from the small cheap crook, that he has something to believe in."

"Let me sleep, I promise tomorrow—"

49

The young man, left alone, undressed and suddenly fell into a very deep, refreshing sleep. When he awoke, he felt like a child again. The sun was shining. He felt exactly as he had the first time that he had possessed Celia, when for three days he had felt he was walking on air and only answered people out of a joyful delirium. But what was it? He turned over on his pillow, pressing his dark face into the clean linen, and tried once more to remember all the incidents of his last evening with Celia. They were somewhat faded. He could not even, in one particular instance, recall the intense emotion he had felt at first.

"I am losing her—"

He tried to feel fear, but felt none. He had gained something overnight—what was it? He was too innocent to think it was the money and his father's little empire. That morning, he agreed to go to the farm and work it for his father without salary, his expenses paid, and to receive an interest in it, and if he did not make a profit the first year, to engage Upton, his cousin, as manager. Upton had married his friend, the young stenographer, and would no doubt come back on better terms for Grant. Gilbert agreed, in a paper he signed, partly to pay for the farm, fifteen thousand dollars out of the twenty-five thousand dollars to come to him next year. He was not quite satisfied with this, but insisted no more when his father said—"twenty-five thousand dollars next year—and if I don't like it, my boy, I wait a while. So wait till you see your check for ten thousand dollars before you get any ideas."

It was eleven-thirty in the morning. Gilbert went to the closet and got himself a drink, smiling at his father's impatient looks. He sat down, crossed his knees. Said he,

"Well, Dad, I'm in a bit of a fog about what happened last night, but I've got the impression you're a whale of an immoralist;

347

an immoralist stuck as full of sermons as an egg is of meat. I really didn't know you had it in you. Fact is, I didn't really know you. Now, I'm a moralist—"

His father laughed sarcastically, "With moralizing you don't understand human nature: that's your weakness. Moralists can only understand injustice. I shall be unjust enough to you to teach you something. That's my idea."

The young man yawned, doddled his head, "I don't understand you, but my compliments, Dad. I didn't think you ever thought anything out. Now last night, I listened to you at great length with some respect to our personal findings, although I can't agree with you and I am sure, from what I know of you, that most of it is just smoke—and it's because I have a favor to ask of you, too. I want you to meet Sergey, the movie director who's interested in setting up a small company to do these educational, technical short films after the war. You can do a lot with it; you can also provide imaginative or surrealist films if you will—for example, I saw a remarkable film made for artists only, from studies of a pneumatic drill in operation; you never saw, well, anything more realistic and sexual—well, not only that, you could distribute to the art movies, but general subjects—then that's a by-product. I have this man Sergey, who's been in Germany and France and who's interested in doing things like Eisenstein, but wants some backing. You could put the money you're thinking of putting into your *Dream Girl* play into this instead, and you're in something modern. I don't believe you're going to make any money on your *Dream Girl*, because it's pure hokum and only written to sell, and make money and, in fact, violates one of your own principles: in doing something, even to sell, one must not think first of the money. Now you first thought of the three million dollars! I am interested in the technical side of these movies and I'm a bit of a technician now, though nothing extraordinary, and if you put a bit of money back of me, I can see that the money is used and at the same time, a technical brain and interest is at work, a real service is being rendered. Now you left out one thing, and that is, that money comes not out of other money, or out of a fertile brain, but out of service. Isn't that so?"

"Who is Sergey?"

Gilbert described him and said he could arrange for a meeting on the next day, that he had already mentioned it all to Sergey, who was about thirty-eight; and continued, "Why not put a few thousand dollars, whatever you can, say, ten, into this and leave it to me? I understand the artisan and working artist and you don't. Now you let yourself be led into all sorts of bypaths you don't understand with people like Flack, that writer without a telephone in Brooklyn, and Karel Karolyi. I understand them, they're easy to handle."

"I understand them, my boy; I employ them. That's the only understanding you need. Can you employ him? Or can you go into business with him? No man is at par. Some don't want to work and some want to buy you. Same with women: you can buy a lot of them, but the others want to take you over. Every man is in the market—but is he a seller or a buyer? Know that first. I don't advise a man like you to go into the market. Let me manage the business end of our undertakings. I'll see your Sergey. I'll put your ten thousand in his business, tell him—ten, twenty thousand, if I like him. I'll employ you, and let him employ you. Then we'll see. Give it a twelve-month tryout, after the war. Even now. Let me talk to him. I'll give him twenty thousand dollars of yours if I like his looks, and he gives me specifications, blueprints. If he can't talk me into it, it's no good. I'm a business man, I'm in the market, I've got to use my money. I want you to look about yourself. Sergey's got a good proposition, talk me into giving him twenty thousand dollars. Fair enough! Here I am. If he can't talk me into it, I lose nothing. I promise twenty thousand dollars but I pay nothing. Fair enough? Let him sell me, eh? Bring him along tomorrow. Eh? I'm through with living here in a hole. Today I'll go out, see the blondine, if I want to, see your mother and the blondine and Livy all together, if I want to. I wish I'd stayed yesterday afternoon. Ha-ha-ha! Must have been a good show.

"My dear boy, it's too early to drink, a vice is only for the public, for your friends. Tomorrow I'll put them all from me. You're right. It'll be you and me. But I'll go through it with the blonde. And you must stand for it. You've seen life, you understand now. Listen, my dear boy, if she has to go through the mud, I will. She paid a dividend. I don't mind. I don't yowl. I'll go through the mud with her. But I'll try to arrange it. I'll see. I heard some good news today. There's an X, a Mr. X who can't afford to lose his good name, in it. I'm not like that. You had pleasure with a woman; you can't get away scot-free! No! You must pay for the honey. A woman always gives more than she gets! I'll tell her, go to him, tell him, if he doesn't want to pay the debt of society, he must pay the debt in money. Let him make

349

a contribution. Why should that 'ooman pay? The debts of society are scaled so high, only men can pay. Ha-ha."

He walked up and down, rubbing his hands, "If we did something wrong, we must pay. Must you get honey free? If you can. But you can't. Only try to make it pay a dividend. Try to get a bonus. But this time, I thought to myself—Rob Grant, you'll go through the mud, get your name in the papers, first time in your life, something to live for! Eh? What do I care? Let her go back to Boston! Let her take a nap. Let her sleep it off! Try and sleep off this one. I'll marry her, good God, I owe it to her. I'm an honest man. I owe it to her. Yes, yes. Never mind the others. I made a mistake. Never mind. Tomorrow I go out and do what I like and see the town and go to the White Bar. I'm not afraid. I see my lawyer. I see her. I say, 'Go to X and tell him, "Pay up ten thousand dollars or you'll have trouble."' He can't afford trouble. He's one of Hoag's Washington fellas. He'll pay. She's free. I'm free. No one in the mud. I'll stick by her. Put this stuff in the closet. Come, help me.

"No Havana. What do they want to do behind my back? That Goodwin? That Flack? I'll stay here. I watch my interests. I stay near the honey. Ha! She's like me. I'll do something for her. She don't expect it. I'm like her. I'll stick by her. They'll see me in the papers. Good! Something got me in the papers! Good. Do I care? They'll see my name—Robert Grant and a blonde, beautiful 'ooman! Good. Let her sleep it off. You're Grant's son. Don't tell me your opinion. Because if I don't like it, I'll push it back in your teeth. If I like it, it don't make any difference. Yes! That's it. Tomorrow I get out of this rathole and we'll shove all this back in the closets. And I'll look for another place where she can visit me. I'm tired of this damn zenana. Go on, go back to bed. I want you to help me pack. I don't want a hangover. Take an aspirin! Take a nap!"

When the young man went out to the bathroom in the corridor, Grant stood a moment looking after him, pulling down his shirt sleeves which had been rolled above his elbows. Suddenly he burst into a boyish laugh, thrust out his open hand toward the corridor, and cried, "Agh! If he— Agh!" He burst out laughing, took a turn, and then, seeing the hatbox, frowned, replaced it, locked it, and put it behind the pile of luggage. He put the key in his vest pocket while he wrestled with the as yet unopened collarbox. When the boy came from the bathroom, he took the hatbox and the collarbox into the bedroom with him.

350

But the pertinacious young man telephoned Sergey after breakfast and arranged a meeting for the next morning with his father, at the hotel, at eleven: "Why not? I know you have nothing to do in your office, Dad. I've seen you lying on the sofa myself."

"Rubbish, I was exhausted, had been overworking and had to rest for a couple of minutes, had to take a little stretch. Wasn't resting when you saw me—was thinking—"

"Well, Sergey is coming at eleven. I told him you would give him ten or twenty thousand dollars, according to how it sounded to you."

Grant went down to the office, telling his son to put the stuff in the closets as far as it would go. He would find a hotel suite today or tomorrow and not go to Havana at all. He would advise the blonde simply to see Mr. X and advise him as to his best interests—"But no divorce, my boy—no; I don't want the 'ooman trying to break up your mother's home."

50

Before Gilbert arrived at the office to confer with Sergey and himself, Grant had a respectful visit from a detective from the police station at Old Slip, two blocks away, saying that a man had been picked up on a road in New Jersey, walking hatless, without a coat and in a bad condition, apparently undernourished, now in a hospital, and that this person had a letter from Robert Grant, cotton broker, in his pocket. This letter said,

Dear Karel,
  I repeat, for the last time, the copy first, the money when I've seen it and accepted it.
                                        Yours, R. G.

"Do you know this man?" asked the detective.

Grant said he did, and said it was a dramatist who had not yet produced a play for which he had paid a reasonable sum. He had a claim against the man's goods. He had seen no manuscript. He said he did not know where the man, K. Karolyi, lived in town; in fact, thought he lived in Westport, Connecticut, in an old, broken-down house, for which, in these hard times, a large premium had been asked. He personally had put up three hundred dollars for Karolyi's premium. He believed Karolyi was behind with the rent. The detective said that Karolyi was in hospital with pleurisy, and delirious, did not know his name, and the New

Jersey police wished to get in touch with his relatives or friends. Grant knew nothing of relatives or friends, but only said, "Call up the Polish Consulate in Sixty-seventh Street, they must know. I don't. Give them something to do."

He sat there jingling his coins in his pockets till the detective went, then called the uptown hotel where Karolyi lived and told the manager, to whom he was known, that Karolyi had gone out of town but had told him to come and get his French silk scarf, Charvet, gray, red, and black stripes. The manager objected, said that Karolyi had been locked out of his room, and had ridden up and down in the elevator of the hotel for two days and nights, changing elevators and when possible sleeping in the angles of the roof garden, now disused, of the hotel, or on the stairs in the uppermost story. The elevator boys had been reprimanded for having allowed this. It was they who in the end had given him away, because, they said, they were afraid he would commit suicide. From the top story of the hotel a magnificent view of New York was to be had. The city looked like a vast number of gulches and ashpits. One of the elevator boys had given Karolyi a packet of cigarettes, knowing he had had nothing to eat for two days. Karolyi had told him that he had twenty thousand dollars in his mattress and a further forty thousand dollars in a mattress in a canyon in Beverly Hills, California, and some more in an attic in a house in Westport, Connecticut. One of the elevator boys had given him the money for a haircut and shave. The elevator boys liked the man and declared that he expected a remittance from an English nobleman, or at least, said the manager, "from a magnificent English gentleman."

Grant at once took a taxi uptown, leaving a note with Miss Robbins for his son and Sergey.

When he got to the hotel, he saw the manager, whom he knew well, offered him a box of Max Schwart's Primadoras cigars, twenty-five, and asked him to let him into the room of K. Karolyi to find his Charvet scarf. He said he had heard Karolyi was out of town, either at Westport or in Florida, he had a bad cold and needed the scarf, given to him by his fiancée. The manager refused the cigars and said that he could not let him in the room. Mr. Karolyi was absent.

"You can come with me," said Grant.

"No, I cannot do this."

"Look, I am his best friend. He owed me one hundred and eighty dollars. He's away. He may not pay his rent, he's an artist,

352

I'm willing to stake him to it, and I don't want to see you robbed, whatever it is—if it's sixty a month, I'll put up thirty dollars, he's not around, you might lose money—I want you to know I'm his friend and absolutely guarantee him—"

The manager refused to do so, however, and Grant went out of the hotel with angry and noble airs, and after some wandering sat down in one of his favorite cafés near Central Park to think what to do. He telephoned his office, the blonde, and his wife. He made, through his son, an appointment with Sergey for the next day. He conducted several small affairs and when five o'clock came, the hour at which the day manager went off in Karolyi's hotel, he went back there, and walked up to the first floor, found the chambermaid who had just come on, and told her, who knew him well for his frequent visits, that he must wait for Mr. Karolyi in his room. He gave her two dollars and asked her to unlock the door. The maid replied that Mr. Karolyi had been absent, and seemed perturbed, but Grant replied cheerfully that he knew very well, Karolyi had been upset by the death of a stenographer, a faithful old friend from Poland, up in Westport, he had gone to the funeral, and had sent him, Grant, a postcard to meet him here tonight, the two of them would go out to dinner, but to a quiet place, as Karolyi, a romantic man like all Poles, felt very upset.

"And this is very important for me, as I am his friend and not only that, regard him as a moneymaker, and what he is doing for me is a play, you understand, and I need a pretty girl as chambermaid in the play, someone who knows the job, and I will recommend you."

The woman laughed just the same at this flattery, took another dollar, and said she did not know when he would be back, but Mr. Grant could wait a few minutes, she was certain.

"I'll leave the door ajar," said Grant.

"Oh, he would not mind your being there," said she.

A few minutes later he emerged with a satchel, closed the door, and went down the staircase, as he had mounted it. The satchel he had found in Karolyi's room. He recognized it as a portfolio K. had received accidentally, by airmail, with a pile of MSS. from Hollywood, "therefore to whom does it belong?" and he wore round his neck his own silk scarf, from Charvet, given to him by the blondine. Inside the portfolio was the play, *The Subway Princess*, in Karolyi's handwriting and only partly typed, without a title page, simply with acts, scenes, and at the end, the words he was looking for, "The End," since he had requested this repeatedly of Karolyi.

Downstairs he met no one. He went to Hugo March's apartment. There he studied the play for some time by glancing at its pages and writing, not very clear. To his mind, it was very poor. He did not see any of the speeches he expected actors to make. In rage and disappointment, he telephoned the Flacks, asked them to dinner, and said he must show them the play, *The Rainbow Girl*. In his own script he wrote in this title on the manuscript.

He was unable to wait for the Flacks, however, who were engaged, until the next day; therefore he telephoned the Goodwins and Dorothea, and asked them to meet him that evening in the apartment. Gilbert would read the play and they would improve it, make it a real play. He had been cheated, he said, by that fellow, and would pay him nothing for these couple of words.

"There's no color in it, no one will know what the hell it's about. I don't myself and I gave him the idea!"

On the title-page he wrote,

BY ROBERT GRANT AND KAREL KAROLYI,
based upon an idea of Robert Grant.

He was pleased by this and showed it to Gilbert as soon as he came in for dinner. Gilbert, however, refused to do the reading, said the script was all right as far as he could see, he had experience of such things, said he would not touch the thing, and recommended his father to send it to a play-doctor. This evening, besides, he had an appointment with Celia Grimm, and his cheerful, rosy face showed his feelings. The father heard his son telephoning Miss Grimm. Gilbert was begging her to put off a trip through the South that she was obliged to make. She was an organizer for a league of northern radicals for the education and liberation of the Negro women still in a state of peonage in the lost South.

Grant came out of the bathroom as soon as the conversation finished and asked his son about this, saying he was sorry to see Gilbert get involved with such a woman, who was no good, and "going native." Gilbert tried to show his father that the whole interest in the Negroes and in Negro women was only a worthy modern continuation of the northern anti-slavery attitude during the Civil War, and that Celia represented those noble women from Massachusetts and other New England states who went down South in those troubled times to educate the Negro. He indicated

354

to his father the itinerary that Celia would follow next week, when she left to address meetings, and told him of the dangers that awaited her. Had his father, going down to Florida, never seen the strange-looking fellows, like trusties, strung along wayside stations where northern trains stopped, looking for Negroes from the North with too swagger an air, for labor organizers and such? Gilbert told his father of some horrifying incidents, and of organizers maltreated, hunted, killed. "You simply don't understand, Dad. You belong to the old world where every woman was supposed to be a kitchen and bedroom type. You're decades, even centuries behind the mind of a woman like Celia."

Grant argued rationally with his boy, remained serious and kind, but asked for a further description of Celia's interesting itinerary and of what might happen to her. He tut-tutted and wagged his head and looked grave, saying, "I underestimated her, had no idea; maybe you're right, I must have a talk with her, give her some money for the League," and asked him to tell Celia to telegraph him at any time, from the South, if she needed help.

Gilbert felt he had misjudged his father, and hurried off joyfully to meet his lady. Grant at once telephoned Flack, pressing him to come and read *The Dream Girl*—he must, he must; and Flack would get his large cut, together they would edit and improve it. Flack, who never resisted his old friend long, agreed to put off his other appointment. He was to have gone with Edda to a meeting in Madison Square Garden to show sympathy for the anti-fascists suffering in the south of France, in internment camps. Flack said, on the telephone, "At any rate, Edda will go by herself; she has become very interested in this lately, and I am glad. She says, in a time like this, everyone must forget personal horrors and do something for the world."

Meanwhile, Betty Goodwin called him to say that she was bringing a friend of hers, a well-known actress, to the reading. This actress was looking for a part: she was a woman once famous, now long past her prime, and even past her scandals, but she felt she could make a comeback with a good vehicle. Grant, that evening, ate and drank prodigiously without noticing what he was doing—for in general he ate and drank lightly in company, as he had been taught by Laura.

When his friends were assembled, sitting on the valises, on the couch, on a few chairs, he handed out some brandy in a very genial mood. The actress, whom he insisted upon calling "Mrs.

Penguin," although that was not her name, blew in very late, in a gust of fur, frock, and perfume. Her figure was that of a fine woman of her epoch, that of Lillian Russell. Her dressing and coiffure were up to date. She was a powerful, corpulent, vain animal, a sort of Grant in skirts. They sniffed at each other, and liked each other at the first glance. The gross man went up to the gross woman, put his arm partly round her waist, and kissed her on the shoulder, "A Polish woman taught me to do that; I was going with her to reconstruct Poland after the war, arrange to supervise spinning and clothes, but she died. You remind me of her."

The fat woman gave a great laugh and plumped down in the desk chair, looking around with satisfaction on everyone, but making a fuss, in a moment, about the appearance of the room, the valises. He began again his flattering; and she said firmly, "No more monkey business; let's get on with the reading—I have only an hour. I have to see my manager at the White Bar at eleven."

"My dear lady, wait till you hear *My Dream Girl*, three acts, five scenes. How do you like *The Dream Girl*, eh?"

"Don't like it."

"My dear lady, it's a selling title. It'll sweep them into the Atlantic. That's what every man wants, his dream girl, that appeals to every man's heart and even his pocketbook, for his dream girl he'd pay out a forchun, just to get the right woman."

"You may be a character, but you're a bad actor. I've got no time for this comedy. Let's get on with it. Do you read?"

Flack began to read, clearly, very fast, with high-school emphasis. When he reached the fourth interchange, which was,

> BERTIE (*to the maid*): *Let any woman in who is less than five feet four*. I advertised for a dream girl. With an innocent air, sweet ways, loyalty. And a waist that can go through a wedding ring!

Grant, who had been shifting his great haunches in his seat, yelled, "It's a smash-hit, believe me: we'll sweep them into the Atlantic. A five-star hit; our name in lights on Broadway. Winchell will give us a write-up for this, we'll invite him to a cocktail party. Eh?"

Flack, after waiting a moment, continued with the reading. A few minutes later, Grant called out, "Eh? What do you think? It's a knockout. It'll knock out their eyes, it'll knock out their front teeth. Put in your reservations two months in advance. No standing room. Eh? Eh? Eh? A knockout. See our names in Winchell. What do you think of it?"

"Shut up, shut your g.d. trap," said the actress, good-naturedly.

"Why don't you listen for a bit?" said Flack.

"Listen, I been sold before this," said the actress.

"All right, go on, go on," said Grant, with good humor.

"Listen, bully-boy, don't let's have any more of those sweet words out of your big puss. Honeybear, remember I've got a black mark against you. Remember the drawers you have to change for me," said Goodwin with obscene, loutish yells.

Flack began,

LULA: *It's a town on the Fall Line.* I'm looking for the right man and when I find him, I'll settle down and forget my ambitions and make breakfast for him.

Grant involuntarily called out, "Heh? Believe me, put in your reservations two months ahead. Eh? A woman's feelings. You get the men and get the women. He has a dream girl. She has a dream boy. Eh?"

Flack laughed, "Say, didn't you put that in yourself?"

Grant muttered, "No conversation; Karolyi didn't do anything. No script, when I got it." He turned to the actress and said, with a big grin, "Eh? What do you think of it? Is my psychology right? It'll knock them for a loop. What's your opinion? You're a beautiful woman, give me your opinion."

The actress, "Can it, O'Toole!"

Flack burst out laughing, but continued.

BERTIE: *I've never been to New Jersey, but I'd love to travel —with you.* I'm looking for the right woman and if you are the right woman, then we'll go when the war is over and re-construct—

Flack stopped, burst out laughing again, and said, "When the war's over we'll go and reconstruct New Jersey. That's a radical line for you, Grant. And a radical comes in and says, 'But why?' The Hague machine draws the line at murder. No murder. They're practically leftists. Then you have a political intrigue with Bertie trying to reconstruct New Jersey and the radicals opposing him because they're supporting the Hague machine. Then, *Deus ex machina—*"

Grant frowned, "Don't put me off. Go on reading."

357

The actress said, "How the hell did New Jersey get into this?"

"Grant's been writing in his own view of the dialogue," said Flack, sighed, and was about to go on reading, when Grant said, "No dialogue; there was nothing there but a couple of words. A couple of words in every scene. The fellow did not give me value. I paid for it and no value. But the idea is mine. Wait till you hear Act Two, Scene Three. It'll wow them. Sold out, no seats for two months. Eight years' run. Beat that *Tobacco Road*, have *Cotton Road*. Wait and see. Leave it to me. I guarantee you. I bring luck. A smash-hit."

"God, he's terrible and it's terrible, but let me hear a bit more of this crap," said the actress.

"Don't you like it?" Grant repeated several times.

"Have I got a waist like a wedding ring?" asked the actress.

"No—no."

"Then where do I come into this picture? Do you mean to say the famous Karolyi wrote this, or how much did you write in with your little hatchet? Go on, go on."

"What's the use?" said Flack.

Grant roared at him, "It's got heart-appeal, it appeals to men and women alike. A man is looking for a woman and he can't find her, he advertises for a fine young woman, healthy, good-looking, intelligent, and she answers. And he has a chance to pick them, but when he sees her he knows she's the right one. Every man would like to do that. Why does she answer? She's looking for the right man! But she's ambitious—"

"I give up, the man would drive me mad, I give up, I can't stand it, go away, take him away, he'll drive me out of my mind," said the actress. She got up.

Goodwin at once got up and said loudly, "Sit down, Madame! I respect your talents. Don't pay any attention to the bully-boy. We're used to him. If he has no brains, if his puss opens too wide, he's got money and he can be an angel to you. Listen, Grant, I don't like you and I'm waiting for you to make good on the pants. I told him, 'Go and get me a set of drawers, the sort I like, roomy in the back.' He said he'd get them for me. He gets me a size too large, large enough nearly for his own ——, and I say, 'Take them back. Listen, bully-boy, you know I'm sick, I can't do for myself. You do that for me or I'll upset your apple-cart. I brought these drawers along in a parcel. You take them and see you change them and leave them for me tomorrow morning at the Pickwick. I don't pay your rent unless you change the drawers.'"

He went into the details again. The actress planted her hands on her knees, which panted apart, and with a sweating face looked with jovial anger at the company.

Grant murmured, "I never did, I never did, did you a favor, you told me the wrong size—" At this point he was interrupted by Goodwin, who cried, "You big steer, I gave you all the instructions. I told you to get 'em for me. I can't do anything for myself. I'm sick. I got a bad heart, bad blood vessels. I told you, 'Get them for me,' and, by God, you'll get them. If you don't change them, I'll leave them, I'll strew them on your hotel steps when I go out. Unless I have your written promise, I know you, you welsher. Now, don't interrupt any more, I got enough on you. I know you now, you slipped on a pair of drawers. I'm not afraid of you. I got more money than you. You thought you'd get my wife. You sang her your song and dance. You thought you'd wear her drawers. Now you got to buy my drawers. Once you thought I was peanuts, now I got more than you. I got ten safe-deposit vaults. So never mind about defaulting, and a little advice, I know your story and never mind going with my wife and talking it out of her, I'm on to you and if I don't get those drawers changed by the morning, I'll write to the District Attorney. I know you, my sweet one. You're my dream boy. Listen to the dream boy. If you don't get me new pants that fit round the waist, by ten o'clock tomorrow morning, dream boy, I'll send you to the District Attorney by special messenger. Now shut up and listen while your sucker over there reads this—"

Flack laughed. The actress and the others put in words, trying to calm Goodwin, pretending to laugh, but unnerved. But Goodwin overrode them with a loud voice and imperious air, shouting, "Do you expect to get anything out of this fourflusher? You got to fight for it, like I got to. If he doesn't change those g.d. drawers by ten o'clock tomorrow, it's an ultimatum, I go to the District Attorney and tell a sweet story of a honeybear. Then it's curtains for him, no Act Two."

Grant laughed very low and murmured, with a modest blush, "What's the matter, Alf? I'll do it, what's the matter with you?"

Goodwin said, weightily, "And do it, you'd better. Because if you don't do it, first I throw those pants all over the steps in your fancy little respectable hideaway, and second, I go to the District Attorney, and third, I go and see the—"

"I'll do it, I'll do it," said Grant. He smiled at the others there and shook his head. He sat with his shoulders bowed and his

359

face lifted. He flushed like a rose. Meanwhile, Goodwin had drawn out a photograph, postcard size, and was showing it to the actress, saying, "That's my son, and I'm getting another son in two months, I always hit the bull's-eye. I'm not a fourflusher like Grant; if I set out to get drawers, I'd get drawers, and remember, I have a serious condition, I can't do anything for myself, but get sons one after the other, year after year I can do. And I married the daughter of a millionaire, ten million dollars. Not bad, eh? But that fourflusher, that welsher, that poor jerk can't get me two pairs of drawers the right size. I'll strew them on your steps to-morrow, you big honeybear, if you don't change them. Why don't you go out now, you dream boy, and hunt them up? I don't want yours—"

He went off into a mad fantasy about Grant's clothing.

At last Flack said, "Well, when do we get back to the reading, or don't we? What we've had here, I admit, is more of a play than *The Dream Girl*."

"No, no, it'll sweep them into the Atlantic. We'll give Winchell a cocktail party and we get a smash-hit, sell to Ollywood—Holly-wood—three million dollars. Go on, the lady wants to hear it."

"The hell I do. I have a date; but thanks for the memory," said the actress, getting up.

They all rose. Grant rushed up, holding her by the arm, beg-ging her, trying his endearments. She only laughed and shook him off, but she said, "Call me some time—dream boy; I'll make a date with you if you'll bring your friends too. I wouldn't have missed it for worlds. Good-bye." And suddenly, elegantly, she sailed out of the door. They stood round her at the elevator.

Grant, returning sadly to the apartment, began to upbraid Flack, but this scolding was broken into by Goodwin, who thrust the packet of new drawers under Grant's nose and repeated his threat. Pretty soon they all left but Flack. Flack and Grant had a long, miserable talk. Why had the actress gone, Grant asked over and over again, and wanted to blame it on Flack. Flack blamed it upon Grant's meddling with the script. Grant walked up and down discontentedly, jingling the money and keys in his pockets and repeating, "It's a smash-hit, she's old, she's worn out, she doesn't see it. She's a has-been. It's a diamond of the first water. It'll sweep them into the Atlantic. It's artistic. It has an idea, it has appeal. Appeal to every man, every 'ooman! I want my dream girl, or dream boy. General appeal. No problems. Nothing un-necessary. No sex, no scandal. Suitable for Hays Code. Broadway hit, first-night hit, and can't get seats for months ahead. Hold out for three million dollars. You get your cut. She doesn't see it. She's an old fool, a has-been. The world's changing. Got to have humor and romance too. Democratic. Every girl, every boy, their dream. She's no good. Turns down a gold mine."

When Flack remonstrated with him and said his additions to the script had turned it from a hit to a misfit, Grant yelled, "You shut up. It's my play. You don't know how to make money."

"No: I hate money. So money eventually hates me," said Flack.

He laughed, dropped his arms, cast his gay, arched eyes at Grant, "Don't ask me to explain the mystery of life; but if money meets a person who not only hates money but actually does not want money, it wants to kill him, but I mean kill—"

Curiously enough, when he said "Kill," Flack's voice became shrill, even hysterical, certainly full of fear, as an honest man seeing the approach of a fascist policeman who had once tortured him.

Grant was touched for the moment, "I respect you for that, my boy, respect you, wish I could be like that. If there's a law preventing me from putting my hand—"

Flack broke in with, "Those who really love, like myself, are hated by the rascals, business men, and peddlers of love."

"Eh? Eh?"

"Anyone who is decent, Robbie, is hated by your rabble. You don't understand because you're naïve, Robbie. Your rabble are monkeys, they're not men yet. They don't like to be decent. If you force them to be decent, they simply crap in the public square when you're not looking and then hide behind a telephone booth to grin at your growl, when you see the neat little pile."

"Not at all, unnecessary, not at all, we must have a constructive view of people," said Grant. He walked up and down once or twice, then burst out laughing, clapped his friend on the shoulder, yelled with laughter and remarked, "That's a damn funny picture, though. Where'd you get it? That's very good."

"I got it from Koehler's apes."

He frowned at once. "H'm? H'm? Never mind."

51

Flack filled in the time for him just the same, but when he had gone at twelve, because Edda would be home and waiting for him, lonely, Grant felt lonely indeed. For a moment, he actually sat and felt lonely, realized his life was empty, that his friends had moved off in swarms, in families to amuse themselves and each other, and that even his son—but his energetic nature refused such moments.

He sprang up from the chair and threw himself into a mood—any mood was not only entertainment, but preferable to the sorrow of thinking of his old age and uncompanioned state. He thought at length of Gilbert. It was two o'clock and Gilbert had not yet returned. He flung himself down on the couch and imagined a series of letters, of unfortunate incidents provoked by him, striking down Celia Grimm, a young woman pretending to be radical, who had gone out with a radical like himself, honest, since after all he had all that money to give to Spain or the Spanish refugees if he chose, therefore, more honest than all of them—an honest radical, he saw himself, with dilated eyes, sitting in Café Society, in some other leftist night club, in the company of radicals, a real radical better than those who spoke too much, even than David Flack who, inexplicably, was a wonderful mass-stirrer at radical meetings—because he had a good heart and could hand them, if he wished, one million dollars—enough surely to solve the problems of a few radicals, of poor men without shirts, with no teeth, and who lived on concentration-camp soup. His million dollars, that could purchase them all back to humanity, made him, of them all, the most radical, a thousand lives in a bankbook—especially as he had a good heart. He lay, being very sleepy, and thought bitterly of Celia Grimm. He had taken the woman out a number of times and received nothing for it—a couple of kisses. She was not a child and she had accepted dinners from a man, they had become intimate, talked a lot about Negroes' rights and Spanish refugees in the south of France; they had had plenty of drinks and he had even once taken a whole party to Café Society Uptown, just to please her, to see Hazel Scott. And what was the result that evening? She had gone home with someone else. She had no honor, then, as a woman, not even any commercial honor, a bargain is a bargain, a woman knows what she is doing. Now she had entranced his young idiot, his son, by romantic talk about the South. He felt his troubles would be over, the woman punished, and his son ridiculed, if he showed the woman up. Thinking it over, his lips became red, he licked them, he smiled, his eyes shone like jewels, and he arose and drew a little map. He then wrote a form letter, more or less in this style,

The Sheriff, Clay County.

Dear Sir,

Our country is at war and we do not want any unrest among our workers. I know that Miss Celia Grimm is leaving New York City on [date] for [place] in order to give Communistic ideas to hard-working local Negro women. I recommend you as a loyal northern friend to look out for her at the railroad station or bus depot, about [date].

Yours sincerely,
A. Goodwind,
Broker,
N. Y. City.

P.S. I met this woman recently in the company of two Negroes. It seems to me she is mad about color. I do not like to see anyone I know in that situation.

When the young man came home, staggering with fatigue and with an expression of bliss and raggedness, about three A.M., Grant, full of his new idea, gave his son a drink, talked again to him about Celia Grimm, and sent him to bed.

He slept soundly that night—the play was finished and read to an actress; he had accounted for the insult to his honor given by Miss Celia Grimm; his son—he knew now where to find him. With some tenderness, he got up at seven-thirty and made breakfast for Gilbert. Gilbert did not rise till after nine. Grant stayed away from his office, and spoke again of Celia Grimm, who was leaving the next day for the South.

In the next week there were some, for him, interesting developments in the "blonde" case. Having once more employed his old friend, Bentwink, a pleasant and modest and tranquil detective, he had found out (what he might have found out, perhaps, by employing a spyglass, a pair of spectacles, or a lawyer) that the blonde's lover, Mr. X, was a highly placed Washington man of Catholic connections, upon which he depended much, married to a rich girl, and that he could in no way allow the scandal to come to light. Grant was delighted at this, and exclaimed several times to numerous persons that, "It is the triumph of decency. No scandal, he made a mistake and he pays, and no scandal. Everyone who made a mistake is sorry for his sins, and no scandal, a profit, and nothing to pay for the rest. For him, he had the most to lose, so he has the most scandal. His weakness is her strength. His weakness—h'm—at any rate, he'll pay the money, and I've advised the blondine not to divorce. That idiot, her husband, does not want to marry, and he says if the blonde deceived him, with that innocent lovely face, any woman can, and he doesn't want that. Well, I don't suppose he's very strong, either. I'm going out to put that in *My Dream Girl*. 'You deceived me, so no other woman counts. I'll never look at another woman again, she hurt me too much.' That will appeal to everyone."

He met the blonde every day, having conferences with her about the amount of money "Mr. X" was to pay and to whom it should be awarded. He was quite happy and forgot about his son. However, the younger man suddenly became fretful and tyrannical, and Grant found out not only that Celia Grimm had left for her Southern tour but that she had told Gilbert she might never see him again, such was her work and such the difference of their views of life. Grant felt he could write his letters of denunciation with impunity. The more he thought of Celia Grimm's tricking, the angrier he became. These letters to sheriffs all sent off, he sat down in a pleasurable quiet and played Russian Bank with his son and the Goodwins.

A week later, Gilbert told him, with tears in his eyes, that Celia was in a southern jail for inciting the Negroes to break contracts, and that he was going down at once. Grant forbade this in a fury, "If you do a thing like that, you'll get nothing from me. Remember your twenty thousand dollars which you will get in a few months for Sergey, or for the farm, it depends what I think is conditional, subject to—"

The young man said harshly, "When you met Sergey you promised money next year in Europe, not here and now; I know you promised to give the farm back to Upton. You are treating me like a child and you let everyone think I am a dupe."

Grant continued without noticing this: "If I don't like you, you don't get a penny. It's my money. Never mind what I promise. I promise here, I promise there, if I see a good thing, if I believe in a man. You bring me something and you'll get your money, subject to my approval and you'll sign for it, and you'll take it all on your own responsibility and not come to me for it afterwards; I'm clean about money, I don't pay twice. You got to respect my money. If it weren't for my money you'd be a laborer, a workman in a mill or a white-collar man in an office with no brains and no chance. You're Grant's son. I'm not saying that to insult you, my boy; I don't consider it an insult. All right, you can't make money. Everyone can't. If everyone could I wouldn't have had such a streak of luck myself. Ha-ha. But no going down with woman who likes colored people. Or go on your pocket-money. Get her out on it. Don't ask me for any. If you ask for my money you have to take my opinions along with it. If you don't, to hell with you, do without it."

"You get on the high horse and talk about yourself and your money when a friend of yours, a woman you knew, is in jail down there. Perhaps they're doing something to her, hurting her."

"She asked for it, it's the risk of the business, isn't it? She can't go into a business and howl afterwards. Everyone knows the risks. Let the committees and councils that are always sending me appeals for five-dollar dinners and twenty-dollar dinners get her out. This is New York. They must have collected thousands. I was at a meeting myself and saw them collect two hundred and fifty-seven thousand dollars! What a business, oh, boy!"

He looked seriously at the young man, then slapped his side, shouted, "Someone got up and just asked for it—I couldn't turn a trick like that. Oh, boy. And he got it. Listen to me, my boy. Flack says to make the revolution you don't need money. You can't buy the revolution on a silver teatray. That's what Flack says. You get high-paid officials, you give them out-of-pockets, you give them banquets and you get corruption. A lot of people think you can buy the revolution like you buy a pound of sugar, and it's as high as that too. Record high prices for revolution. Now revolution is pure, my boy, take it from me, I was a socialist as a boy. Don't try to buy your way into the revolution or way out. If she's sincere, and we'll see, my boy, I don't say she isn't, now is the time for us to find out. She's a nice girl. I don't say she doesn't mean it. But she took me for a ride. She's not straight."

"I've got to go down there, it's a question of honor."

At the young man's crestfallen air, he triumphed, but worked himself into a greater fury, saying, "You don't know the woman, it's blackmail, it's social blackmail, that's all the radicals and leftists are good for, social blackmail. I did maybe something she didn't like, why not, it's none of her business, and now she goes out of her way to involve you. Revenge, an old song. Ha, you're a mouthful to her. Nothing doing! She's got no respect for the rules of the game. To hell with her. Let her stay in jail. And when she comes out, I don't want you near her. That's all play-school stuff, playing round with—"

Seeing his son made no response, he continued for some time. At last, feeling he had won him over, he began to reason with him paternally. Gilbert went to bed very quietly. Grant, full of affection, went out to the kitchen and set Gilbert's tray for the morning. Grant thought to himself that now he had a reasonable young man—why not take a new apartment for the two of them with separate entrances, not as gaudy and expensive as the Pickwick, and so spend his remaining years decorously, with the love of one member of his family? He spent a few of his usual sleepless hours working it out. There were embarrassing details, but the young man had grown up; he too, for example, had affairs— Grant even thought, "My God, I should forgive him for wanting this girl gone native; I went with a real black girl myself."

When Grant got up in the morning, there was a note for him next to the letter which they had both written to Maxwell and Flora in Florida demanding $1,000. This note was from Gilbert, and said he had taken twenty-five dollars from his father's pocketbook, which, together with some money of his own, he calculated would get him down to Celia.

"I will expect you to send the rest, as you promised to Celia; and in the meantime, please take this as a general I O U for any expenses for myself and Celia. Please get Sam Banks for Celia."

Grant folded the note, went to the hatbox, and locked it in it. Then he started to think about the situation. He reviewed what Gilbert had told him, about the trusties, about the danger of organizing Negroes in the South, the terror and backwardness of the country. The town in which Gilbert would be, within twenty-four hours, was very violent, famous not only for its oppression of the black people but for its murder-rate. Grant at once telephoned his most serious radical friends, the Flacks. Gilbert had got himself in a jam just as bad as Claud March, and he wanted their advice before he went to a lawyer.

Flack said, "What do you want me to do? I'll take the train tonight. Is that what you want?"

"We don't want to act hastily. Let's give it our consideration. The young fool got himself into a jam. Let him learn. If I get him out right away, he'll follow her round, get in another tomorrow. He's got to learn his lesson. I learned mine. I got my fingers burned with the blonde, now I know. Let him learn."

"Get him out, with a lawyer, and get her out, too," said Flack.

"Boloney. Nothing doing! That's just what she wants. She wants to marry him. She found out he has a forchun. Let her

366

learn something too. I don't pay for women I take out to a couple of dinners and not even a kiss. They know why you take them out. You're married. They know why! Nothing doing. I'm not a sucker. She couldn't get me so she got her claws onto him. Nothing doing. We'll get him out, if they put him in."

"Good God, you can't go and bail out your son, the son of a rich man, and leave her in— The whole press will have it. What will you look like? He'll never forgive you."

"To hell with him! But the press—to hell with the press. I'll ring up a couple of journalists, tell them, give them a couple of brandies, tell them she went native and tried to get in my boy—"

They wrangled for a long time. At last Grant, furious with the world, yelled, "O.K.! O.K.! He wanted it this way. Let him stay there and find out what it's like. He won't be so romantic. He's a romantic. He's got to burn his fingers. She's a blonde, too. Let him stay there. There's a Southern Negro Congress, you say, is looking after him. Let them look after. They put up the money? Let them. I don't put up a cent. I didn't know they had any money. What kind of funds have they?"

"Not too much—about one hundred thousand dollars—at the utmost, not that."

Grant became thoughtful. He said at last, "Well, if I go to them and I say, 'Here's my son, a fine boy, but romantic, doesn't know that he's burning his fingers, some woman, a blonde, nice man, no doubt, but he's naïve, doesn't know—get him out and I'll give you a contribution'—how much, Flack? Eh? Twenty dollars? I give them a contribution, no check, in bills, twenty dollars, and I say, 'Get him out, he doesn't know what he's doing, just a Huck Finn, an escapade.' Eh? 'Young fellow got loose, lot of sympathy, don't take it seriously'—eh? 'Get him out. You have influence and here's my twenty dollars, no discount, the affair's a bonus to you.' Eh? 'And if you do it I'll tell everyone about your work, get you converts.' I'll get you lady converts, especially. Eh? No, I won't go there myself and you won't go there as my agent. We'll teach him a lesson and we'll go to them and give them a song and dance and say, 'A naïve young fellow, a Huck Finn, wants to save the world, whole responsibility of the capitalist monopolist system isn't on his shoulders, but he has no theory, and he runs after a blonde,' eh?—that's an intimate touch, a romantic touch, they'll get him out. I give them twenty dollars in bills. You go along, Flack, you say—'Here's fifteen dollars—

and he'll send a check—ten dollars and ten dollars if you get him out—' "

"Twenty dollars for a man and woman: in slave days they got more."

They wrangled.

Grant became very angry with Flack, whom he thought of as standing in his way. He shouted, "You're trying to get me and Gilbert into this. Your idea is not to get him out but to get me in. All you radicals are social blackmailers. Not to get him out. It's a simple thing, isn't it, to go to them and say, 'Here are ten dollars and you get ten dollars when you get him out'? Why won't you do it for me, as a favor?"

They parted in irritation. Flack said he would go down South and get the young man and Celia out himself with his own money, with the permission of the Congress. Grant was soothed by this and told Flack to telegraph him from the South—"Telegraph to Miss Robbins, not to me, for the boy's sake, I don't want the name mentioned, and call him—call him—Jack."

"All right, if you want it that way."

"Telegraph to Miss Robbins and call him Jack. And her, Barb—I said she was a red, by God," he said, and burst out laughing, but would not explain it.

The morning Flack left for the South, Edda telephoned Grant at David's request to say good-bye and promise that they would telegraph Miss Robbins with the name "Sinclair," which Grant had requested. After delivering this message, Edda said, "And here is a message from me. Do not weep for me, I am going along. I'm calling in at Washington where I have got a job in the foreign-language service of the Commerce Department. I hope to get through the interview successfully, and then, Robbie, we'll wipe your dust from our boots. I'm going to tell you now what I think of you—you ruined Papa and you ruined a lot of people. You promise them joy in the Never-Never but they work for you in the here and now. I know your game. I know your Land of Canaan. My memory's good. I'm taking charge of Papa and I substitute myself for Robert Grant. You don't have to bother about us any more. Keep your farms! Keep your honey. I saw enough etchings at any rate—"

"Don't say that, my girl, don't talk like that, I understand you, when it's a question of your father you're up in arms, you'd do anything, it's just like a tiger with her young, I understand

368

perfectly, you misunderstood me completely with the Land of Canaan—"

He stopped, laughed a little, tenderly, proceeded, "Rely on me, my dear girl, and don't get bitter at your age. If you need anything, I understand you, you're young, you're bitter, no boy-friend, you're Presbyterian you say, thin hair, big nose, you're bitter, if you need anything, telegraph Miss Robbins and sign Sinclair. I'll see about it. I'll take it to the Congress. I'll tell them, 'Here are two impartial outsiders taking your side, get in touch with Marcantonio, get in touch with anyone you like, send a telegram to Congress, I'll pay for it, they're helping out my boy, they're outsiders, you got him into this, you help him; I'll do what I can.'"

"I'm dying laughing! I can't help it. Well, good-bye," said Edda.

"Look, my dear girl, if you've got some grievance against me, let me know, I don't like things done in the dark."

"I'll let you know, you'll hear from me, we'll have a little chat," said she. Laughing, she rang off.

Grant had a bad day. In the evening he saw the blonde Mrs. Downs, told her the whole story of his relations with the Flacks. He said, "Flack's all right, in his way; I sort of like him, but I hate her, she's bitter and she has no romance. She doesn't understand me and she's bad-natured."

"You shouldn't have let them mix in this Southern affair, they'll involve you," said the blonde.

This idea kept him awake many hours.

"You keep right out of it, they'll only involve you and it'll cost you thousands. What is he but a spoiled young swine who never listens to a word you say, but goes off with all kinds of women, leads a libertine life, and calls it some idealism? Are you really taken in by Gilbert? You spoil him, I don't blame him, I don't say he's bad, and then when he gets in a jam you allow two people I wouldn't trust, two leftists, to go down South and represent you. You must be mad. You'll be in this for thousands, I say. Keep out of it. Wipe your boots and say good-day. If they telegraph, don't answer. Don't go near the Congress. They'll get the boy out, but let it be on their own hook. I'm tired of seeing you throw your money at everyone who asks for it, and buying cocktails for every bought woman and man like Goodwin. Keep out of it. They'll survive. You can't save the whole world. They'll get on without you. Take my advice."

He was torn between his duty to his son and the good sense

he found in the blonde. He had not realized that the Flacks would expect a contribution from him for their services, and for lawyers for Gilbert and Celia and probably later, if it became a newspaper item, for the Congress. How would he get out of it? People would come round sympathizing and asking for checks. He resolved not to go to the Congress and not to offer them ten dollars in a check or in bills. He had no foresight. He arose in great physical misery, dizzy, his heart beating wild. He walked up and down his disordered apartment, thinking of his ruined hopes of having a quiet place with his son, of Celia Grimm who had denied him, of everything that had happened. From what did all this misery come? From whom? He was a rich man, with plenty of friends and a good business, people came to him for loans. From whom did it come? Some enemy? Some fool? Some bad luck? He suffered. Upton wanted to give up the chicken farm for some girl. Gilbert was in jail for some girl. Flack was a slave of his daughter, this adder-tongued Edda. The blonde wanted *him*—she should have him. She alone had shown loyalty. He could actually feel his brain burning, it seemed to him; he could feel a network of fire. Would he get brain fever? Everyone deserted him. What harm did he do—ever? To anyone? He only thought of doing kindnesses to people. He promised them this, that, and the other, whatever they needed, in the kindness of his heart. If he couldn't perform, it was physically impossible. Who else had worried that much about that crowd? He laughed bitterly, "To hell with them all; I don't mean them any good and they'll get no good out of me. What did any of them do for me? It's all out of cupidity they stick to me. I have the art of waking up their cupidity even if they have none. If they have none I plant it in them. To hell with them."

When he got to the office, he found Miss Robbins with one telegram addressed to her and signed "Sinclair." He said, "It's a mistake, burn it, and if any more come, burn them. Don't let me hear any more about it."

52

He bought all the papers but was too impatient to read them. The blondine, whom he saw at night (putting off Mrs. Grant and the Goodwins, who were having a party), irritated him beyond endurance, in detailing the crimes of his friends. When he went home he determined to punish the Flacks for having got him into this intolerable situation. He wrote a letter to the Department in which Edda was to be a foreign-language secretary and told them what he knew about her, that she was immoral and a Communist and had gone down South to join a friend of hers, Celia Grimm, at present in jail in —— County. He told the views of Celia Grimm which he had heard, he said, from Edda Flack. When this went off—he walked far to post the letter so that it would not appear to have come from the district of his present hotel—he felt easier in mind and that night he slept better. It was the Flacks, he thought, who had tormented him and led Gilbert into this. To the blonde alone was he able to tell what he had done, he knew it would have her approval.

"Get rid of them, get rid of them," she said several times, and suddenly burst into a denunciation of him, putting on his shoulders all her sorrows as a woman. He was unable to bear it in his present lonely, bare state, and kept repeating, "Tell me what to do and I'll do it."

She at once told him certain things he must do: get rid of the Flacks, for good and all; get rid of Spatchwood, a man now whining and begging for the payment of the outstanding bills for the partly remodeled house in the St. Lawrence; send Mrs. Grant back to Boston; send Gilbert to the farm and not even $5,000 unless—and so forth.

He was pleased to have a program, for his affairs had reached an unhappy, aimless state. In the morning he wrote letters in his own style, to fill in the program they had made up the night before. He also wrote a letter to Laura telling her that he hoped the house was in order, for he hoped to come and see her after the war, talk things over with her and try to get themselves back to the old happy basis.

The next day Flack came back from the South, twinkling with his diplomatic and oratorical success in getting young Grant and Celia, too, out of jail. He had brought them back with him. He sat for an hour in Grant's office and vociferated joyously, that young Grant was a credit to the family, like those young fellows who—sensing the turn of opinion, sensing that a disunited country, a set of old realms, was turning into a modern democratic nation—started to give up privilege and profit, were real men, "Don't tell me men can't change—or perhaps they can't, but give them only a chance to prove they're human beings, with decent feelings, and they'll give up money, and even their future and even their homes, to do something creative, constructive, as you

371

say, Robbie, for the world—you've gone and got yourself a son like that. I'll wager you didn't mean to, you old bastard, but you shouldn't sow words on the wind, someone hears. You talk daily about socialism and now you've got yourself an honest son. And so whatever you do with your money, Robbie, one day it'll have a good use. Of course, I don't guarantee the future of any young man with Gilbert's expectations. A young man's a liberal just because his father is sitting on the dough, and he can become stricter than ever the old man was, once he pockets it— I don't say Gilbert is an angel, but he shows good signs. It just shows— free. people from pecuniary worries, without spoiling them, and they're good-hearted, willing to brave terror for a cause—or even a woman, as you're always saying. Why, he's your son, after all. You wanted to reconstruct Poland for a woman and he wants to reconstruct the South for a woman—if you want to put it in those chivalrous terms."

"For a woman, for a woman," said Grant a number of times, frowning and looking ill-pleased. When Flack left, he dictated a couple of letters to Miss Robbins, and then muttered to her energetically, "That man's no good, always trying to involve me, very inconsiderate. Sticks to nothing. Has no sense of measure. Question is sense of measure. I don't want any monkey business with Gilbert. Let him attend to business; he got me in plenty of jams. No sense of measure. Take this letter:

Dear Spatchwood,

I am sorry you let yourself in for a lot of expense about a house in the St. Lawrence, I never saw this house and could not have been interested in it and am sorry, as I see that you were so unbusinesslike as to go ahead and get specifications, etc., from architects, plumbers, carpenters. I must tell you that I am sorry to see an old friend in trouble, but I do not see that I am responsible. I see the letter you enclose. This letter was signed not by me but by David Flack. Kindly get in touch with him. He may have been undertaking this business on his own account, and I see he uses my letterhead, but believe me, I can do nothing for you. My commitments are large at present and I receive no monies from abroad. I have many dependents and many people expect me to help them out in a bad season. If you have no funds you should not have gone ahead on a project like this without confirmation from whomever you supposed to be your principal. If you did it for yourself, then those who went in with you must, I regret to say, suffer financially from having acted without proper commercial inquiry. Please do not write to me again about this house matter.

In the business of furs, you went beyond your instructions, Goodwin tells me, and have no written order from him, you acted on a telephone message: I know nothing of this. Your hard luck, you're an old business man. Re the jobbing in steel construction bars, look around for my friend Delafield, see what you can do, I want you to give us some ideas.

Yours,
R. O. G.
[Initialed illegibly only.]

He then went on to consider the situation of Di Giorgio, one of his managers from Italy, who had just arrived in the United States from Milan and apparently believed that Grant would recompense him for his loyalty during years of trouble, and even think favorably of him because he had been an anti-fascist. He mentioned some promise of Grant's which Grant could not call to mind, to employ Di Giorgio in one of the new businesses Grant would cause to be established in Brazil, the Argentine, or South Africa. Di Giorgio had been befriended by Laura, had actually lived in her attic for several years, and by her his life had been saved from the fascists, and he was doubly grateful. He had at last escaped to the mountains, then to Milan, and now to Grant, in whom he believed profoundly. He had come to him as an old soldier with scars to his captain.

Grant first muttered for some half hour about this rashness of Laura, sheltering enemies of the State in his house, where would it get him if reactionary powers took over? He thought there would be ten years' civil war in Europe before any state settled down. What did Di Giorgio mean by expecting gratitude after having put him in jeopardy like that? Nevertheless, he wrote a curt, vague, sentimental letter to Di Giorgio. His ex-manager replied at once, effusively; he would work for very little, in order to get a start, and would work at anything in Grant's employ.

Grant liked this letter, carried it about with him, and thought of it. Miss Robbins had the key to all his files, and even knew most of the material in the hatbox, for he had had Laura's letters all copied by Miss Robbins, and other such letters. Not only

Livy Wright, but the blonde too, had insisted that it was unsafe to let one woman know so much and an unmarried woman at that—"One day she will take you over, that'll be the cake of soap you slip on." He was becoming more timorous, had begun to notice, as he had never noticed, Miss Robbins' objections to his various small and, to him, amusing, innocent conspiracies. She was stiff, starched "Presbyterian," that was true. Supposing she met some man? She was still very good-looking in a Presbyterian way. Grant had quite enough of petty blackmail, with the Goodwin affair. Thus he presently reasoned himself into dismissing Miss Robbins, with three months' pay, saying, "I want to be fair to you, but I don't have much business now, it doesn't pay me, I'm going to Rome, too."

He had paid Miss Robbins $50 a week for some years past. He now was able to install Di Giorgio in the office, at $35 weekly, promising him a job in New Orleans or Buenos Aires very soon, as soon as things political quieted down.

Grant kept on occupying March's flat; meanwhile, Walker and Goodwin used the Pickwick Hotel place. This was the first Christmas that Grant did not go to Boston. March paid the servants at the flat and Walker and Goodwin gave the traditional tips to the people at the Pickwick: thus Grant had little reason for putting himself out so far as to go home. He also felt he could not leave the neighborhood of the blonde in the continuing crisis. She announced to him every day that Downs was going to sue on such and such a day, that the lawyer had filed papers, that the matter was coming up in court, that it was actually on the calendar and such things; and although advised by everyone to fly, Grant found it impossible to do so. He could not give up the excitement of this danger, and he did not want to leave the blonde: he actually wanted to submit to this ordeal with the blonde, even if she had caused the whole trouble, even if he suspected her motives from beginning to end, even if she did not love him, even if he was a laughing-stock to all his friends. It did not seem to be love, for he had a schoolboy's and seducer's tin pan alley view of love; but it was the outcome of his deep union with this woman. He was true to her, in their fashion; he was one with her. He could not depart and leave her to this foul and great experience, public shame, by herself. He had left other women to disgrace, and divorce, and had felt no emotions about the previous divorces of Mrs. Downs. He did not even ask himself why he was different, nor know that he was different. At times, the threatened public disgrace with all its side-issues seemed to him the greatest experience he could hope for. It would prove to everyone he was a lover, he was not the kind of man they thought, he was greater than they thought. Meanwhile, the blonde woman, with her peculiar hats and handbags, and her flat gleaming eyes, her hollow temples, her childish mask, went about from café to restaurant telling all her intimates the details of the story. Wherever Grant went, he met people who knew the story. It was a base but general triumph. He could not leave it. Yet he still fancied himself "in hiding" because he was in March's flat; and imagined somehow, that he had to go back to the March-Hoag society, where he could more freely discuss this affair. Here, naturally, they discussed the threatened divorce and gave their advice or offered to act as go-between. In the end, Hoag did apparently settle the matter, by arranging for Downs to withdraw his complaint, for Mrs. Downs to go once more to Reno, and for Grant to pay all expenses of any kind appertaining to this embroiled affair. It was not fair; but Grant had been having these dismaying, enthralling daily conferences with Mrs. Downs for weeks, even months on end, and was incapable for the time of getting out of it.

He had a strange dream about this time. He dreamed he was walking across muddy fields in wartime. The landscape was dreary: it was winter. He slipped into a mud-wallow and the more he struggled, the deeper he sank, till the slime filled his mouth, ears and nose, and approached his eyes: but he kept on seeing the heaving field. He felt the filth folding him in, in his armpits, round his waist, his limbs. He kept sinking but was not yet submerged. The dream did not fade. He told it to people. He believed it meant, "I am getting lower, I am sinking in mud."

53

Meanwhile, he became possessed of some more property. One day in June, 1944, Livy came from Philadelphia to meet him and begged him to lend her $4,000, which was the sum she owed on the houses she had contracted for in Montague Street, Brooklyn. She had not been able to meet payments and could borrow no more money against her own business in Philadelphia. As the houses were a sort of gauge from her to Grant, she hoped Grant might help her out. She was worn out with anxiety and business cares. She spent her strength, went down as fast as she came up. For old time's sake she thought Grant would help her, had no doubt: he risked nothing, if the worst came to the worst, he would get the houses from her. Grant, however, refused the loan. He reminded her that he had already been good to her, had done business through her, paid her her commission on the Swiss watches; and that he had warned her against pyramiding, a thing he had never done. He knew she had done it to get him, but why? He had no need of houses. He wanted a woman, not houses. He had too many houses and no real refuge.

Livy had counted on him. She knew him for a straight dealer in business, a joker in personal affairs, but a lover; they had spoken often of their future, their marriage and the arrangement of their properties to suit both parties. She went home and showed quite a different side of her nature. She sent him passionate, pleading letters, and passages of denunciation. He read them with intense interest and even ardor, but at the same time, arranged through an agent to take over the houses unknown to Livy. Presently he had a letter from her in which she said she was losing the houses as she had lost him and would lose her business perhaps; that she had lost heart, did not believe in life, if he could treat her in this manner; that if he did not send a check to save her within forty-eight hours, all would be lost and she would never see him again; that she was brokenhearted. The note was final: she had really given up hope. Grant did not answer the letter; and became possessed of two well-built, somewhat old-fashioned houses in Montague Street, which were sold to him at bargain prices. Livy knew real estate excellently. She had sifted the real estate offerings of the same kind in all New York and had picked out these as a rarity, a real acquisition. Each had at the bottom of the garden, a brick garage with an apartment above it. Each house had been used as a lodging house, and could soon be renovated so as to yield apartments for which he could charge high rents, especially in the present housing hunger. Grant knew all about the houses and their possibilities from Livy. He surveyed the houses and made arrangements for prudent alterations, putting Di Giorgio in charge of all this business. He was gradually getting out of the cotton business, selling out to his partners at an excellent price, and had now enough to employ Di Giorgio. He decided to use him as his factor, at the same salary, but with a promise of ten per cent on rental receipts at the end of the year.

In June, 1944, Rome fell and it became again possible for him to open a weekly correspondence with Laura Manganesi about the house on the Pincio. He told Laura that manifold business affairs kept him from visiting Rome, and put her off when she spoke of visiting New York to settle her financial affairs with him. Although their arrangement about her American property (which had been alien property and which he had been able to take over) were inavowable, she seemed to have perfect confidence in him and to expect him to give her some reasonable price for what he had taken over. He put off the discussion from month to month. At one time, in the autumn of 1944, when this discussion had been going on in weekly letters for some months, Grant had a letter from Laura's maid, Lina, a devoted servant of many years' standing. Lina, a plain, square-set, honest and pious old woman, had always sympathized with Grant and felt that her frivolous mistress had done him too much wrong: "You were a simple, affectionate man and she was a society woman who had too many admirers," she had told him after their break-up. Lina, in her letter, told Grant that she had served Laura during the war and all the troubles, because it was the best thing to do, and Laura had suffered bravely for her loyalty to an unpopular cause; she had earned the hatred of an elderly police official who had expected to win her at a word. She was still suffering, just as everyone was: she was cold, did not even eat enough. She could have let their house out in small apartments, in rooms, half-rooms, as they did in Rome at present, but she wanted to keep that house, which was Grant's and hers, in decent condition for Grant's sake, so as not to destroy its value. It was hard for her. She had a few faithful tenants from before the war, but she could not earn enough; she had taken a job as nurse, and still could not earn enough. She could not afford to keep Lina or even the man who did the heavy work, and was obliged to stoke the furnaces, sweep up the coal, and do the cooking. She did all this very cheerfully and like a brave woman, said Lina, but she had grown older, and now she seemed to have lost hope: she did not believe that Grant would come; or she believed that he would come too late. She believed her old lover would not pay her anything at all, or would only pay her five per cent, which would never be enough. She had actually been to a lawyer and the lawyer had said he could do nothing, her title was not clear. For, said Lina, Mme. Manganesi had thought of selling the house and dividing up the price fairly between Grant and herself. Then she would go to her cousin's farm and die there. Things were bad. Everything was black-market. Laura could not live. Lina begged Mr. Grant to think about this urgent matter.

Grant did not answer this letter, but presently wrote to Laura that he could not come to Rome for some long time. Conditions were unsettled, he had to assist his son Gilbert in a new business Gilbert had taken up, technical films, "and you know that I am glad to see some idea take root in that virgin skull." Following upon this, he wrote to Laura that he had contracted a very unpleasant, even disgraceful, disease and would not be able to frequent honest society for a considerable time and could not think of traveling. The week after this, he wrote to Laura that she must not think of coming to New York, that nationals of enemy countries were hated in the city, and that she would never get her permission in any case. He followed these by other letters. He knew that Lina knew her mistress very well; he trusted to Lina's letter. He believed Laura could easily die of a broken heart now, and then his title would be clear in Rome.

He was busy: his days were full. He was even getting enough mail to divide between Di Giorgio and Flack. Flack had established himself with his daughter in a small flat near 125th Street and Broadway, for which the rent was $45 monthly. Edda had not got the job she hoped for in Washington, but on returning to New York City had at once got another job at $60 weekly, so that the Flacks were in no way dependent upon him. From time to time, Grant would take them out to dinner or go to a newsreel with them. Their relations were much as before. Edda was a little more friendly to him than before, having suffered, and needing Grant more than before. Her father was now permanently feeble, with a dangerous, though never painful, malady, and could only work intermittently: the work Grant gave him, Grant's quarterly accounts, Grant's personal letters, the affairs of Largo Farm, was quiet work, and although he received no ordinary payment, it was understood that presently, when things were fixed up in Europe, Edda and David would go with Grant to Rome, live there peaceably. David would do Grant's accounts, act as general factor, and Edda would get a job somewhere, with the Americans no doubt: she knew French and Italian. David needed this security in his present state and Edda now partly trusted Grant. They had no attraction for each other as man and woman, but each was tired of the long contest of wills.

One day, when lunching with March and Hoag at the Bankers' Club, March smiled between his hanging jowls and said quietly, "There's a fellow in town asking for you, Mr. Hilbertson, seems anxious to meet you, seems very anxious to meet you. I didn't give him your address: not my affair."

After a hesitation, Grant replied, with a slight flush, "Can't have anything to say to me: a hasbeen, oldtimer; knew him twenty years ago. Lost touch."

"He said, his opinion seemed to be, that he had some unfinished business."

"Don't remember any. If that's so, let him come to me, let him come to me."

"He was very anxious to come at you, he said."

"Let him come to me, then."

"He seemed to have something on his mind, not my affair. I didn't tell him your address. Said he was in Boston, you weren't there. He seems genuinely anxious to meet you."

Grant was silent, but looked suspiciously at March. March added, "He had a band on his arm: I hear his wife passed away last month."

"Sorry to hear that, sorry, sorry! He was very fond of her." Grant became as if doubtful and drooping.

There were days when Grant, released from business and with too much spare time on his hands, had fits of depression. In one of these he wrote to Laura:

My dear Laura,

Here is five hundred dollars which I send you because I heard you were not too well off. Spend it wisely. Money is never too easy to acquire. I have been very sick with headaches, and wish I could see you, you always had something for that. Also, my wife is here, so much to do. My son, Gilbert, I never depended on him, suddenly left me with the farm on my hands and went to Hollywood with a certain Sergey, to make educational films. He won't do anything by it. I know him: he'll soon come begging. In the meantime, much expense. Must get someone else to run my farm, I have in view Upton, a reliable person, who got married recently to a woman who wants money. As to Di Giorgio, you know him, but I think he has degenerated during the war. It happens: we mustn't ask too many questions of those who went through fascism. He told me much about you and so I send you the five hundred dollars, a present, why not? I am glad to do something. I don't expect to be in Europe for a year. I am not well. Something spinal. Better look out for a buyer, sell the best you can and we will discuss the results. You will get your percentage on the sale.

[Signed illegibly] R. G.

Laura, upon receiving this, went to bed, could make no business deals, and was very easily persuaded to sign all necessary documents to get rid of the house to the third party. She then went with a friend to Tripoli, in Libya, with the intention of not returning, thus leaving her farm in the hands of her incompetent relatives. It was thought generally that soon she would have no place to come back to. Grant instructed Santelli, a former Roman employee, who had been hiding in the mountains from the fascists, and had now returned, to look into the matter. If one could save it for Laura, well and good; if it were sold at public auction, then one must take care of it, see it did not pass into alien hands. He would give Santelli the money to buy it in, though not Laura, for he did not "want Laura to get any ideas."

54

He began to see something in certain kinds of women that he had not seen before. A woman had laughed at him one evening when he had come into Manetti's, looking haggard. He now saw that in certain types, these befurred and strange-hatted types, the ringed and powdered ones, their "hard laugh showed their hard hearts." He never looked at young girls: he had met a few recently with rough tongues. He met every day Mrs. Goodwin, Gussy, a few modest women like that, but the blonde was too much for him. Her way of life was not his. She never rose till twelve or two in the day and he could not help rising, as he had always done, at six-thirty. By three he was fatigued, he wanted to "take a stretch." And the blonde saw little of him; she was very much in the power of Alexis at that moment. Grant's wife kept coming to New York to find out what he was doing and had written a letter of complaint to Gilbert, which Gilbert had sent on to his father, with a polite note.

Grant suddenly gave up the March flat in which he had been all this time and went to live in one of the two Brooklyn houses. This one had already been altered and made modern. He now began to live quietly in the first floor of the house in Montague Street, with Mrs. MacDonald downstairs, a whole apartment to herself. She made his meals, pressed his clothes, darned his socks, "like a mother," and did all for $40 a month, his theory being that if she wished she could work for the other bachelors in the house. She found the basement humid, could hardly make the beds for the others, had to employ a young schoolgirl to help her, out of her money, yet she stayed with him because he promised that very soon, in the summer, they would go to the farm with Mrs. Goodwin. Mrs. Goodwin would run things and Mrs. MacDonald would have little to do.

His affair with Mrs. Goodwin continued. He could see she was really in love with him. He was able to get along with her, never giving her anything: this astonished and flattered him. He often felt a bit queer about this relationship and would promise her that she and Alfred would soon go on the chicken farm, Alfred as the manager, she as housekeeper, so that she could look after Alfred's health. He was very strange, "psychopathic" everyone said, perhaps partly mad—at any rate, almost uncontrollable. Betty would cry to Grant that she had so many, many terrible scenes with Goodwin, and would have left him, as she had threatened, but that Goodwin either à propos of this or of nothing at all, would say, "If you make a move to leave me, not that I want you so much, but I don't intend to let that whoremaster get you, if you do, I go to the District Attorney."

"What have you on him?" Betty asked many times.

He had not told her until recently, very inflated, convinced that he had done many things of state, for example, that he had supported General de Gaulle and this was the reason for the General's success. Grant had better beware of him. Grant trembled at this notion, though Betty would clutch his sleeve and repeat, "Don't you understand that Alf is half-crazy! He told me he is going to finish Mussolini and that you and that blonde are like Mussolini and Clara Petacci and he'll sell you for tripe."

Grant said, "She's only a woman, not her fault: if a woman's at fault, it's the man: she loves him, she can't tell him, 'You're a four-flusher,' can she?"

"Robbie, old boy, don't argue with me. I'm telling you Alf's crazy. He says you're a Red but he wants to see if your blood is not white, one day he'll just try and see. I wish you'd go away, even if it's to Rome."

Grant shivered horribly and said, "Don't say things like that."

"I know; but Alf's crazy and that's what he believes. Now, I've got to keep him quiet for your sake."

"Yes, yes, I know. What does he say?"

The devoted woman said, "It's a terrible story, but this is what he says: That he learned it all from James Alexis and that this is the real reason why you are partners in the blondine."

"In the blonde!" He started and moved away from her.

"I'm only saying what I heard; I wanted to tell it to you weeks ago. We were at home and Alf had one of his fits on him, it's terrible, I don't know how I stand it, but I do it for you, for he keeps up this song, 'I'll go to the D.A. I'll be crazy. I know you think I am. You all think I am. I'm not so crazy. I can get fifty per cent dividend out of being crazy. That's the kind of crazy I am.' You know the way he goes on. Then he says, 'I know you're sweet on the bully-boy. I kept tabs on you. You both made a fool of me. I'll see he gets it where the chicken got the ax. I take my own good time. He'll buy my drawers and toothpaste and prophylactics, till the statute of limitations, and then some.' I felt very bad, Robbie, I felt very bad, I can't stand the man, but he said often, if I leave him he'll go straight to the D.A. about you. I said to him about two weeks ago, 'But tell me, Alf, finally, what you know about him? I really think you're crazy. Don't you know he wants you to go out on his chicken farm, be his manager—what can you have against him?—you mustn't be neurotic.' He said, 'Oh, don't worry, you won't get it out of me till I want to tell it,' but at last, Robbie, he did tell me, and I'm telling you what he thinks he has on you. I don't think for a moment it's true, but a letter of denunciation can say just one thing that's true and the rest is carried along with it. And they have that file on you in that affair with the blonde. They'll put Alf on record and they'll just add to your file, even if it isn't true: what do they know? My dear, I'm so sorry—"

"It's all right, what does he say? The point is, what does he think he's got? Don't hold you responsible—"

"He says, Grant Associates sent bales of cotton from Brazil which contained small scattered pieces of rare alloys essential to the Nazi war effort. I'm sure that's right, for I listened very carefully, you can imagine. You said you exported only cotton and they put the alloys in when your back was turned. And Alf goes on, 'And the bully-boy has a long and big back so that's possible, though not probable.' The British let it get through to Cadiz. Ultimate destination was some place in Nazi Germany."

"It's a terrible story, he can't prove it," said Grant.

"He says he can. I asked him, naturally—such a fantastic story! He says the German bank paid the Spanish bank two checks, one for alloys and one for cotton. They paid somewhere about one million Spanish pesetas; roughly two hundred and fifty thousand pesetas for cotton and roughly seven hundred and fifty thousand pesetas Spanish for alloys. The Spanish bank—just like the Spanish says Alf, only I think there might have been a friend of the resistance in it, myself—paid two checks to Rio, one equaling the amount paid for cotton and one the amount paid for alloys. And all paid like that, in that incriminating manner, to Grant's Associates. Now there are two reasons to examine this story, Robbie. Is it true? Who made it up? A third reason, my darling —is there someone in your business, or among your awful friends, say, March, who has power and who hates you, is out for blood?"

"Look, glad you told me, correct, correct thing to do, but very upset. A great shock. Alf shouldn't say things like that. You better get him put away. Look, in every organization there is someone thought you trod on his toes once. You don't know who it is, don't know how to put your finger on him. Got to watch out with anyone. Everyone has an inflated ego, is greedy, wants what you have. A lot of people don't like me, I did no harm, but they don't like me. Got nothing on me; but don't like me. It could be anyone. Did he say anything else? James Alexis—James Alexis—it couldn't be—nonsense—"

"Well, listen, Robbie, this is what he says he's going to tell the D.A. I know he's crazy. I'm frightened for all of us. You had better know, whether it's dream-stuff or not. I don't ask; I don't want to know. I'm only thinking of you. Alf says they have the goods on Grant Associates if they want to come down on you. He says, 'Some slip-up, eh? Robbie didn't know. Where did I hear a commercial like that? Some line. Let him tell it to the judge.' And, Robbie, he knows about us, he keeps on about it, he's a very coarse man; he said, 'I hear it from James Alexis, your sweetie's best friend, and does that explain their fifty per cent partnership in the Honey?' And he means Mrs. Downs, Robbie. He said last night, 'The other day, I gave you the straight tip,

I tipped you off, you better not tell Grant. I got his number and I'll know if you tip him off. He's going to buy me drawers until the statute of limitations and then some more.' That's his mania now. Oh, watch out for him, Robbie, and watch out for James Alexis, he sold you out."

"Thanks, darling," said Robert, very gruff and greatly disturbed. Between them, they arranged for Betty to watch Alfred Goodwin at every hour of the day and night. Grant would arrange for the holiday at the farm as soon as possible. But he had decided to give Upton a free hand, as Upton had improved considerably since his marriage, and the young wife was an excellent cheap drudge at the farm. They wrote letters every day, now, about the questions of new boilers, new bed linen, new brooms, new wire netting, new curry combs, and this kept Grant in an agreeable fever. He did not mind the Goodwin danger if nothing at all happened, and he sweetened Goodwin by going into numerous small businesses with him.

55

This went on till the spring of 1945. He once more stayed in New York for Christmas. He as usual spent New Year's Eve with the Flacks, his luck. Mrs. MacDonald was now pottering about in the basement and Grant was happy with her. She gave him sour and sage advice and occasionally came to him with her hand out, asking for extra money for the housekeeping or saying he must pay her more. He enjoyed going into these matters for hours, reducing her to tears, hearing her bitter, honest remarks about himself, and at length giving her a few dollars. He would always chuckle and feel tender. He never allowed Livy Wright to come to New York, but went to visit her in Philadelphia occasionally, and pretended in fact, that he was living in town with his wife and Andrew but that out of terror of his wife he could not give anyone his address.

He allowed the blonde to visit him there, but only because James Alexis was now living at the Pandulfo Hotel in Brooklyn Heights, very near him, and he wanted to keep James Alexis sweet. He paid no more weekly salary to the blonde and rejoiced at what he saw in pencil in the back of a little book he kept for expenses.

The blonde had, however, a key to his apartment. It happened one day that he had been looking through his papers in the old yellow leather hatbox, and had gone to the bathroom for a moment to look at his complexion. If it was an effect of the harsh, virgin light of this spring day, he really looked so bad, he did not know; but in the shaving mirror, he saw himself, a hangdog, ash-gray, baldheaded man with vacant eyes: he was old at last. Yet he had bathed and perfumed himself this morning as other mornings. It was perhaps that he had been up too late with the wrong woman the night before. At other times, he would have dismissed this face with that excuse. Today, he felt a return of manhood. He looked at the face he saw in the shaving mirror, and thought, "That is I: that is how I look to them; I feel the same: but I have known for a long time how old I am—the things they say in stores when they are not trying to insult me. I am old and it is only a day or two since I was a young man. This spring I will be an old man, with yellow hanging chops: they won't even look at me, wonder if it is worth while playing me for my pocketbook." In business he had always seen clearly, not deceived himself: of course, he had this perspicacity. He now did not use it in business and it came back like a sharp knife, cutting the cataracts of dream from his eyes, painfully, in his private life. He had only his private life to live for: he had become a small man.

Grant looked profoundly at himself, passing his hand over his jowl. He thought of many things. He became a little puzzled, as at a distance, as a man who tries to puzzle out an accident five hundred yards off at the end of the streetcar line. He did not know what it was he was puzzled about, some moral question? He had never thought of such things: it had all been clear to him: it was settled. He had always been gay. He had done wrong things and made mistakes, but nothing wrong "in a biological sense."

The house in which he lived had formerly been a private residence with a large drawing room on the ground floor, and this large salon was still entered by two magnificent sliding doors which he never kept locked. It amused him to be able to slide the noiseless doors apart and pad out in his slippers and pad downstairs or upstairs, and make no noise, or merely to look out when the mailman came.

Thus he had left his doors on the slide, in forgetfulness, this day, with the papers from the hatbox strewn on the large oval center table, and when he came back from creaming his face, found the blonde in the apartment, seated on a divan and putting on make-up. The papers appeared to him to be the same as before, which alone to him appeared unnatural, for he knew the blonde's curious and acquisitive nature. The blonde Mrs. Downs showed her small damp elastic swimsuit, of an emerald green, an almost unobtainable black-market item which he had got for her, and said she had been having a suntan with James Alexis at the Pandulfo, and had dropped in for tea, but had just remembered an appointment with her dear mother, who was suffering from twinges of rheumatism; and so she went.

This departure seemed very odd to Grant, who was used to the blonde at least asking for some simple thing, like a cake of soap or a stick of chewing gum, before she went; and he went very carefully through his papers. She must have been already in Manhattan when he discovered that she had taken from the strewn documents a letter from some solicitors at Charlottetown, Prince Edward Island, dated some years back, which revealed quite clearly that Grant had in 1936 arranged for his total property, save in potentially enemy countries, to be vested in two corporations, the first ultimately to be controlled by Gilbert, his son, and the second by Andrew, his young son, in Prince Edward Island. The ostensible offices of the corporations, called Timber Wolf Furs, Ltd. (Gilbert), and Positive-Bitkoff Corporation, Ltd. (Andrew), were both at Charlottetown, in a solicitor's office. This was all, of course, to avoid estate taxes and to minimize American income taxes. However, in order to make the whole situation correct, and no trouble when the estate passed into his boys' hands, these corporations had actually long been the property of the two boys, and he actually had had the share certificates issued by the secretary, in the names of, respectively, Gilbert Grant, and in the name of Andrew Grant, a minor, for whom he was a trustee, only to the age of twenty-one. Seventy-five per cent of the estate was in the Timber Wolf Furs (Gilbert) corporation, and twenty-five per cent in the Positive-Bitkoff (Andrew) corporation. If the blondine were to reveal this situation to the boys or to their mother, she would, of course, gain absolutely nothing, and she could not denounce him to the income-tax authorities since it was strictly legal. But Gilbert, very dissatisfied with his father, his wretched salary, and oddities of accounting at the day-old chick farm, had run away to Hollywood with his friend Sergey and was dunning his father for a loan for his films, the $10,000 promised having never been paid. He was very angry with his father. He believed sincerely in his educational films

386

project and was trying to get money for it. If the blondine were to reveal to Gilbert that he owned outright seventy-five per cent of his father's estate, Grant would at one stroke be reduced from $1,800,000 to $450,000, and from his point of view would be ruined and have to go back to work.

As soon as he could suppose her at home, Grant called up the blonde and said, "Sweetie, the wind blew in and disarranged my papers when I was sorting them. You didn't see a bit of any on the floor?"

She said, "Yes, I did, dear; and I have it with me, I kept it for you, you're so careless. I think you need a keeper. I think you hedged yourself out. You want me to look after you. Now, I'm a good housekeeper, and I think you need someone with you, not an old woman, because you're all alone and I know Alf Goodwin is threatening you. Let's meet for a little chat at the Pandulfo tomorrow."

When they met the next day, Grant said angrily, "You can't do a thing, it means nothing, it's worth nothing."

The blonde only said, "To me, darling, it's worth nothing, and to you it's worth a great big loss, but Gilbert has only to go to Prince Edward Island and identify himself and you would be in the soup. He wants to go to work. He wants to run his own corporation."

"Look, darling, we must have a little chat."

"Robbie, you know I have a rent problem."

56

The upshot was that Grant ejected Mrs. MacDonald, telling her she was a very fine old lady and must go and live with her daughter and giving her half a month's pay. The next day the blondine came to live with him, in the large basement apartment, and became his superintendent and rent-collector. She was an excellent superintendent. She saved money, begged milk and Coca-Cola bottles from their tenants, in order to get the deposit money, had Grant's old shirts and suits turned. Grant was enchanted and kept saying that his wife had never thought of that.

Meanwhile, Grant kept his office going downtown, but now it mainly existed to receive letters he could not receive at the Montague Street house.

Once a week, usually on Sunday, he visited the Flacks for lunch or dinner. Edda was a good cook and prepared a quantity of food for him. He had contracted the curious habit of taking his old-fashioned yellow leather hatbox with him whenever he went out. David, who spent his time in the apartment and on Riverside Drive, when the weather was mild, reproached him with, "Robbie, why don't you put the blamed papers in a safe deposit and then you won't be afraid of the blondine or anyone on earth."

And Grant laughed powerfully at this, repeated, "I'm not afraid of her, nor anyone on earth, but the Government: one day they'll come down, open all the boxes to hook out the black-market money, and something will stick to their fingers. I'd do it myself. I wasn't so innocent myself, ha-ha."

"Don't carry it about with you, Robbie."

"Look, Davie, I know what I'm doing. I go along that terrace. I go down by the steps to the quays by the East River, and I think, ha-ha, if I dropped the whole bunch of papers, what a bouquet for the crabs and smelts, I don't know what they have down in that mud. Once I saw a young man about twenty, in a blue shirt, floating down that river, and only his back showed. He had white skin, a thick neck and blond hair like me when I was like him. I'll give the whole lot to him. Did I work for that piker with his Sergey, for that 'ooman with her sofa, for a neurotic, draws white horses and pink marguerites? It'll be the only fun I will have after—when I'm—after—in the hereafter— seeing them scrambling for it, maybe they'll employ a diver, or a steam-shovel, get up the hatbox from the crabs. Ha-ha."

"I'm not worrying about that, I'm not worrying about what happens to them; I'm thinking about you, Robbie; I love you. One of these days, someone will think you have something in that box you always carry about with you, and they'll do you in. I know damn well you'll never throw it in the East River. I know you. But the yellow blonde may do a little thinking about the yellow hatbox; I'm worried about you. And don't go and get it in your big empty head I'm thinking about the dough. Profit has been the ruin of you."

"I'm with you, my boy. If I'd been in a place where they had a law prevented me from putting my hand in your pocket, I would have been a good commissar for pushcarts. Ha-ha."

One evening in the late spring, Grant went home with his hatbox from the Flacks'. The Hudson was almost red with the setting sun. Grant took a taxi to Brooklyn, but paid the man off before his home as he always did, in a foolish, unthinking notion of precaution, and walked along the heights to observe, as always, the East River. Of course, he would not throw his hatbox in, but he laughed and thought of the divers, the cranes, the Bucyris: but perhaps it would float? He got home before the blonde, and began, as several times before, to search in her apartment, among her valises and closets, for the missing paper. What a smart fox she was!

From now on, the former Mrs. Downs lived in the basement apartment which she had as Grant's superintendent. She had a good deal of freedom, collected the rents, at which she was very exact and agreeable, paid the taxes, at which she was as neat and hairsplitting as an accountant, and spent most of her evenings with Grant.

Grant's apartment was on the first floor, raised slightly above street level. A grand sitting room led into a large, airy back room used as a bedroom by Grant. A hall ran past the doors of both rooms to an apartment in the back, containing a kitchen and bathroom. The windows from both their apartments looked out over a small plot. Mrs. Downs and Grant managed both buildings, and were about to buy an excellent house in the same district for $10,000. This house, with some $3,000 improvements and similarly constructed, could be built up to the same condition and would bring in considerable rents from wealthy employees and artists.

In the evening, Grant lounged in the sitting room or parlor, by the big windows overlooking the street, his shirt sleeves rolled above the elbows, his horn-rimmed spectacles on, and his legs stretched out like felled trees, beside him a bottle of beer. Mrs. Downs, who was fond of knitting, would often sit opposite him in the opposite pair of windows, with a half-jersey already knitted on her needles, wearing an unbecoming knitted jacket buttoned up to the neck. She did not have to look at the clock in the hall. She knew the exact hour by the goings and comings of people, sounds in the house—someone who went down and came upstairs, even the fall of shadows, the cries of birds, a child bouncing a ball, a cat mewing. When a certain hour had come, she would put on some extraordinary red hat she had bought, or else knot over her head some odd cheap square of cotton she had bought for a bargain at a local department store in the Heights, and would go out to buy some provisions for the evening, meat, beer, milk, vegetables. If she was too long away, Grant would frown and ask her roughly upon coming in, "Did you go to the Pan-dulfo?"

She would show him her swimsuit, and say, "Yes, I went to get a suntan and a swim and I met James Alexis."

James Alexis, now an old man but lively and vain about his love affairs, still kept an apartment in the Pandulfo for his New York visits. But now he came rarely. Grant knew that the blonde woman met him there, but constantly hoped for business from him. Unlike himself, James Alexis had gone out to make money, and now was worth about $5,000,000.

Sometimes, as in the old days, when Grant did not want to sleep in the evening, he, Alexis, Mrs. Downs, or he and Alexis and two young women would have a party. The situation pleased him very much. Mrs. Grant had retired to a long silence in Boston. The young boy was declared to be a great painter in embryo, and Grant would write one letter a week, adjuring the boy to work hard and do well, and to think a little also about earning a little money, there were all kinds of things today—comic strips, the movies, educational films, like Walt Disney, and even war factories, during war times painted to look like fields of cotton.

Grant still kept his office in Hanover Square. He would arrive there later than before, about ten, and say to Di Giorgio, now raised to $37.50 a week, "Where's the mail? Let's see the mail."

There was rarely any mail. At each mail-hour he would spring up from his easy chair or couch, rush to the outer office, and say, "What's in the mail? Let me see the mail at once."

Very often he sent Di Giorgio on long errands through the city, and when he came back he would find Grant "taking a stretch" on the sofa and would say, "Well, you have not much to do, Mr. Grant. Why don't you take a walk?"

Grant would then spring and say angrily, "I'm exhausted with work. I have everything to think out, you do nothing."

And he would dictate some letter which must be sent out to two hundred or so correspondents, not multigraphed, but typed by a typist, offering goods which no longer existed, or could not now be handled internationally on account of local tariffs, exchanges, or nationalization. If he sent out six hundred letters he would get back two hundred answers, and be happy for a day or two—but no business resulted. Sometimes he resorted to misquoting prices and materials, so that some correspondence could ensue about these mistaken figures or quality. He would take on partners, old friends like Delafield and Goodwin, and lose them because there was no more business. The world was a monopoly or the commodity was controlled or the product was under Government control or black-marketeers were shot or the exchanges were closed. The world had moved away from old-line private enterprise.

After a very wearing day, he would go uptown to some bar for a tea and chat with some new woman, but rarely found one to "give him a thrill," as he thought of it. At night he went home and sat in his shirt sleeves, reading a great number of fresh-smelling evening papers, with the blonde opposite.

Night would come. The blonde would put on the lamp. There were many lamps. The expense was considerable, but Grant preferred this light for he did not know what was in the shadows. It seemed to him that he could not make out what was there, that people were concealing things from him. Also, Death might be there. He believed really in Death. He believed that when Death came for him, Death would knock on the door and he would hear the rap. Sometimes when he and the blonde sat there they would laugh, talk some gossip, and sometimes concoct an anonymous letter between them—the world, they knew, was a vile, dishonest place, and no man could go before the police and say, "You have nothing on me," and if he could—there was more fun in their denunciations; for as Grant had reasoned one day, "The Flacks, you know, three times in succession lived opposite a church, and suppose a bomb had burst in that church—eh? What does it look like?"

But this intellectual pastime would only come to them at the change of season, toward Christmas-time or New Year, when the world began to stir. Most times they sat by the window, Grant handed the comics to the blondine, and they went to bed about nine o'clock.

All the evening one of the lamps would have been shining on the old-fashioned yellow leather hatbox standing on the marble mantelpiece. At night Grant, who still, as always, slept alone, put it beside him, removing a pillow for the purpose, and locked the door. The window had iron bars on it.

A fine-looking Negro woman, strong, young and severe, now came to do the household chores for Mrs. Downs; they called her Marsha. One day, when Grant came home and found Mrs. Downs out, Marsha told him that an old man came to ask for him and asked a lot of questions about him, spent half an hour at the door,

"I didn't ask him in, not knowing who he was. He asked who you were and how old you were and what you did, in business; and I said, Mr. Grant, that I didn't know at all. He didn't give a name, or he said something but I couldn't understand the way he said it. Something like Gilbert."

"Like Gilbert!" screamed Grant.

"I don't know, Mr. Grant, he had a funny accent."

"Was it like a Southern accent?" said Grant.

"I don't know." She became surly. Grant who knew that he had once earned her dislike by saying he had lived in the South, looked dubiously at her but did not dare to press her. Yet he knew that with her ear, she must have known the origin of the man. After a moment, he said, gently, "It wasn't Hilbertson?"

"I don't know."

He felt faint, but he had suffered much from his heart for several years. He liked the strong, handsome woman, and did not want to alienate her. He had made one faux-pas by saying he had business in New Orleans and had once known a lovely woman there. Since that moment, Marsha had had no more confidence in him. He was disturbed and could do nothing till the blonde came home. By her sharp, suspicious discussion, she soothed away his fears. Still, at present, he suffered too much. For several years he had been under the tyranny of this heart anguish. He did not suppose the old man was Hilbertson, but still he would wake at night and hear his heart beating. He had peculiar dreams. He would wake up to hear his heart beating fiercely. He suffered. Sometimes in the daytime, when he was out, and he managed to make an appointment with some woman, not too young, not too old, he would feel the sun shine on him again. He always went with working women because they needed more, they expected less, and, in his parlance, "sued him less."

One day, while he was out, and the blonde was at home, a man came to the door and asked for Grant. He was a very tall, strong, but bent, old man, with blue eyes and big hands. He looked the blonde over for a while, smiled, and asked her if she would come and have some tea and a little chat with him, one day soon, in some place quite near, say the Pandulfo, and what day would she be free, Sunday? The blonde invited the man in. He said, to begin with, that he was a very old friend of Grant's, a friend from way back, and he had been looking for a long time to renew relations with his old partner; but he had not been able to, his wife had been sick for a long time. Now, his poor dear wife was no more; and he was free to come up North and look up old acquaintances. The blonde said she led a quiet life here and Grant was not the man that he had known, no doubt. He stayed in all day Saturday and Sunday reading the papers, even the comics, not at all like him, never went to a cabaret, hardly ever went out to dinner; and one of the reasons was that he was getting foolish— he took everywhere with him his old yellow hatbox. It made them conspicuous and he wouldn't even check it."

The old man had said, "What is in the yellow hatbox? Love-letters, I suppose?"

"Oh, no. He only carries things worth money in that."

The old man, who was well dressed and had that imposing air of a man who had once had great charm and not wasted it with prostitutes, a man who still carried in him his passion, smiled charmingly at the blonde, "Then perhaps on Sunday, when he is at home, you can slip out for an hour or two. To the Pandulfo— or you name the place? I would rather you named the place."

The blonde was attracted to this splendid old man; and on the Sunday morning, she dressed carefully, putting on her newest and most strange red hat, and went out, leaving Grant alone. He was sitting in his shirt-sleeves before the long windows, as usual, and paid no attention to her.

When she had been gone about fifteen minutes, the doorbell rang and Grant answered it. He was at ease. He had his spectacles on and was still in his shirt-sleeves, with his shirt open at the neck showing his strong hairy chest. He had rested. He looked fresh and his eyes were gay and clear. He still had the Sunday supplement in his hand when he opened the door.

At the door was a strong, bent old man with large eyes, intense as jewels.

"Hilbertson," said Grant.

"Not a bad memory. You remember what I said?"

"It's a great mistake, it was all a mistake," said Grant. The Sunday supplement fell from his hand, he stepped back without thinking. He became pale with fright.

"You're quite an old man now," said Hilbertson.

"You are old too," said Grant, but he gasped: he could hardly get the words out. He watched Hilbertson, whose hand was in his pocket. Suddenly, Grant fainted. Hilbertson looked a while and closed the door.

When Mrs. Downs came home, about an hour later, she put her key in the door, opened it and gave a short cry when she saw

Grant lying in the hall, in his shirt-sleeves, with the paper near him and his horn-rimmed spectacles fallen off, without being broken. She went up to him, listened to his heart and then sat on her haunches beside him, thinking, her brilliant eyes large and gleaming. What should she do? She had only $15 in her purse, the rent coming for next Saturday, her luggage, a few things she could at once take from Grant's apartment—some bottle returns. That was the total. Suppose she took the hatbox? That would be a bright idea. But she had few friends but her mother. Alexis had gone away, and at present his friendship was rather dangerous than otherwise. She was friendly with the police and yet did not want too many inquiries. At her age, when with her hard struggles and the unkindness of men she sometimes looked like a faded working-class forty, she must be careful. She did not want to go back to some Peacock Alley or other and wait, wait—Grant had been close to her. She got up and looked for some time at the hatbox lurking on Grant's other unused pillow in the double bed he always occupied. After thinking a long while, without touching anything, she rang up the police.

THE END

Other VIRAGO MODERN CLASSICS

SYLVIA ASHTON-WARNER
Spinster

MARGARET ATWOOD
The Edible Woman
Surfacing

JANE BOWLES
Two Serious Ladies

KAY BOYLE
Plagued by the Nightingale

ANGELA CARTER
The Magic Toyshop

BARBARA COMYNS
The Vet's Daughter

ELIZABETH HARDWICK
Sleepless Nights

EMILY HOLMES COLEMAN
The Shutter of Snow

ROSAMOND LEHMANN
Invitation to the Waltz
The Weather in the Streets

TILLIE OLSEN
Tell Me a Riddle
Yonnondio: From the Thirties

GRACE PALEY
Enormous Changes at
   the Last Minute
The Little Disturbances of Man

STEVIE SMITH
The Holiday
Novel on Yellow Paper
Over the Frontier

CHRISTINA STEAD
Cotter's England
For Love Alone
Letty Fox: Her Luck

SYLVIA TOWNSEND
WARNER
Mr. Fortune's Maggot
The True Heart

REBECCA WEST
The Return of the Soldier
The Judge
Harriet Hume

ANTONIA WHITE
Frost in May
The Lost Traveller
The Sugar House
Beyond the Glass
Strangers

Virago

If you would like to know more about Virago books, write to us at Ely House, 37 Dover Street, London W1X 4HS for a full catalogue.

Please send a stamped addressed envelope

VIRAGO ADVISORY GROUP

Book Tokens

Give them
the pleasure of choosing
Book Tokens can be bought
and exchanged at most
bookshops